BLOOD·ALONE

ALSO BY THE AUTHOR

Billy Boyle
The First Wave

BLOOD · ALONE

A Billy Boyle World War II Mystery

James R. Benn

Copyright © 2008 by James R. Benn

Published by
Soho Press, Inc.
853 Broadway
New York, NY 10003

Library of Congress Cataloging-in-Publication Data

Benn, James R.
Blood alone : a Billy Boyle World War II mystery / by James R. Benn
p. cm.
ISBN 978-1-56947-516-4 (hardcover)
ISBN 978-1-56947-595-9 (paperback)
1. Americans—Italy—Sicily—Fiction. 2. Amnesiacs—Fiction.
3. Mafia—Italy—Sicily—Fiction.
4. World War, 1939-1945—Campaigns—Italy—Fiction.
5. Italy—History—Allied occupation, 1943-1947—Fiction.
I. Title.
PS3602.E6644B66 2008
813'.6—dc22
2008013300

10 9 8 7 6 5 4 3 2

For Debbie,

"Love goes toward love."

—WILLIAM SHAKESPEARE

"Blood alone moves the wheels of history."

—BENITO MUSSOLINI, December 12, 1914

CHAPTER · ONE

I WAS HOT. And my head hurt. Heat shimmered up from the ground and sat thick on my chest. Dust blew in under the loose canvas flaps, riding a warm breeze that died as soon as it hit me, leaving a thin layer of dirty yellow-brown grit to settle into layers of khaki cloth and bright white bandages oozing pink.

Pain sent sharp stabbing messages to my brain, coming from somewhere on my left arm. I lifted it so I could see, the weight of my own hand heavy in the pressing heat. A thick dressing was wrapped around it below the elbow. A thin line of blood had soaked through the bandage. I touched my head, feeling gauze over a sticky gob. A cut on the head is never as bad as it looks, someone once told me. Who? I couldn't remember, but I liked the idea. It can't be too bad, I thought. A conk on the noggin and stitches in my forearm. The arm didn't hurt much but my head felt like one of those things you hammer into wood was stuck in it. What was that word? You bought them for a penny a sack. Nails. That's it; my head felt like it had a nail in it, a red-hot one at that.

My hand flopped down onto my chest and I stared at the brown canvas above me, exhausted from my efforts. My eyes began to close. I tried to keep them open, a faint, distant voice in my head telling me I needed to figure out where I was, what was what, and who was who.

Other questions I couldn't quite form into sentences, or even put into words, swarmed around in my mind, but the fog was too thick and heavy for them to join together. I stopped struggling. What harm could there be in a little shut-eye? My eyelids slid shut, and I felt a faint, fluttering fear, realizing it might be impossible to open them up again. Then nothing.

I awoke, dull with pain and confusion, with no idea where I was. Other than that I was in a tent, my head was banged up, and it felt as if the tent were an oven. I tried to focus, to lift my head, but I couldn't with that nail through it. I groped for the nail but my hand came away red. I felt a warm trickle down my right temple.

No, there's no nail, I told myself. It only feels like a nail. First, I couldn't remember the word, and then I thought a nail was stuck in my head. Was I crazy? Was this a nuthouse, a canvas loony bin out in the desert? There was no nail, I knew that. I was a little mixed up, I figured, could happen to anyone, nothing to worry about.

My head hurt. I wanted to call out, to ask for a doctor, but I couldn't. I was sure the sound of my own voice would split my skull wide open. I couldn't lift my head but I could turn it. Moving produced a feeling like broken glass behind my eyeballs, but I managed. I realized some of my pain came from noise. It had been one big jumble before, but now I could distinguish different sounds. Yells, groans, brakes screeching, metal doors slamming, all swirled around, dove into my head, and bounced around my brain, looking for a way out. At least I knew what one source of my pain was. Noise. It hurt.

Guys carrying stretchers came in, dressed in brown wool clothes and wearing helmets with red crosses on them. Wool, like the folded blanket my head rested on—hot, coarse, and itchy. It smelled like mothballs and road dust. I looked at my chest, then my legs. I wore khaki too, but light khaki. Everyone else wore a different . . . suit . . . no, outfit—like what all the guys on a team wear.

What's that word? I wondered. Why is mine different?

"Sorry, buddy," a guy said as he knocked against my cot. I winced as the pain sent a jolt up my neck and into my skull, where it exploded into white-hot fragments. He and another fellow left a stretcher next to me.

". . . 's OK," I croaked, glad that at least we spoke the same language. But he didn't hear me. I looked at the person on the stretcher, his clothes cut away, his chest torn to red ribbons. Compress bandages taped below his rib cage turned a darker pink with each heavy breath he took. He was a kid, pale as a ghost, put there to die while they worked on the ones they could save. He had sandy-colored hair and a few faint freckles around his eyes. He never opened them. I watched the final lift of his chest, heard a last gasp, a harsh sound as air escaped his dead lungs. I looked at him a long time, his mouth open, chin tipped up, one hand palm down in the dry dust, and I realized where I was. This was Sicily.

I was in Sicily, in a field hospital. And these stretchers bore casualties. I must be a casualty.

It all made sense, sort of. I still had a lot of questions. But the trouble was, I didn't know what they were. Maybe it was the fact that I wasn't dead like the kid on the stretcher, but my head didn't hurt as much as it had. Words began to come together, and as my confusion receded, the worst of the pain went with it. I tried to remember how I'd gotten here. I didn't know exactly where *here* was, just somewhere in Sicily. Which is an island shaped like a triangle getting kicked by the toe of Italy. Naturally, there were a lot of Italians who didn't want us here. And Germans. I felt a shiver of fear, a shudder, a trembling in my gut. Who was I afraid of? A little voice, a tinny, distant echo in my head, tried to tell me something, but I couldn't make it out.

I'm in Sicily. There's a war on. And I'm scared of something. I got that far.

My eyes scrunched as I tried to think harder, remember how I'd been hurt, where I'd been before I came here. Where had I been before Sicily?

The dull sound of thunder distracted me, but it wasn't really thunder, I knew that much. Artillery. I watched two doctors in stained white coats stop and look at each other with that worried look you get when you hear enemy artillery creeping closer and you know things aren't going well at all.

How did I know that? How had I known it was enemy artillery? I tried to remember a battle. I tried to remember crossing the ocean. It's a long way to Sicily, right? "It's a long way. . ." A song from another war drifted across my mind and I faded out, dreaming of water sliced by the bow of a ship. "It's a long way . . ."

"Hey, kid, you asleep?"

I felt his presence looming over me as I awoke, the loose chinstrap of his helmet brushing my cheek as he moved. I felt his hand on my chest, a gentle push, maybe to feel if I was still breathing. He patted my pockets as the odor of cheap cigars and stale sweat wafted down, foul smells made worse by the stifling heat. I opened my eyes, the pain now a dull throb where before it had been a searing slash.

"Yeah," I said. "What are you looking for?"

I thought about raising my head and decided against it. I could see his face, encircled by the helmet pushed back on his forehead, glistening with an oily sheen of sweat. The netting on the helmet was new, none of the threads broken or frayed. He was short, kind of round but beefy, and an unlit stub of a cigar was clamped in the corner of his mouth. He looked like he was used to hard work, but he wasn't a combat soldier. The trace of softness in his face told me he slept in a rear-area tent, not a front-line foxhole.

"Nothin', kid. Just wanted to be sure you was still breathing."

"I am."

He raised an eyebrow, waiting for more. How did I know so much about him? Everything else was blurred and confused, but I could zero in on this guy. He was crystal clear to me. It was strange, automatically cataloging and judging him at a glance. Strange but comforting. There were questions I was afraid to ask, things I didn't want to think about, so it felt good to focus on what was right in front of me. I watched his eyes dart left and right, tracking the movement of medics scurrying around us. A chaplain knelt next to the dead kid, murmuring prayers as if he were in a hurry.

"You—you look familiar to me," I lied. "I know you, right?"

Dull booms echoed across the landscape, followed by a screeching sound high above us that made my new pal duck and put one hand up to steady his helmet. He was a buck sergeant, three stripes, silver on black against his brown wool shirt.

"Jesus," he said, "them cruisers sound like they're shootin' fuckin' freight trains at the Krauts."

"Where?"

"Where what?"

"Where are the Germans?"

"All over the goddamn place, that's where. Supposed to be nothin' but a bunch of guinea wops ready to give up, except for a few Kraut technicians, they told us. Well, they forgot to tell our paratroopers them technicians was all driving Tiger tanks. Nearly kicked our ass off Piano Lupo yesterday and made it down here. Can you imagine that, kid? The fuckin' Hermann Göring Panzer Division! If they'da made it down to the beaches, we would of been screwed, blued, and tattooed. And they'd be headed fer yours truly, lemme tell ya."

Piano Lupo, main drop zone for the 505th Paratroop Regiment. A hill mass seven miles northeast of Gela, landing area for the 45th Division. The words raced through my mind as if someone had turned on a radio. Clear as day, then nothing.

"Piano Lupo, right, Sarge?"

He was watching the padre, and it took him a second to pull his eyes away. He was nervous. Maybe he was thinking about a Holy Joe squatting over him, if those Tiger tanks made it to the beach.

"I knew you was a headquarters boy," he said, wagging his finger at me. "First time I saw you, I knew. Yeah, that was the fuckin' plan, but they all got scattered to hell and gone. Just a handful of boys ended up there, maybe a hundred instead of a full regiment. Stopped those goddamn Krauts, though, stopped 'em dead. Before they got to me and my supplies."

"Your supplies?"

"Quartermaster Company, 45th Division, kid. We got a captain, he ain't worth shit, and a lieutenant too, I don't pay him no mind. Rocko Walters, kid, that's who to ask for if you need bullets, beans, or blankets. They call me Rocko 'cause everyone depends on me. I'm the rock in this outfit, see, since the officers are total screwups. You ain't an officer, are you?"

I gave a little laugh and rolled my eyes, hoping he'd settle for that as an answer.

"So, Rocko, when was the first time you saw me?"

"Geez, it was yesterday, don't you remember?"

I raised my hand to the bandage around my head.

"Yeah, well, you was pretty banged up. That Italian who had you musta whacked you one good."

"What Italian?"

"How the fuck do I know, kiddo? The place is crawlin' with 'em. All I know is me and two other guys took off to Gela in a jeep to rustle up a couple trucks. We didn't get all the transport we was supposed to, so we figured to get us some civilian trucks. Right outside town, we see this Eyetie who's got you, and we holler at him to let you go. Louie speaks the lingo from his old neighborhood, enough to make himself understood. The Eyetie lets you go, but pulls a gun, so we hadda shoot him."

"You kill him?"

"Naw, Louie's a lousy shot. Creased his side, I think. Got his attention, though. He dropped the pistol, and we gave him to some GIs who were herding about a dozen POWs down to the holding area."

"How did I get here?"

"In a jeep. A medic heard the shooting and pulled over. When he saw the shape you were in he grabbed you and brought you here. I wanted to come visit you, but couldn't get out from under my asshole captain until now."

"And when did all this happen exactly?

"Yesterday morning, a few hours after my outfit landed. How long you been on the island anyway? And what's your name, kid? You must've lost your dog tags. They couldn't figure out your blood type or nothin'."

How long had I been here? I puzzled over that one so I wouldn't have to think about his other question.

"I don't know, Rocko. I really don't know."

"You dunno where you been or you dunno your name?"

He kept his eyes on me as I lay there, not answering his question. The longer he waited and stared at me, the harder it was not to answer. I felt the words form and rise up as if I had no control over them. Orderlies brought in more stretcher cases, transferring the wounded to cots and cutting away grimy blood-soaked bandages with practiced ease, revealing the awful truth of combat. The louder the artillery, the busier this place got. The chaplain moved around us, kneeling and praying with the wounded waiting for treatment.

I lowered my voice. "I have no idea where I've been or how I got here. I don't remember you or any Italian or anybody else, for that matter. I don't know my own name."

"No shit?"

"No shit, Rocko. Help me up, will you?"

Rocko grabbed an arm and I swiveled my legs off the cot. I pushed off with one hand and sat up straight. Everything whirled, then calmed down. Rocko was looking at me with a mixture of confusion and disbelief, his eyes darting over my clothes. My uniform, that was the word. "Nail." "Uniform." I wondered what else I'd remember.

"Jesus, kid," Rocko said, sitting down on the cot next to me. "You got any other ID on you? What about that jacket?"

"What jacket?" I said as I patted my empty pockets. My eye caught the shoulder patch on my shirt. Blue triangle with a yellow A, filled in with red. Seventh Army, I knew that much. So I was a headquarters guy.

"That funny jacket you was wearing. I almost thought you was a Kraut or maybe a Limey at first."

I tried to remember a jacket. A funny jacket. Maybe my next one would be a straitjacket. I saw Rocko reach his arm under the cot and feel around. He came up with a faded khaki jacket, neatly folded, where the medics had left it.

"This is it, kid. See what I mean?"

I took it from him and let it fall open. No insignia, no rank, no labels. The buttons were plain brass, tarnished and worn. It was rumpled and sweat-stained, the original color faded by the sun until only traces of dark khaki showed along the seams and under the pocket flaps. It could've been a German or Italian tropical jacket, maybe British. Or a U.S. Army field jacket, all insignia stripped off. Four buttons, four pockets. Your basic standard-issue design. Except everyone here was wearing brown wool. Dog-shit brown, someone had called it recently. Who was that? Words flashed through my mind—drop zone, Piano Lupo, dog shit, Licata—but they didn't connect. They were only words.

"You ever see an army uniform without all sorts of numbers and labels inside it, Rocko?"

"Never saw anything like this. No size, no serial number; you could never fill out a requisition for this rag. I'll check yer pockets, kid."

Rocko reached for the jacket, feeling around in the large lower pockets. He obviously had taken me under his wing. He'd probably saved my life. I realized he was the only guy on this goddamn island whose name I knew.

I dug my fingers into my shirt pocket, felt something soft and silky, and pulled out a handkerchief. Not plain white, not army-issue khaki cotton, but a silk handkerchief, the fabric a deep, rich yellow, almost gold. In the middle the letter *L* was stitched in black thread. It felt strange to hold this elegant item here, surrounded by dust, canvas, wool, and gauze. I had a strange urge to get rid of it, to distance myself from whatever that initial stood for. Unless it stood for my name? But then why did I feel like getting rid of it?

Harsh noises drove those thoughts away. Not the dull thunder of distant artillery but the crack of cannon fire. Tanks. The drumbeat of machine guns echoing off ridgelines. Not too close. Not yet. I wondered who was taking a beating out there, and I was startled to feel a pull on my hand as Rocko grasped the handkerchief. I looked at his face, and for just a second, I saw the golden silk reflected in his wide-open eyes. I snapped my hand back, stashing the handkerchief in my pocket, as Rocko looked away, glancing at the wounded, doctors, and orderlies crowding around us. More wounded came in, one guy screaming for his mother. Rocko looked nervous, and I can't say I blamed him.

The doctor didn't care what my name was. He told me I had a mild concussion and abrasions on the right side of my head. A gash on my left arm, like a knife slash, that he had closed up with half a dozen stitches. He ordered me to get a new set of dog tags and to get out, not in that order. They were busy, and since I could walk away, that's exactly what he wanted me to do.

"I'll take him back, Doc," Rocko said, leading me by the arm. I didn't know where back was, but I didn't want to admit it, so I let Rocko walk me out of the tent. Stretcher cases, lined up in rows, waited outside. Some of the wounded were grimacing in pain, some softly moaning, while others stared straight up, their mouths open, gasping for breath in the hot air. Across the dirt road a line of scraggly pine trees shaded the scorched ground. The walking wounded sat quietly, smoking cigarettes, cradling rifles and bandaged limbs. Waiting. Two paratroopers, baggy pants stuffed into jump boots, sat apart from the other dogfaces. Sounds of the battle to the east came over the rise again, signaling a renewed attack. As the harsh echo of cannon fire boomed through the heat, the paratroopers looked at each other and, in silent agreement, flicked their butts into the road and rose up painfully. One of them used his M1 as a crutch as they hobbled down the road toward the sound of gunfire. While his pal limped along, the second paratrooper discarded the sling that supported his left arm, letting it fall to the ground as he grasped his rifle with both hands, at the ready.

"Saps," Rocko muttered to himself. "C'mon, kid, I'll get you a cup of joe and you'll feel better in no time." I let Rocko lead me, his hand on my arm, guiding me like a nursemaid. I looked back to watch the paratroopers disappear over the rise and wondered again who the hell I was.

Trucks rumbled along a dirt track, churning up yellowish brown dust. The smell of salt was strong in the air, and I could see shimmering light blue where the road curved to the sea. Tents of all shapes and sizes were set up along the way. Jeeps spat gravel, pulling onto the road with gears grinding. Everyone was in a hurry, everyone except Rocko and me. Camouflage netting was strung up over stacks of fuel drums and cases of artillery shells. GIs stripped to the waist shoveled sand into burlap bags and stacked them around the explosives.

"Welcome to Service and Supply territory, kid," Rocko said as he nodded at the work crew. "See why I don't like the idea of fuckin' Tiger tanks roamin' around down here? Come on, we got a mess tent set up."

Gritty dirt turned to hard-packed sand as we approached the beach. A long line of vehicles snaked along tracks of steel grating laid to support the heavy stuff driving off the beach. Trucks and jeeps that had tried to drive around the metal mesh in their haste were sunk axle-deep in the sand. Engines roared as tires and treads fought for a foothold to pry themselves loose from the beach's grip. Scattered among the moving and straining vehicles were darkened, smoking wrecks, overturned amidst craters where bomb blasts had found them. Huge LSTs, their massive thirty-foot doors opened wide, disgorged more vehicles weighed down with supplies onto the shore. It was a swirling mass of confusion as jeeps, half-tracks, trucks, and tanks crossed paths, driving off the beach and onto the narrow road inland. Far out into the Mediterranean, I could see warships cruising, the hot North African winds pushing their smoke toward us. Between the ships and the shore, a parade of smaller craft scurried back and forth, heavy coming in, light going out, their only cargo the wounded. The living and the dead stayed here.

Rocko sat me down on crates of K rations under camouflage netting that had been hung from the front pole of the mess tent and tied off to a tree for shade. It wasn't cool, but at least the sun wasn't broiling the top of my head. He came out of the tent with two cups of coffee in one hand and a sandwich in the other.

"Here's a bacon sandwich, kid. You gotta be hungry. It's left over from breakfast, but it's good." He handed me the bread stuffed with crumbling strips of bacon, and I realized I was starving. I couldn't remember the last time I'd eaten, but then there was a lot I couldn't remember. He handed me an enameled steel cup and I sipped the black, sweet coffee. It tasted good, so I figured that's how I liked it.

"Thanks, Rocko," I said with a full mouth. "I appreciate it, but I can't hang around here."

"Where you gonna go, kid?" Rocko sat on another crate and drank his coffee.

It was a good question. "Headquarters, I guess. Somebody there has to know who I am."

"Seventh Army HQ is out there on one of them cruisers. I heard Patton's comin' ashore today, but where I got no idea. Stick around, kid. Another day or so, they'll have HQ set up in a palace somewheres and you can go see who remembers you. Or maybe you'll wake up in the morning and it'll all come back."

"Yeah, maybe," I said. I couldn't think of anything else to do right now anyway. I didn't want to tell the doctors about my lapse of memory and risk getting thrown in a loony bin. Or whomever I reported to at headquarters either. It would be a lot better if things were to come back to me in the morning. And better still if they were good things. If they weren't, then that was another reason to lie low until I knew what the deal was.

"You think your name starts with an *L*, like on that fancy hand-kerchief?" Rocko said, looking out toward the ocean. He seemed inter-ested in that handkerchief, but working hard not to show it.

"Doesn't ring a bell," I said. "Probably just something I picked up."

"Lemme have a look, willya?"

I hesitated, trying to think of a reason not to take it out of my pocket. Maybe I was naturally distrustful, and maybe he was simply curious, but something told me not to hand it over so easily. A jeep braked hard in front of us, spewing sand as it swerved to a halt.

"You! Sergeant!" A paratroop captain wearing the double-A patch of the 82nd Airborne pointed at Rocko.

"Yessir," said Rocko, setting down his coffee cup. "What can I get you, sir?"

"You can get your ass over to the weapons depot and load this jeep with grenades and ammo. Then you're both coming with me. Move!"

"But my pal just got out of the hospital, Captain. . . ."

"I said move, Sergeant. Now." He said it quietly but there was no mistaking the determination in his eyes. Powder marks darkened the skin around his cheekbone. This guy had been doing his share of shooting, and it looked like we would too. He waited while Rocko trot-ted down the road to another nest of tents, then put the jeep in gear and watched me as I followed. A corporal with a clipboard emerged from the main supply tent. Rocko spoke to him and gestured toward the jeep with his thumb.

"You too, Corporal! Load up and get in the jeep." The captain looked around for other candidates but the road was empty. His voice carried pretty far.

"Captain, I need my clerk here. What if—"

"Shut up, load up, get in," the captain said, picking up his carbine and making a show of checking the clip.

"OK, Captain, OK. I'll get my gear." Rocko disappeared into the warren of stacked supplies. His eyes wide, the corporal set down his clipboard and picked up a crate of grenades.

"Rocko says you can have whatever you need," he said, indicating the tent in back of him. He was a skinny, tall kid, dark black hair, long chin, wearing a pair of army steel spectacles. He looked more like a clerk in a hardware store than a candidate for the front lines. His two stripes had a *T* underneath for technician fifth class, junior to a regular corporal. His hands, gripping the heavy crate, were long and slender, like maybe he played the violin. His nails were clean and even. He might need a manicure after this.

The paratroop captain grabbed boxes of ammo and began loading the back of the jeep. I pushed aside the tent flap and went inside.

Rocko was nowhere to be seen. Crates of M1s and ammo were stacked along one side of the tent, and everything else an army ran on along the other. Cases of scotch and whiskey, cartons of Luckies, canned food—not K rations, but the real thing—piled alongside boots, helmets, and every issue of clothing the army allowed. A clawfoot bathtub, oddly stark white in the midst of all the brown and green, stood behind a wall of crates. It was filled with large green glass jars of olives. Baskets of fresh figs were set among cases of Italian wine. Now I understood why Rocko had gone out looking for more transport. He had a nice little sideline going here.

I picked up an M1 and a couple of bandoliers of ammo. There were plenty of helmets, but I had to dig to find one with the netting already on it. Why? Was it important? I could almost hear someone telling me it was. I put on the helmet and winced as it pressed against the bandage on my head.

At the back of the tent was a table on trestles set up as a desk. Forms and requisitions littered the top; empty crates turned on their sides served as filing cabinets. On top of the table was a web belt with plenty of extra clips and a .45 automatic in the holster, along with a combat knife and a full canteen. It was obviously somebody's, maybe Rocko's, but right now I needed it more. I put it on and grabbed a Parsons jacket from where it had been thrown on the table. I'd left my jacket at the hospital, preferring something that more clearly showed which side I was on. Stuffing this jacket through the web belt as I walked out of the tent, I felt a flash of recognition. Something about that other one and how it didn't seem to belong to any particular army. . . how it could pass for either side. What did that mean?

"Hustle, soldier!" the captain barked at me as he backed up the jeep to turn around. "And grab some of those bazooka rounds."

I gathered half a dozen black cardboard tubes from a pile and did my best to jump into the jeep without losing anything. The skinny corporal was in the back, cases of ammo wedged all around him. A wooden crate of grenades was on the floor in front of the passenger's seat, and I gingerly rested my feet on it as I got in, grabbing the metal edge of the jeep with one hand and wrapping my bandaged arm around the tubes holding the bazooka shells. It hurt. My head hurt too, and my gut was starting to quiver, but that was from fear.

"That supply sergeant gone?"

"Looks like it, sir," I said.

"Rocko said the captain wanted him," the corporal said, hanging on as the jeep climbed the incline up off the beach. "Our captain, I mean, sir."

"What's your name, Corporal?"

"Aloysius Hutton, sir."

The paratroop officer nearly cracked a smile. "Well, Hutton, when we get back, I'll bust Rocko and give you his extra stripe. He just lost his."

"I don't think Rocko will like that much, sir." Hutton shook his head as if the captain had been foolish not to consult Rocko first on the matter.

"Where are we headed, Captain?" I cut in before he decided to ask me my name.

"Biazza Ridge."

"That where all the firing's been coming from?"

"Yep. Slim Jim has been holding on all day up there."

"Who, sir?"

"Colonel Jim Gavin, commander of the 505th Regiment. There were only six of us when we started out. We were lost all day yesterday. Today we found some other paratroopers and some boys from the 45th Division. We started walking toward Gela and then hit that ridge, kicked a few Krauts off, and dug in."

He blasted his horn as we passed a column of trucks, pressing the accelerator to the floor, and kicking up a plume of road dust as we sped by the hospital. The rest of the walking wounded were gone, probably already headed up to Biazza Ridge.

"Then we saw tanks and lots more Krauts headed down from Biscari, on the road that leads straight into Gela and our beachhead. That ridge is the only high ground around."

As we sped around a curve, I had to lean and hold onto my helmet and the bazooka rounds. It wasn't easy. It didn't leave me with a hand to hold onto the jeep, and the way he was driving I worried about ending up in a ditch. He picked up speed on a slight downhill run as we passed a dried-up lake bed, hot air rolling over us like heat from a blast furnace. From what I had seen of Sicily so far, fresh water wasn't one of its attractions. I squinted my eyes against the wind and wondered if I'd remember anything useful about bazookas, fighting, and killing. Or maybe running.

"Uh, sir, how many are you, up there on that ridge?" Hutton said from the back. I could hear him gulp.

"Couple hundred by now. Lots of our guys headed that way when they heard the fighting. They've been showing up all day."

"But no tanks. No Shermans," I said.

"No. Plenty of Kraut armor, though, mostly Mark IVs. A bazooka can take one out if you hit 'em in the ass or take out a tread."

"What else they got, sir?" asked Hutton, his gulp getting louder as fear dried out his mouth.

"They got Tigers, son. I loaded a round for Slim Jim not ten yards from a Tiger, and he hit it square on the side. Damn thing ricocheted off and didn't even scratch it."

"You got a colonel goin' ten yards from a Tiger tank? Jee-sus!" said Hutton. He was impressed.

Me, I wondered what they made the privates do.

CHAPTER TWO

"DIG IN, DIG IN!"

The voice carried over the explosions and harsh *cracks* as 88mm shells from a Tiger tank split the air and thundered into the ground. Shrill whistling sounds arcing across the sky trailed mortar shells as they found the backside of the hill. Shrapnel was everywhere, zinging against hard rock, filling the air with razors of hot metal. The ground thudded, and I felt the vibration in my stomach. A machine gun fired quick bursts, sounding like a chain saw warming up before it took down a big tree. It was German. Ours made a series of dull pumping sounds. I imagined the German slugs knocking our few pitiful rounds out of the way. More bursts and a crackle of rifle fire. Dirt kicked up all around us, bullets cutting into the ground, shattering loose rock and showering us with dust and grit. Hutton was a few feet away, making love to the ground just like me.

"Dig in, goddamn it!"

I wanted to turn and look at whoever had a set of lungs on him powerful enough to make himself heard over the pounding we were taking. But that would have meant lifting my head a fraction of an inch. My face was flat against the ground, my hands wrapped around an entrenching tool that was doing no good with me on top of it. I'd have to raise my arms to use it, and I knew there were bullets up there. I could feel the air *thrum* as they passed over. Not moving felt sensible.

"Dig in, soldier!"

I felt a rifle butt whack my thigh and turned my head as little as I could. Kneeling down behind me was a tall guy, all knees and elbows. He had to scrunch himself up to stay low. But he wasn't facedown in the dirt. He held his M1 up and hit me in the boot heel with it to make sure he had my attention.

"Dig in. Long and narrow. When those Tigers move in, lie down, let 'em pass over, then hit the infantry coming up behind. Got it?"

I looked at his face. It was dirty and his eyes looked hollow, but there was still something boyish about him. He wore a jump jacket and his pants bloused over his boots. Paratrooper.

"Got it, Slim Jim."

Colonel Gavin didn't hear me. He was already off, running low, M1 gripped in both hands like any GI. "Dig in, dig in." I turned on my side and started scraping a hole in the ground as two paratroopers with a bazooka scurried up next to me and began some serious digging of their own. They ignored the bullets whizzing by as their entrenching tools bit at the dry, stony ground. I looked down the hill at a dark form visible beyond the sloping terrain. I could see the shimmering heat above black metal as the Tiger swiveled its turret, the long, smoking muzzle searching out another target. If that thing was getting any closer I wanted to be underground. I got up on my knees and dug, swinging the entrenching tool in rapid, swift strokes.

"Shit!" One of the troopers held up his entrenching tool. The shovel was bent, yet all he had to show was a pile of broken shale. He threw it away and lay down flat behind a scrubby bush, the bazooka hidden in the branches.

I wasn't doing much better. The ground was as hard as rock. Which it was, gray shale beneath hard, crusty earth. The edge of my shovel bent too and I tossed it, settling down as deep as I could, which wasn't very far. Hutton had done a little better. He had the shovel from the jeep and could do more with it. Lying down he almost filled his hole, except for a helmet at one end and boots sticking out the other. I looked back at the Tiger. It hadn't moved or fired. I could see Germans in desert khaki and dusty brown helmets running for cover behind it. Raising my M1,

I closed my left eye and tried to find one in my sights, but they were moving too fast and low. The weight of the stock against my shoulder felt familiar. I'd done this before, filled my sights with the form of a man, felt my heart beat faster with forbidden excitement. The idea of killing didn't seem to bother me a bit. And that bothered me.

"What do you think's gonna happen?" Hutton's eyes darted over the landscape. We were a few yards below the top of the ridge, and a steep gully ran to our right. In front of us the ground rose up a bit about thirty yards out, which made it hard to see the enemy. I wondered why Gavin hadn't placed us up there, under better cover.

"We'll be OK," I said to Hutton. "This Slim Jim fella seems to know what he's doing." An explosion punctuated my answer, followed by a scream and cries for a medic. I didn't make any more promises. We'd passed the aid station in an olive grove as we brought up the ammo and doled it out. Corpses were lined up behind it and the wounded waited on the ground in front. Not knowing my name didn't seem so bad to me after I saw that. As a medic patched up the lightly wounded they went right back to the line. The colors up here were brown, dirty white, and rusty red.

Hutton was watching a medic dodge bullets to get to the wounded man.

"Look ahead of us, not to the rear. Watch the Tiger," I said to Hutton. "So, what's your job with Rocko?"

He looked at me and I pointed forward as I swiveled my head left and right, taking in as much of the scene in front of me as I could. I wanted him on the lookout, but I also wanted to distract him from dwelling on the wounded behind us. Bad for morale.

"I'm with the Signals Company," he said, eyes front. "Guess because I worked for the telephone company back home. I like to work with radios too. Built my own from a kit. When I was a kid, that is."

Hutton was still a kid, but old enough to need to let me know he didn't play with kits anymore.

"But Rocko's Quartermaster Company. What are you doing with him?"

"Rocko does favors for people. When he needs something, they do favors for him. What's that?" He pointed to a clump of low green shrubs, and I saw a flicker of movement. We both opened up, emptying a full clip each to no visible effect. Tracers from the machine gun behind us sprayed the bushes too. Nothing moved.

Beyond the small rise in front of us the ground was dotted with swaying stalks of knee-high grass. Or was that wheat? The stalks were topped by seeds or grains or something. Guess I didn't grow up on a farm. Yellow wildflowers gathered in clumps all the way down to a dirt road that snaked around the ridge. The road to Gela. The road to Rocko's riches. The road we couldn't let the Germans pass.

I laughed. A memory had popped up and it seemed funny. Hutton noticed I was smiling and gave me a look.

"I remember why you should wear a helmet with netting," I said, raising my voice over the machine-gun chatter.

"Why?"

"Because a plain helmet gets shiny when it rains. Gives you away."

I lay my face down on the warm ground and laughed as the bullets flew overhead. It felt like everything was wired wrong inside my head. The things I could remember were useless. Or terrible, like lining up a man in my sights and feeling the thrill of it. Yeah, now I was all set if it rained. Lucky me.

The Tiger moved. It backed out of the ravine and started up the slope. Lines of Germans came forward at a steady trot, rising up from behind what cover they had. I saw a Kraut, pistol in one hand, waving his men on with the other. The pistol marked him as an officer and within seconds he was cut down, a dozen guys zeroing in on him. Red sprayed from his chest as he toppled backward. Slim Jim was pretty smart to carry a rifle.

I raised my M1 and filled the sight. I fired, and fired again. A figure dropped and I was glad. I looked up again. It was important not to get tunnel vision, to remember to look up from the sight.

Finally, a useful memory. I searched for the closest Germans and fired at a group of them clumped together. Stupid, they were being stupid. I cursed them as they dropped. I could only see them from the waist up with that rise in the way, but it was enough. Turned out I was a good shot. They kept coming, trotting through the yellow flowers, stopping to fire while trying not to get out in front of the Tiger. I heard bullets ricocheting off it as it drew fire like a corpse draws flies. Its machine-gun muzzle swiveled and bright sparkling bursts sought out our firing positions as it tried to protect the infantry around it.

I let loose my last round and the stripper clip ejected, hitting the ground with a metallic *ping*. As I grabbed another eight-round clip and slid it in, I remembered someone saying that was what he didn't like about the M1. That sound could give you away, and you couldn't reload until you were all out of ammo. Same guy who told me about wet helmets. Some guy who played every percentage. Who?

I aimed again. Germans filled up more of the sight as they got closer to the rise in front of us. I heard our machine gun and watched as men went down, hit or seeking cover. Yellow flowers were clipped by flying lead, scattering bouquets over the dead and dying. The Tiger was almost to the rise. It halted in front of it, raking the ground as its turret swung and fired in the direction of our machine gun. A loud explosion hit behind us and the MG went silent. I heard the hydraulic *whir* of the turret, as if the dark machine were thinking, calculating. Gears ground and it lurched forward, tilting back as it began to mount the rise. In a second it would be over the top and free to kill us all. It made no sense, but I began firing at it. I should have been scared, but there was no time. I should have run. I don't know why I didn't.

The paratroopers next to me sprang up, and I saw two more come from the other direction. Two bazooka teams. Then I knew why we were positioned here. The German infantry was down, waiting for the Tiger to get over the rise and finish us off, none of them wanting to risk getting killed when the Tiger was a sure bet. Each bazooka man knelt while his partner fed a rocket in, tapped his helmet, and ducked. They waited for the tank to reach the maximum angle, its front up in the air and its unarmored belly showing. They fired, bright orange flashes blossoming out from the metal tubes. One missed. The other hit square between the treads, a white flash followed by a searing explosion that blew the hatches off. Flames roared out of the tank as it lurched forward, falling hard, nose down, silent except for the roar of contained flames. Roiling black smoke from burning fuel and flesh filled the sky, and I cheered. I clapped Hutton on the shoulder. He didn't move. His head rolled toward me and his helmet tilted off. There was a hole in it dead center that matched the one high on his forehead. One hand lay flat on the ground, the long fingers splayed out as if he'd tried to ward off the shot that got him. His nails were still clean.

Some of the paratroopers crawled to the rise and began firing at the retreating Germans. I didn't know what to do about Hutton. Aloysius Hutton. A good solid name. A bit old-fashioned, but he'd said it like he didn't mind. I took his ammo bandolier and went forward. I saw Germans, more distant now, giving us their backs. I shot two and wondered what their names were.

I slumped against the rise, drank half the water in my canteen, and wished I had enough to wash my face. I couldn't have moved if my life depended on it, and it damn well might. My legs felt weak and I thought the water I'd swallowed was going to come right back up. I lay at the bottom of the rise, Hutton dead behind me, the enemy in front. I tried to get up, but the ground was spinning and I couldn't. I closed my eyes and felt the sun beating on my eyelids. Through a haze I heard medics moving the wounded out and felt someone start to grab my legs until one of the bazooka guys said to let me be, I was alive, I just didn't look it.

I woke to the sound of tank treads. I grabbed my rifle and looked around to get my bearings. The Tiger was smoldering, and Hutton was gone. One of the bazooka team raised his hand, palm up, as if to calm me.

"Don't worry, buddy. Those are ours. We got six Shermans coming up."

"Finally," his loader said, and tried to spit. It looked like his mouth was too dry and dusty to work anything up. I crawled over and gave him my canteen. He nodded his thanks and took a careful mouthful, then handed it back.

"How long was I out?" I asked.

"Couple hours," the loader answered. "You looked pretty banged up to start with, so we left you alone. Nothing much happened here since Joe popped that Tiger."

"What outfit you with?" Joe asked, eyeing me.

"Headquarters Company," I said, a plausible lie that might even be true.

"Jesus," the loader said. "They got everybody up here. Truck drivers, cooks, clerks, even some navy guys from the shore party."

"You shoot pretty good for a straight leg," Joe said. "Calm, not all shaky like some of these other guys."

"Straight leg?"

"He means everyone but paratroopers," the loader said. "After we qualify we stuff our pant legs into our jump boots."

"Straight leg. I get it," I said. "And straight legs can't shoot straight?"

"Some do," Joe agreed. "Some hunker down and don't do anyone no good. Some fire at anything. You took your time with aimed shots. Makes a difference."

I could hear someone else telling me about aimed fire. The helmet guy. He thought the same way. Like a professional. Who was he?

"Thanks," I said. The blurred image of a face swam through my mind. I could almost hear him. *Aimed fire.*

"Name's Clancy," the loader said, his hand extended. "This here's Joe."

I shook their hands. Joe lit a cigarette and they both looked at me, waiting.

"Aloysius Hutton," I said, my mind blank, as if that were the only name in the world.

"Pleasure," Clancy said after a moment. Joe drew on his cigarette and gave it to his buddy. We watched and listened. The Shermans clanked into position about fifty yards away on our left. Firing broke out intermittently along the line. Nothing as ferocious as before, only a rattle of rifles and short machine-gun bursts. We waited as the sun dipped down behind us and more GIs and paratroopers came up from the direction of Gela.

At six o'clock the Shermans roared forward and we got the signal to advance. I followed Clancy and Joe down the slope, jumping over dead Germans and wilting yellow flowers. Gunfire was heavy to our left, but in front of us all we could see were flashes of khaki running low, darting from cover and then going to ground again. We made it down to the road, to an abandoned pillbox situated to cover the road in the opposite direction. Inside was a lone German, dead, bandages swathing his abdomen. He looked a lot like the kid who had died next to me in the field hospital.

For about an hour we hunkered down by the pillbox and listened to the Shermans firing over the next hill. The shooting slackened, then died away. We walked out into the open, standing upright, which felt strange. The Germans were gone, except for a couple dozen prisoners being marched up the slope. No explosions, no machine guns. The quiet was so sweet no one dared speak. Clancy, Joe, and I wordlessly climbed back to the top and looked out over the plain below us. A trail of dust marked the retreat of the remaining German vehicles, and plumes of smoke marked those that didn't make it.

The top of the ridgeline was the collection point for the dead. We watched bodies being laid out in neat rows as POWs were put to work scraping graves out of the shale. No different than the holes we'd tried to dig. It looked easier to do standing up. A paratroop chaplain knelt, saying a prayer over each body. There were thirty-four of them. Someone started knocking K-ration cartons apart, forming makeshift crosses and a couple of Stars of David. Everyone was silent, and the noise of shovels biting the hard ground seemed even louder than all the fighting. *Chink, chink,* metal against rock, flesh against the earth. I turned to walk away and saw Slim Jim himself standing at attention, tears washing the dirt from his cheeks. Thirty-four good names were going to be written on those wooden planks, many of them belonging to boys he knew. All of them he'd put on this ridge to fight and die. I was glad I didn't have to make decisions like that, and then wondered if I ever had.

Joe put his hand on my shoulder and moved me away from the group, walking me down the slope toward the olive grove and the aid station. The light was fading, but I could still see his eyes moving back and forth, looking to see who was around. He stopped and grabbed the front of my shirt, ripping it open.

"I know you aren't Hutton," he said. "I helped bring his body over here and gave the lieutenant his dog tags. I doubt there's two Aloysius Huttons on this fuckin' island. And you don't have no dog tags."

"Listen, Joe—"

"Never mind. I got enough troubles with the Krauts, I don't give a crap about yours. If I hadn't seen you drop so many of them I would've shot you myself when you gave that phony name. But you stood your ground, helped us out, and we owe you. So scram. Grab a jeep before things get organized here. Go back to Gela or wherever you came from. And keep your head down, straight leg."

He nodded toward the road. Clancy stood a few yards away, keeping a lookout. "If you run into trouble with any guys from the 82nd, ask for Joe and Clancy of the 505th. Everyone knows us, we're a team."

He gave a little wave. I waved back and watched them trudge back to the ridge and their buddies, alive and dead. I headed down through the olive grove, past the aid station, to a jumble of vehicles pulled off the road, and wondered exactly where the hell it was I had come from.

CHAPTER • THREE

"HOLD STILL, DARLIN', let me get these bandages off.
They're filthy," a woman said.

"OK," I said. I had been swiveling my head around, on the watch
for officers or anybody else in the business of collecting stray GIs. Back
at Biazza Ridge I had collected four wounded from the aid station and
brought them down to the field hospital. I had wanted to get out of
there as fast as possible, but it didn't seem right to steal a jeep just for
myself. It was good cover, I'd figured. No one would stop and question
me with four bleeding men crowded in the jeep.

"Not infected, thank goodness," she said, pulling off the once-
white bandages, stained with blood, dirt, and sweat. She was dressed in
army fatigues about five sizes too big for her, sleeves and pants rolled
up to fit. Wisps of brown hair stuck out from beneath her helmet.

"I didn't know there were nurses here already," I said as she put a
new dressing on my head. I was still sitting in the jeep. I had been
ready to take off as soon as they got the casualties out, but she refused
to let me go until she had checked my head wound.

"We landed this morning. They sent us up from the Evac Hospital
to help out. We would've gotten here sooner but we ran into German

tanks. We hid and watched them go by. That's as close as I ever want to get to those things," she said, shuddering, her shoulders bunching up.

"Yeah, you and me both."

A few tanks had broken through, but they were stopped short of the beachhead. I had passed two of them knocked out by the side of the road, black greasy smoke curling up out of their hatches. Plenty of our vehicles had been destroyed too, and dead bodies bloated in the heat amid twisted steel. The smell of smoke, death, and decay left a metallic taste in my mouth I could not quite shake.

There was more of everything coming ashore now, and long tents had sprouted everywhere since I'd been here last, more targets for the German planes buzzing overhead. They concentrated on the ships and landing craft, but every now and then a low roar of engines flared across the horizon, followed by a string of explosions. Something was burning not too far off, sharp crackles sending showers of sparks into the evening air.

"There you go, darlin', just get those bandages changed in a day or so. You can head back to your unit. You take care now."

"Thanks," I said, and gave her a grin. "Thanks a lot."

There was something comforting about being taken care of by a woman with a soft, sweet voice and a gentle touch. I hated to see her go. She smiled back, disappearing into the tent filled with the cries and groans of the wounded. That lingering smile left me feeling more alone than I had since I'd woken up this morning. I sat for a minute, wishing everything would come back to me—the people I knew and cared about, my own name, some clue as to who I was. And why I was here. But nothing came, and all I had was the thinnest of all possible human connections. A nice nurse doing her job. A smile. *Take care.*

I held onto the steering wheel and rested my head on it. I could've stayed like that all night. I could have cried me a river. I could've asked her name. I could've done all those things, but I knew I had to move out before someone else started asking questions.

I raised my head in time to see two MPs emerge from another hospital tent across the road. One held a clipboard, the other a carbine. A hand waved and I looked in the direction the MPs faced. Down the road, two officers walked out of another tent. One American and one

British. The American pointed to the other hospital tents on my side of the road. They seemed to be looking for someone. Maybe me. Probably me. I thought about giving myself up to them, but then wondered why the American military police and the Brits would both be out hunting for me. I decided I better find out more about what kind of trouble I was in first. I didn't have a clue as to what I might have done to deserve such attention, but I didn't want to find out from these guys. For all I knew, they might use the carbine before the clipboard. I grabbed a field jacket from the back of the jeep, tilted my helmet down over my eyes and hoped the bandage around my head would help to further disguise me. I backed up the jeep and pulled out into the road, cutting across their path. A plane droned in the distance and antiaircraft fire lit up the sky in front of me. I looked up and hoped they did too as I sped by. I waited for shouts or shots. Did those guys know me, I wondered? Or were they working from a picture? Where would it have been taken and how long ago? I doubted my bandaged, unshaven face resembled any photograph they might have. I drove into the smoke and left them behind me, fear choking me worse than the black smoke from a burning truck.

Who was I running from? Was I a fugitive due for a court-martial? A deserter? A crook? A coward? Or worse? I could still see the men filling my sights, still feel the M1 steady in my hands, hear each shot, see the bodies drop, fold, crumple, spin, stumble, and fall. There were so many ways for a bullet to take a man down, and none of them had seemed to surprise me. God help me, what kind of man was I?

I turned onto the beach road. Rocko's empire of tents had grown, canvas and rope covering the ground along the shore. Camouflage netting covered it all, blocking out the stars that had begun to shine in the night sky. Wires ran from one tent and up the poles supporting the netting, then split off in different directions, draped on tree branches and makeshift poles. Antennas sprouted from another tent, reels of black wire stacked all around. Probably Hutton's Signals outfit. I wished I could have stopped and told them about him, but this wasn't the time. Beyond the Signals tent I drove the jeep behind a stack of wooden crates and hoped they held something nonexplosive.

I tried to figure my next move as I headed for Rocko's tent. I needed a place to rest, to eat and catch some shut-eye. And to think.

Rocko was the only guy I knew on this island who could provide all that, barring a trip to the stockade, even though he seemed too interested in me by half, and had showed himself to be a real louse when he skipped out on the Biazza Ridge dragnet. It wasn't a good combination, but what better hideout than a supply dump? Everything I needed within easy reach. Of course, that meant I'd be within easy reach of Rocko too. I slung my rifle over my shoulder and unholstered my .45. The pistol was better for close work if things didn't go well.

Close work? Where did I get that from? I seemed to know my weapons and the mechanics of killing. I gripped the automatic tightly, feeling the crosshatch marks on my palm. It felt familiar, and damn if it didn't calm me right down.

Light seeped out along the edges of the flaps of Rocko's tent. I went down the side, stepping over taut ropes, listening. I stopped and concentrated. Snatches of conversation drifted in from the road. Cigarette smoke mingled with the salty smell of the beach and the odor of dead fish. Engines rumbled and gears grinded. No one saw me as I lay flat along the edge of the tent. I eased the canvas up, slow and silent, to peer inside. A row of wooden crates, stacked four high, blocked my view. I took off my helmet and rifle, laid them down, and rolled under the flap. Everything sounded loud—my canteen as it hit the gravelly soil, the crunch of stiff canvas as I held the tent flap up, my own breathing. I fought down panic, telling myself it really wasn't that loud, it was my nerves. I heard voices from inside the tent but the blood was pounding so loudly in my temples that I couldn't make them out. I reached for my helmet and pulled it in, then my rifle. There was about a foot of space between the stacked cartons and the tent flap. I gripped my .45 tightly as I strained to listen. I needed to know the lay of the land before I stood up and said hello to Rocko. I took a few silent, deep breaths, willing myself into a state of calm and quiet.

Staring at the canvas above me, I saw water. It was as if I weren't flat on my back in a tent in Sicily but walking on a sidewalk, along the water. Then it was gone, replaced by the dull, dark green canvas, which was as blank as my mind. That had to have been a memory, though it felt real. I thought about today, about waking up, about Biazza Ridge, and all the things I'd done. Those scenes in my mind played out like that jaunt along the water. The water. It hadn't been clean like at the beach. It must've been in a city, a harbor someplace. I tried to replay that vision and get myself to turn, to see what was behind me, but I couldn't.

The *whir* of a field telephone being cranked up brought me back from wherever that place was.

"Lieutenant Andrews." That was Rocko, asking for someone at the other end of the line. I heard a match flare and smelled cigar smoke. "Yeah, it's me. You find that guinea prisoner yet? No? Well, I found out where he came from. The 207th Coastal Defense Division, based in Agrigento. We ain't there yet, so there shouldn't be too many—"

I heard his fingers drumming on the table as he listened and filled the tent with blue smoke. "I don't give a fuck if they're giving up by the thousands! You find that wop and bring him to me!"

He slammed the phone down. I knew of only one Italian POW Rocko would give a damn about—the guy who had been trying to shoot me when Rocko and his pals found me. At least, that was Rocko's story. I decided to wait a few minutes so he wouldn't think I had overheard his conversation.

"So, do we have a problem?" That was another voice. Smooth, relaxed, not like Rocko, who sounded like he was on edge.

"No, no problem at all. It'll take some time for Andrews to sort through the Eyetie prisoners."

"How long?"

"I dunno. He can't leave the Signals section anytime he wants. And he's gotta get that German dialer workin' with the BD 72—"

"I am disappointed in you and your Lieutenant Andrews. I did not expect this delay."

"I can't help it that there's so goddamn many POWs! They're giving up by companies now. Includin' a couple hundred from the 207th, and they're about a hundred miles west of here, in Agrigento."

Lieutenant? I might not remember things perfectly, but I knew noncoms did not talk to officers the way Rocko had spoken to Andrews. Unless, maybe, they had something on them.

"I know where Agrigento is. The food there is almost as good as in Palermo." He said the names like a native, the syllables gently rolling off his tongue and sounding like a threat at the same time. His voice was deep and low, with a raw power to it.

"What I don't know is why you didn't kill him when you had the chance," the man said, as if Rocko had forgotten to do the simplest of chores.

"There never was a chance, honest! First the medic shows up, then at the field hospital there was always someone around. I tried searching him, but he woke up. There was a chaplain right next to us the whole time. I couldn't do a thing! So I brought him down here, where I figured it'd be easy. But then that paratroop officer came along and shanghaied him. I couldn't help it, really."

"You have many excuses," the other voice said, with an icy edge of irritation.

"Don't worry, I'll take care of things," said Rocko, a defensive whine creeping into his voice.

"I do worry," the voice said and I heard a chair move. He spoke quietly, in a voice that carried authority. "I worry about finding this prisoner. I worry about our friend with the handkerchief on the loose. I worry that by now he may have found the note. I worry about our yegg. And I worry about you. Charlotte worries about you, too."

Footsteps, the rustle of canvas, a jeep engine turning over, and he was gone. All I heard was Rocko's exhalation, as if he'd been holding his breath through that little speech.

Charlotte? Who the hell was she? Yegg? Note? Did I have a note? Yeah, maybe I did. That web belt with the .45 I had snagged was probably Rocko's. It held a couple of pouches with extra clips for the pistol and a first aid kit, besides the .45 itself and a knife in a leather scabbard. I opened each pouch, praying the sound of the metal snap wouldn't carry. Nothing but what was supposed to be there. Nothing in the holster either. I couldn't maneuver quietly enough to check the canteen pouch. I lifted the helmet and checked inside. No note tucked away.

Only one place left. Another metal snap, and I pulled the M3 knife from its sheath. A slip of wrinkled white paper was wrapped around the blade. It was soft and worn, but the penciled sentence was clear, printed out in shaky letters, as if the writer was very old or very young. *To find happiness, you must twice pass through purgatory.*

What? I almost laughed. This was insane. Here I was, my memory shot, hiding in a tent from a supply sergeant, with a fancy silk handkerchief in one pocket, wondering what a yegg was, and holding a secret note telling me how to find happiness. The only trouble was, I would have to die twice. Unless this was purgatory, in which case I would only have to die once. Always look on the bright side. It was a great joke on me, and I was afraid I'd burst out laughing, or maybe cry hysterically. What the hell was next? Bob and Bing on *The Road to Sicily?*

"Is that water ready yet?" Rocko bellowed. It sounded like he'd opened the tent flaps. I took the handkerchief out of my pocket and wrapped the note in it. Then I stuffed the handkerchief between two crates of grenades. I holstered the .45, keeping the knife in my right hand. I rose to a crouch and eased my head above the top crate. Rocko was opening the flap for a private struggling with big pot of steaming water. I ducked down as they passed me, moving farther back into the tent. I heard the sound of water being poured.

"You want anything else, Rocko?"

"Yeah, you outta here, and no one else in. I been lookin' forward to this bath all day."

The private left. I peered over the crates again, hearing Rocko move around. I stepped out from my hiding place and crept closer, knife at the ready. I heard a grunt as one boot struck the ground, then another. There was a break in the stacks of cartons to my left. The sounds came from in there, where Rocko had a private bath set up for himself. That clawfoot bathtub was filled with hot water this time, hold the olives.

I took two steps into the gap in the wall of cartons. There was Rocko, in all his pink glory, his backside to me, pouring himself a drink from a table next to the tub. He took a swallow, put down the glass, and lifted one hairy leg into the tub. My knife was ready.

I stepped up to him, lifted my arm, and brought down the butt end of the hilt against his skull. It was all in the wrist, a quick snap. You didn't want to follow through—that could kill a guy. You had to hit him just right, hard enough to knock him out, not hard enough to crack his skull. Funny how some things came to me right when I needed them. Not funny that they all had to do with killing or hurting people.

Rocko crumpled, thankfully not into the tub. That was for me.

CHAPTER · FOUR

ROCKO LOOKED GOOD tied up. I was pretty sure he didn't feel so good, but the khaki undershirt I'd gagged him with was keeping him from complaining. It was my undershirt, and as I began to pay attention to my own personal hygiene, I felt bad about that. The truth of the matter was I stunk, and so did that shirt stuck in his yap.

Even after the fresh delivery of hot water, the bath was lukewarm. I guessed his visitor had been more important than a hot bath. Which was saying something, because as hot as it was during the day, at night the mercury plummeted. I poured some more scotch in the glass—real glass, no aluminum cup for Rocko—and decided it was OK but probably not my first choice. Rocko's eyes bulged out at me as he strained against the rough rope I'd bound him with. It wasn't a pretty sight, but it was satisfying.

"Calm down, Rocko," I said. "Sorry about the tap, but you avoided much worse by running out on us. You might've ended up like Aloysius."

Rocko's eyes bulged even farther out. He tilted his head and raised his eyebrows, asking me a question.

"Dead. Never knew what hit him," I told him.

Rocko's head fell back. He looked shocked. I remembered how he had tried to protect Hutton from being shanghaied that morning. It didn't seem possible, but Rocko actually seemed to have cared about Hutton. Strange. I wondered what Hutton had done for him other than carry a clipboard.

Leaving Rocko to his grief, I concentrated on getting clean. I scrubbed my face with soap and water and felt the hair on my chin. I looked at the pile of my discarded clothes. They had the crumpled, greasy look of garments worn for days. My entire body smelled like it was covered with layers of dried sweat. Every fold of skin revealed a thin line of grime, and I felt sorry for the private who'd brought the water in. It was probably his job to clean the tub.

I might not know my name, but I did know my own whiskers. Something didn't add up. We'd invaded yesterday, during the night and early morning. I'd awakened in the field hospital this morning. Now, it was maybe 2300 hours. Eleven o'clock, civilian time, I reminded myself automatically. Was that a habit of mine? It felt familiar. I liked that.

Two days ago, paratroopers had just begun to drop over Sicily. Infantry was offshore, getting ready to load into landing craft. I rubbed my chin again, and had a vague recollection of being in a small boat, rolling on the waves. It was dark, and it was dangerous.

That was it. Water! The things I remembered both had to do with water.

Never mind that now. I was a straight leg, right? So I hadn't jumped during the night. I must have come in by landing craft or small boat before dawn two days ago. D-day for Sicily. Operation Husky, scheduled for July 10, 1943. The code name and date popped into my head, another sudden revelation, followed by nothing.

I would've been clean shaven and wearing a fresh uniform. So why did I have a week's worth of beard? Not stubble but longer hair beginning to feel soft, like a beard growing in.

I must have arrived in Sicily *before* the invasion.

I scrubbed the dirt of days away, scouring my body, wishing the hopelessness I felt would fall away too. I lathered my face and shaved, using the small mirror and razor that had been set up next to the scotch. It was hard going, and I cut myself. Drops of blood fell into the dirty water, blossoming red and disappearing. I pressed my fingers against the cut and they came away wet and sticky. I stood and poured a pitcher of fresh water over me, rinsing off soap and lather and pale pink droplets. It was cold, but I didn't care.

I'd been here before the invasion.

The conclusion was plain but I didn't want to think about it. Mechanically, I dried off. Rocko made some noises but I picked up the knife and he quieted down. I gripped it in my palm, blade pointed at Rocko this time, as if I were about to stab him.

The knife. The knife in my hand was bloody, glistening wet. I felt it slide between someone's ribs, my hand twisting and cracking bone while a hand flapped uselessly against a holster, trying to draw a pistol, too late.

I gasped and dropped the knife. I blinked, half believing the man in uniform whom I had stabbed would be standing in front of me, breathing his last. There was no one but Rocko, though, naked and hog-tied, watching me with more fear than I'd yet seen in his eyes. I picked up the knife, felt the handle and looked for blood, scarcely able to believe it was clean and dry.

I'd been here before the invasion. And I was a killer.

I gathered up clothes and gear, leaving the M1 where it was and exchanging it for a Thompson. I liked the thought of a spray of .45 slugs between me and trouble, and there was plenty of trouble on this god-damned island. Italian trouble, German trouble, and whatever brand of trouble I was in. I grabbed a M1928 field pack—oddly enough, I could remember all sorts of army nomenclature—and stuffed in socks, a shaving kit, anything I thought I might need for the next few days. I found an open carton of D rations and threw in some of the vitamin-fortified chocolate bars. Then I retrieved the handkerchief and the note from where I'd stashed them. I folded the handkerchief and stuck it under my T-shirt, against the small of my back. I located a sewing kit, picked up my shirt, and pulled a chair over in front of Rocko. I took out my knife. Rocko was shaking. I pulled the shirt from his mouth.

"Don't. . . ," he started to say, then spit on the floor. "Don't kill me. You aren't gonna kill me, are you, kid? Jesus Christ!" He spit again, that last curse directed at the taste left in his mouth, not me. Not directly anyway.

I sat back and began cutting the stitches from my Seventh Army shoulder patch on the khaki shirt I'd been wearing. I figured it might

come in handy to stay a Headquarters GI if I had to talk my way out
of a fix. I got the patch off and pulled at the little threads, wondering
if this was a clue to my identity or another subterfuge.

I didn't like the way things were going, and I needed to find out
what I was involved in. So far, it all seemed suspicious. I mean, who
would have been in Sicily prior to the invasion? Secret agents, maybe,
but somehow I doubted I was one. Did secret agents let themselves be
led around by Italians? Weren't they trained to remember things? I
almost had to wonder if I was really an American. But outside of a few
curse words in French and Italian, I couldn't come up with anything
but English. So I was sure I was a genuine Yank. What did that tell
me? Even if I was an agent, it didn't mean I was safe, not until I knew
what my mission was.

"I heard some guy leave before I sneaked in here, Rocko," I said as
I threaded the needle. "Who was he?"

"I dunno. Some officer who wanted a case of scotch."

"Really?"

"Yeah."

"Rocko, I think you were going to deliver me to someone dead or
alive when you brought me down here this morning. I think I got out
of here just in time."

"I dunno what you're talkin' about," Rocko said. "Say, what happened to Hutton? Is he really dead?"

"Yep," I said. "He a pal of yours?"

"Yeah, you could say that."

"Sorry for your loss."

"Fuck you, buddy," Rocko snarled. "You better untie me now! I
could holler my head off—"

The knife blade was at his throat before he could finish. He didn't
say another word.

"Rocko, the things I remember are all pretty nasty. I've killed
before, up close, like this. I killed people today. It wouldn't bother me
to add one more."

"Jesus, kid, we're on the same side!" He croaked out the words, his
eyeballs swiveling down, trying to see the blade.

"If that were true, Rocko, you would've gotten in the jeep with us
this morning."

"The captain, he ordered me—"

"No, no, no," I said, pressing the blade against his neck. "Don't lie to me, Rocko, don't do it. I'm on edge right now, and I really don't care if you leave this tent under your own power or toes up."

"OK, kid, geez, take it easy with that thing. I keep it pretty sharp, y'know."

I moved the flat of the blade away from his throat, leaving the tip resting just below his Adam's apple. A tremble scurried through the muscles of my arm and settled in my gut. Was I a killer? A close-in killer? Not like up on the line, where you did what you had to do to stay alive, following orders. No, not like that at all. Was I a killer who could lay the blade of a knife against a throat and use it like a professional? A remorseless killer. Was that who I was?

Had I been sent here to kill someone—not the unknown enemy but someone with a face and a name? Was I an assassin? Had I done my job?

My arm was tired. As I sheathed the knife my hand shook.

"Rocko, save us both a lot of trouble and tell me what the deal is," I said. "Why are you so interested in me? What's with the handkerchief? And who else is looking for me?"

"Everyone's looking for you, kid. But I haven't turned you in, have I?"

"Who's everyone?" I asked.

"The army, for one. And friends of *the friends*."

"I thought some MPs and officers might be looking for me. But what do you mean 'friends'? Whose friends?"

"Not yours, kid. If you're smart, you'll untie me and let me take care of everything. I can hide you until you get your senses back, then we'll set things right. You still got that fancy handkerchief? It could be your ticket out of this mess if you hand it over." He said it with a smile, his head cocked to the side, eyebrows up, oozing sincerity and concern. I had tied his arms tight at his waist, crossed over and knotted at the wrists. His hands stuck out and he twisted them, palms up, beseeching me to listen to reason for my own good.

"It's somewhere safe. I'm smart enough not to trust you. Now tell me who these friends of yours are."

"They ain't friends of mine, they're friends of the friends, know what I mean? Jesus, I told you too damn much already. Now untie me, willya?"

"No, I don't know what you mean! Who's Charlotte? Where is this Lieutenant Andrews?"

"I can't tell you anything, don't you understand? They'll kill me. Forget what I said. I got connections, kid. You can trust me. You gotta. Now be a pal and untie me." A desperate, pleading tone had crept into Rocko's voice. His hands clenched, then steepled into a parody of prayer. He was afraid of these friends of his, whoever they were. I wanted to trust someone, I needed to trust someone, but if this guy was my only choice, I'd take my chances alone.

"No thanks, Rocko. Sorry about this." I gagged him again with the T-shirt. He shook his head, making muffled, growling noises, then a low, resigned moaning. I felt sick at the sound, disgusted with Rocko and his naked pleading. The reality was that this was all I knew of my life: a petty thief and coward, mysteries of purgatory, and dangerous friends; the comfort of a knife in my hand, the practiced ease with which I'd held it, and the nightmare vision it cut across my brain. I had to leave.

I grabbed my gear and squeezed behind the stacked cases of grenades, figuring the way I came in was the best way out. I lifted the canvas flap. The cool evening air washed over my face. It was quiet. I pushed my helmet, pack, and Thompson out under the flap, then slid myself out. On one knee, I blinked, trying to adjust to the darkness. I reached for the helmet. My hand felt the netting and the steel beneath it. With that touch, a name came to me. Harding. Major Harding. Sam Harding. He was the one who had told me about shiny helmets, and aimed fire, and. . .

The surge of joy at recalling this name ended as a sharp stabbing pain erupted at the base of my skull. Then, darkness.

CHAPTER ▪ FIVE

I AWOKE WITH A throbbing head and a name on my lips. Harding. I opened my eyes and found myself back inside the tent, face-down on the ground. I'd been hit by someone who knew what he was doing. It had been a sharp rap, the same as the one I'd given Rocko. All in the wrist, enough for lights out followed by a pretty good chance of waking up again.

Harding. Sam Harding. Major Sam Harding. I saw his face, sharp angles and squinty eyes. Close-cropped dark hair, traces of gray flecked across the temples. I knew him. I remembered him.

Great, but what was I doing here, and who'd given me that smack on the skull? And why? I pushed myself into a sitting position and rubbed my head. There was a bump behind my ear that hurt like blazes when I touched it. I had to stop getting hit in the head. That's what Punchy had always said.

Punchy. Pauly Hawes, but we called him Punchy from the pounding he'd taken in the ring. I saw his face, broken nose and all, but that was it. I didn't know where he was from or where I'd seen him fight, but I knew he was a welterweight, and that I was right about those hits to the head.

My arms were wet. Soaking wet, it dawned on me, as I felt my sleeves. Water dripped from the cuffs. I stood, trying to make sense of things and how I had gotten here. *Here* was in the back of the tent, near the opening in the wall of cartons that led to Rocko's secret bathtub. Steadying myself with one hand on a pile of crates, I took tentative steps around the corner. I was dizzy. I stumbled.

Rocko was in the tub, feet sprawled out over the sides, face up, eyes and mouth wide open, underwater. His hands were still tied, palms facing out, in that same supplicating gesture he'd made to me. The expression on his face was pure surprise. But it could also have been panic, when he realized his next breath was going to be of water. I'd seen drowned faces before, in that water scene that had flashed through my mind. Water, Harding, Punchy. I was building up quite a scrapbook of memories.

Water puddled at my feet as I stared dully at Rocko. I knew I shouldn't be standing here. Something was very wrong, but with the strange images and hints of memory that were all I had, I couldn't think clearly. My one specific memory, of Harding, felt like a crack in an old wall; the others crowding behind it were building up pressure, ready to flood through. But not yet. I was confused and afraid. Afraid of what would come tumbling through that crack when it opened.

Later, I told myself; now you've got to get out of here. You've been set up. As the idea took hold I got my feet to move. There were voices in the darkness outside, then inside the tent, advancing on me. There were two of them, and in a heartbeat, they'd reached the narrow passageway, blocking my only way out.

"Hey, who the hell—" The first guy, a PFC, stopped in his tracks. The second, a lieutenant, almost knocked him over. The lieutenant had a .45 automatic, but the unarmed PFC was between us.

"Omigod, omigod," the PFC said, staring at Rocko in the tub, then at me, standing there, soaked to the shoulders. He backed away from me, maybe afraid I was going to grab him too and give him a bath. He bumped into the lieutenant, who started swearing, waving his pistol in my general direction. I knew I had about five seconds before he shot me or took me prisoner; it was no accident he'd come in with his weapon drawn. I put my shoulder down and ran forward, crashing into the wide-eyed PFC and knocking them both to the ground. I stepped on one body and heard a cry as I pushed off and ran as fast as I could out the front of the tent. I didn't have time to worry about who might be waiting out there or if they would follow me. Panic took over as I imagined the lieutenant steadying his aim and lining up the sights on my backbone. I kept going, digging my heels into the sand, keeping my head down, fleeing from the murder scene, my pursuers, and the growing crack in the wall that held back my memories.

I ran onto the hard-packed road leading up from the beach, straight into a crowd of GIs. Some were coming up from the water, others running toward it from tents and bivouacs strung out along the coast road. They were yelling, pointing up toward the night sky over the Mediterranean.

No one was chasing me; no one paid me any mind. I stopped running and fell in with the throng moving toward the beach, melting into the crowd of dogfaces. I felt oddly safe and secure in the midst of dozens of guys dressed exactly like me, cloaked by darkness, a formless mob, moving without orders or direction. We crossed the steel mesh laid down by the engineers, left the trees behind us, and got the first view of what the fury was all about.

Our ships were letting loose on a group of German bombers. I couldn't see them, but tracers lit the night sky, reaching from the flat of the sea across the wide curve above. Steady *booms* and fainter *rat-tat-tats* echoed over the water as the faraway drone of aircraft engines came closer, growing louder and more ominous. I thought I saw a meteor, then realized it was a bomber going down, a trail of yellow flame glowing in its descent until it vanished suddenly into the dark water. An explosion ripped the sky, closer now, a huge fireball falling in a gentle arc, disintegrating into a thousand pieces, each drifting its own slow way down to the waiting sea.

All the ships in the fleet must have been firing every weapon they had. Close to the horizon, the air was electric, bright white phosphorous tracers shining like neon lights on Main Street. Reflections from exploding and burning planes glowed in the awed, uplifted faces all around me. Except for involuntary gasps, everyone was silent. The firepower dancing across the star-drenched sky was too awesome, too catastrophic, too thick with death for words.

I watched the antiaircraft fire and wondered why the German aircraft hadn't dropped any bombs. I didn't see a single explosion near our ships. The planes were headed our way, but why would they fly over the fleet if they were coming to bomb us? They would've come from the opposite direction anyway—north not south. They only thing south of us was more of the Mediterranean, then Tunisia.

No, it couldn't be.

"Look, look, look!"

Hands pointed, heads swiveled, searching overhead to pick out what someone was yelling about in the midst of all the noise and explosions. I saw it, coming in low, less than a thousand feet off the water was my guess, a twin-engine plane trailing a long flame from its port engine. As it neared the shoreline, white parachutes blossomed behind it. Five, six, seven. Then, with the plane's engine on fire, the wing, folded up and broke off, pieces flying off wildly. The plane corkscrewed over our heads, spinning out of control as it vanished behind us. An explosion thundered in my ears, the sounds of steel hitting hard earth, and gas and ammo erupting, mingling into a horrible, unbelievable, wrenching sound.

"German paratroopers," someone yelled. "There's Krauts landing all around us." The group scattered, the previously quiet spectators screaming and firing their weapons into the air, fear replacing their sideshow glee.

"No!" I hollered, as loud as I could. "No, they're not Germans!"

No one listened. Guys pushed past me, running for cover, sprinting off the beach to save their lives. I watched the parachutes descend over the water, their bright whiteness as clear as if they'd been lit from beneath. One by one the canopies flattened, floated on the surface, then disappeared, each pulled under by an American paratrooper carrying his body weight in gear, weapons, and ammo. We were slaughtering our own.

I fell to my knees. I knew what this was. A reinforcement drop of the 82nd Airborne Division's 504th Regimental Combat Team, over two thousand men carried to the Gela Plain drop zone on C-47 transports. I ticked off the facts in my mind as if I were reading them from a report. I must have, before I came here. The navy was supposed to have been alerted. Whatever the plan was, it hadn't worked.

The firing died down. The transport planes had either made it over, or been scattered or shot down. How many, I thought. How many dead? I pounded my fist in the sand, the thought of our guys killing our own men a poison inside me. My skin went clammy. I gasped as if the wind had been knocked out of me. I cradled my head in my hands and cried, gushing tears and sobs. A small voice in the back of my mind asked, *What's the matter with me?* I didn't have an answer. What I'd seen was terrible and tragic, but why was I doubled up in agony, bawling like a baby?

That little voice didn't last long. I was sick to my stomach and vomited until dry heaves racked my body, while tears and snot ran down my face. I cried at the agony of useless death, then I cried for myself, scared I was losing my mind. I crawled off the beach, into a patch of scrubby brush, and curled up, hands tucked under my armpits. I was cold. I didn't want to think about it. I squeezed my eyes shut, but I couldn't hold it back. The wall was cracking, and names and faces flew at me. One of them was a friend of mine, I was sure, and I had killed him.

CHAPTER • SIX

I WATCHED THE DAWN light the soft, fluffy clouds over the Mediterranean, slowly turning darkness into red-tinged daylight. Sitting on a crate of mortar rounds I drank coffee, cupping my hands around the aluminum cup to take in the warmth. I blew on it, but the hot rim still burned my lips.

It had been cold last night when I left the beach and made my way up the road to find a place to sleep. A navy shore-party crew let me bunk in their tent, no questions asked. I fell asleep in a minute but an hour ago I'd awakened with a start, bolted upright, heart racing, not sure where I was, but certain I was being chased. A bad dream, I guess. I left before the swabbies woke up and thought of any embarrassing questions to ask me.

There were always guys walking around the rear area. Some of them belonged, some didn't. I looked like I didn't belong anywhere. No helmet, no weapon except my .45, and no unit I could claim as my own. I pinched an M1, a bandolier of ammo, and a helmet, then walked into a mess tent for some joe, filled my cup, and took some hot biscuits. At least I looked like I was going somewhere.

The sun was fully up. From behind me came the noises of a waking army—clanks, grunts, footsteps, curses, splashing water—rising in volume, accompanied by the sound of gear being buckled on, the soft tinkling and clinking of grenades and canteens and ammo clips that signaled a new dawn, an awakening to the possibility of death, maybe only one last day of life.

Out at sea, ships still moved back and forth, ferrying supplies and men, breaking the waves with purpose, cutting across water where hours ago helpless paratroopers had drowned. That was yesterday, this is today. That much I remembered about war. That was then, and it was horrible. This is now: Get some hot chow while you can, you have a chance to live another day.

There was something else I remembered but I was afraid to say it. Not actually *say* it, since I was alone. I mean even to think it. It lurked in the back of my mind like the aroma of a sweet strawberry ready to be eaten. I liked strawberries, especially when my mom served them with cream flavored with powdered sugar. At the kitchen table, in our home, in South Boston.

I let the words come, speaking them softly in my mind.

I like strawberries. And my name is Billy Boyle.

That was enough. There was other stuff, other memories, but they weren't from my mom's kitchen. I blinked and shut the door on them. I didn't want to know more, not yet. I drank some more coffee. It had gone cold.

Three British Motor Torpedo Boats sped across the bay a few hundred yards offshore. Their engines were deep and throaty, their wakes high, white, and frothy. They cut across each other and sent angry foam lapping against the beach. My stomach knotted, and I closed my eyes, scrunching them up tight. I felt my hand shake as coffee spilled out over the rim of the cup. I dumped it into the sand and packed my gear, my back to the sea. The sea. Flashes of ocean water flitted across my mind. The dirty harbor. Bone-chilling cold water. Scrambling over sharp rocks to the shore. Hot sun, palm trees. Then nothing. Pieces of a story that still made no sense.

Forget about it, I told myself. I knew I had to move on before some officer or sergeant starting asking questions or put me into a work detail. I had an idea; it wasn't much, but I had a couple of names. I had Harding, but somehow I knew he wasn't the first person I should approach. I listened to the MTBs in the distance, their motors growling low as they faded away. My thoughts were jumbled, and a wave of confusion and sweat broke over me. More images I couldn't make out flashed through my mind. Not water this time but a fire. Something about a fire, and an explosion.

I couldn't think about it now. I had to focus. Focus on Harding, yeah, hard-ass Harding, the last guy I'd want to run into. Unless I was going to turn myself in. West Point, by the book, a professional soldier. Not one to cut corners, and I needed a lot of corners smoothed out for me. I had to have help, but it had to come from someone who didn't live by U.S. Army field manuals. I trudged up from the beach, head down, M1 slung over my shoulder. Another GI heading up to the front or on some chickenshit errand for an officer. I thought some more about Harding. He was a lifer, but he didn't enjoy lording it over the enlisted men either. OK, Harding was all right for an officer. But I still couldn't go to him. I was surprised by my own thought: I respected him too much to put him in that position. It was odd learning who I was in bits and pieces, through fragments of dreams, splintered memories, names bubbling to the surface. A lot of it worried me, some of it frightened me, but finally this was something worthwhile I could hang on to. Something that wasn't bound up in dirty water, fire, and death.

Kaz. That name surfaced as quickly as I could say it. I could go to Kaz. I was amazed when I managed to remember his full name: Lieutenant—sometimes Baron—Piotr Augustus Kazimierz. Real Polish nobility, and there weren't many of them around anymore. I wasn't worried about putting Kaz in a tough spot. He didn't do things by the book, at least not anymore. Why was that?

I knew Kaz had been studying languages at Oxford when the war broke out, and that his entire family had been butchered by the Nazis. He'd talked his way into a commission with the Polish Army in exile, despite his bad eyes and bum ticker. They'd given him a job as a translator with Eisenhower and somehow he'd ended up working with me. There were memories with cobwebs around them and others down a deep black hole I couldn't even get close to. Kaz still wore cobwebs, and the dark hole blotted out my vision whenever I thought too hard about him. But I knew I could count on him. We were close, closer than I would've ever thought I could be to a skinny little four-eyed Polack genius.

I stopped. There it was. He was Polish. *I was Irish, Boston Irish.* I hadn't even thought about my family. Of course I was Irish, goddamn it! I kicked at a stone and kept going. Something in my head wasn't right. I kept thinking in circles, avoiding things, even the most obvious, natural facts of my own life. It felt like there was a barrier around some dark hole, filled with lost memories.

Lost? Or terrible? I trembled, afraid of finding that dark hole filled with nightmares. Instead, I thought about strawberries and walked onto the shore road, picked a direction and started off at a brisk march, rifle slung, just another GI under orders. The heat reflected up from the road and shimmered ahead of me. A few yards away from the breeze off the water and I felt the sweat begin to soak my wool shirt. A convoy of deuce-and-a-half trucks thundered by, each towing an artillery piece. Tires kicked up dirt and the wheeled artillery bounced on the uneven road, creating a dust storm as they went by. I shielded my eyes and pressed my lips together as dry, chalky particles settled on me. Head bowed, I didn't notice a column of soldiers on the other side of the road, standing back and waiting for the trucks to pass. It was the Italian they spoke that drew my attention.

There were over fifty POWs, most of them complaining about the bastards who got to ride in trucks that left them covered in dust on a hot road. I couldn't understand their Italian words, but I didn't need to. The long-suffering tone of the infantryman was universal, along with the hand gestures offered to the trucks disappearing around a corner. Two dogfaces guarded them, one at the front, the other at the rear of the column.

The Italian prisoners looked like a parade of happy hobos. With their lethal potential stripped away, they were nothing but a bunch of unshaven, smelly guys wearing all the clothes they owned. Some carried blankets or canvas bags, but most had nothing but the smiles on their faces. They were out of it. No more Germans at their backs, no more Americans gunning for them. They looked relieved as their two guards signaled them to move out.

One of the Italians looked at me and gave a mock salute, shouting out, "Brooklyn!" at the top of his lungs. He and his pals laughed. Did he imagine he'd be joining a cousin or brother in Brooklyn? Or was it joy at his overwhelming luck at being safely in American hands?

"Boston!" I yelled back. Someone whistled and more laughter rippled through the group. The tail end guard looked at me and shook his head, smiling wearily.

"What a war," he said, running his sleeve across his face, vainly trying to clear the caked dirt and sweat away.

The gesture nearly knocked me over. I envisaged another guy doing the same thing but in fading evening twilight. He was coated in grimy blackness and he drew his sleeve across his face just like this GI had. Except he was wearing an Italian uniform.

"Hey, buddy, where're you taking these guys?" I asked as I trotted across the road. I was looking at the GI but seeing the Italian soldier leaning over me, helping me up.

"POW center outside of Gela, place called Capo Soprano," he said. "They're givin' up faster than we can take 'em in."

As he spoke, I could hear another voice, a voice I recalled from days earlier.

"Come, my friend. I help you, yes? Come, my name is Roberto. Do not fear, I will take you back, then you help me get to America, yes?"

Roberto Bellestri. Late of the 207th Coastal Defense Division, a machine gunner who preferred dancing with American girls to killing American GIs. An Italian who chose to live rather than die for Mussolini. A deserter who was looking for safe passage to a POW cage at the first sign of invasion.

Roberto had talked incessantly as he took me—where? "I like Americans very much, I talk with the American ladies in Firenze, which you call Florence, every day in the *piazza*. They teach me their English better than my teacher at school, yes?" I could feel my arm across his shoulder, I had been hanging on to him as he led me down steps, to a street. Where?

"You OK?" The guard snapped his gum as he stared at me, concern, curiosity, and boredom mixed in his quizzical expression.

"Sure, sure, been out in the sun too long, that's all," I said.

"Ain't that the truth." He trudged off, his carbine, held loosely, pointing in the direction of his prisoners. They weren't high escape risks.

Roberto. Who only wanted to go to America and dance with rich women and learn better English. I couldn't picture where he had picked me up, but I knew it was where I'd gotten hit on the head and cut up. We'd gone down a dirt path and onto a street. The next thing I remembered, Roberto was lifting me into a cart, tossing out cauliflowers to make room, hollering in Italian and waving a pistol at a short guy in a dirty shirt and black vest who obviously owned the cart. He'd reached into my jacket pocket and pulled out fistfuls of lire, throwing them at the cart owner, who stared in amazement at the shower of cash, pulling them out of the air with meaty fists. The gold handkerchief with the *L* had come out with the lire and lay in my lap. I'd known it was important, and that I shouldn't lose it. As I stuffed it back into my pocket, the Sicilian caught sight of it. This loosed a torrent of apologetic Italian, directed at me, with little bows and an abashed smile. His hands, stuffed with lira notes, waved us off and he ended his outburst with the sign of the cross. Roberto climbed onto the seat and grabbed the reins, clucking at the donkey, who ambled off with a slow gait that led us away from his former owner, now richer than the donkey could have ever made him, but more frightened than he should have been by the sight of an ordinary silk handkerchief.

Capo Soprano, outside of Gela. I had to find it, and find Roberto. Because not only had I remembered all this, I remembered he'd been shot. Three GIs had come toward us, one of them pointing at me. Roberto had called to them from the cart, "Here, I save your wounded friend, Bill-lee Boyle from Boston, yes? Come help us."

In response, one of the soldiers had raised his carbine and fired. Roberto had gone down, clutching his side, blood seeping through his fingers. "Why have you shot me? I am a friend, your friend, yes?" His eyes looked up to me, wide with shock and surprise. Then some other vehicles had arrived, and some GIs had taken Roberto away as medics bundled me into their jeep.

Next thing I knew, Rocko was hovering over me in the field hospital. And I realized it was Rocko who'd aimed his carbine and shot Roberto. I couldn't remember the face of the guy who'd pointed at me first. But it told me something: Rocko and his pals had been out looking for me, and they'd known where to look. Since I was coming in from enemy territory, they had to have been in touch with someone behind enemy lines.

For that matter, the same went for me. I felt the handkerchief under my T-shirt and wondered at the power it had wielded over the fellow who had given up his cart so willingly, lire or no lire.

Yegg. A yegg is a safecracker. It came to me as easily as an apple from a grocery stand back on the beat in Boston. My memories were beginning to fall into place. A safecracker. The guy in Rocko's tent, he'd wanted to find their safecracker. Why? It didn't make any sense.

Sure it did. A bank heist in the middle of a war. Who'd notice?

CHAPTER ▪ SEVEN

I'D HAD ENOUGH OF walking. When I came to a cluster of tents, I strolled into the vehicle park and found a jeep screened from view by a supply truck. In the back were a couple of packs, which I left on the ground in case the owners had anything personal in them. I'd been a policeman, that I could recall now. My father and uncle were on the job in South Boston, too. Being a cop was in my blood, which meant I'd steal a jeep, but not somebody's letters from home or the souvenirs they'd scrounged or traded for. The army is impersonal, like an insurance company or the Boston Harbor Authority, so it didn't matter.

I gunned the jeep out of there and soon passed my Italian friends, slogging it out on their way to Capo Soprano. I almost waved but figured they'd be cursing me because of my jeep, so I passed them with all the indifference military drivers show for the common foot soldier on either side.

Minutes later, I saw the familiar white-banded helmets of the military police at an intersection about one hundred yards ahead. I braked and found myself trapped in a slow line of traffic. No roads led off to either side, only pine trees and cactus to my left and a row of bombed-out buildings on my right, their faded red brick scorched by fire. The MPs were looking anxiously up the other road, letting vehicles through the intersection one at a time. It didn't seem as if they were searching for stolen military property, but I knew they had a way of sniffing out suspicious characters. So I tried to play it as normal as I could when I approached the intersection.

"Hey, Sarge," I yelled to one of the MPs standing apart, obviously in charge of the detail. "What's the holdup? My captain'll have my ass if I don't get this jeep to him on time."

"Tell him to complain to General Eisenhower," the noncom growled back at me as the vehicle in front of me went through the intersection. The closest MP held up his hand.

Uncle Ike. *What?* Shock registered in my head and plunged down to my gut. *Uncle Ike?* It sounded right and true, and yet impossible. I felt the blood drain from my face as I tried to keep up with all the new information flooding into my brain.

"Hold up, you got a front-row seat to see Ike," the MP sergeant said. "That's gotta be worth a pissed-off captain any day, am I right?"

"Worth a dozen of them, Sarge," I managed to say.

My mom and Ike's wife were second cousins but I'd called him uncle since he was so much older. That had never meant much, until my folks had cooked up a scheme to get me a safe job.

Sitting in a line of jeeps and trucks, gripping the steering wheel until my knuckles whitened, it all started to come back, memories of my family rising up like heat from the road.

Dad, Uncle Dan, and me in Kirby's one night, soon after Pearl Harbor. They had laid it out for me, how the Boyles had already lost one man fighting for the British and they didn't want the same to happen in another generation. Frank, their older brother, had been killed in the trenches during their own world war. To the Boyles, the British were nothing more than oppressors, and they weren't worth a single Boyle life, much less two.

While my father and uncle came up with the solution, it was my mother who made it happen. Massachusetts politicians, all owing the Boyles for various favors granted over the years—especially on Election Day—were called. I rapidly found myself at Officer Candidate School, then assigned to Uncle Ike's staff, which I thought would mean an easy posting in the nation's capital. None of us could ever have guessed that this unknown general would be called upon to lead our armed forces in

Europe. And that I'd end up going with him from London to North Africa and now to Sicily. Holy shit! I was an officer. A lieutenant. Not much as officers go, but I was one. Not my first surprise of the day, but a big one.

So, I'm Lieutenant Billy Boyle, special investigator for General Dwight David Eisenhower. I look into military crimes for the general to be sure justice is served, but quietly, so as not to harm the war effort. How that had led me here, I still couldn't tell. I wondered if I'd gone bad, if I'd gotten in over my head in something on the wrong side of the law.

Two U.S. Army motorcycles roared through the intersection. One halted, pulling over to the side of the road, as the other continued. A small crowd of GIs had gathered as word spread that Ike was coming through. He wasn't a general people got excited over, like Patton or Montgomery, but he was in charge of the whole shooting match, and he was one of ours, a regular American guy. He had a calm determination that was more impressive than Patton's bloody exhortations or Montgomery's posturing for glory.

Had I failed Uncle Ike? Had I gotten mixed up in something that would make him ashamed of me? I remembered once, when I was a kid, I'd been caught breaking the windows of an old shed in an alleyway near our house. It had been a dare, and once I'd broken one, I was too caught up by the feel of the rock in my hand and the sound of shattered glass to stop. It was Mr. McGready's shed, and even though it was ready to fall down, he hadn't taken kindly to my efforts. And he knew my dad. It wasn't the spanking I'd gotten that bothered me or being sent to my room with no supper. It was the look of disappointment on my father's face. I didn't want Uncle Ike to look at me like that.

A jeep with a mounted .50 caliber machine gun slowly made its way through the intersection. A DUKW followed. The Duck, a new addition to our invasion arsenal, was a wheeled amphibious vehicle that traveled through water, climbed up onto the beach, and then drove on inland. I could see a bunch of brass, American and British, but no Uncle Ike. I found him in the next jeep, stopped short of the intersection so he could get out and talk to the troops. He wore a khaki uniform with a fore-and-aft cap, his general's stars lined up and gleaming. He returned salutes and shook hands, mixing with privates and noncoms like he was one of them. No one cheered or hollered like they might have done if it had been Patton barreling through in a tank. They just gathered around and chatted.

"Billy! Billy? Is that you?"

I heard a familiar voice call out from the DUKW and watched Captain Harry Butcher climb out, looking natty in his tropical navy uniform, even in this heat. Harry had been commissioned a U.S. Navy captain, but his nautical experience was strictly limited to cocktails on yachts. Harry was Uncle Ike's aide, which meant he had a variety of duties, mostly revolving around keeping visiting dignitaries, politicians, admirals, generals, prime ministers—anyone important enough to rate time with the general—happy. Harry was one of the busiest men on Uncle Ike's staff. I waved back, resigned to having been spotted.

"Billy, good to see you," Harry said, shaking my hand. As usual, military formalities were forgotten. I was Ike's nephew, I was among the anointed. "Haven't seen you around HQ, Billy. Where'd you disappear to? General, over here, look who I found!"

He waved excitedly, not waiting for an answer, and I counted my blessings. I got out of the jeep and stood at relative attention, snapping off a nervous salute and wondering what Uncle Ike knew about whatever I'd been up to.

"William, what a surprise!"

The general returned my salute and grinned broadly. His face lit up with affection that did little to hide the dark bags under his eyes and the lines of stress across his forehead.

"Good to see you, sir. I didn't know—"

"We arrived this morning by destroyer, straight from Malta," Harry put in. "The general wanted to see things firsthand. With everyone accompanying us, it's turned into a bit of a road show."

"Captain, would you excuse us for a moment?" Uncle Ike asked as he put his arm around my shoulder and steered me away from the crowd that hovered around us.

He gave my shoulder a quick squeeze as the smile on his face dropped away, leaving nothing but worried lines. We stood in the middle of the road, the sun beating down on us. I struggled to keep my voice normal while trying to remember the last time I'd seen Uncle Ike. Algiers? Was it Algiers? I could picture him at a desk, windows at his back, tape crosses on each, to protect against flying glass in case of an air raid.

"I haven't had a report yet from Sam," he whispered. That had to be Major Sam Harding. "Did everything go as planned?"

"Pretty much, General. I just have to wrap a few things up. I'm headed down to Capo Soprano now to find an Italian POW. He's important," I added hastily. I figured a vague answer mingled with the truth might sound convincing.

"Good. We've been out of touch with headquarters since we landed. There will probably be a report from Sam waiting for me on the cruiser. We're returning tonight on the *Vincennes*." Uncle Ike glanced at the bandage sticking out from under my helmet, and then studied my face, his eyes searching mine. "Are you all right, William?"

"Yes sir, I'm OK. Not much sleep the past few days, that's all."

He looked at me as if he saw into my soul. Uncle Ike was a good judge of character. You had to be if you were in charge of the entire war in the Mediterranean, balancing egos like Patton's and Montgomery's while keeping the brass and politicians back home happy. He knew something was wrong.

"Did you run into much trouble?"

"A fair bit," I admitted. I took off my helmet and wiped the sweat from my forehead with my sleeve. I thought about taking out the handkerchief and seeing what Uncle Ike's reaction would be, but that was too risky. "I got pulled into the fight on Biazza Ridge the other day."

"Is that where you got that?" Uncle Ike asked, pointing to the bandage wrapped around my head.

"No, that happened before. Just a scrape."

"How did you end up that far east?" His eyes narrowed as he watched me and waited for an answer.

Again, I figured the truth was the best way to lie. Part of me wanted to tell him everything and ask him what I was supposed to do, but the other part couldn't face letting him down. Not to mention the fact that I wasn't sure if I was mixed up in something a commanding general would take kindly to.

"I was in a field hospital getting bandaged up, and some paratroop officer shanghaied me. Next thing I knew I was on Biazza Ridge, trying not to get run over by a Tiger tank."

"Well, William, that's not what I intended when I sent you on this mission, but I'm glad you were there to lend a hand, and lived through it. Jim Gavin and his boys saved the day, I'll tell you that."

"Do you know about the paratroopers last night, sir?" I didn't know why I said that. Maybe I wanted to steer the conversation away from me. Maybe I was still haunted by visions of C-47s in flames arcing across the night sky. Uncle Ike's lips tightened and he looked away. He shook his head slightly and spoke to the ground at his feet.

"It shouldn't have happened, William. It shouldn't have happened. Men die in war, like those boys you fought with on Biazza Ridge. I accept that my role is to send them where they may well be killed. But to have so many die through a goddamn *mistake....*" He clenched and unclenched his hands. I saw his eyes race around the GIs surrounding us, perhaps wondering which of them would be dead before nightfall.

"I'm sorry, Uncle Ike, I didn't mean—it's just that I saw it all. I was down by the beach, and I saw it happen. We thought it was an air raid. It was awful. I'm sorry," I said again, turning away. I felt as if I were confessing, another burden he didn't need. But I couldn't help myself, I couldn't stop the words. "Some of the planes exploded, and some burned as they fell. I watched men jump and parachute into the water. Their chutes were the only things that floated. They all drowned. I was so close but I couldn't help them. I'm sorry."

I looked at the crowd around us, scanning it for MPs who might be out hunting for me, avoiding Uncle Ike's eyes.

"William. Look at me."

I did.

"I have to ask you to focus on the job right now. Can you do that? I know it's tough, and it's a lot to ask. Can you do it?"

I wanted to say no, that I needed a good night's sleep and to get off this damned island. I wanted to tell him there were things I couldn't remember, and that I was afraid of that dark hole in my mind. That I feared there were memories waiting even worse than those pitiful white parachutes floating on the water. I looked away, then back into his eyes.

"Yes. Yes, sir. I can. I'm close, General. Not too much longer."

"That's good, William. This is very important. What you do over the next few days will affect the rest of the campaign here and save lives. Plenty of these Italian troops are ready to give up, and I want to hurry that along as much as possible. I'm sorry to put all this on your shoulders, but I know you can do the job. I can't excuse a member of my family from danger, not when I have to send so many of these boys straight into it. Do you understand, William?"

For a second, I thought I saw pleading in those eyes, a desire for me to understand his burden.

"Yes, I do. Don't worry, Uncle Ike, I do." I spoke in a whisper, so no one else would hear, and I gripped tightly as we shook hands.

He smiled, his eyes lighting up, almost overcoming the dark circles. We stood in the middle of the hot, dusty road, and I knew I had to find out what it was I was supposed to do, and then finish the job for my weary uncle.

"OK, I've got to go," he said. "I've caused enough of a traffic jam already. Come back with Harry and tell me all about it when you're finished."

He slapped me on the back and made his way to his jeep, waving to GIs as he did. Harry Butcher stood a few yards away, where we'd left him. I looked at him and wondered what Uncle Ike had meant. Was I supposed to go somewhere with Harry Butcher?

"What's the matter, kid?" Butcher asked as he saw me staring.

"Ike said I should go back with you when I'm finished. Why would he say that?"

"Wrong Harry, pal. You've been out in the sun too long."

The small convoy pulled out, and the MPs waved me on. I drove, looking for the road to Capo Soprano, wondering who the other Harry was. And what the hell it was I was supposed to be doing that was so damned important. Not to mention how to do it before they threw me into a loony bin or the stockade.

CHAPTER ∎ EIGHT

CAPO SOPRANO WAS the perfect POW compound as long as you didn't care whether your prisoners escaped. A wide promontory, it was covered with ancient ruins, situated below groves of palm trees and stands of flowering cactus. Thick stone walls stood amidst dunes that swept up from the sea, and I wondered how tall the buildings that once stood here had been. In some places the crumbling walls were only a few feet high; in others, more than five. Columns and towers dotted the landscape, the walls dividing the sands neatly into open compartments, each containing Italian POWs, seated in the shade or stripped to the waist, enjoying the sun and soft sand. The breeze off the water was cool and lent a festive feeling to the gathering, as if it were one big beach party. GIs walked along the tops of the thick granite walls, surveying hundreds—no, thousands—of Italian POWs. They hardly needed guarding; it was more crowd control to keep them from rushing the landing craft that beached along the shore to take them aboard and off to the real POW camps in North Africa. *For you, the war is over.*

I went down the path from the roadway, walking toward a cluster of tents, wondering how I could possibly find one Italian POW among thousands. I stepped into the shade of the first tent I came to and caught the eye of a noncom with a clipboard and a harried look. His shirt was sweat-soaked, sleeves rolled up to the elbows. Other GIs sat at makeshift desks piled with mounds of paperwork. Tent flaps were up, and rocks served as weights for the papers that fluttered and struggled to be released to the winds. Two MPs, their helmets off, ate K rations and eyed me indifferently.

"Hey, Sarge, where do you keep the wounded Italians?" I asked the noncom.

Sweat plastered his hair over his forehead, and he brushed it aside with a beefy forearm. He was a staff sergeant, maybe thirty-five or so, and he had the steady look of a bull who knew his way around a cell block.

"Who wants to know, sonny?" He took a long drink from a canteen then set it down on a table made from a door and two crates with an empty, hollow sound.

"You a cop?" I asked.

"Yeah," he said. "Kansas City. That obvious?"

"You look right at home surrounded by prisoners," I said.

"That's what the lieutenant said when he stuck me here. What about you?" He narrowed his eyes and studied me.

"Boston PD. But don't tell my lieutenant. I don't want to get stuck babysitting POWs."

"Smart choice, rookie. OK, what do you need?"

"G-2 wants me to find a Roberto Bellestri, wounded and captured a few days ago. They think he has the dope on some gun emplacements." I turned so the Seventh Army shoulder patch was visible and hoped he wouldn't ask for orders or identification or the name of the officer who'd sent me on this errand.

"Wounded bad?"

"I don't think so. Graze along the ribs. But maybe a bit worse."

"Well, you're welcome to try the Italian aid station. Badly wounded cases are treated in field hospitals, only the walking wounded are sent here. We've got a bunch of Eyetie medics and doctors. We fixed them up with supplies, so they can take care of their own. Most of the wounded head down here to the beach as soon as they can."

"Why's that?"

"They say the Krauts are going to kick our ass off this island, and they want to get away before the Germans take over again. Ain't that somethin'? Except for the locals, that is. You hear about Bradley's order?"

"I've been a little out of touch," I said, with a fair amount of truth.

"Just came in," he said, pulling a sheet from his clipboard. "General Bradley's got some smarts. Any Sicilian who surrenders will be immediately paroled and allowed to go home. We released a couple hundred who left laughing and singing."

"The Vichy French shot at us when we came ashore near Algiers, and we ended up kissing them on both cheeks. The Italians shoot at us here and we let them go home. It's a crazy war."

"Well, only the Sicilians are cut loose. The other Italians are a close second when it comes to surrender. I never saw so many guys eager to get to North Africa."

"Odds are they haven't been there before. I have. Where do I find the aid station?"

"Take this dirt track," he said, pointing up a small rise. "See those palm trees? That's where it's been set up. Good luck."

"If I find him?"

"He's yours. I got plenty."

Three whitewashed stone houses stood along the narrow track, nestled under the shade of tall palms. Behind them were U.S. Army tents and what I guessed were Italian Army tents, some marked with red crosses. Though they were not guarded, no one looked as if he was about to sneak off to fight to the death for Mussolini. The first house held supplies and two orderlies playing cards. The next two were set up as makeshift operating rooms, but no one was on the tables.

"Can I help you?" The voice from behind startled me. I nearly brought my rifle up as I turned, then I steadied myself.

"Sorry," I said. He was Italian, and his English was precise, with that faintly British accent of Europeans who learned English from the source. He was drying his hands on a white apron worn over his uniform. He wore khaki breeches with puttees and heavy brown leather boots. His light khaki jacket was almost a dead ringer for the one I had been wearing, only his collar was more pointed and showed the insignia of the 207th Coastal Defense Division, a white patch with a blue triangle. Funny how those little things popped into my mind, things I didn't even know I knew.

"Are you a doctor?"

"Yes. Captain Dottore Enrico Sciafani. What can I do for you?" He cocked his head as if it was an invitation for me to introduce myself.

I let that vague request for rank and name hang in the air. "I'm looking for an Italian soldier who was wounded in the side three days ago. It wasn't too serious, and he may have been brought here. His name is Roberto Bellestri."

He nodded, as if Americans came calling for their Italian cousins every day. "Names mean very little here. We take care of light wounds and injuries then send the men down to the boats as soon as we can. They are most eager to go. We keep no records ourselves. That is now a matter for your army."

"Does the wound sound familiar, Doctor?"

"They all sound familiar, my friend. Where did you get yours?" He removed my helmet and peered at the dirty bandage.

I felt oddly comforted and at the same time disturbed. Doctor or not, he was supposed to be the enemy prisoner, not the one in charge.

"I don't remember." I was tired of lying; it felt good to come out and say it. This guy wasn't about to cause me any trouble.

"It happens, more often than you think. With some wounds, it is better not to remember. When did you last have that dressing changed?"

"Yesterday, I think."

"Come, I will give you a new bandage, then you can look for your man."

I followed him and sat down. It was cool inside, and I let him remove the gauze and clean the wound.

"This is not so bad," he said. "You have no recollection?"

"No. And I was hit in the arm too." I rolled up my sleeve and showed him those bandages. He cut them away and shrugged.

"Superficial. That makes your memory loss more interesting. What were you doing before the injuries were sustained?"

"I don't know that either. I woke up in a field hospital. I didn't remember anything, not even my name."

"Which is why you haven't told it to me?"

"No, it's come back. A lot has come back, but not everything."

He surveyed me as he studied my injuries. He worked quickly, wrapping my arm in gauze and tape, and putting a smaller dressing on my head, tying it off with a torn strip of white cloth. He was young, under thirty, with thick black hair, a narrow nose, and dark eyes. A small triangular scar marked one cheekbone; other than that, his skin was smooth except for fine lines at the corners of his eyes.

"Where'd you get your scar?" I asked.

His hand automatically went to the scar and brushed it faintly.

"My younger brother. We were sword fighting with sticks and he gave me this. My father stitched me up and then thrashed us both. With the sticks."

"Your father's a doctor?"

"Yes, in Palermo," he said, tying off the bandage and standing back to check his work.

"Is your brother still there?"

"His submarine never came back from patrol last year."

"I'm sorry."

"Ah, yes, so am I." He fingered the scar and sighed. "So am I. Now tell me what do you want with Roberto Bellestri?"

"I believe he saved my life. I remembered him a while ago, lifting me up and taking me away. . . from wherever this happened. Some men—Americans—found us, and one of them shot him. That's all I remember."

"You say your memories have been returning since this happened? When was that?"

"Three days ago, maybe four."

"Four days ago, the invasion had not occurred."

"Yes," I said.

"Very interesting. You think this Roberto may have some answers for you?"

"I hope so. I'm looking for him because I don't know what else to do."

"Why not do nothing? Your memories are likely to return fully, since they have started already."

"Because I'm not sure of what it was I was doing. And why."

"You know, my nameless friend, you are the most fortunate of men," he said, laughing as he poured water over his hands and dried them again on his apron. He pulled up a chair and sat next to me. "In some respects."

"How do you mean, Doctor?"

"What did the philosopher say? Something about the unexamined life not being worth living? Most men live an unexamined life, and have little interest in truly knowing who they are. Most go through life untested, with no need even to understand what they are capable of. They get up, eat, go to work, eat, make love, sleep, and get up again. Do you understand?"

"Yes, I do," I said, surprised that I really did.

"We, though, we have seen war. We know there is more to life than a meaningless cycle of tasks, do we not? We know the day is here to be savored."

"Yes," I replied, thinking of the placid sea the morning after the paratroopers dropped into it. "Yes."

"But you have another gift few men receive. You must discover who you are. You are unsure of what you will find. You are about to examine your life, once it is fully known to you, from the distance of your amnesia."

"It doesn't seem like much of a gift," I said.

"No, I doubt if it does. Do you have cigarettes, by any chance?"

I dug through my pack and found a pack of Luckies. "Here, take them. I don't smoke."

He lit one and inhaled, leaning back, closing his eyes as he exhaled. "Ah, that is good. American cigarettes, very good. Now, I have some things to tell you."

"What?"

"I do not think it likely that the wound to your head caused your amnesia. It certainly gave you a slight concussion, but nothing more. Real damage to the brain would have caused a serious organic amnesia. Your memories would not be returning so rapidly if that were the case."

"So what caused it?"

He drew on the cigarette and waited a moment before he answered.

"It sounds like what is called psychogenic amnesia. There are many references to it in recent literature. Recent meaning before the war. I had studied in Vienna and was starting my psychiatric residency in Rome when I was drafted. This is an area of interest for me."

"Are you saying I'm crazy?"

"No, no. It has nothing to do with mental illness, trust me. But personal identity may be lost for emotional or psychological reasons. An event may be too traumatic for the brain to process. So it obliges by not remembering the event. Our minds are quite inventive in this regard. Then, as time passes, the memories return. It is very unusual for such memory loss to last more than a few weeks. It usually comes back suddenly."

"So I'm only temporarily insane?"

"Yes," he laughed. "If you define loss of memory as insanity, then yes, you are temporarily insane. Rest assured your sanity will return. Although, as events all around us demonstrate, sanity and awareness are not always to be desired."

"If there are things I still can't remember. . ."

"Then they are likely the most distressing memories. The precipitating event might be any traumatic event you endured. No shortage of those in wartime."

"Sounds like things are going to get a lot worse before they get better," I said.

"Yes, when these memories return, you will have to deal with them. I would recommend you talk with a qualified doctor when they do."

"Maybe I'll come back and see you, Captain Doctor Sciafani," I said as I stood and gathered my gear. "Thanks for the first aid. I'll go look for Roberto now."

"Sit, sit down. There is no need."

"You know where he is?"

"Yes. I am sorry, but he died last night."

"Why didn't you tell me before?" My voice rose in anger and disbelief.

"Because I didn't know why you wanted him. And because he was found this morning in bed, his throat cut from ear to ear."

CHAPTER NINE

"WE BURIED HIM RIGHT away. The heat, you know."
Sciafani stood respectfully at the mound of sandy soil marking the
grave of Roberto Bellestri. There were only two other graves.

"You're sure this is Bellestri?" I asked. The wind drifted gritty dust
up from the mound and coated the toes of my boots.

"Yes. His name was on his identity disk, and his wound was as you
described. A bullet grazed his side, breaking two ribs but passing
cleanly through. He was in pain, but would have recovered fully."

"He wanted to go to America. Said he had cousins in Chicago."

"Every Sicilian has a cousin in New York or Chicago, my friend."

"A few in Boston as well," I said.

"Ah, Boston. Excellent hospital facilities there, I understand.
Massachusetts General Hospital, do you know it?"

I thought about that. Images of flashing red lights, blood, and
handcuffs raced through my mind.

"The emergency room, at least. I'm a police officer back home. My
name is Billy Boyle, by the way." I extended my hand and he shook it
with a firm, sure grip, but he hung on to me as he looked down at the
grave.

"He spoke of you. He said you would help him get to America, that he saved your life. Is that what happened?"

I pulled my hand away and rubbed my eyes, as if that might focus my memory. "I don't know. He may have. I could've told him I'd help him. Somehow, maybe, I don't know." A small pebble rolled down the side of the pile and bounced against the toe of my boot. Something had passed between Roberto and me, something important, my life and safety for his future. Had I promised him a ticket to the States? Had I lied to him? I kicked at the stone, wondering if I'd ever know, and walked through a stand of prickly cactus into the cooling shade of the palms. Two men, murdered. One was a bum, out for no one but himself. Even so, Rocko hadn't deserved what he got. And Roberto, eager and excited, had survived the invasion and hoped he'd found his ticket to the promised land. Maybe he had saved my life, or maybe that was a line designed to get him in good with the Yanks so he could make it to the States. Maybe he'd lied to me or I'd lied to him.

Anger pulsed through me and I felt. . . like myself. Rage felt familiar and close. It felt like desire. For what? Vengeance, justice? No, those words were too fancy. I needed things to be set right, that's all. And it felt like something I knew how to do, although I couldn't have said exactly how.

I was electric, awake, vibrant now as if everything else before had been someone else's life or dream or nightmare. Was this who I was? A flash of fear and shame swept through me and I let it go. This was better than not knowing, always wondering, merely guessing at who I was. I decided to take myself as I found me. I was dog tired, hot and dusty, but I was here, savoring the day, and that was enough.

Sciafani stopped at the first two tents we came to, chatting with bandaged Italian soldiers who laughed and shook his hand. It sounded like he was saying his farewells, and it hit me that, as a Sicilian, he had had his ticket punched. He was a free man, and he knew the island.

"Captain Doctor Sciafani," I said, mustering all the military courtesy I could, "are you leaving? Going home?"

"Yes. What is your rank, may I ask?"

"Lieutenant, sir. Lieutenant Billy Boyle."

"Well, yes, Lieutenant Boyle, I am. I have my parole. There is another doctor, from Milano, which is unfortunate for him. He will remain here. There is little to do that will challenge him. And you need not call me captain. I am once again simply a *dottore*, which is quite enough for me."

"I guess that makes me your first patient as a civilian," I said, following him into his tent.

"Yes, Lieutenant Boyle, perhaps it does. I am sorry I will not be able to see you again, as yours is a most interesting case." He began to stuff a few items of clothing into a knapsack, pausing to inspect a shirt that was covered with stains where it wasn't replete with gaping holes. He dropped it to the ground and put on his knapsack. Collecting a canteen of water and his khaki *bustina*, the soft wool cap the Italians wore, he looked at me as if I were a houseguest who couldn't take a hint.

"I have a jeep," I said. "I can drive you part of the way."

"That is very kind, but I do not think so. Not far from here, being with an American will make me a target. Alone and on foot, I can avoid the *tedeschi*. I know the hills and back roads. Please excuse me."

He hung the canteen from his shoulder and pulled his *bustina* on, angling by me sideways to get out of the tent. I couldn't blame him for wanting to steer clear of the Germans. I scurried after him, knowing I needed a local to help me figure things out but also aware that the last one who had helped me had been rewarded with a mouthful of sand for his troubles.

"Just up to the main road then," I said, feeling like a high-school kid asking to walk a girl home. He nodded his acceptance and I led him to the jeep, cutting across the rocky slope, directly above the tents and enclosures on the beach.

Below us, landing craft picked up Italian POWs while the lucky Sicilians among them trudged away in the opposite direction, toward their homes. As we sat in the jeep I remembered the odd note I'd been carrying around.

I gave it to Sciafani. "Does this mean anything to you?" I asked him.

"'To find happiness, you must twice pass through purgatory,'" he read. "Yes, I have heard this. Why?"

"It has something to do with where I was when Roberto found me, I think."

"Then you were some distance away, my friend," Sciafani said. "In Agrigento, perhaps 130 kilometers east of here."

I started to ask him how he'd reached that conclusion when two jeeps full of MPs raced down the road and braked in front of the tent where I'd been. They were in such a rush they didn't notice the vehicle park or the jeep. The two MPs who'd been eating K rations came out to meet them and they all looked at some papers while one MP pointed up the path I'd taken to the Italian aid station. They took off at a trot, an officer, his hand on the .45 in his holster, leading the way. The MPs behind him carried Thompsons and carbines.

"Must be a dangerous war criminal up there," I said as I started the engine, put it in reverse, and backed up the road as quietly as I could. When I was out of their sight I turned hard and floored it, kicking gravel out from the rear tires and praying more reinforcements weren't headed for me.

"Yes, Lieutenant Boyle, if that is who you really are. Perhaps he is a very dangerous man."

Sciafani hung on as the jeep bounced over the ruts up to the junction with the main road. I didn't want to lose any time getting away from the MPs, and I wasn't slowing down enough to let him jump out.

Then I saw the truck blocking the road ahead. They'd sealed it off when they came to look for me. Two guys in nondescript khaki leaned against a Dodge WC-52 Weapons Carrier parked sideways across both lanes. On either side rocks and cacti blocked escape. I slowed and wondered if I could make it out of there on foot. We came closer, and I saw the two men more clearly. They were lounging against the truck as if they were casually waiting for someone who was late for an appointment. One of them was smoking and for a change no guns were pointed at me. It didn't make sense. Then it did. One of the men was Kaz. I pulled to a stop within a few feet of him and couldn't keep myself from smiling. He looked grim, which was unusual. The scar that split his face from the corner of one eye down to his chin didn't tend to make him look cheery, but his usual expression was carefree, or at worst nonchalant. I knew it was a pretense that pleased him, and that the look on his face now was a truer reflection of his heavy heart.

"Kaz," I said, leaning over the steering wheel. He was my friend, and I was glad to have met up with him. He was only person I could trust to believe me and not turn me in.

"Who is this?" Kaz pointed at Sciafani, his eyes still on me.

"I am Dottore Enrico Sciafani, late of the Italian Army. I have my parole papers."

"*Lei è siciliano?*" Kaz asked.

"*Sì, sono siciliano.*"

"All right, both of you in the back of the truck. Banville will take the jeep," Kaz said in sharp, clipped tones.

I had questions, plenty of them, but hearing the snarl of engines behind us I decided they could wait. Kaz took Sciafani by the elbow and hurried him along. The man he called Banville took my place at the wheel of the jeep, eyeing me strangely as we passed, but there was no time to wonder if I knew him. I thought I might, but it was like seeing somebody who resembled someone you knew, yet not closely enough for you to feel OK about clapping him on the shoulder and telling him it had been too long. Banville wore crumpled, faded British naval khakis and a weather-beaten white naval cap with threadbare gold braid. Unshaven, with a huge knife and a revolver on his belt, he looked piratical.

"Hurry," was all Kaz said as he hustled me into the back of the truck. Kaz was a slight guy, thin and reedy, and wore steel-rimmed spectacles that he really needed. But he wasn't afraid to use a pistol for close work, that much I remembered from North Africa. He'd gotten me out of a jam in Algiers. I recalled a Vichy French jailer tumbling down the stairs and Kaz strolling into the cell block with a ring of keys in one hand and a smoking Webley revolver in the other. He'd been smiling then, but today the expression on his scarred face was grim.

Canvas covered the rear of the truck, a small three-quarter-ton job that was handy for transporting weapons or a few men tightly packed. It was bigger than a jeep, but not by a lot. What it did have going for it was that no one could see me, and that Kaz had stashed gear, weapons, food, and water in the back. I lifted aside the canvas flap and saw Banville following us in the stolen jeep, far enough back not to be choked on our dust. Banville. That name was familiar. I did know him. A British sailor. From where?

As we rounded a curve I noted a group of tents with aerials thrusting toward the sky, protected from overhead view by camouflage netting stretched between palm trees. Wire ran up one tree and across the road. I wondered if Lieutenant Andrews—Rocko's pal—was in there, working on a German dialer, whatever the hell that was. And if he'd taken a walk down to Capo Soprano last night with a sharp knife. And Charlotte? The voice in Rocko's tent had mentioned a girl. What was a girl named Charlotte doing mixed up in this?

"They are friends of yours, these English?" Sciafani asked from the bench opposite, jolting me from my thoughts.

"Yeah, yeah, I know them. Kaz is Polish, though."

"Ah, the Poles," Sciafani said. "As unfortunate in their geography as we Sicilians. Destined to be overrun by armies from the east and west, just as the Greeks, Carthaginians, Romans, Moors, and Normans have conquered us. They have all come here, but only the *siciliano* remains."

I barely heard Sciafani's history lecture. I was remembering what I hadn't wanted to remember about Kaz. His scar. And Daphne Seaton, who had loved him and had been my friend. Daphne, who'd been murdered to keep her silent, a car explosion immolating her and ripping Kaz's face and heart. I remembered my resolve to keep Kaz busy, to keep him from blowing his brains out. Based on the look on his face I realized I hadn't been doing my job. Kaz liked to be amused, and he had often said that working with me made him interested in what tomorrow might bring. Now he didn't look much amused at the prospect of today, much less tomorrow.

Something else ate at my gut, but I couldn't tell what it was. I knew that I hadn't remembered everything yet. Daphne had been killed, Kaz badly injured, and when he'd returned to duty he'd become a killer who took chances with his life. I didn't want to think about what else there might be. I rested my head in my hands and tried to quiet the rage in my mind as the unfairness of Daphne's death and Kaz's loss overwhelmed all other thoughts.

Daphne and Banville. There was more, about them both. What?

"Lieutenant Boyle, are you weeping?" Sciafani asked.

I didn't realize I was until I looked down at the floorboards and saw tiny drops, fading in the heat and vanishing as quickly as they appeared.

CHAPTER · TEN

WE DROVE FOR NEARLY an hour, mostly at a crawl, in the midst of a convoy of trucks and tanks. I tied back the rear canvas flaps for some air, but loosely so they gave us shade and cover from prying eyes. We passed an artillery unit, the short barrels of their 75mm pack howitzers sticking out beneath camouflage netting. Dappled shade cut across the backs of the crewmen kneeling to fire and feed new shells into the smoking breech as each empty casing was rapidly cast aside. The roar of cannon fire was followed by dull *crumps* on a far hillside where brown dirt puffed into tiny explosions that looked harmless at this distance. But I knew there were small red-hot shards of metal flying through the air, rending flesh wherever they encountered it. Sciafani sat with his head in his hands, and I knew he too was thinking about the men on the ground, his comrades of yesterday, still suffering today. Perhaps he couldn't bear to watch, with his parole in his pocket and thoughts of safety, home, and a life to be lived vying with his sense of duty. The war had made it possible for *me* to think and believe entirely contradictory things. I knew I wanted nothing more than to go home, and yet I was willingly being carried to the front lines, the only place I would find what I was missing, what I needed to feel whole again, to understand what home really meant.

The sound of artillery fire faded as we drove. I put it out of my mind because to think too much about what we were doing to the enemy did no good at all. The same kind of bombardment could land on me tomorrow, so it was best not to imagine the results or think too deeply about it. Shrapnel didn't care about the color of the uniform it shredded.

Occasional rifle fire rippled across the landscape, but it was impossible to tell if it was from the side, front, or rear. A few quick *pop pop pops* and a burst of machine-gun fire here and there—the sounds of tentative skirmishes rather than a full-scale battle. Traffic slowly thinned out, vehicles taking turns or pulling over and stopping to disgorge GIs in fresh uniforms, their clean shirts and full packs marking them as replacements for units chewed up since the landings.

We drove a while through silent, gently rolling farmland, the soil almost black where it had been recently turned. Kaz took a side road, little more than a dirt track, and pulled over. Banville pulled the jeep off the road and into a field of ripe grain. The stalks fell away from us, the wind from the sea carrying the faint smell of salt as it brushed our backs. Banville took a gas can from the back of the jeep and sprinkled gasoline over it, then lit a match and tossed it into the backseat. A soft *thurmp* and flames burst over the vehicle, shimmering in the hot air, red-yellow brightness quickly dulled by black smoke from burning rubber.

Banville got up front with Kaz and we drove off, leaving the harsh sound of an exploding fuel tank behind, the smell of gas and rubber trailing us. Sciafani looked at me. But I was a stranger here myself. Or maybe not. The burning wreck disappeared as we turned a corner. There was something familiar about Banville and fire. I wondered what it was. Thinking about fire caused a pounding in my chest, so I tried not to dwell on it.

We drove on, the road winding and rising as we passed more farmland. Grain was everywhere, ready to harvest, but farmers were scarce. So were farmhouses, for that matter. We drove through one small village that could've passed for a heap of stones if it wasn't for the blue daisies neatly bordering small vegetable gardens. The houses were squat and square, built from white-gray rock that looked like it had been bleached in the sun for a hundred years. A woman dressed in black, squat and square as her house, fed an outdoor oven from a stack of firewood. The oven, made from the same stone but blackened by smoke, looked like a charred entrance to the underworld.

"She makes the bread *di campagna*," Sciafani said. "They cook outside to keep the house cool."

"They?" I asked.

"The peasants," he said.

"So I guess your mother cooks inside the house then?"

"It depends upon which house. But never mind about my mother. Tell me where we are going."

"Sorry, Dottore, but all I know is that Kaz can be trusted."

"Is he a relation of yours?"

"No," I said. "He's Polish, I'm Irish."

"You have known each other for a long time?"

"No," I said, "about a year."

"A year? Then he is a *staniero* to you. As you are to me. A stranger. You cannot know a man well enough to trust him if he is not a relation, or if you have not known him since you were both *bambini*."

"You wouldn't trust anyone except a blood relation or childhood friend?"

"Why should I?" He looked at me, his dark eyes steady as the truck rumbled over the dirt track.

"Because you have to, when there's no one else. Kaz and I have gone through a lot together, maybe a lifetime in that year."

"Yes, perhaps," he said. "Perhaps. Was the vehicle stolen?"

I was surprised by his sudden shift in conversation, and wondered if his command of English was all it seemed. "It was," I said.

"Then he is a smart friend, at least. He speaks Italian like a Tuscan, but, still, he is smart."

"I think he studied in Florence before the war."

"Ah, yes, that would explain it," Sciafani said, as if bemoaning a sad but inescapable fate.

I lifted the canvas side of the truck and stuck my head out. The ground had changed from gently rolling fields to steeper hills and deep gullies. No entrenchments, supply dumps, or burned buildings marred this landscape. It was oddly quiet, and I realized how accustomed I had become to the sounds of an army at war: the echoes of fighting as well as the rear-area noise of machinery, engines, shovels, shouts, and curses.

Here, it was calm and peaceful, and that worried me. Kaz slowed as the road narrowed where a small stone bridge crossed a stream. Beyond the stream he turned onto an even smaller path, lined with lemon trees, their yellow fruit ripening in the sun. On either side were fields of purple cauliflower, their huge heads looking ready for market. Bushy green trees flourished along the streambed. More color surrounded me here than anywhere I had seen before on this island.

"Now you begin to see the real Sicily," Sciafani said.

The truck slowed to a crawl as Kaz turned a corner, halting in front of a stone barn, its double wooden doors swung wide open. An elderly Italian man, wisps of white hair flying out from under his cap, hobbled out, hitching his suspenders up over a worn gray collarless shirt that might once have been as white as his whiskers. He nodded to Kaz, who spoke to him in Italian, with his Tuscan accent.

"He asks if anyone has been here. The old man says no, not since last night, and asks if he brought the American cigarettes," Sciafani said, translating the exchange.

Apparently Kaz had, so the old man motioned him to drive the truck into the barn. As we got out, the old man stopped short when he saw Sciafani in his Italian Army uniform. He pointed at him and spouted off at Kaz, but Sciafani interrupted him. All I understood was *siciliano, siciliano,* which seemed to do the trick and calmed the fellow down. Sciafani introduced himself, not mentioning his discarded rank.

"Dottore Enrico Sciafani," he said somewhat formally, straightening up as he did so. The old man removed his cap and murmured what sounded like apologies.

"*Mi chiamo* Filipo Ciccolo, Signore," he added with a bit of a bow as he backpedaled and stuck his cap back on. Kaz handed him four cartons of Lucky Strikes, which he took and hid under a tarpaulin.

"Filipo did not wish to have a Fascist under his roof," Sciafani explained. "I assured him that as a Sicilian neither would I."

It made sense, as far as it went. I had been told that Sicilians were not too fond of Mussolini and his Fascists. But there was something about old Filipo's reaction to Sciafani that interested me. It was as if he acknowledged him, respected him, and maybe feared him. And now, for the first time, I noticed that the truck we'd been riding in didn't have the regular army paint job. No white star, no serial numbers or unit designations were stenciled on it. It wasn't even army green, more of a nondescript tan color. At a distance, covered in dust, it might pass for any small truck in any army.

"It's like my jacket," I said to no one in particular.

"Exactly," Kaz said.

We filed out of the barn, Filipo shutting the double doors behind us. Kaz led us around the back to a house made of the same stone as the barn. It was larger than the ones I'd seen in the village, but still square, with thin slits for windows. A small patch of peas and beans stood outside a side door, surrounded by more of the familiar blue daisies. A grove of orange trees, growing near the stream, shaded the front of the house.

"We will stay here for the night," Kaz said as he stood in the doorway.

Above the door frame, a little niche had been carved out of the wall. A ceramic tile bearing the image of the Virgin Mary was surrounded by cut flowers, a small candle flickering in front of it. Framed in the dark doorway, with the religious symbols floating above his head, Kaz looked menacing, a small but dangerous holy warrior.

"Dottore," he added, "I believe you would find civilian clothes more to your liking?"

"Certainly," Sciafani answered.

"For now, we must insist on your company, Dottore. May I have your word you will accept our hospitality, or will it be necessary to impose it upon you?"

Kaz had a way with words. No one else I knew could tell a guy he was still a prisoner and have it come out so nicely.

"You have my word, for now."

"Good. It will make for a much more pleasant evening," Kaz said, walking into the house under the Virgin's gaze as the candle sputtered out in a sudden, sharp breeze.

Signora Ciccolo showed us to the well, where we could pump water to wash up, and then led Sciafani away to give him the couple's son's Sunday suit. The son was missing. If he was in an American POW camp in North Africa, he was in the safest place he could be, she told Kaz. They hoped for the best. She reappeared minutes later carrying the discarded uniform, which she put into the smoldering fire in her outdoor oven. Smart woman, I was sure Sciafani was thinking.

While Sciafani was changing clothes inside, Banville, Kaz, and I sat at a wooden table under a grape arbor attached to the rear of the house. An earthenware jug of red wine and four cups waited for us, but the time didn't feel right for a toast, although the smell of grapes filled the shaded air and I could almost relax.

"Well?" I said. "Does Harding know about this?"

"You know Major Harding," Kaz said. "He wouldn't approve, so I didn't ask. Nor did he ask why I went with the MPs this morning."

"Why are those MPs after me?"

Kaz and Banville exchanged confused looks. They'd gone to a lot of trouble to snatch me and hide me out here, but they hadn't seemed too happy about it. Now they seemed at a loss for words.

"Don't tell me you don't know?" Banville said, an edge of anger creeping into his tone. I was about to assure him I didn't when Kaz broke in.

"For desertion in the face of the enemy and for the murder of Sergeant Rocko Walters. Both offenses are punishable by death. Which is why we are hiding you. The road we came in on is a dead end. There is nothing of military value here, so we should be unmolested."

"Good, because there's probably another charge against me by now. An Italian POW, Roberto Bellestri, was murdered last night. I went to the POW camp to talk to him, but it was too late."

"Was it to silence him, Lieutenant?" Banville asked.

"No. I needed him to tell me what had happened. Who brought those charges against me? Was it Harding?"

"No," said Kaz. "He defended you, but in the end a JAG officer filed charges."

"What the bloody hell is that?" asked Banville.

"The American army legal branch," Kaz answered. "The Judge Advocate General's Corps."

"How did JAG hear about me?"

"First, you need to explain what's happened. The whole truth," Kaz said, his expression giving away nothing.

"OK, guys, I have to start from the beginning. I don't have every-thing straight, but here goes. . . ."

I told them about waking up in the field hospital and not remem-bering a thing. About Rocko appearing and his story about finding me with an Italian soldier and bringing me to the hospital. About Biazza Ridge, Slim Jim, Clancy and Joe, and Aloysius Hutton. About how I made it back to the field hospital and saw them looking for me, except I didn't know who *they* were. About sneaking into Rocko's tent of treasures and what I heard there: Andrews, the yegg, Charlotte, every-thing. About the note, the bath, and Rocko's fear of what would hap-pen to him if he squealed. How I was clobbered on the head and woke up to find Rocko dead in the tub. How the paratroopers were shot to pieces and fell to the sea in flames. About remembering Roberto Bellestri and Harding, and how things were coming back to me, but not everything, and that the good *dottore* had said the things I hadn't yet remembered were the worst of my vanished memories.

"You remember me, it seems," Kaz said, disbelief battling with hope on his face.

"Yes, you came back to me. But there's something else, something about a fire. When I look at Banville I see visions of fire."

"Do you remember Banville from before?" Kaz asked.

I studied Banville's face a long time. I connected him with a build-ing or a car or both, on fire. But where?

"No. You're familiar, but I can't place you," I said to Banville. I looked at Kaz, and his face was ashen.

"Can't place me? What the hell are you up to? And where's my captain, that's what I want to know!" Banville's voice rose with his anger, and his last words were accompanied by his fist slamming on the table. He still meant nothing to me. Kaz turned his head to avoid my eyes. He knew. I wanted to ask but I was afraid of the shattered look on his face. I was scared of what I didn't remember, but it was easier to lash out at Banville.

"I don't know who you're talking about, goddamn it! If I could remember I'd tell you, don't you get it?" I wanted to grab Banville by the collar and take out all my frustrations on him. It felt good to get angry. And I was glad of the distraction for Kaz.

"Did you leave him somewhere? Don't tell me you can't remember your good friend Lieutenant Harry Dickinson? The fellow you almost got killed up in the North Sea? The man who captained the Motor Torpedo Boat that took you to Bône? Where he got shot in the leg, helping you?"

Banville was up now, his clenched fists resting on the tabletop as he leaned over me.

"I was in the hospital, Billy. In Algiers. You saved my life, do you remember?" Kaz asked.

"No, I don't. I don't remember being in Algiers. There are all sorts of gaps in my memories. I have no idea who Harry is. Ike mentioned Harry somebody this morning—"

"You saw General Eisenhower? Today?" Kaz asked, surprised.

"By accident, on the road to the POW enclosure. Harry Butcher was with him. I remembered Butcher, but Ike mentioned another Harry, said I should bring him with me to see him when it was all over."

"Eisenhower knows only the bare outline of the original plan, nothing about what has actually happened," Kaz said.

"Kaz, what was the plan? What was I supposed to be doing?"

I wanted to ask if I was an assassin, a murderer made legal by a state of war, but I didn't. If it was true, I knew Kaz would dress it up in nicer words, but I wasn't ready to find out.

"You do not remember coming ashore?" Kaz asked, avoiding my question.

"No, nothing before the field hospital—wait, no—at first that was all, but then I did remember Roberto leading me away from somewhere. He wanted to surrender, and helped me to our lines. Rocko found us and shot him."

"Rocko Walters, the soldier who was killed?"

"Same guy. He babysat me in the field hospital. He was very interested in this," I said as I drew out the silk handkerchief.

"Put that away!" Kaz said, thrusting out his hands to cover it. "And thank God you still have it."

"What the hell is it, and why did Rocko want it so badly?" I asked as I stuffed it into my pocket now, wishing it had gone into the fire with Sciafani's uniform.

"It might be best not to give Lieutenant Boyle too much help, medically speaking." Sciafani's voice surprised us as he approached to sit at the table. Kaz glanced at me, probably wondering the same thing I was. Had Sciafani seen the handkerchief? He seemed not to have noticed, as he was busy pulling and tugging at the black suit that had replaced his uniform. It was a bit too large on him, but he was the kind of guy who could look good in most anything. He adjusted the cuffs of the threadbare white shirt as if they were gleaming white linen with ivory cuff links.

"How do you mean?" Banville asked. He scowled at Sciafani with as much distrust as he showed me.

"Well," Sciafani said, with the confident air of a man in a new suit when his previous garments have been khaki or gray-green, "I am not an expert in these matters, but I have studied in Vienna with students of Freud. And it is best if the patient recalls the missing memories on his own. Which has begun already, Lieutenant?"

"Yes, as I told you—"

"How much have you told him?" Kaz said, his eyes darting between Banville and Sciafani.

"Only that I had memory loss. I was keeping it a secret from everyone else, but it seemed as if it couldn't hurt to tell a POW the truth. He told me I had some sort of psycho amnesia."

"Psychogenic amnesia," Sciafani corrected. "The result of witnessing a traumatic event. It is not permanent, as I said."

"The whole war's bloody full of traumatic events," said Banville, his face turned away from me but not so far that I couldn't see his mouth turned down in a sneer.

"Why did you keep it a secret?" Kaz asked.

"I didn't know what I had done before I arrived at the field hospital," I said. "Things didn't add up, like that jacket I wore instead of my uniform, and amount of time I must have been on the island. I didn't know if I was legitimate or—"

"Enough," Kaz said, holding up his hand. Signora Ciccolo entered the arbor bearing a bowl filled with steaming pasta with cauliflower and anchovies. Filipo followed with plates and bread and they set the table, serving Sciafani first. They chattered in Italian, and I watched Kaz as he watched them, worry creasing his forehead once more. Banville poured himself wine, his grim eyes focused on me. Suspicion and secrets hung in the air, mixing with the smell of fresh bread, making me hungry and anxious at the same time.

"I don't speak the Sicilian dialect," Kaz said to Sciafani. "What were you talking about?" Sciafani shrugged, an entirely Italian gesture, lips down turned, shoulders and palms up, head cocked slightly to the side.

"Family," he said. "Who our fathers, uncles, and cousins are. Sicilians always seek to find what we have in common, what binds us to each other. It is all we have."

"And what do you and the Ciccolos have in common?" Kaz asked.

"His nephew lives in my village, about thirty kilometers from here."

"Village?" I asked. "I thought you were from Palermo."

"Palermo is where I have my medical practice. But I was born in a village in the mountains."

"Which village?" I asked.

"Sciafani."

"You're named after a village?" I asked.

"Um, no," Sciafani said as he chewed on a piece of bread. He washed it down with a drink of wine and smiled at me. "In the fourteenth century, the honor of the village name was given to my family."

"What are you then, this fellow's lord and master?" Banville asked.

His dislike for me seemed to transfer to Sciafani automatically. He drained his third glass of wine, staring at Sciafani as he tilted his head back.

"*Il signor* Ciccolo is his own master, as is any Sicilian man. He would not be alive today if he were not. He is a good *mafiusu*, and knows his own worth."

"He's in the Mafia?" I asked.

"No, no, he is *mafiusu*. It is not a gang of thieves, although that may be the case in America. To be *mafiusu*, a man understands who he is, and is ready to stand against all outsiders. We do not depend on others to give us justice. A man makes his own. In any clash with authority, Sicilians stand together; that is to be *mafiusu*, a man of honor. As I said, it is all we have. But do not worry. *Il signor* Ciccolo is a man of his word, even to one who speaks with a Tuscan accent."

Kaz nodded, and ate the food in front of him. I tasted the wine, and it was harsh.

CHAPTER · ELEVEN

KAZ AND I SAT alone. Banville had drunk too much and stag-
gered off to sleep in the barn, where he was to keep watch on the truck.
Sciafani was taken to the room of the Ciccolos' son, the bed of honor
in their meager home. Signora Ciccolo brought out a candle in a glass
chimney and set it between Kaz and me on the table. It lit most of
Kaz's face, casting a deep shadow along the scar on his cheek.

"Tell me—"

"The doctor said it would be best if you remembered on your own."

"You don't want to talk about the past?" I said.

"No. I do not."

"My mission, though, you have to tell me about my mission, and
this Harry Dickinson. What does it all mean? Why am I here?" I
glanced around, whispering, as if there were spies and eavesdroppers
surrounding us.

"The handkerchief was a message, a token. You were supposed to
deliver it."

"Who to?"

"Wait, Billy," Kaz said, holding up his hand.

It was the first time he'd called me by name, the first sign of friendship from him, and it filled me with a startling joy. After losing all

memory of friends, it was like a drink of cool water on a hot day, re-freshing and reviving my soul.

"I will tell you a few things, and we will see if that helps you remember on your own. It is very important, and I don't want to set you back in any way."

"Maybe we should ask the doctor?"

"No. It would be too great a risk. We don't know much about him, not even if he really is who he says he is."

"You don't trust him?"

"No, of course not. He has a piece of paper saying he is no longer our enemy, but that is all it is. Paper. And Filipo treats him as some-one to be obeyed."

"Can you trust Filipo? How did you connect with him?"

"Let me start at the beginning," Kaz said. He removed his steel-rimmed spectacles and cleaned them with a white handkerchief. He adjusted them carefully, looking a bit like the studious bookworm I had first come to know in London. Back when. . . when what? A memory of London, of headquarters in Grosvenor Square, the sound of foot-steps on marble stairs. . . .

"Billy?"

"What?" I snapped at Kaz, the thread of memory gone. "Sorry." I waved my hand at him to continue and took a drink of wine. I set the glass down and felt the wood of the table, worn smooth at the edges, patterns etched in the grain like the contours of the hillsides. It was very old, dark and stained with spills from meals served decades, maybe a century ago. I ran my thumb across the shiny surface and wondered at the years of talk, food, and drink it had witnessed, and who had made it, and how long ago.

"Billy, do you need to rest?"

I shook my head.

"It was hard not knowing, not remembering," I said.

"But perhaps not as difficult as remembrance?"

I barely heard the words. It was a beautiful night. Through the grapevines I could see the twinkling of stars. The air had cooled and the wind brushed through the grove of orange trees, *whooshing* the leaves like waves lapping at the shore. It was pleasant here, as I was poised on the brink of recall, but terrifying too. I was like a child at the seashore, fascinated by the water but too frightened to go in.

"Let's find out," I finally said.

"Harry Dickinson and Nicholas Cammarata. Do those names mean anything to you?"

"No. Banville said I knew Harry. Is that true?"

"Yes. He's a Royal Navy lieutenant, captain of a Motor Torpedo Boat." Kaz watched me, looking for the lightbulb to go on, but I couldn't even find the switch.

"Nothing," I said. "The other guy?"

"Lieutenant Nick Cammarata, U.S. Naval Intelligence."

"Zilch. Tell me more."

"Lucky Luciano?" Kaz lifted an eyebrow, as if to dare me not to recognize this name.

"Sure, Mafia boss, serving time in a New York state pen. Prostitution charges, I think."

"Correct. He was born Salvatore Lucania, in a village not far from where we are now: Lercara Friddi, about fifteen kilometers northeast of us."

"So?"

"Luciano has been cooperating with your government, through the Office of Naval Intelligence, to provide assistance to the war effort. At first, he used his Mafia and union connections to keep watch on the waterfront docks, to prevent Axis agents from gathering intelligence or committing sabotage. After the SS *Normandie* burned at her moorings in New York Harbor, there were questions, and ONI began to rely more on Luciano's sources."

"I remember that; it was right after the war started."

"Right after America entered the war," Kaz said. His family had been killed when the Nazis invaded Poland in 1939, so the war had already been old in 1942 when the *Normandie* burned and capsized in the Hudson River, and I had still been learning how to do an about-face in basic training.

"Of course," I said. "Go on."

"When the invasion of Sicily was planned, ONI got Luciano to provide contacts in Sicily to assist our forces."

"Mafia contacts, you mean."

"Naturally," Kaz said. "Mussolini tried to wipe out the crime families in Sicily, so of course they hate him, not that Sicilians would be too friendly to any government in Rome."

"What does Luciano get out of all this?"

"There are rumors," Kaz said, "that he will be released from prison once the war is over. Even that he is here in Sicily already. Or that he is running his criminal operations openly from prison, take your pick. I doubt he is here, but his influence is very important."

I pulled out the silk handkerchief with the large *L* and laid it on the table.

"Luciano?" I asked.

"Yes. The night before the invasion, Harry brought you and Lieutenant Cammarata ashore secretly in his Motor Torpedo Boat. Banville is his petty officer. Cammarata is Sicilian-American himself, one of a team of intelligence officers sent in to make contact with those who could be helpful to us."

"Why was I along for the ride?"

"General Eisenhower was leery of doing business with gangsters. He thought with your police background, you would be useful in assessing their honesty and worth. Harry went along as added security."

"What was I supposed to do with this?" I laid my hand on the yellow silk square, feeling the supple fabric between my fingers as I gripped it. In the fire, I thought, in the fire.

"You are to deliver it to Don Calogero Vizzini, head of the Sicilian Mafia, in a little mountain village called Villalba. It is a sign that the bearer has the blessing of Luciano. This method of communication has been used by Don Calo himself."

"No wonder Rocko wanted it," I said.

"The dead supply sergeant?"

"The same," I said. "I could tell he had more than a casual interest in it. How could he have known what it meant?"

Kaz shrugged. "Do you have any idea who killed him?"

"There was a guy in Rocko's tent the night he was killed. I didn't see him but I heard him talking. He was putting pressure on Rocko to find me and to find Roberto Bellestri, the Italian who helped me.

They were in contact with a Lieutenant Andrews at the POW camp by field telephone, and Rocko was practically ordering Andrews to find Bellestri."

"Did the sergeant address this man by name or by his rank?"

"No, but it was clear he was scared of him, and that this guy was used to intimidating people. He didn't have an accent exactly, but when he said the name of a place here it came out smooth, like he knew how to say it the right way."

"Was he in uniform?" Kaz asked.

"I couldn't see him. But I heard a jeep start up after he left the tent, so he had to be. He mentioned something odd, though. Is there a safe that needs to be cracked in all this?"

"What?" I knew Kaz had heard me, but I'd thrown him with that one. "No, not exactly."

"What do you mean, not exactly?"

"One of the ONI agents who went ashore got into the Italian naval headquarters and blew open a safe. He brought out the operational plans for Axis naval operations around Sicily. But that had nothing to do with your mission."

"Right, since he used dynamite. Rocko and this guy talked about a yegg—gangland slang for a safecracker who works with his fingers."

"Billy, we have to put that aside for now. I don't know what it means, but we have to figure out what happened to you and complete your mission, if at all possible."

"Not that I suppose it will be easy to find the head of the Sicilian Mafia, but why did you say that?"

"First," Kaz said, counting off on his fingers, "prior to the invasion it was easier to move about on the island with the proper precautions. Your jacket, for instance. At night, it would make it impossible to tell if you were American, Italian, or German."

"Sure. It would give *everyone* a reason to shoot at me."

"Secondly, Cammarata knew the location of the rendezvous with the contact who was to take you to meet Don Calo. Something must have gone wrong, so unless he told you and you can remember it, we have no way of contacting Don Calo, short of walking into Villalba and asking for him. And that would be a bad idea."

"Why?"

"Because we have heard rumors that Don Calo has put out a contract on you. He wants you dead."

"Jesus, Mary, and Joseph!" As the words came out I could hear my father speak them. It was the worst blasphemy he could utter, and he saved it for those times when simple anger wouldn't do, when he needed a string of names to signify total, stunned disbelief in the face of overwhelming bad news.

"Indeed," Kaz said. "Which is one reason we cannot trust the good doctor. With all his talk of *mafiusu*, he may be one himself."

"What about Ciccolo?" I asked.

"He wouldn't have been a problem, *mafiusu* or not, if the doctor had not known about your situation. Now we must keep Sciafani with us. It would have been easier to shoot him."

"But you didn't." I was glad to hear it, remembering that Kaz had not only grown careless about his own life, he had become more casual than I liked about killing.

"No. Banville was adamant about not shooting prisoners, especially a doctor."

I took a drink. The wine had grown less harsh, but it still bit my tongue and left a taste of sour grape skins in my mouth.

"All right," I began, trying to summarize. "I failed in my mission. Harry and Cammarata are missing, and the MPs want me for one murder, maybe two. The Sicilian Mob has a hit out on me. I don't remember most of the key events surrounding any of this, and—let me guess at this one—the mission is critical to the war effort and we need to get this damn yellow snot rag to Don Calo, toots sweet."

"*Tout de suite*, yes. A task made difficult by the fact that he apparently wishes you dead."

"Goes without saying on this island. Can you tell me why this is so important?"

"Don Calo can influence the Italian soldiers, especially those in Sicilian units. The island is dotted with pillboxes on every hillside overlooking the main roads, mostly manned by Italian troops. If they fight, we lose lives and days. If they disappear or surrender. . ."

"We save lives. And time."

"In war, those are nearly the same thing," Kaz said. He was right. It was more of the terrible mathematics of war, which was all too familiar. If these few men die today, fewer may die tomorrow. If I risk my life, I can save other lives. Tough part was, the guys doing the dying didn't give a damn about the math. I didn't either, but I couldn't deny that saving GI lives was worth a risk. I just wished it was someone else's neck on the line.

"OK. At least we have one advantage."

"What is it?" Kaz asked.

I took the wrinkled note from my pocket, and placed it on the table, smoothing it out.

"Dottore Sciafani knows where paradise is."

"Where did you get this, Billy?"

"Rocko had it. When I was shanghaied into that fight at Biazza Ridge, I grabbed some gear when he turned tail. It was his gear, and this note was hidden in it."

"That is the same message Lieutenant Cammarata received about the rendezvous. His family is Sicilian, and he recognized it immediately."

"He didn't explain it to anyone?"

"No. Security."

Of course. The military loved security. That way, if I'd been caught, the Nazis could have tortured me all night long and I'd never have given them a thing. So thoughtful.

"I have a feeling this mystery man from Rocko's tent knows where it is. You know, he mentioned Palermo to Rocko, and said it with an accent just like I heard a guy in Boston say it."

"Who was that?" Kaz asked.

"Phil Buccolo, he was born there. Last time I was home, he was the head of the Boston mob. Lucky Luciano put him there."

"The navy and army intelligence services were recruiting everyone with a Sicilian background they could find, right up to the invasion," Kaz said. "There are probably quite a few native-born gangsters on the loose now. It could have been anyone."

"Yeah, well this character knows how to use a knife, doesn't mind killing, and is smart enough to frame me for it. That makes him someone to worry about in my book."

"I am too tired to worry, Billy. We should sleep." Kaz took a final drink of wine, winced at the taste, blew out the candle, and stood. "I'm glad you're alive, Billy. And that you didn't desert, or worse."

"Thanks, Kaz. Thanks for coming to the rescue."

We locked eyes for a second, no more. I sensed he was repaying a debt, one that was tied up with things I hadn't remembered yet. I followed him to the front of the house, wondering what were the ties that bound us, and if I deserved the payment. Desertion? Or worse? How could I be sure I was free of guilt? We entered the house. The small candle above the door had been relit and glowed in the carved niche, a timid, faltering flame that I supposed was an offering to the old gods or the newer saints, or perhaps simply a light to guide their son home from the wars, to sleep safe in his own bed once again.

CHAPTER ▪ TWELVE

I AWOKE FROM a dream. I'd been standing at a window, or maybe it was a door to a veranda overlooking sparkling blue water. Sunlight glinted off low, rolling waves as soft breezes wafted through palm fronds in the garden below. It was beautiful, except for the twin-engine German bomber, smoke and fire trailing one wing, dropping its bombs as it headed straight for me. They struck, one by one, first in the ocean, then the beach, then closer to where I stood, and right before the last one, I felt someone by my side. We were holding on to each other, watching the last bomb hurtle toward us as the burning plane, nearly at treetop level, zoomed over the building and vanished.

I awoke before the bomb hit and before I could turn to see whom I held.

I awoke and wished I could go back to sleep, even if it meant dying in the explosion, if only I could see who was standing next to me. It was a woman, but not just any woman. She was the woman of my dreams. I realized she'd been in my dreams the past few nights, in the shadows, out of sight but always there, a presence, a reality I could never turn to fast enough to glimpse.

I sat up on the thick straw pallet that was my bed. Kaz lay across from me, covered in a rough wool blanket. We were in a bare stone room at the back of the house. I felt my way down the narrow hall to the back door. My mouth was dry and my head thick with the wine we'd drunk. I stood over the well, pumping up water to drink and rub over my face. It felt good to breathe in the cool night air, refreshing and cleansing. Off to the east, a line of light blue appeared at the horizon; dawn was not too far off. It was quiet, the kind of deep late-night quiet that seemed to hold the promise of a better day, or at least the chance of one.

Then it wasn't quiet. A scuffling of feet, a hushed whisper. I couldn't make it out, but it was Italian, or Sicilian, not that I'd know the difference. All I knew for certain was that it was a sound that didn't belong in the quiet hours before dawn. A suspicious sound, wrong in every way, in its haste and hidden nature. I walked around the side of the house, my hand on the cool stone, steadying myself as I watched each step to avoid the slightest stumble. I peered around the corner, my face in the shadows. Two stooped figures, one hurrying the other, tottered off into the grove of orange trees, and disappeared in the dark. Signor and Signora Ciccolo, beating feet for all they were worth.

I walked around in front of the house, not worrying about being seen by the old couple, swiveling my head, listening. I looked at my watch; the luminous dial and hands showed a quarter to five. What did the Ciccolos know, and at what time was it going to happen? No other sounds carried in the night. No heavy boots on gravel, no engines, no grunts from armed men running to surround the house. They wouldn't cut it so close, would they?

A tiny, distant grinding noise came from the main road we'd come in on. Gears. Someone was grinding his gears as he shifted. Nothing else, but the mechanical grating sound hung in the air, and I thought I could hear engines, two or three, coming closer. The Ciccolos must have overslept. I ran into the house.

"Kaz, Kaz, wake up!" I ran up the narrow steps to the small bedroom on the top floor. The door was open and Sciafani was already up.

"What is it?" he asked. "*Tedeschi?*"

"I don't know, but let's get out of here before we find out."

Sciafani knew the Germans might shoot him as a deserter, parole or no parole. I flew down the stairs and Kaz was up and ready, revolver in hand.

"What?" he asked, his eyes darting around the room.

"The Ciccolos are gone; they went off into the woods a minute ago. And there are vehicles headed this way."

Kaz exited, Sciafani following. I dashed back into the bedroom, grabbing what little gear I had, glad to have my .45 in its holster and the rifle in my hands. I went to the open door, straining to hear the engine noises to judge their distance. It didn't matter. As I stepped outside, I felt cold metal, the business end of a double-barreled shotgun pressed against my neck. I froze. Out of the corner of my eye I saw Kaz and Sciafani off to the side, a big guy in a black suit standing behind them, a sawed-off shotgun raised to their heads.

"*Pezzu di carni cu l'occhi,*" said the big man, pointing at me with his shotgun.

"*Sì,* Muschetto," my guy said, laughing, as he pushed me toward the others. Two more men, wearing cloth caps pulled down over their eyes and black vests over rough farm shirts, appeared from in back of the house. Sporting sawed-offs on straps hung around their necks, they nodded to Muschetto, the all-clear sign. No trouble from us, we'd been easy pickings. The engines were closer now, and I figured these mugs had been here all along, waiting for us to run outside to see what the fuss was about and be gathered up, one, two, three.

"What did he say?" I asked Sciafani, glancing at Muschetto, who was grinning beneath his thick black mustache. He had a broad chin and small deep-set eyes set close together. He was at least six feet tall, and he could have rested his arm on top of Kaz's head if he got tired of holding the shotgun on us, but it looked like not much would tire out Muschetto.

"It is hard to translate exactly. He said you are a piece of meat with eyes, meaning that you look like, well, a shocked idiot, perhaps."

"Thanks for the translation. Next time make up something nice," I said.

"*Silenzio,*" Muschetto said.

I obliged as the others relieved us of our weapons and stacked them inside. Two vehicles came down the dirt track leading to the farm, past the field of cauliflowers, then past the barn, which I avoided looking at. Muschetto waved to them. In the lead was a little Fiat 500, one guy at the wheel. Behind that was a U.S. Army jeep, the driver and passenger both wearing khaki uniforms like officers, with the summer service cap, leather visor, and shiny brass eagle insignia.

They drove right past the barn. I shifted my eyes away, not wanting to tip them off. Banville was in there with the truck, and unless he was a heavy sleeper, he had to be watching us through one of the narrow windows of the stone barn. Old Man Ciccolo was playing an angle with these guys. He had to have betrayed us, but why should he give up a nice truck? He must've told these palookas there were three of us in the house, and left out the part about stashing a truck in the barn.

Muschetto motioned the three of us to back up against the house, and held his shotgun on us casually as he waited for the men in the jeep. I didn't hold out any hope this was the cavalry coming to the rescue since our captors were relaxed and confident. They didn't look much like the Mafia gang members I knew from Boston. Back home, they were togged to the bricks, always clean, shoes shined, colorful ties like garlands around their necks. These guys wore dusty black or dingy gray, with a few days' growth of beard, and evidently had spent longer than that between baths. But the sawed-offs said Mafia, real down-home Sicilian *mafiusu*.

The jeep pulled up in front of us. The passenger wore a .45 automatic in a shoulder holster. He was short and stout, not a picture of military elegance in his rumpled khakis, maybe forty or so. He displayed no rank or insignia, but Muschetto jumped to as if this passenger was royalty, offering a hand to help him out. Muschetto bowed like a servant, then quickly eyed us to make sure no one moved a muscle.

It was only when the passenger tipped his cap up and I saw his eyes that I made the connection. Deep set, they were surrounded by dark bags and shadows cast by his heavy brow, the whites of his eyes looking lost in bluish gray caverns. I'd seen them gazing at me from wanted posters and glossy photos sent by J. Edgar.

"Vito Genovese," I said, not by way of introduction, but out of astonishment. He stood in front of me and smiled, a meaningless expression on the face of a major crime boss.

"You know me, that is good," he said. It was the same voice I'd heard in Rocko's tent. The kind of calm self-assurance that comes from having a pack of Mafia gunsels to back you up, and at the same time knowing you don't need them. "Let's go inside where we can talk."

He brushed past me and I got my third shock of the morning. First came the Sicilian Mafia, then the American Mafia shows up, and now here was Joey "Legs" Laspada, enforcer for the Boston Mob. He was the driver, looking natty in his khakis and service cap, worn at a jaunty angle over thick, wavy black hair. He gave us all the once-over, but I could tell he didn't recognize me.

"I thought you were dead," I said, locking eyes with him even as Muschetto herded me to the door with the butt of his shotgun. That caught Laspada off guard, as his eyes widened in surprise, then narrowed again into his permanent look of suspicion. They constantly darted about, gauging the chances of threat or enrichment wherever he went. His mouth was long and thin, a match for his narrow eyes. He had a wide, high forehead, a sign of intelligence according to some. On Laspada, it looked like a wall behind which deadly secrets were forever held.

"I ain't," he said, as he followed Genovese into the house, not giving me a second look.

I followed meekly, knowing what these men were capable of and wishing I didn't.

"*Fa'il caffè*," said Genovese, and Muschetto, towering over us all, made himself busy at the stove. He did so with ease, pulling a tin of coffee from a shelf without looking for it. He was no stranger to this house. Genovese sat at the head of the table, and Kaz, Sciafani, and I were shoved into the other three chairs by Muschetto's goons, who left without a word. Laspada leaned against a wall and lit a cigarette, peering at me through the smoke.

"Boyle," he said, snapping his fingers. "Your old man's on the Homicide Squad, right? Hey, Vito, this one's a bluecoat from back home. Kinda makes me homesick."

"Seeing you makes me plain sick, Legs," I said. Laspada stood, a scowl on his face and one hand on his holstered pistol.

"Gentleman," Genovese said, his hands up in a gesture of calm. "There is no need to revive old animosities here. We have come to help you, but first we need to know exactly who you are and what you are doing here."

"How did you know we were here," I asked, "so you could help us?"

"We have come, at great risk, because we heard of two Allied soldiers traveling with an unknown civilian, out in front of our lines,"

Genovese said, drumming his fingers on the table in irritation. "Think of this as a rescue mission. You should be thanking us, not questioning us as if this were a police station. We are a world away from all that, my friend. This you would do well to remember."

"Billy," Kaz said. "How do you know these people? Who are they?"

Genovese nodded to me, as if I should make introductions. I started with our little group.

"I'm Lieutenant Boyle, and this is Lieutenant Kazimierz. *Il dottore* Enrico Sciafani was just released from a POW camp and has his papers to permit him to return home." I watched Sciafani as I spoke. He looked nervous, and I wondered if he'd heard of these guys before. But then any Sicilian would recognize these men with their sawed-off shotguns.

"You'll be interested, Kaz, since you like American gangster movies so much, to meet Vito Genovese, one of the top Mafia bosses in New York City. Word has it that he killed his former boss, Joe Masseria, on the orders of Lucky Luciano himself. Luciano took over all the Mob operations in the city, and Vito rose up with him. Until 1937, anyway, when he left the country ahead of a murder charge."

I could see Kaz was actually interested in all this.

"You head one of the Five Families," Kaz said, sounding a little like he was meeting a movie star.

He and Daphne had loved to watch gangster movies and learn American slang. I rubbed my eyes, trying not to think about it, trying to focus on what was happening and how to get free of these mobsters.

"No, no," Genovese was saying. "That is all nonsense the newspapers print. I am simply a businessman who wished to visit the old country, and then was trapped here by the war. How could I be facing a murder charge? I work for AMGOT."

I could see Sciafani didn't understand so I broke in. "That's the American Military Government of Occupied Territories."

"Yes, exactly. I met some of the first American troops in Gela and soon found a Senior Civil Affairs officer and volunteered my services. I am employed as a translator and for whatever special situations may occur."

"Him too?" I jerked my thumb in the direction of Laspada. I tried to think only about Legs back in Boston, not about Daphne, not about Kaz and his pain. And not about mine.

"Joey is my driver, also officially employed by AMGOT. So you see, we are all on the same side."

Genovese spread his hands and laughed. All one big happy family, with Vito at the head of the table. Muschetto set down a small cup of steaming coffee in front of him, and handed one to Laspada. I guessed the distant relations didn't warrant any java.

"Joey 'Legs' Laspada," I said to Kaz, nodding at the other American. "Chief enforcer for Phil Buccola, head of the Boston Mob, or syndicate, as they call themselves. Back in '39, we found a badly decomposed body on the incoming tide in Boston Harbor. Had Joey's billfold on him and two slugs in his skull. We figured Joey had done something to anger Phil, who'd had enough of him. But it looks like Joey found a way out of that mess."

"Like Mr. Genovese, I am an American citizen who was trapped in Italy when the war started. I've been hiding out in the mountains here, waiting to be liberated. Now I am eager to assist in any way I can."

It was a nice little speech, one I was sure appealed to the AMGOT bigwigs. They were desperate for Italian speakers, especially anyone with an intimate knowledge of Sicily. When these two showed up waving their arms and welcoming GIs, I bet AMGOT's brass fell over itself to sign them up and let them play soldier. And they had contacts among the locals; their own private Mafia army was proof of that.

"Why do they call you Legs?" asked Kaz, ever the eager student of American gangland slang.

"Guess because I ran track in high school," Laspada said.

"I doubt he ever went to high school," I said. "They call him Legs because that's his trademark. A pair of broken legs for the first offense, whether that's a late loan-shark payment or shorting the numbers receipts."

"What's the penalty for the second offense?" Kaz asked.

"Two bullets in the brain."

"There will be no more talk of these things," Genovese said, in that calm and grave voice, as he drew his .45 from his shoulder holster and laid it on the table. It gave off a solid *clunk* as it hit the wood and drew my attention, especially since the barrel was pointed straight at me.

I stared at the muzzle. I wanted to tell Kaz I remembered Daphne, to tell him I was sorry, but we'd been through all that. I'd already made good on my promise to avenge her death. It didn't matter now. I needed to drive those thoughts out of my head.

"What do you want?" I asked, folding my shaking hands in my lap. Genovese stared at me as he slurped coffee. I met his eyes but was drawn back to the gun barrel. Anguish rose in my throat and I choked it down, understanding for the first time the allure of a quick end and a journey to a place without burned bodies in blackened cars, where no flowers, plucked by bullets, fell on the dead and dying. Everything in the room narrowed to the small circle of steel pointed in my direction, as if every step I'd taken in the past days, weeks, maybe even years had led me here. I was amazed to be calm. I forced myself to look at Genovese and caught a glimpse of feral surprise. He'd expected to see fear, and instead saw something else. I was beyond a Mafia bully and his pistol. I'd watched a Tiger tank crest a rise in front of me, seen plane-loads of paratroopers flame out into the sea, killed men close up and far away, some of whom I knew, most of whom were unknown, and except for one, I was sure they had all been better men than Vito Genovese.

"We want to know why you are here. We want to know who you are looking for," Genovese said as he picked up the .45 and holstered it. He knew its threat wasn't working.

Except for one. Who was that? Why had I thought that? Images and words swam through my mind. I saw Harry Dickinson and recognized him instantly, even though hours ago he'd been a stranger. Harry, who'd taken me to Norway under forged orders on my first assignment for Uncle Ike. Click. Another memory fell neatly into place. Click. Harry at the MTB base in Algeria, swinging his fist and threatening to kill me. That had been on my next assignment. Not every memory was a happy one.

Except for one. Who was that one?

"I am speaking to you!" Genovese shouted, a white gob of spittle hanging from his lip. He wiped it and slammed his hand, palm down, on the table.

"We are deserters," Kaz said, with a quick glance at me. "The *dottore* was going to hide us in the mountains. We thought we could sell cigarettes on the black market. We have connections."

"What, are you going to sell Limey smokes?" Legs thought he was a comic.

"No, we have someone in the American supply services. He has access to everything—cigarettes, penicillin, liquor."

"What about this one?" Genovese asked, pointing to me.

"He is shell-shocked. He's been in the fighting. The man in supply is his cousin, so I need to keep him safe. That's why we're hiding out here."

I had to admire Kaz—it was a good story. A little truth, a little lie, and told with no hesitation. Liars usually hesitate, even for a fraction of a second, but the truth comes out smoothly, since people don't have to think about it. It just is.

"How did you choose this farm?" Genovese asked.

"I have access to reconnaissance photos. I picked it out because there are no main roads, no intersections, nothing of military value. The track turns to a trail and winds up into the hills. No one, German or American, should be very interested. So I offered the Ciccolos payment for a few days' shelter."

"How did you get here?" Legs asked.

"We had a jeep, but a Messerschmitt came out of the sun and strafed us. We jumped out, but he got the jeep. We left it burning in a field a few miles from here."

Legs looked at Genovese, reluctantly conceding that they'd seen the wreck.

Except for one. My mind raced, and I felt the woman of my dreams close by.

Except for one.

"How much penicillin can you get?" Legs asked. He'd bought the whole line and was ready to cash in. He was a solid enforcer, but that didn't make him the brightest guy in the room.

"Stop," Genovese said. "They are lying. Don't be stupid." He caught Muschetto's eye and pointed at Sciafani and the door. The big Sicilian grabbed Sciafani and led him outside.

"No," Kaz said, "don't . . ."

"Don't worry," Genovese said, his voice calm again. "We need doctors in Sicily. It is time for us to talk, just among soldiers."

"What do you want?" I asked. My hands were still in my lap, but they weren't shaking. When Legs said penicillin, there'd been another click. The hospital in Algiers. Kaz had been shot in the arm while rescuing Harding and me from the Vichy jail. Click. I was somewhere else, watching a newsreel of my life play out in my mind, each new episode a revelation.

"I respect a man who can focus on the business at hand," Genovese said, the smile playing across his face a mask, broad and false. "So I will tell you what I want. I want the man who was put ashore before the invasion to meet with Don Calo Vizzini. I want to help him to complete his mission. Do you know such a man?"

"He sounds like a failure," I said. I tried to concentrate on Genovese, but I was seeing a woman raise a pistol to her head—who was she?—echoing the thoughts I'd had earlier. An end to all this, an end to suffering and pain. I understood what she'd wanted. To go to that other place, where the suffering had not yet reached, and never would.

"Not yet. He still can complete his mission, and I can help him." Genovese sounded like a pal. "Even though he has done 'many bad things'."

I laughed. "Many bad things? We're in the middle of a fucking war, and you talk about 'many bad things'?"

"Billy," Kaz began.

I cut him off. "'Many bad things'. You don't know, Vito. Even in your blood-soaked dreams, you have no idea." I couldn't stop laughing.

"Where is the handkerchief? Search them," Genovese said to Legs. "Find it and we will all bring it to Don Calo."

Legs lifted Kaz up by the armpits and started to pat him down. It was just the four of us in the kitchen now, and while Legs was searching Kaz, Genovese drew his .45 again, but this time held it cradled close to his chest.

"Do you know who Don Calo is?" he asked me.

"Somebody who needs to blow his nose?"

He snapped his hand holding the .45 at me, slamming the barrel against my temple. He was fast, so fast that before I noticed the blood dripping from my head he had brought the pistol back, a satisfied smile on his face.

"I believe you are the man we have been looking for," Genovese said. "I believe that you know where the handkerchief is. And I believe you will give it to us, and we will all be heroes."

"He's clean," Legs said after thoroughly searching Kaz, who was lacing up his boots.

Genovese, gestured at me with the pistol. "Search him, then the house, if he doesn't have it."

I thought about going for the gun, and then there was another click. Harry, going for a woman's gun, coming up from behind her, and snatching it away.

Diana. The woman had been Diana, Daphne's sister. *She* was the woman of my dreams. Diana, who'd been kidnapped, drugged, and raped by a Vichy rat, Luc Villard. Except for him, I was sure every man I'd killed was a better man than Vito Genovese. Diana, who wondered if I still loved her, if I'd be man enough to stand by her.

I'd killed Luc Villard in Algeria with a knife slid between his ribs. He wasn't resisting or shooting at me. But I'd deliberately pulled a knife and ended his life. For a brief time, he had been the enemy, officially. But when I'd killed him, he was technically an ally. I'd had murdered him. I'd had to murder him. It was impossible to let him go on living after what he'd done. It was my decision, and all the blood in his veins couldn't wash away the fear and shame I'd felt, not knowing for certain if I would be man enough to take Diana into my arms and love her after what had happened.

Harry had saved Diana, stopped her from ending her life, and as certain as pulling the hammer back on a revolver, the next click fell into place. Harry Dickinson. I owed him for that, but I'd repaid the debt by killing him. Here in Sicily, in the Valley of the Temples, the night before the invasion. Click. I felt Legs lay his hands on my shoulders. My head was pounding, I was dizzy, and it felt like there was a weight pressing down on my chest. I didn't know if I could stand, but Genovese had his .45 leveled at me.

"Up," he said.

"Fuck you," I told him. I had nothing left but a curse.

Vito's mouth curled into a sneer. He was about to speak when the door flew open and Muschetto stepped into the room. "*Molti tedeschi,*" he spat out. "*Andiamo.*"

"Germans?" Genovese said in disbelief, his eyes wide. Muschetto vanished outside and we heard the sound of the Fiat motor starting. I jumped up, the dizziness gone, grabbed Legs by the arms and threw him at Genovese. The two of them collapsed to the floor as Genovese's chair tipped back. I knew Kaz was following me as I ran out the rear door, but I didn't look back. I ran—past the grape arbor, around the house, trampling beans and daisies as I went, diving for cover behind a jumble of rocks.

I squeezed my eyes shut, but I could still see Harry, coming around the stone column of an ancient temple, not knowing that I'd just rolled a grenade in his direction. I'd hesitated a fraction of a second, but that was all the time it had taken for the blast. That was the last thing I remembered, except for fleeting glimpses of Roberto helping me.

I'd killed Harry.

CHAPTER ▪ THIRTEEN

THE SUN WAS RISING at my back, lighting the far hillside, illuminating figures in tan desert uniforms and rimless helmets scurrying down the stony slopes. German paratroopers. I didn't care. The burden of memories weighed me down, and I wished I'd never recalled a thing. Remembering what Sciafani had said about my being fortunate to be able to examine my life, I spit in the dust.

"Billy," Kaz whispered, "what should we do?"

"Good question."

I eased my head around the boulder we'd hidden behind and looked at the house. The Fiat was puttering toward the road, weighed down by Muschetto and his men. Not far behind was the jeep with Legs at the wheel and Genovese hanging on, fleeing from an encounter with a gang far tougher than theirs. Dust roiled up from the vehicles, leaving a swirling marker showing the direction in which they were headed. I heard soft thumps in the distance and a short whistling sound, then a pair of small explosions near the main road, followed by another salvo. Mortar fire, hurrying the enemy convoy on their way. The Fiat, with the jeep close behind, made it to the road between rounds and faded from view.

"The truck?" Kaz asked.

"We'd never make it to the barn. Besides, the Krauts have zeroed in on the road now."

"Where do you think Banville is?" Kaz asked, squeezing himself small behind the boulders.

"Unless he got out of the barn in the confusion," I said, "he's trapped."

I tried to think it through, figure out what to do next, but everything was mixed up—Genovese and Villard, Harry saving Diana, then Harry at the temple. There were too many memories, too soon, too terrible. I wanted someplace to rest and think, to sit out again under the grape arbor in the cool night air and let the memories come again and again until I could absorb them, until they were no longer razors slicing through my mind. I rested my cheek on the warm, rough, chalky rock and wished the Germans would keep on going, simply march down the road and let us be.

I heard the muffled sound of an engine.

"Look!" Kaz shook my arm. The barn doors had swung open. The truck emerged at top speed and careened toward the road, tires spinning and gravel flying. Banville. He fishtailed, regained control, and flew by the rows of purple cauliflower, heading for the main road. As he slowed to turn, the explosions started again, the mortars leading him and concentrating their fire on the road. Banville couldn't stop in time. He hit the brakes, sending up clouds of dust, but he slid directly into the next rounds, the small truck lifting up and toppling over, the gas tank exploding as it rolled into the ditch at the side of the road. He should've stayed in the barn, he shouldn't have braked, he should have sneaked out on foot. What did it matter? In this war there were enough shoulds and should nots to get any man killed sooner or later.

A scuffling sound, shoes stumbling over stones, came from our rear. I was glad of a reason to look away from the burning wreck. It was Sciafani, peering at us from behind a prickly cactus. I pressed my finger to my lips, then waved him over to us, motioning him to stay low, my palm down to the ground. He'd been at war long enough to understand, and to know that those mortar crews were watching the terrain for any other movement, covering the advance of their pals.

"They let me go," he said. "They gave me this." He handed me a revolver.

"You don't want it?" I asked.

"No, I am done with war."

"Those Germans are not," Kaz said, keeping an eye out at the edge of the boulder.

"No, but one revolver will not do much good against them," Sciafani said sensibly.

"Why did they give it to you?" I asked, wondering at the generosity of the thugs who had held us at gunpoint.

"Muschetto said I might need it to get home. They did not seem to have any argument with me."

"No, they wouldn't, I guess. Listen, I'll help you get home, but I want you to help me too."

"Help you with what?" Sciafani asked.

"Help me find happiness."

"Ah, yes," he said, grinning. "But first we must twice pass through purgatory. Happiness is not too far off my path so, yes, I will show you the way." A burst of machine-gun fire interrupted us. We all ducked, but it wasn't aimed in our direction. Bullets struck the stone house, then played over the barn, then returned to the house. They were making sure there were no more surprises.

Shouts from the orange grove rose up as the machine gun stopped, and Germans slowly advanced from the foot of the hill toward the house. I could pick out German commands and pleading words in Italian as I watched Signor and Signora Ciccolo come into view, prodded by rifles out of their hiding place in the trees. A German officer, waving his pistol, was yelling at the old man, who was shaking his head in denial, clutching at his shirt, then extending his arm in a Fascist salute as he kept moving ahead of soldiers behind him. The officer stopped, turned on Ciccolo, and pointed to the open barn.

Oh Jesus, no, I thought. No, don't let it be true. Was the old man so greedy as to betray us to the Mafia, then betray the Mafia to the Germans, all while trying to keep the truck in the barn secret from both? Ciccolo extended his arms toward the barn and shrugged, as if to say the appearance of the truck was a total surprise to him too; how could he have known?

The officer didn't buy it. He raised his pistol and shot him twice in the chest. Ciccolo collapsed as if his legs had turned to jelly, sprawled with his knees up in the air, the rest of him laid out slackly in a way that said dead, dead, dead. His wife shrieked and fell to the ground, her hands lifting his head to her bosom, as the officer holstered his pistol and walked by her. The other soldiers ignored her, and soon she was left alone with her dead husband, his blood soaking into the ground at the edge of his peaceful orange grove. *Many bad things, Vito, many bad things.*

"You weren't the only one who picked out this secluded spot, Kaz," I said as I watched the officer walk into the farmhouse. Other Krauts checked out the barn, and one squad walked up the track to check on the still-burning truck. "It looks like they're settling in."

"They'll be setting up a perimeter soon," he said. "We have to leave."

"Head back to our lines," I said, handing him the revolver. "Someone has to take back word of this position. There's at least a full company of Germans here, and who knows how many others getting into place in these hills. You're elected." I saw Kaz about to protest, but then he nodded, accepting the logic of it.

"You're right." He looked at me a moment, then spoke again. "You remember now, don't you?"

"Everything. Daphne, Diana, and Harry," I said, hesitating over the last name.

"What about Harry?"

"He's dead. I killed him. In the Valley of the Temples."

"Agrigento," Sciafani put in. "It is a large field of temples, all kinds of ruins, right outside the city."

"Are you certain?" Kaz asked me. "How?"

"A grenade. He walked into the explosion. There was a fight with some Italians there, we got separated, and when I tossed a grenade behind a column, Harry stepped right into it. I didn't know he was there. Then—well, I guess I don't remember everything yet—then I blacked out."

Kaz held up his hand. German voices grew louder, in that relaxed, joking tone of soldiers who feel they're on safe ground. I could smell their cigarette smoke. They were headed our way. We eased back, staying low, entering a stand of small, thin trees that bordered the cauliflower field.

"Dottore," I said. "Before we split up, tell us both what the message means." I took out the worn slip of paper. To find happiness, you must twice pass through purgatory.

"It is silly really, not even a joke, but something one tells the *turisti* in Agrigento. You see, there is a small plaza, the Piazza del Purgatorio, and on that plaza is a church, the Chiesa Purgatorio."

"So you pass through the plaza, and then the church?" Kaz asked.

"Yes. If you take the side door out of the church, it leads you up a flight of steep steps to the Duomo—the cathedral—and within is a small chapel to San Felice, where he is buried. Saint Felice de Nicosia was a Sicilian, made a saint in the last century."

"Where does happiness come in?" I asked.

"Felice means to be happy," Kaz said, the dedicated student of language.

"OK. So our contact is in the cathedral, or the chapel of the cathedral." Seemed logical to me.

"Perhaps," said Sciafani. "Or perhaps that person was there, and is now gone."

"Either way, it's all we've got. I need to finish this mission, if only to find out what happened, and why Harry died. I owe him that much."

"Remember, Billy," Kaz said, with a nervous glance at Sciafani, "the mission is still important. We must have the cooperation of Don Calo and the Sicilian Mafia, especially as we advance into the mountains."

"Yeah, just make sure those American mobsters don't get in the way. When you get back, check around and find out who the hell in AMGOT hired those two goons. And be careful. JAG runs Civil Affairs and Civil Affairs runs AMGOT."

"Do you think there is a link between the charges against you and these mobsters?"

"I don't know what to think, but don't take any chances. And look into a Lieutenant Andrews in the Signals Company that's set up near Capo Soprano. I think he's on Vito's payroll too, just like Rocko was. And see if the name Charlotte comes up. Whoever she is, she's heavily involved."

Kaz nodded his agreement, then spoke to Sciafani.

"Dottore, we are depending upon you to lead Billy where he needs to go. You must not abandon him. If you leave or betray him, I will find you, in Palermo or in your village. Now, or after the war. And I will kill you, do you understand?"

"Certainly. A man would be honored to have such a friend avenge him. To say this does you credit. I will guide your friend, and not because of your threat. I am not a Fascist, and I do not care to watch the *tedeschi* shoot any more old men." Sciafani appeared proud to have been threatened with death.

Kaz extended his hand, and Sciafani shook it. Then I did, and held on to Kaz for an extra heartbeat, grasping him by the arm. "Stay safe," I said.

"Good advice," he said. "I will follow you with the cavalry, like in your Western movies. I have already gone through purgatory, so perhaps it will be easy for me to find where happiness hides."

He let go of my hand, locked eyes with me for a moment, and left us at a slow trot through the trees until he disappeared in the leafy green.

CHAPTER ▪ FOURTEEN

WE WALKED, CAUTIOUSLY AT first, keeping to the bushes and small trees that divided the cultivated fields, blending in with shadows and staying low where the ground rose and fell. Periodically we stopped to listen, swiveling our heads to catch the sounds of booted feet hurrying after us, but all we heard was the chattering and warbling of sparrows and starlings as they flitted among the plants and trees. We walked for hours, avoiding the few workers we saw in the fields and crossing dirt roads only after checking to see that no one was in sight. We walked east, by the sun. As it rose in the blue sky so did the heat. We crossed a stream, and drank from it, lying flat and letting the cool, clear water soak our chests as we gulped it down. We talked, at first in whispers. Then we grew bolder and spoke up, our own voices giving us strength, proving to ourselves that we were not afraid. But by the time the sun was directly above us, we were reduced to grunts and fingers pointing the direction to take, a single word serving where a conversation had earlier. We walked.

The ground changed from rich soil to crumbling, gritty reddish dirt mixed with stone. Dust coated our legs and floated up to choke us. We were higher up now, where there were no streams to drink from, less growth to hide in, and no low-lying gullies to walk along.

We followed a trail that left us outlined against the hill that rose in front of us. I turned and saw the landscape below, green folds of cultivated fields and the yellows and browns of weeds and wild growth wilting in the arid heat. Anyone below could as easily see us. But Sciafani had chosen his route well; there was not a single person in sight, as well as no water or shelter from the sun. At that moment, I would have surrendered to a German or Italian patrol for the promise of water. I had to remind myself I could get a bullet just as easily, and that even if I didn't, I'd still be facing murder charges.

I tried to think about other things as I followed Sciafani up the trail. My breath came in big gulps that never seemed to get enough oxygen to my lungs. I kept my eyes on the ground in front of me and thought about home. About birds, actually, and all the things my mom had taught me about them. She had a feeder set up outside her kitchen window, and when I was small it was my job to put out the bird food and pieces of old bread she'd saved. Starlings, like the ones in the field below, were always pecking around the ground and sitting in the tree in our small backyard. She didn't like starlings much, since there were so many of them and they drove away the other birds. She loved cardinals, who always traveled in pairs, the bright red male and the gray female with her flecks of red. I liked them too, the mom and dad cardinals, as they flew in together and nibbled at seeds, then swooped off in unison, an invisible command driving them both. I always wondered how they knew when to fly away, and where they went.

I wished I had some of that stale bread I used to crumble up in my small fingers and scatter on the flat feeder Dad had built. Maybe at this moment, early morning in Boston, Mom was opening the window and tossing out seed and bread crumbs, maybe watching the cardinals flutter in for a landing and remembering how we used to watch them. Funny, I'd been away from home for more than a year, and that was the first time I'd thought about those birds. It was nice but sad too. I decided the jury was still out on the value of remembering things. Everything that had come back to me was either a mixed bag or very bad news.

I realized we weren't climbing anymore. We'd come around the crest of a hill and the trail continued on flat below it. Sciafani sat on a rock by the side of the trail, and I joined him, thankful for a rest. Below us, rows of olive trees curved downward to a sluggish stream that drifted through the valley.

"Ravanusa," Sciafani said, pointing to the next hill. "A small town. We should go around it."

"Germans?" I asked.

"Or Fascists," he said. "It is all the same. We must find water."

I watched Sciafani rub his eyes with the palms of his hands. He had an odd habit of shifting the conversation in midstream, as if he didn't want to think about any one thing for too long. He raised one hand to shield his eyes and gazed at the horizon to the west.

"It will be dark soon. We need shelter too," he said.

"Do you know anyone in Ravanusa?"

"Yes, but no one I could trust."

"No family, you mean," I said.

"Exactly, my friend. You are beginning to understand Sicily perhaps."

"It's not so different really. That's how I got my job back home. All the men in my family are policemen. My father is a detective, and so was I."

"And what are you now?"

I opened my mouth to answer, but there were no words. I remembered that I was Uncle Ike's special investigator, but that sounded hollow, nothing but a title. Who was I now? A killer, an assassin, a deserter, a coward, maybe all those things.

"Let's go," I said. "We need water."

Sciafani led the way into the olive grove.

Who am I? I knew my name, knew my rank, but didn't seem to know myself.

Remember who you are.

I heard my father's voice, saw him leaning over the table at Kirby's, his tie loose the way it always was at the end of the day. I was still in my patrolman's blues, a rookie, still walking the beat in my neighborhood so folks could keep an eye out for me. They had.

It was all because of Al. Alphonse DeAngelo, a guy I went to school with. He was Sicilian, and I'd known him since the fourth grade when we'd had a fistfight at recess and ended up in the principal's office, each of us telling the other he was lucky Miss Bayley had broken up the fight before it really got started. We both had hot tempers.

We were sent home with notes for our parents. Al ripped his up in the street and tossed it over his shoulder. I brought mine home, and Dad got out the strap. I should have known right then and there Al was going to go in one direction and me in the other. But before our paths diverged, we became pals, the original beef between us forgotten as we ran through the streets and parks, fished in the bay, played hooky, and caused all sorts of minor mischief. That summer after fourth grade, we'd play mumblety-peg with our jackknives, flipping them into the ground out of our hands or off our heads or whatever the rules of the game demanded. Al could always make the tough casts, his knife flying through the air and slicing into the ground at just the right angle. He was good with that knife.

Four summers later was our last as pals. When it was over I went up Telegraph Hill to South Boston High School, and Al went to work. His old man had something to do with the numbers, which didn't mean much to me at the time, but I could tell that my old man was glad to see the last of Al. I'd run into him on the street every now and then, but it wasn't the same. He looked and acted older, which he might've been by a year or two. He was almost grown-up, and I was trying to act grown-up, so there was no room for memories of childhood play. All that was behind us; we were nearly men now.

High school over, I joined the cops, started walking a rookie's beat. That's when I started seeing Al every day again, walking his own beat, collecting numbers receipts just as his old man had, while I wore the bluecoat, just as my old man had. We'd chat a bit, then we started having a cup of coffee together at Noonan's Diner, where we'd cross paths about ten o'clock each morning. That's what did it.

"That bum takes people's hard-earned nickels and dimes every day," Dad had said as soon as we sat down at Kirby's. "Next he'll be shaking them down for protection, just like his old man over in Dorchester."

"Everyone plays the numbers, Dad, there's no harm in that. No one forces anyone to play."

I was sure about myself on that subject, but I didn't know what to say about protection. There were rumors that the mob was expanding its activities, and for all I knew, Al and his numbers were the start of it in our neighborhood. But childhood loyalties die hard. I watched as my father drew in a deep breath, as if he were filling his lungs for a long speech.

"There's something you have to understand, Billy. There's three kinds of people in the world. First, there's the people out there, everyone you see each day on your beat, the rich and the poor, the bastards on Beacon Hill, and the Irish folk in Southie." He stretched out his hand, palm up, and drew it around, the gesture taking in everyone in the tavern and beyond.

"Then there's those who feed off the poor and helpless, who use their strength to take from others with less strength, or courage, or luck. Finally, there's them who stand up for the weak and the helpless. I'll be the first to say that I'm no angel, but I know who I am. I'm not one of the helpless, thank the Lord, and I know I'll never take advantage of a man worse off than me."

I remember thinking how that left a lot of leeway, while at the same time feeling glad of having enough wit not to point it out.

"What do you think the folks on your beat think when they see you and Al drinkin' coffee together, and he pays each time?"

"I'm not doing anything wrong, Dad. I'm not on his payroll." There were cops who were on retainer with mobsters, paid regularly to pass on tips about arrests and snitches.

"It doesn't matter," he said, with a sad shake of his head, speaking in a low voice. "We're the third kind of people, you and me. What matters is that you are supposed to protect the common folk. If you're going to do that, you can't buddy around with someone who takes from them. It's only the numbers now, but someday soon, mark my words, it will be more. And then, boy-o, how can these poor folk come to you if you're still pals with the one threatening to burn their store down if they don't pay protection?"

"You think that's why Al is being friendly?" I'd asked.

"It doesn't matter, Billy," he'd answered, leaning in close to me so I could feel his breath on my cheek. "What matters is that you remember who you are."

With that, he slid out of the booth and left me there, before a pint could be served. The next day I told Al we weren't kids anymore, and that he should watch his step on my beat. Part of me felt like a bum, and part of me understood that there was more to growing up and being a man than height and weight.

Remember who you are.

I wished I was sitting at Kirby's, a cool pint in front of me, feeling the glass sweat into the palm of my hand, and having my old man explain it all to me again. I'd forgotten so much.

"Here," Sciafani said, shocking me out of my thoughts. I realized I hadn't been paying attention to anything around me. We were still in the olive groves, but nothing looked familiar. How long had we been walking?

"Here," he said again, his voice rising with excitement. In a clearing ahead stood a stone building covered in stucco painted a pastel orange. The setting sun cast its rays from the side, illuminating it, in stark contrast to the greenery all around it. Our long shadows ran ahead of us, straight to an ancient rusty pump in front of the building. Sciafani grabbed the handle and worked it madly, both of us oblivious to the noise as it clanked and squeaked, waiting for the first gush of water. It came, and I gulped handfuls down, then took over at the pump and let Sciafani drink and stick his head under the flowing water. We took turns, laughing like kids, and I thought about Al and how we'd opened fire hydrants on hot August days, laughing in the cool spray and feeling like the world was our playground. It was, until the world split us up. I'd heard Al had tried to go straight and joined the navy. He'd been stationed at Pearl Harbor and caught in an explosion. Lost one leg, ended up back in Boston doing the only thing left for him to do. The numbers, and anything else to make a buck.

"*Chi la sono?*

The voice surprised us, and I jumped nearly a foot. A heavyset older man leading a donkey, weighed down with two baskets filled with olives, looked as surprised as I felt. His white shirt was open and he wore a handkerchief on his head and two or three days' worth of gray stubble on his cheeks. Sciafani walked toward him, speaking calmly, but the old fellow backed up, his eyes searching the trees behind us for signs of any more strangers.

"*Amici,*" I heard Sciafani say. Friends. That seemed to calm the guy down, or maybe it was hearing Sciafani's Sicilian accent. He pointed to me and rattled off a quick question. Sciafani shook his head no, and they talked some more, settling into a friendly conversation.

Finally the old man nodded. Sciafani reached into his pocket and took out a green fifty-lira banknote. Allied Military Currency was printed boldly on the front, and Sciafani pointed to it, seeming to explain what it meant. The old man took the money, folded it, stuck it in his shoe, and pulled at his donkey to get him going again. He didn't give me a second glance.

"What was that all about?" I asked.

"He will bring us food and blankets. This is a storehouse; no one else will be here tonight. It should be safe, he says."

"Do you believe him?"

Sciafani shrugged. "What choice do we have? I choose to believe him. But we should wait in the trees and watch."

"Where did you get the money?" I asked as we walked back up the hill.

"They gave me two fifty-lira notes when they released me. They said this currency would replace all Fascist-issued currency. Is that true?"

"Yep," I said as we settled down in the olive grove, a safe distance from the building but still with a good view. "The plan is to replace all the money in the banks with this, and have people turn in their lire for occupation scrip. It's supposed to stop inflation, I think. The official rate, set by AMGOT, is one hundred lire to the dollar."

"This is the American Military Government you spoke of with the other *americano?*"

"Yeah, but those guys are no good, don't go by them."

Sciafani shrugged again, with that soulful expression of not expecting too much from life. I wondered about AMGOT. If Genovese and Legs had been able to talk their way in, was AMGOT up to the job of governing an island the size of Sicily? Replacing the currency alone—wait, how much money was that? Enough for all the banks on the island, plus all the lire stashed under mattresses, buried in backyards, and in the wallets of every Eyetie there?

Millions. Millions of dollars worth of lire. How were they bringing AMGOT currency ashore, and how was it being guarded? I didn't know, but one thing was certain, it had to be in safes. Just the thing for a yegg to crack. What had I heard Genovese say to Rocko? *I worry about our yegg.* Had Genovese found him before he killed Rocko? Or had it been Legs who'd done the dirty work? Much as I wanted to think all this through, I was too beat. I lay on my side and tried to keep my eyes open to watch the house, but I didn't last long.

I knew I was asleep and could feel the rocky ground digging into my side, as odd dreams flitted through my mind. First Al was playing mumblety-peg with a stiletto, then I was lost in a strange city, then in the kitchen at home, but there were no bread crumbs to put out for the birds, and then the woman of my dreams was back. I realized I'd forgotten about her and then remembered, but I lost her again.

Sciafani shook me by the shoulder. The old man was returning.

Only the part about Diana had been true. Early this morning I'd remembered everything, and it had descended upon me like an avalanche of sharp stones. Diana being taken prisoner by the Vichy French while on a SOE mission. Taken by Luc Villard as part of his ransom scheme, drugged, beaten, and raped. I'd found her, brought her back to Algiers to heal, and worried that my best wouldn't be good enough when it came to loving her. All day, while we'd walked, I'd filled my mind with thoughts of home and birds and old friends, but I'd suppressed my memory of Diana. I was ashamed of myself.

"He seems to be alone," Sciafani said, oblivious to the emotions raging inside my head. I tried to sound normal and focus on the old man and the house.

"How long has it been?" I asked. The sky was darkening as the sun dipped below the horizon.

"One hour, perhaps."

"Not enough time for him to reach the Germans and get back here, I don't think."

"Well, if it was, then at least we will meet them with full stomachs. Come," Sciafani said. I did as I was told.

This time, the donkey's baskets were full of blankets and food, along with a jug of wine. The old man, Signor Patane, was very talkative. He kept up a conversation with Sciafani as he helped us unload. He unlocked the padlock on the door and led us inside the building. Farm implements hung from the walls and hay for the donkey was piled up in one corner. He spread out the blankets and set down the food and wine. A chunk of yellow cheese, two rounds of bread, and a jar of olives. It looked like a feast.

"*Muffoletta, provola,*" he said proudly, pointing to the bread and cheese. I got the impression he was saying he made them, or more probably, his wife. I smiled and nodded.

"Are these his olive trees?" I asked Sciafani, as I smiled at Signor Patane.

"No. A rich Fascist from the mainland owns all this land. Signor Patane works for him, as do most people in his village. He hopes the Americans will take the land from the Fascists and give it to the people."

I thought about the three kinds of people in the world. "So do I," I said.

Signor Patane left us with his good wishes. From what I could understand, unless he was a terrific actor, we were safe here tonight. We ate, ripping the bread and biting into pieces of the sharp cheese. The plump olives were a rich green, marinated in their oil. We drank from the jug of strong red wine. By the time we'd eaten our fill it was dark. Before I fell asleep, I tried to see Diana's face, but the only vision before me was of her in that dusty courtyard, right after I'd freed her, her face twisted with rage and tears, lifting the revolver to her head.

Remember who you are, I wanted to say. You're not what somebody did to you, you're not what happened to you.

It occurred to me that I had said that to her, later, in Algiers, after the bruises and physical wounds had healed. My father's words. They'd helped me once, and I hoped they helped her too. Now it was my turn again, and as I drifted off to sleep I imagined I was back at Kirby's, watching my dad lean in on his forearms and whisper to me, so close it was almost a kiss.

CHAPTER • FIFTEEN

THE SUN WAS OVER the horizon when I awoke. Sciafani was washing up at the pump. We drank water, ate the bits of bread and cheese left over from the night before, and prepared to set off in the direction of Agrigento.

"But first, we must make a stop," Sciafani said, as calmly as if he were giving me a lift to work.

"Where?" I didn't like the idea of stopping anywhere, or the fact that he had surprised me with it. I was supposed to be in charge here.

"At the house of Signor Patane. His wife is ill. Yesterday I told him I was a *dottore*. I thought it might make him less anxious. He asked if I would examine her this morning." He combed his wet hair back with his fingers and set off, the country doctor making his rounds.

"Why didn't you tell me before?" I asked, quickstepping to keep up with him.

"Because I thought it would make you more anxious."

"Listen, hiding out here is one thing, but going into a village, isn't that dangerous? What if there are Fascist sympathizers?"

"See, you are more anxious already. Be thankful I did not tell you last night and ruin a good night's sleep. There will be no Fascists there. Do not worry, my friend."

"Did he say what was wrong with her?"

"She is weak, and coughs up blood. He is very worried about her."

"Hasn't he taken her to a doctor?"

"There is no doctor here. This is nothing but a little village where people work as they always have for the very rich, who pay very little."

"What about in Palermo or Agrigento?" I asked.

"That is the other side of the world to these people," he said. "They would have to walk there, and she is in no condition to do so. And there is the war. Even if there were no war, there would be bandits on the road. No, there is no way out for them."

"Sounds like the stories of Ireland under the English my uncle used to tell me. There was nothing there for the Irish but hard work and death. No way out, except to leave for America. Uncle Dan never forgot his grandfather telling him about digging for potatoes and coming up with nothing but shrunken, rotted things not fit to eat. He was the only one of his family to survive the potato famine."

"Did not your father speak to you about this? Only your uncle?" Sciafani didn't miss a beat when it came to family. His view of the world didn't seem that far off from the one I was brought up on. Family first, which meant your father, then the rest of them, then the rest of the world.

"My uncle is the older brother. He remembers those stories better, and he's never stopped being angry about it. He's a policeman too, and he's also IRA." Sciafani raised an eyebrow in a silent question.

"Irish Republican Army. The IRA fight the British to free Northern Ireland."

"Ah," Sciafani said. "You come from peasant revolutionaries."

"I don't know about that," I said, not happily.

"No, do not take offense. Peasant is a class, not an epithet. And to be a revolutionary in such circumstances is natural. Some say this is how the *mafiusu* came to be. Still today, when a young man is inducted into *cosa nostra*, he takes a blood oath to protect the weak from the powerful."

"That doesn't sound like the mobsters I knew in Boston," I said, wondering how he knew so much about this.

"No, I am certain it is quite different in America. And the reality is different here also. But what is important to remember is how these men see themselves. Look, ahead, there is the village."

We turned a corner in the rutted dirt road and I saw a clump of low buildings. A small church at the far end anchored the cluster against a slide down into the ravine that curved in front of us. As we crossed a small stone bridge, the smell of human waste slammed into my nostrils. A ditch by the side of the road carried a sluggish flow of brown, foul liquid from the village to the ravine, where it spilled over into a dark pool and fed the small stream at the bottom.

"It is better when it rains," Sciafani said.

"I bet," I said, not wanting to open my mouth any farther to tempt the swarming flies.

The church was nothing more than a gray dome surrounded by grayer walls, the stucco long since peeled away to reveal the lines of rough-cut stone, fitted tightly together. The houses were all the same—low squat buildings, some of plain concrete blocks, others of stone, but all in the same square shape, with crumbling, faded orange roof tiles. They radiated out from the church, as if each home wanted to be as close as possible to their priest and prayers.

The first house we walked by was abandoned, shards of roof tiles bleaching in the sun where they had landed on the ground. It stood alone, away from the rest, as if it had fallen out of favor, the tragedy, bad luck, or both of the last residents still clinging to it. The doorway showed traces of soot, and the faint smell of smoke drifted in the air. The rest of the homes were hardly in better shape. No flowers or little gardens decorated the landscape. It was uniformly gray—the hard-packed dirt road, the stones, and the dust on my shoes—all the color of granite crushed down to powder.

Doors were shut, and no curious villager peeked out at the two strangers walking in their street. One of the doors was painted with a black streak, over which *per mia madre* was written in white.

"For my mother?" I asked Sciafani, guessing at the words.

"Yes. It is a sign of mourning in these villages." He looked at the ground as we walked, avoiding my eyes and the scene around him. He seemed uncomfortable, and I wondered if the poverty and grimness we had encountered was embarrassing to him or if it reminded him of part of life in Sicily he didn't want to think about.

Another door was hung with black cloth. Another had nothing but a slash of black paint, weathered and cracking in the dry air. Death was everywhere, even far from the battlefield. A low rhythmic sound echoed from the stone walls. A chant. We stopped, and a priest in a black cassock came from around a corner, his hands holding up a prayer book, his skirts brushing the dirt. Behind him four little children held their hands in prayer as they followed in line. Six men held a plain wooden coffin on their shoulders. The wood had a fresh-cut look to it, and I could smell it, the aroma of pine and sawdust lingering as they passed by. Women dressed in black wept as they brought up the rear, shuffling along with veils covering their faces, the only brightness evident in small white handkerchiefs fluttering from pockets and disappearing beneath gauzy black veils. We watched the small procession make its way across the *piazza* and around the church, probably to a graveyard where someone had hacked a hole out of the stony earth.

"Pleasant little town," I said.

"This way," Sciafani said, ignoring me as he turned right at the entrance to the central square. He strode ahead of me, eyes on each house, looking for Signor Patane's. Then he stopped short and fixed me with his eyes, his face flushed.

"I come from such a town as this. It is a very difficult life, one you should not mock."

"I wasn't mocking," I said, holding up my hands in protest, or perhaps surrender. "I didn't mean it that way, I'm sorry."

"Very well. Come, this is the house."

"Wait a minute," I said, grabbing him by the arm. "I thought you said your father was a doctor in Palermo. I don't see many doctors coming from a village like this."

He pulled his arm from my grasp and turned away from me. He wiped his face with one hand and breathed deeply, as if readying himself for a difficult task. "I did come from a village much like this one. I was adopted by a husband and wife who could not have a child. He was the doctor from Palermo. As often happens, as soon as they adopted me, she bore a child. But it did not matter to either of them—we were both treated as blood."

"What happened to your parents?"

"We should not keep *il signor* Patane waiting." With that, he knocked on a bare wooden door, the grain bleached to a light gray by the harsh Sicilian sun. It seemed odd to me that a guy who was adopted would be the same one who preached about only trusting family. Trusting them to do what, that was the question.

I followed the good *dottore* in as Patane opened the door. The room was cool, a relief from the heat. An old tasseled rug covered the stone floor, and the walls were bare of decoration, except for a picture of the Virgin Mary, her immaculate heart in flames. The furniture was old and worn but clean. A side table gleamed, a thin coat of dust starting to coat the glossy wax shine. Signora Patane took her housework seriously. Her kitchen was spotless too. I waited there while Sciafani and Patane went into the bedroom off the kitchen, where I could hear a harsh cough that wouldn't stop. The coughing continued through softly murmured words, and I knew she was very sick. I got up and looked around the kitchen. Pots on a shelf gleamed. Iron skillets still damp from oil rubbed into them hung from hooks on the wall. Jars of seasonings were lined up full along the counter. Dried peppers and garlic cloves hung in twisted strands from a rafter. Everything was ready, clean, and in order. Irish or Sicilian, it didn't matter. I knew a woman who kept a kitchen like this yet didn't greet her company on her feet with cakes at the ready was in bad shape indeed. From the look of how stocked everything was, I thought maybe she didn't expect to be back on her feet any time soon.

I wandered to the rear door to check for an exit. Another row of houses backed against this one, a wide alley separating them. Plenty of room to run. A wash bucket on the stoop caught my eye. Water had splashed onto the stone and hadn't dried yet. Patane must've put it out here as we knocked on the door. In the bucket, floating in sudsy water, were white handkerchiefs, spotted with blood. I thought about the white handkerchiefs in the funeral procession, and wondered if he'd be able to clean these. And if he'd paint his door black, or drape it in cloth.

A wave of sadness passed over me. This village was awash in death, an everyday occurrence. Not from the war, but from a lifetime of killing labor and poverty. This was what my family had left Ireland to escape. This was what Sciafani couldn't escape, even with his position and education. The life of suffering of the peasant. It had descended upon him as he walked into the village, apologizing for the smell. *It is better when it rains.*

Sciafani and Patane came into the kitchen, shutting the door behind them. Patane looked to the *dottore*, hope battling with fear in his eyes. Sciafani shook his head gravely as he put his hands on the old man's shoulders and spoke to him, softly, gently, masking the harsh words with an apologetic tone.

Tubercolosi was all I could make out. It was enough. Patane nodded, receiving the news he knew was coming with as much dignity as he could. His eyes welled with tears, but he did not give in to the emotions playing across his face. Sciafani dug into his pocket and pulled out the other fifty-lira AMGOT note. Patane refused, but Sciafani pressed it into his hand, nodding his head in the direction of the bedroom. It wasn't much. Four bits, but that would buy some good food for Patane's wife. He took it.

I waited while they spoke more in Italian. Patane pulled a bowl from under a counter and gave us each an orange. He smiled at me as he said something I didn't understand. I shook his hand and felt it tremble in mine. I could tell he was proud to be able to give his company something, and probably right now, with the war about to appear on his doorstep, a couple of oranges were one helluva gift. I felt the handkerchief as I stuffed the orange into my pocket, and for the first time realized that it could mean something for the people of Sicily as well as for the GIs who might have to fight their way through this town. If the Mafia boss could keep enough Italians out of it, villages like this might not be caught up in heavy fighting.

I thought about Signora Patane. She had a right to die in her own bed without artillery shells and machine guns all around her. She should have a nice funeral, with the chanting priest and small children leading her to the grave. Signor Patane should come home and smell the herbs his wife had collected for him, sit in their kitchen, and remember all the meals they had shared there. None of that could happen if tanks rolled through here, if bombers dropped their loads on Italian soldiers barricaded in houses, their polished furniture thrown up against doors and windows to protect them.

"Let's go," I said.

"Yes," Sciafani agreed. "There is nothing I can do here." It looked as if the thought pained him, or maybe it was memories. Having said goodbye to Signor Patane, he squeezed through the narrow doorway as quickly as he could and stood in the street, letting the sun wash over him. There was nothing he could do, about the dying woman or the ghosts of his own past.

CHAPTER ▪ SIXTEEN

WE PASSED THE CEMETERY in the rear of the churchyard as we walked out of town. The funeral was over, the little group of mourners clustered under the shade of a beech tree. The tears and wailing were past; sadness had given way to quiet talk and closeness. Some wandered among the markers. One woman led a little girl, pointing to a grave, telling the story of her family. I couldn't hear her words, but I knew the gestures. *Here is your great-grandfather. Here is your poor cousin, only a baby.*

"How long will it be for Signora Patane?" I asked Sciafani.

"Difficult to say. Too long at the end. I pray she can die in peace."

I was about to protest that Italy was not at peace, but I understood what he meant. Their young men had been taken away to war, but the people of this village knew little of the outside world. If life was hard, it was also tranquil. Unless and until the armies decided to fight over this piece of land. Could it be important? It was on a back road through the mountains. Ahead of us was an intersection with a wider road. Good place for a pillbox. The church didn't have much of a tower, but it still would make a fair observation post. Put a couple of machine guns at the stone bridge we crossed, snipers in a few houses, and in no time we'd be calling in artillery coordinates.

As if in echo of my thoughts, the drone of engines drifted from the south. Four, no five, twin-engine planes, maybe a thousand feet up. I shielded my eyes from the sun and tried to make them out. One trailed smoke.

"German," I said, as soon as I saw the black crosses. "Probably coming back from a run at the beaches." They turned in a wide arc, passing over us, headed northeast.

"There is some good news," Sciafani said. "I wanted to wait until we had left the house to explain."

"OK, tell me."

Sciafani looked a bit more relaxed as we put our backs to the village. He glanced at the now distant aircraft, and I was relieved his mind was focused on more current concerns.

"Signor Patane was most grateful and asked if we needed transportation. His nephew is leaving for the market at Agrigento with a load of olives. He is waiting for us there, at the main road." Sciafani pointed to a skinny kid next to a cart painted every color in the book and then some.

"You didn't tell him we were going there, did you?"

"No, no, no," Sciafani said, shaking his finger. "I told him we would be glad to accept a ride to Favara, which is on the way. It is better than walking."

"Yeah," I said doubtfully. "But what if we're stopped? I stick out like a sore thumb in this uniform. At least if we walk we can stay off the main roads."

"That is a problem for you, yes. But not for me, since I am now a civilian. So, we will hide you." With that, he was off at a trot, waving to the kid and jabbering in Italian.

The two-wheeled cart was painted with flowers and hearts and every damn thing under the sun. It wasn't that big, and was crammed with baskets filled with olives. The donkey that pulled the cart stank. The kid wore a cloth cap with a dark vest over a collarless shirt. A sawed-off shotgun hung by a leather strap from his shoulder.

"Billy Boyle, this is Salvatore Patane." Sciafani spoke our names slowly so we could each understand. We shook hands. I eyed the shotgun.

"Ask him why he carries a sawed-off shotgun, like those other guys." I didn't want to say Mafia out loud.

Sciafani spoke to him, and I could tell it wasn't a question. They both laughed.

"It is a *lupara*, a handmade shotgun. The name means 'wolf-shot'—shepherds carry them to protect their sheep. And it is a good weapon to protect oneself from bandits since it can be hidden."

"Are you a shepherd?" I asked Salvatore, waiting for Sciafani to translate.

"He says he is your shepherd today, and you should get in back and be quiet," Sciafani said, not trying to hide a smirk.

I didn't like it, but there wasn't much choice. Even a donkey pulling a load on a dirt road would be faster than walking cross-country. The cart was jammed full with six tall baskets of olives, each slightly wider at the top, leaving a very narrow space at the bottom.

"In there?" I asked, knowing and not liking the answer.

"In there. It is a good thing you are no taller. There is barely room."

"Yeah, so I noticed." I slithered in between the baskets. With my feet drawn up, they were able to close the rear panel on the cart.

"Hey," I said. "I can see you fine. Anyone who looked could see in here!"

Salvatore thrust in a worn green blanket.

"He says to cover up," Sciafani said, laughing as he picked up something from the front of the cart. I did the best I could as I heard the sound of burlap ripping and the two of them chuckling like school-boys. Then came the avalanche. Streams of almonds flowed in from the spaces between the baskets.

"Sweet almonds for the Festival of San Calogero! May you be blessed, Billy!"

"Yeah, bless you too," I said, glad I had covered my head with the blanket. I felt the cart creak as they got on it and jolt forward as the poor donkey pulled its heavy load away. I realized I had never heard the name of this village, and I didn't care to learn it.

I could see out through a tiny opening between the front of the cart and a basket, where the almonds hadn't completely filled in. I watched slivers of sky and landscape go by and listened to the slow, methodical clip-clop of the donkey's pace. Sciafani and Salvatore chatted. I dozed. The weight of the almonds was like a heavy blanket, and the sweet nutty smell was pleasant, sending me off to sleep with thoughts of almond cakes tantalizing my appetite.

I awoke to the rumbling sound of powerful engines in the distance. The little cart vibrated as the sound drew closer. I wanted to leap up and look. But I stayed pinned down by bushels of almonds and baskets of olives.

"We are pulling off the road, there is a German column coming up behind us. Do not move," Sciafani said as softly as he could and still be heard.

"*Molti tedeschi*," Salvatore said, and that I understood. Many Germans.

I felt the cart shift as Salvatore brought it to a halt off the road. I could tell we were in the shade, and that Salvatore and Sciafani had both gotten off to stretch their legs. Salvatore was talking to the donkey, patting it down, checking the harness. Then came the vehicles. Watching through the small space at the front of the cart, I tried to guess each kind by its engine sound before the vehicle came into view. First, motorcycles. Then trucks of all sizes, with staff cars mixed in. The dust rose up, churned by the never-ending wheels, and blew over us like a desert storm. Sciafani walked by, a handkerchief covering his nose and mouth, cursing into it. I started to sweat, and was tempted to kick my way out of the cart and make a run for it. It was irrational, I knew. The smartest thing was to lie still and wait it out, but I wanted out from under.

A whining, insectlike noise intruded upon the others. The orderly, steady movement of the column changed to a panicky revving of engines. Shouted commands, voices tinged with fear or anger or both raged up and down the road. I saw a truck fly by us, crushing small trees as it charged off the road, looking for a place to hide. The whine increased, and I knew it was the sound of fighter planes, lining up to strafe the convoy. And us, since by now parts of it engulfed our little cart.

Sharp *rat-a-tats* repeated themselves as the planes—two of them, maybe—sent machine-gun bursts into the column. A faint ripple of half-hearted return fire rose from the road, but two massive explosions smothered it. One was incredibly loud, a sharp thundering blast that nearly lifted the cart up off the ground, likely a hit on an ammunition truck. The other was less contained—a *whump* that sounded like a truckload of gas cans igniting. The crackling fires, shouted commands, and the moans of the wounded were the only sounds after that. Engines turned over, gears shifted, and the smell of gasoline and burned flesh mingled in the warm air. I heard somebody crying, but no sound of returning fighters.

German soldiers walked through the trees, some calling out names, others laughing with the relief of being alive. It was a nervous kind of laugh, the same in any language: a little too forced and high-pitched, a false joy trying to seal off what has just happened and what could happen in the next minutes, hours, or days. An engine revved high, followed by a crunching sound as a vehicle was pushed off the road. Treads clanked and I knew tanks were going by. If I remembered my briefing correctly, from the Fifteenth Panzer Grenadier Division.

"*Oliven? Olive?*" A German voice, then two more joined in, asking Salvatore about the baskets. Blurs of khaki passed by and I heard Salvatore and Sciafani protesting to the Germans.

"*Mircatu, mircatu,*" Sciafani answered. "*Mi dispiace, no.*"

I figured he'd said that they were meant for the market, and he was apologizing. From the scuffling, I sensed more Germans gathering around. If they searched the cart I was done for. Salvatore and Sciafani would be shot on the spot and I'd be lucky to end up in a POW cage with a cracked skull. I closed my eyes and tried not to move a muscle, feeling the sweat drip over my face.

"*Olive siciliane, molto buone,*" I heard a German say slowly and proudly, as if he'd mastered a difficult phrase. It didn't sound like a search party. I eased open one eye and saw the barrel of a Schmeisser MP-40 pointed at me. But it was slung over the shoulder of a Kraut who was standing sideways to me. In his hand was a bunch of lire. They wanted to buy the olives. I almost laughed out loud. Minutes ago they'd almost been killed and now they were shopping for roadside treats, lined up like obedient children.

"*Olive, no,*" Sciafani barked. "*Mandorle dolci, sì.*"

Dolci? Didn't that mean sweet? I didn't know the other word, but I figured it out as soon as Sciafani dug his hands into the loose almonds and began giving each German a double-fisted handful.

"*Grazie, danke,*" I heard over and over.

"*Lire, no, mi amici ,*" Salvatore said, giving away the almonds to his *tedeschi* pals.

By the time they were done, the level of almonds was down a fair bit, but the Germans bid friendly *Auf Wiedersehens* as they climbed onto the last of the tanks. Sciafani had played that one smart. I was glad more Krauts hadn't stopped by or else he would've come up with a fistful of me pretty soon.

"That was close," Sciafani said, after the last of the vehicles had passed.

"Do you mean the Allied strafing or the German soldiers? There's so much to chose from."

"I would say the Germans. They were closer. Do you need to get out for a few moments? It looks safe."

"Yeah, I gotta see a man about a horse. Pull me out, willya?"

They each reached in and grabbed a leg. Almonds poured out with me and I had to grab onto Sciafani to keep from falling as the circulation came back into my legs.

"A horse?" he asked.

"It's an American saying," I explained as I walked to the nearest tree.

"*Pisciarsi addosso dalla paura,*" Salvatore said, and they both laughed.

"You must not have been too scared if you have that much left," Sciafani said.

"I'm glad you boys are enjoying this," I said as I finished up.

Walking back to them, I saw figures come out of the woods and head for the wrecked German vehicles. They both followed my glance. Salvatore retrieved his *lupara* from where he'd hidden it. There were about a dozen people, some of them women. The men were armed with shotguns, German Mausers, Italian Mannlicher-Carcano carbines, and pistols. They were all ragged, their clothing dirty and patched. The women stripped the dead Germans where they lay in a row at the side of the road.

"Bandits," said Sciafani, the smile gone from his face.

"Mafia?" I asked. Salvatore shot me a glance then returned his gaze to the nearest group of men.

"No, *mafiusu* do not look like that. Bandits. There is no time to hide, we should leave now."

It was too late to leave. Three men had detached themselves from the group and were walking toward us. One held an automatic pistol— a nice Beretta, it looked like. The other two were armed with short Italian carbines. Salvatore stood still, his right hand on the leather strap of the *lupara* that hung from his shoulder.

Harsh words and angry gestures came from the guy with the Beretta. He pointed to the cart, then the donkey. I thought he was going to shoot it, but then understood. He was saying it was his now. He waved his hand toward the road. Maybe he was in a good mood today, and we could go free, simply leave the donkey and cart behind. Or maybe he preferred shooting his victims in the back. He looked the type—narrow little eyes, a broken nose, and crooked teeth rotted nearly black. I'd want to shoot somebody too if I looked like that.

At about ten feet, they were too far away to rush. It didn't look good, but Salvatore didn't say a thing as he stood his ground. Sciafani looked as worried as I was, and took an involuntary step back, holding his arms out at his side, palms out. None of the three bandits had their weapons pointed at us. There was still the threat of Salvatore's *lupara*, and they seemed to prefer that he walk away with it. Silence filled the space between us as the man with the Beretta raised it, a half-threatening gesture that went nowhere. I could see Salvatore lock eye-balls with him, and very slowly lift his left hand to his shirt. The other men shifted their weight, but the movement was so deliberate that it didn't surprise them into action. He unbuttoned the top button, then the next, then another, until his shirt fell open. Now it was the bandit's turn to take that step back. I couldn't see what was on his chest, and thought it best not to move into the line of fire for a better view. The two men with the carbines took another two steps back, lowered their rifles, and took off. The Beretta guy with the bad teeth stood with his gun hand still half up, looking too mean too run, too uncertain to shoot.

"*Cazzo!*" He spat out the curse as he raised the Beretta. In one fluid motion, Salvatore pulled on the leather strap with his right hand and the *lupara* appeared in it, a blast from both barrels knocking the ban-dit onto his back, two neat blackened holes, seeping red, right over his heart. As he reloaded Salvatore walked over to the dead man and picked up the Beretta. He found a spare clip in the man's jacket pocket and brought both over to me.

The other bandits stood quietly at a respectful distance, their weapons slung over their shoulders. The grove of trees was quiet as the coppery smell of fresh blood rose from the ground.

Salvatore handed me the Beretta and the ammunition clip. "*Un regalo*," he said.

I was too busy reading the tattoo on his chest to react. In a bold arc across the top of his chest were the words VIVA LA MALAVITA.

"What does he mean?" I asked, looking at Sciafani.

"A gift, he is giving it to you as a gift."

"*Grazie, grazie*," I said to Salvatore with sincerity. "But what does this mean?" I tapped on the tattoo. Salvatore smiled and buttoned up.

"Long live the underworld, the life of crime. It proclaims who he is, a man of honor."

I watched as the band of bandits made their way back into the woods, carrying German boots and uniforms and other debris the convoy had left behind. They could have massacred us. But they were afraid, afraid someone would see, or simply afraid of killing a *mafiusu*.

"He's a member of the Mafia," I said.

"It is only the newspapers that use that word, although it has become more widespread now. The entire purpose of the organization was to be secret. It was never really named. You have heard of *cosa nostra?*"

"Sure," I said. "That's another name for the Mob."

"Here in Sicily, it is called a society. And members of that society refer to it as 'our thing.' Which translates as *cosa nostra*. So you see, there is no real name for it, other than the labels outsiders create for it. The life of the underworld. That is what it is."

"How do you know so much about it, Dottor?"

"Let us bury you again, Billy, under the almonds."

"Are you part of *cosa nostra*? Are you *mafiusu?*"

"You ask too many questions. In Sicily that can be unhealthy," Sciafani said.

"It's been nice getting to know you so well, Dottor," I said as I slipped into the cart and pushed away almonds from my hiding place. "How far to Agrigento?"

"Two or three hours, if you do not have to see a horse again."

"See a man *about* a horse," I corrected him as I pulled the blanket over me and they piled on the almonds.

I was certain there was something Sciafani was keeping from me. I didn't know what it was, but I figured it was about his past, reaching back into his childhood. What worried me was why he would bother lying about anything to me. What could it possibly matter?

I may be nuts, I thought to myself, but I felt a whole lot safer with the Beretta in my pocket. I might be *nuts*? It would have been funny if it had not been such a distinct possibility.

CHAPTER ▪ SEVENTEEN

I SPENT THE NEXT three hours thinking about the last time I had been in Agrigento, or at least what I could remember. It was a bit hazy. I had met Nick Cammarata before the mission. He was a Naval Intelligence officer, recruited for his knowledge of Sicilian. He'd been born in the States, but his parents had emigrated from Sicily so he'd grown up speaking the Sicilian dialect at home and English on the streets of Brooklyn. There was even a village with the family name somewhere in the mountains, not far from Villalba. Nick had hoped he could get there when the shooting was over to look up his aunts and uncles.

Some navy commander had brought Nick and four other agents to Allied Forces HQ a month before the invasion. They each had a different mission. Nick had been paired with me, since Uncle Ike wanted to keep tabs on the Mafia angle. The whole thing had almost been called off when one of the guys let slip he'd been brought to the attention of the Office of Naval Intelligence by Joe Adonis, head of the rackets in Brooklyn, who worked for none other than Lucky Luciano himself. While some of the brass was nervous about the Mob connection, others would have been glad to shake hands with the devil himself to get the upper hand in this invasion. Uncle Ike wasn't sure either way, except I remember him telling me how Don Calo's cooperation would save lives.

I could see Nick's face, but no matter how hard I tried, I couldn't place him on this island. The last thing I remembered was seeing him on the deck of Harry's MTB, leaving the dock in North Africa. Harry's face came to me easily enough, especially that last moment when he came into view rounding the stone column before the grenade exploded. I could feel the cool darkness of the night and the pressure of the explosion in my eardrums, see the bright flash, and hear the frantic yelling in Italian and English. Had Nick been there? How had we ended up at the Valley of the Temples, shooting up the ancient ruins? Had we been betrayed?

English. If there had been yelling in English, it must have come from Nick. Harry would have been standing right where the grenade went off. The cry I'd heard hadn't been one of pain, it was more controlled and urgent than anguished. What had Nick been saying?

Nothing came to me and I tried not to think about it too hard. That was the best way to remember. Let it roll over in your mind a few times, my dad used to say. Your mind is busy all day, he'd told me, so don't expect too much of it. It's got a lot to handle, so let the problem roll around in there for a while, and maybe your subconscious will earn its keep. It doesn't have anything else to do.

My dad said a lot of things. Some of them made great sense, and some were just to have something to say. Others I wasn't sure about. This was one of those, but I had to give it a try. So I thought about something else.

The note. The note about purgatory and happiness really bothered me. It matched a message Nick had been given for his Mafia contact, a code of sorts that only a Sicilian would understand. A Sicilian from around Agrigento. That little village of Cammarata was no more than twenty miles north of here. Nick wouldn't have needed to keep it written down, so how had that piece of paper gotten into Rocko's hands? More important, how had the message itself been communicated? The only people besides Nick who would have possessed this information were in North Africa, unless you counted the Mafia contact who had passed it on in the first place. Which was interesting, since the *mafiusu* were in the mountains and Rocko would have been stationed at the beachhead. I couldn't figure that out either, so I took my father's advice again and let my subconscious work on it.

Late in the afternoon we climbed a steep hill, the donkey clip-clopping up switchbacks slowly. Salvatore and Sciafani both got out of the cart to lighten the load. Lucky me, I got to stay buried under the almonds. We pulled off the road, and Salvatore unhitched the donkey to let him feed on the grass.

Sciafani lowered the rear of the cart. "We are almost to Agrigento. Look."

I got out, thankfully for the last time. I brushed almonds from my clothes and tried to straighten up. As I did, I saw Agrigento, the setting sun hitting its walls, turning them to gold as shadows reached like greedy fingers across the rooftops. It was a beautiful city set high on the next hillside, a small valley of green split by a wide stream beneath it. I could hear church bells chiming the hour.

Salvatore closed up the cart as he and Sciafani exchanged words. I shook his hand, said *Grazie*, and smiled. He gave me a little salute and then went to tend to his donkey.

"We should wait until dark before we enter the city," Sciafani said. "Salvatore must go to his relatives now. It is too dangerous for him to take us further."

"Where should we—" Sciafani stared at something over my shoulder, and I turned to see what he was looking at. A cloud of dust kicked up from the road down in the valley, and the sound of an engine downshifting painfully and straining up the hill toward us echoed from below. He grabbed my arm and pulled me behind a line of thick shrubs. We flattened ourselves and waited. Salvatore held on to the donkey as he stood in the open, his shotgun hung carelessly from his shoulder, his lethal speed hidden by a posture of peasant lethargy.

An ancient truck heaved itself up over the crest of the hill. It had no military markings but was crammed full of khaki-clad soldiers standing in the back and on the running boards, hanging onto the truck, grasping short Italian carbines.

"Fascist militia, MVSN," Sciafani said in whisper, even though at this distance, with all the noise the truck was making, he could have yelled it.

The truck stopped as soon as the road leveled out, and the soldiers burst into activity, handing down cases of ammo from the back of the truck, and lifting out a heavy machine gun and tripod. An officer, his dress uniform complete with the official Fascist black shirt, stepped from the passenger seat and scanned the horizon with binoculars. He looked east, to the left of the city, which I judged to be due south of us.

"We must be making a move," I said, my voice a whisper now that the truck was silent. I imagined GIs advancing up that hill into machine-gun fire.

Then I thought about Sciafani. Fascists or no, these were his countrymen. There was still no "we" between us, no matter how friendly he'd been. I wondered if he would want to stay with them, to tend their wounded, if it came to that. I wondered if he was tempted to turn me in. I glanced at him but his expression gave nothing away. For the first time, I felt a shiver of mistrust. Sciafani had been a willing traveling partner at first, but after the encounter with Vito Genovese and Legs, something had changed. Was it seeing the German shoot Signor Ciccolo? Perhaps. But there was something mysterious about the story of Sciafani being adopted, especially after all the talk about trusting only blood relatives. I realized he was here for his own reasons. They coincided with mine for now, but I needed to pay attention and be alert to any change.

The Blackshirt pointed at Salvatore and yelled. Two soldiers marched over, waving their hands for him to leave. He argued with them, gesturing from his cart to Agrigento, probably complaining about not getting to the market. They shook their heads, and he resignedly hitched up the donkey, complaining the whole time. He did a good job of maintaining their focus on him as he moved away, keeping up a stream of Italian that sounded like insults mixed with bewilderment. As he passed our hiding place he winked.

We watched the militiamen set up the machine-gun emplacement. There were about twenty of them. They dug foxholes on either side of the road and a firing pit protected by sandbags for the machine gun. Off in the distance, to the east, a dark plume of smoke appeared. The officer turned his binoculars on to it, then got into the truck and took off, back down the hill. For reinforcements maybe.

"Are these Fascists good fighters?" I asked Sciafani. I was hoping they were nothing more than local militia who might skedaddle for home as soon as the first shots sounded.

"I have seen a battalion of Blackshirts attack British tanks with hand grenades," he said. "I have seen others cower in their holes. Some Fascist units are very well trained, others less so. Most of the Blackshirts here are not from Sicily."

"So they'll probably fight?"

"It is a good position. I would say yes, they will fight."

"We should get out of here." I stated the obvious while looking to our rear.

"That will be difficult," Sciafani said. He was right. While we had cover between us and the militia, there was nothing but bare rocky ground behind us. Once we left the shrubs, we'd be in the open long enough for them to spot us, either going down the hill or back the way we had come.

"We have to stay put until it gets dark," I said.

"Yes, and pray one of them does not walk over here to see a man and his horse," Sciafani said. He had the basic idea, so I didn't correct him.

We waited. The truck came back and more men got out. The truck was towing a 20mm antiaircraft gun, and the crew hustled to unhook it and set it up. As if to taunt them, a single aircraft zoomed out of the western sky, the sun at its back. I couldn't raise my head high enough to identify it, but the machine gun gave it a few ineffective bursts before it climbed out of sight. They moved the 20mm gun to the side of the road opposite the machine gun so their positions formed a semicircle, facing east. We'd have to move around to the right and hope there wasn't another unit doing the same thing on the other side of the hill. We waited some more, listening to the sound of digging and idle chatter that could have come from enlisted men in any army. Nervous laughter, jokes, complaints about the hard ground, bad food, and indifferent officers. I'd been in the army a little more than a year and already the rhythm of daily life in camp or at the front had become part of me. It was easy to recognize the sounds soldiers made, their ability to show contempt for the service while at the same time quietly demonstrating their bond to each other. The tone and tempo of the words didn't sound any different in Italian, and it almost made me homesick for life in a GI camp.

Memories of North Africa flowed unbidden through my mind. Uncle Ike had his headquarters in a fancy villa. I was in a nice tent with a wood floor up off the sand. It wasn't as nice as the Hotel St. George, where Kaz had managed to get us a room when we first arrived in Algiers, but we weren't living in foxholes either. There were dinners and receptions at the villa, and once in a while Kaz and I would be invited, especially if the guest was a visiting congressman from a Polish or Irish ward. Uncle Ike didn't like having to entertain politicians, but when he did, he did it right. Harry Butcher would show them around, make sure they met some GIs from their district, take their pictures, bring them to a villa on the beach for a swim, then for a fancy dinner with the general, plenty of booze and cigars all around. There might even be one going on right now, I thought. Cocktails, maybe. Perhaps Diana was there, wearing her brown FANY uniform as if it were a gown, the wide leather belt polished to a gleam, the brass buttons sparkling like diamonds. She loved that uniform. It had been tailor-made for her, sent from England after she decided to accept the posting SOE had offered her in their North African operation. The first time she tried it on after her last mission, it hung off her thin frame, a wide gap between collar and neck. We both pretended not to notice.

FANY, the First Aid Nursing Yeomanry, was an outfit that provided the Brit army with women trained to operate switchboards, drive trucks, that sort of thing. It also was a source of agents for the Special Operations Executive. Diana had volunteered after she had served as a switchboard operator with the British Expeditionary Force in 1940, and made it out of France at Dunkirk. The destroyer she was on was sunk by Stukas, and by the time she had been picked up, she'd watched the wounded who had been on stretchers slide off the deck and disappear beneath the waves. Diana had told me about that the first day we met. She'd clung to me, crying her story out, reliving the helplessness she had felt watching everyone around her die.

She'd been courting death ever since and almost caught up with it in Algeria. She was OK now, but I didn't know how we were. We'd fallen hard for each other, back in England. But after I pulled her out of that Vichy prison camp, drugged and half dead, I focused more on getting my revenge on the bastard responsible than on being with her. Not that she didn't want him dead too, but once that was taken care of, I should have stepped up and let her know I still loved her. But I'd been scared, unsure of myself, and she knew it and thought the worst: that I didn't want to be with her after all she had endured.

I'll admit, I didn't like thinking about it. So I tried, tried my best, and as the weeks passed, and she grew stronger, so did we. But I was never sure I had her full trust, and had no idea how to get it back. That's the way things had been when I left for this island voyage. We were still in love, I guess. Something was missing though, and I was man enough to understand it was something I didn't have, but not man enough to know what it was.

Sciafani shifted his weight as he lifted his hands to put them under his arms. A rock rolled loose and started a noisy fall, dislodging gravel that flowed downhill after it, the stones hitting each other at the bottom with a sharp *click-clack* sound. We flattened ourselves even lower, not daring to look up to see if the soldiers heard.

"*Che ciò è?*" The sound of boots on gravel came scuffling across the ground, drawing closer, murmurs of cautious curiosity evident in the tone of the militiamen as they approached.

A sound like a long sheet being ripped rose in a crescendo from the sky, too fast and fierce to allow for any response. The ground shook as one shell hit, thundered, and cracked on the hill. More shrieking sounds descended, explosions that spewed earth and fire around the Italian positions. Naval gunfire, I thought. That aircraft, a spotter, had caught a glimpse of the antiaircraft gun being unloaded. Right now, sailors miles offshore were reading coordinates and loading huge shells into the cannons of a cruiser's gun turret, while a few dozen Blackshirts were being blown to kingdom come. I pulled at Sciafani, motioning down the hill. We had to get out of here now, while we could, before a shell found us.

"No," he said, shaking off my hand. Screams pierced through all the other sounds, and he started to stand, but I pulled him down again. The awful shrieks and explosions continued, punctuated by the agonized calls of the wounded, until they were drowned out, perhaps ended, by the next round of shells. A series of smaller explosions marked a hit on the 20mm ammo, a column of flame coloring the darkening sky as the truck's gasoline tank went up. One soldier unhurt, but with wide, panicked eyes, ran right through the shrubs, tripping on my legs as he barreled by. He rolled partway down the hill, then looked at me and screamed, running crazily away, weaving and nearly falling as he held his hands over his ears.

The shelling ended abruptly. Sciafani and I looked at each other, unsure what to make of the sudden silence. It took a few seconds for other sounds to be heard, the aftermath of a violent bombardment. The crackling of flames, moans of the wounded, the *pop, pop, pop* of rifle ammunition going off in the fire. We raised our heads and looked. It was nearly dark but the burning truck lit the scene with a flickering orange light. Craters filled the area where the positions had been, smoke curling up from the bottom of the ten-foot-wide holes. We stood. The machine-gun emplacement was simply gone, the men, heavy weapons, and sandbags erased from the landscape, replaced by overlapping circles of smoking dirt. The antiaircraft gun, a blackened heap of twisted metal, had been thrown ten yards from where it had been set up. I stepped over a severed leg.

"Here," Sciafani said. "Help me." He had a man by his arms, buried up to his chest in debris thrown up by the explosions. He didn't seem to have a mark on him. I grabbed one arm and Sciafani took the other. We pulled and fell back, holding the top half of a man, cut through by shrapnel. The sailors who had loaded shells minutes before were probably drinking coffee by now.

We finally found someone alive, huddled in a crater where he had taken shelter after the first round of shells. He had shrapnel fragments in his back, which Sciafani picked out by the light of the fire with a knife he'd taken from the body of an officer, a sharp dagger that he sterilized in the flames before he worked the shrapnel out. The guy never blinked. He stared out into the night, his mouth open as if to speak, but he made no sound.

I searched for other wounded while Sciafani worked. I found a soldier, younger than me, younger than my kid brother, by the side of the road. He was crying as he lay in a pool of blood. I called for Sciafani as I knelt beside him. He looked at me with a question in his eyes that I didn't want to answer as he held his hands clamped tight to his abdomen. I knew what shrapnel did. It was seldom clean. Blood seeped through his fingers. I didn't know enough Italian to say anything and it didn't seem right to speak to him in English.

"*Je suis désolé,*" I said as I smoothed the hair away from his forehead. I am sorry. "*Je suis désolé.*"

"*Mi dispiace,*" Sciafani said as he knelt next to me and put his hand on my shoulder. He took the boy's hands to pull them away from his wound, but stopped as a raspy, jagged breath came out. With it, all movement ceased. The hands relaxed, and Sciafani placed them crossed on the boy's chest.

"He is gone."

I didn't know what to say or feel. I didn't want these guys firing into the GIs who might be swarming up this hill tomorrow, but I also didn't want this kid to have to suffer and die. I put my head in my hands, and repeated Sciafani's words as best I could.

"*Mi dispiace*," I said.

"Look," Sciafani said. "Look at me. His blood is on my hands." He held his hands out, palms up, coated in dark red blood. "These are the hands that did this. I did nothing to stop the Fascists, and now they are sending boys out to be killed for Mussolini. Do you know what Il Duce says about blood?"

"No."

"Blood alone moves the wheels of history," Sciafani quoted. "He said that in 1914. We had quite enough warning, don't you think? Blood alone."

CHAPTER ▪ EIGHTEEN

"DON'T SHOOT!" I HELD my hands up and stepped in front of the three bandaged Italians on the floor. I knew what a glimpse of an enemy uniform might mean to the GI who had stuck the snout of his Thompson submachine through the door, not to mention what it could mean for me. "I'm an American."

"*Non sparare, non sparare,*" sobbed one of the wounded Italians. I guessed it was basically the same request.

"Come out where I can see you," the owner of the Thompson barked. He still wasn't showing more than the muzzle of his gun. Smart guy.

"Coming out," I said, holding my hands palm up, slightly forward, so the first thing he'd see was that they were empty.

"Who the hell are you, Mac?" The guy eyeing me was a buck sergeant, and while he didn't keep his Thompson leveled at my gut, he didn't exactly practice firearms safety with it either.

"Lieutenant Billy Boyle. I got separated from my unit. There's three wounded Italians in there," I said, pointing to the abandoned house where Sciafani and I had taken the survivors from the night before.

Over his shoulder, I saw GIs darting from cover and making quick dashes, staying low in the long early-morning shadows. The only sound was the rapid tread of boots and the slight clinking and clanking of gear as a platoon of heavily armed men moved swiftly around us, wraiths descending from the hills.

"What unit, and where's your weapon?" He eyed me with suspicion.

"Seventh Army HQ," I said, turning so he could see the patch on my shoulder. "We ran into some Germans and barely got away. All I have is this Beretta." I patted the pistol stuck into my belt.

"Hey, nice. Can I see it?"

"That's 'Hey, nice, Lieutenant.' Or has the army given up on that in the last couple of days?"

"I got no idea if you're a lieutenant, a deserter, or a Kraut. What I don't believe is that any headquarters punk got here ahead of Rangers." His eyes narrowed beneath the steel rim of his helmet as they studied me.

"Purely by accident, Sarge. We were trying to make our way back last night and got trapped up there when the Italians started setting up emplacements." I pointed to the top of the hill, the dark craters draped in shadows cast by the morning sun.

"Yeah, the navy blasted that for us yesterday." He turned and signaled to someone. His shoulder patch said First Battalion Rangers.

"You're Darby's Rangers, right?"

"That's right, Mac. You sure you don't want to trade for that Beretta?"

I knew he believed my story when he started hustling me for a souvenir. If he thought I was a deserter he would've taken it outright. If he really thought I was a Kraut, I'd be dead.

"No, Sarge, I might need it. You'll probably find a few more up ahead."

"OK, our medic will look at your wounded prisoners." A Ranger with a red cross on his helmet and armband ran up to us.

"Got some wounded Eyeties in here. Hang on, Doc, lemme check 'em for weapons."

He disappeared into the house, but it didn't take long. It was one long room, and the most badly wounded man was on the single bed, the others on the floor. We'd washed their wounds as best we could and ripped up clothes and the single sheet for bandages. It wasn't much, but Sciafani said they'd live. I'd scrounged canteens and rations from the debris at the top of the hill, and even found some brandy in the house, but that had gone to the wounded.

"They're all yours, Doc. One looks pretty bad. There's a civilian who had this, said he was a doctor." The sergeant held the dagger Sciafani had picked up the previous night. The sheath had MVSN engraved on it and the Fascist symbol.

"Nice souvenir, Sarge, but he really is a doctor. He used that to dig shrapnel out of one of the wounded last night." I held out my hand for the dagger.

"If you say so," he said reluctantly, slapping the sheathed dagger into my hand. "Yeah, and I know, there'll be lots more up ahead."

The medic went in the house and I heard Sciafani talking with him, asking if he had sulfa, giving him an update on each patient.

"You headed into Agrigento, Sarge?"

"Well, I guess with that Beantown accent you ain't no Kraut spy," he said as he spat. "We're going around it, to take Porto Empedocle from the rear. Then the Third Division can move into Agrigento real easy. You seen any Germans around here?"

"None, just those Italians, Fascist militia. These are the only survivors," I said.

"Good." He flicked a finger close to his helmet in what might have been an attempt at a salute or a wave goodbye. I figured only a sucker wants to be given a salute when there's a chance of enemy snipers around, so I didn't make a big deal out of it.

"See ya in the funny papers, Sarge."

"Where?" Sciafani asked from the doorway of the house.

"It's just an expression. It means I think he's a funny guy, in a sarcastic sort of way."

"I did not think him amusing. We can leave now; the medic is setting up an aid station here. The men will receive good care."

It's odd, the things that divide men in a war. Sciafani had been talking with the medic like a colleague. He and I were getting along OK. But that one word, one comment from the sergeant about the bombardment last night: *Good.* It made all the sense in the world. Who knows how many of these Rangers would be dead or writhing in pain right now from machine-gun bullets or 20mm shells if the navy hadn't hit that position? It was logical. But Sciafani didn't see dead and wounded Americans. He saw his own people blown to pieces, and it was gnawing at him. Did he feel guilty for being alive and in the company of an American?

"Good," I said, studying his face. The word hung like a challenge in the air. I handed him the dagger and he tucked it into his belt.

"Come," was all he said, brushing by me, a brief look of disgust on his face. I followed, and thought about the leg I'd stepped over, and the boy clutching at his stomach, and I felt small, ashamed, and insignificant. Who was I to judge him or the sergeant or anybody else? The Ranger sergeant knew what he had to do, and so did Sciafani. Me, I was still following ghosts.

But the ghosts were getting closer.

I grabbed a full canteen and followed Sciafani. The Rangers veered off to the left, circumventing the hill in front of us that led up to the backside of Agrigento. The city ran along the crest of the hill and then descended the slope toward Porto Empedocle, a few kilometers away. Between them was the Valley of the Temples, acres of ancient crumbling temples built by the Greeks and who the hell knows else.

From here, we could make out the tops of a few tall buildings, their orange tile roofs blazing in the hot morning sunlight. It was as if no one wanted to build anything out of sight of the sea or the ruins. We climbed up rough paths through stands of cactus and trees, waiting at one point for a goatherd to pass with his mangy flock. Following a streambed, we made it to the crest of the hill, taking a dirt path that emptied out into the Piazza Vittorio Emanuele, according to Sciafani. We passed a massive, rounded building set off by pink marble columns and a statue of heroic-looking Italian soldiers. It was from my dad's war, when the Italians were on our side. Two dogs slept on the stone steps beneath the statue, too lazy in the warm sun to take notice of us. Otherwise, the plaza was empty.

After the steep hike in the growing heat, it was odd to suddenly find ourselves in a city, surrounded by green trees and neatly trimmed hedges. A fountain gushed from stone cherubs and we stuck our heads into the spray, the cool water cleansing us of dust and sweat.

Two old men walked into the park, identically dressed in black suits, vests, and collarless shirts. They stopped to look at us, their eyes wide in surprise, whether at my uniform or simply our general appearance, I couldn't tell. The worn suit of the Ciccolos' missing son hung like tattered rags on Sciafani's thin frame. His once white shirt was filthy now with stains of dried blood across his chest. I didn't know if the men knew I was an American, or cared. They scurried away, turning a corner and disappearing up narrow stone steps.

"This way," Sciafani said, pointing to a plaque that read VIA ATENEA. It was a wide street, running straight into the center of town, large buildings with ornate facades on either side. Several of them were bombed out. The debris spilled out into the street, where only a lane wide enough for a single vehicle had been cleared. We walked quickly, not wanting to linger or attract attention by running. A window opened above us, and a frowning gray-haired woman looked down at us and slowly shook her head, as if she found the sight of us in her city pitiful. I felt eyes on us from all around—windows, doorways, alleyways, and rooftops. I shivered in the heat.

"There's no traffic, no one up and going to work," I said. I glanced at my wristwatch. Just past seven. "Is it Sunday?"

"No. I think word has spread. They know the Americans are coming."

The eerie silence was broken by the growl of an engine echoing off the buildings. We eased back into a doorway, keeping to the shadows as much as possible. I heard the vehicle turn onto Via Atenea as the sound grew louder. A stream of shouts in Italian and the hard thuds of boots hitting pavement followed the squealing of ancient brakes. I chanced a quick glance from the doorway. The truck started up, coming toward us with men still in the open back. MVSN.

"Fascists," I said to Sciafani. "It looks like they're going to drop men off at the other end and search the entire street."

"Those old men must have informed," Sciafani said. He put his hand on the doorknob to try to open it. As he did, the knob turned slowly and the door creaked open. The gray-haired lady who had looked at us so sadly from the window grabbed me by the sleeve, the strength of her grip a surprise.

"*Entri rapidamente.*" She pulled me in and Sciafani followed. She put a finger to her lips and shut the door slowly, holding the latch so it wouldn't make a noise.

"*Bastardi di fascista,*" she whispered, cocking her head toward the street. Then she gave a wheezy little laugh, and her cheeks flushed red. She liked this game.

"Bastards," I said, pointing too. She laughed some more. The truck rumbled by and boots echoed on the empty street. She beckoned us to follow her to the rear of the apartment, and we ended up in her kitchen.

"Chicago?" she asked me.

"No. Boston," I said, slow and clear. She shook her head and fired off some Italian to Sciafani.

"Her brother lives in Chicago. She wanted to know if you know him," Sciafani translated.

I shook my head. She shrugged and opened a low wooden door that led out to steep, narrow steps in an alleyway. We nodded our thanks and she laughed again, shooing us out like troublesome neighborhood kids. I pulled the Beretta and kept my back against the wall as we edged up the stairs. The stone was cool against my palm, but soft, worn down by centuries of Sicilian hands.

"Is the church far?" I asked Sciafani.

"No. We must turn soon and that will take us into the Piazza del Purgatorio and the *chiesa*. We go into the church, out the side entrance, then up stairs much like these. They will take us to the Duomo."

"The cathedral, where happiness awaits."

"Let us hope so, my friend."

Explosions sounded in the distance as we climbed the stairs. Soft, muffled sounds, *thump, thump, thump,* followed by ripples of small arms fire. At the top of the steps, I looked back between two buildings and saw plumes of black smoke billowing up from the direction of the harbor. Rangers at work.

Sciafani led us down a narrow street and up another set of stone steps between two buildings. Wash was hung out to dry on lines strung overhead and from balconies, the clothing limp in the hot early-morning stillness. On the next street, we saw a line of old women, their black shawls pulled tight over their shoulders, bowed heads and stooped shoulders leaning toward the *piazza* ahead of us. A large church on our right dominated a tiny square. Its great wooden doors were open, swallowing the tiny stream of worshippers.

"Welcome to purgatory," Sciafani said. "La Chiesa del Purgatorio."

The bell in the church tower began to ring, as if to announce our arrival. Two American fighter planes zoomed low over the town, the roar of their engines drowning out the bells for a moment, disappearing over rooftops as the bell tolled its last few rings. No one looked up.

As I scanned the ornate facade of the church, I wondered why I didn't remember it. Harry and I must have come through here with Nick. Built from blocks of light brown stone, it was decorated with white marble pillars and statues on either side. The bell tower ran up the left side, giving it an oddly unbalanced look. Why didn't I remember it? I looked around the *piazza*, suddenly nervous. A nun came from a side street and hurried ahead of us; I nearly jumped a foot.

"Are you all right, Billy?"

"Yeah, I think so," I said. "I don't remember this, and I think I should."

"Some memories take longer than others to return. Things that remind you of that incident may be the most difficult memories to recover."

I stopped to lean against the corner of a building and watch the church entrance. I didn't like this. I felt light-headed and dizzy. I wanted to slump down and close my eyes. Instead I kept them on Sciafani. Was he the one making me nervous?

"What happened to your parents?" I asked. The words came out without my thinking about them.

"What? Why do you want to know that now, even if it was any of your business?"

I licked my lips and looked around again. My mouth was dry and I could feel my heart pounding. Something wasn't right and I had no idea what, so I had to work at the one wrong thing I knew about, and that was Sciafani's story.

"You told me all about your family in Palermo, and lectured me on how you could only trust family, those closest to you. Then it comes out that your real parents were killed and you were adopted, but you don't want to say anything more about it. Seems strange to me. What are you hiding?"

If he had told me to go to hell or called me crazy or even socked me on the jaw, I would've known things were on the up-and-up. Those were all normal reactions to some guy sticking his nose too far into your private business. Sciafani didn't do any of those things. He stared at me with wide, startled eyes, like he'd been hit with a two-by-four. He blinked a few times and looked away.

"Come," he said. "We have to pass through the church and leave purgatory behind."

I had no choice but to follow.

CHAPTER • NINETEEN

OUR FOOTSTEPS WERE LOUD on the stone floor, echoing down the narrow dark interior of the church. Solitary women on their knees fed their rosaries through their fingers like soldiers feeding ammo through a machine gun. Intent on their prayers, they didn't look up as we passed. We didn't belong here, and they ignored us with profound indifference. I had stopped at the entrance to dip my fingers into the holy water and make the sign of the cross. I wasn't exactly a Holy Joe, but I knew what was expected of a good Irish boy in any Catholic church. Sciafani had walked right by.

You would have taken him for a bum fresh from a couple of days riding the rails and the dagger stuck through his belt gave him a look made more menacing by his dark features and black-whiskered face. My uniform wasn't much cleaner, and the Beretta in my waistband probably didn't give me a peaceful churchgoing appearance either. I was sure Sister Mary Margaret would give me a tongue-lashing whenever I saw her next for going to church not only dirty but armed, no less.

"This *chiesa* is famous for these statues of the eight virtues," Sciafani said to me as we passed through the nave, pointing at the four statues on each side. "Charity, Love, I forget the others." He was playing the happy native tour guide, as if the exchange outside had never happened.

"Justice," I said, pointing to the one holding scales.

"Bah! In this world, justice is hard to find."

A priest swept by us, his long black cassock dusting the floor as he walked. He glanced at us sourly and put a finger to pursed lips, more offended by our voices than our attire and armament. Someone began playing the organ, the energetic pumping echoing almost as loudly as the *Gloria Patri* itself. Exiting by a side door, we left the darkness behind and stepped out into the bright sun.

"You're not religious?" I asked Sciafani. He shrugged, which seemed to be the most common reply to any question asked in Sicily.

"Do you get on your knees and pray to Cristu?" he asked me, taking the steep stairs that led directly up from the plaza.

"Yeah, I go to church. Pretty often, when I'm home."

"I have no wish to beg on my knees, to whisper words after a priest to beg crumbs from heaven. You may as well beg a rich man for his land."

"You wouldn't pray for an end to the war?"

Sciafani broke his long stride and turned on me, his smoldering anger barely contained as he punched his finger at my chest. "Pray? To whom? It would take a giant to end this war, not the pale Jesus in the church paintings. He wasn't even much of a man, if you ask me. He had no wife, and gave up carpentry to go around giving speeches and begging for food. Sicilians revere his mother, Mary, more than him. Or our Sicilian saints, like Saint Lucia, who saved Catania from Mount Etna's eruption. Stopping lava—now that miracle I would get down on my knees and pray for. But where is this Jesus now that we need the great Son of God? Where is he since he chased some fish into a net and got himself crucified?"

He made a trembling fist and held it to my face, his eyes looking beyond mine, to some distant pain. I took his fist in both my hands and pulled it to my chest, recalling how I used to pray as a child.

"Who was it, Enrico? Your father? Your mother?"

His eyes widened in rage, then compressed as he worked to hold back tears.

"All of them, damn you!"

He pulled his hand from my grip violently, throwing me back hard against the stone wall. I stumbled a few steps, and then had to take the stairs two at a time to catch up with him.

"What do you mean, all of them? You spoke of your father as if he were still alive in Palermo. What's the truth?" He stopped again, the look of rage that had played across his features gone, replaced by weariness. He let out a breath and shook his head as he smiled, as you might at a small child who kept asking questions beyond his understanding. He put his hand on my shoulder gently.

"Why don't you pray to Christu, Billy? Ask him for the truth. Who better to tell you? Come, we are almost to the Duomo." That struck him as funny, I guess. He dropped his hand and climbed the steps, laughing as he went, the echoes rattling in the narrow passageway between stone buildings until it sounded like a hysterical mob on our heels.

Sciafani slowed as we reached the top of the stairs, gesturing to the wall of pink stone in front of us. "The Duomo," he said, beckoning me on. We turned left and walked along the south wall of the cathedral. His outburst had tempered my earlier sense of suspicion, replacing it with satisfaction at hitting my target. I still didn't understand him, but at least I knew now that there was a story behind his evasions. The emotion with which he had turned on me made that clear.

It was one of the little rules my dad had drummed into my head. When something doesn't feel right, find out why. You'd be surprised, he used to tell me, how many times people get that little gnawing sense of something wrong and ignore it. A guy says something that contradicts what he said an hour ago, and you figure, I must've heard him wrong. People want everything to fit in with what they know, and they twist the facts to make things match. The trick—he told me a couple of dozen times—is to recognize that thread of wrongness and pull at it until you unravel the truth. And to keep at it until you do.

He never told me to pray to Jesus for it.

At the west end of the cathedral we turned and went up the steps to the main door. It wasn't a fancy cathedral like the ones you see in pictures. It wasn't even as nice as the Cathedral of the Holy Cross in Boston, with its tall stained-glass windows, bright red doors, and massive bell tower. This bell tower was short, squat, and looked like they'd stopped working on it long before my granddaddy was born. The walls were soft limestone, the blocks uneven and worn, crumbling away in places. Carvings in the stone were unrecognizable, hazy with blurred edges, like my memory. The front was plain, nothing but a single round window above the door, a cross set in the stained glass the only decoration. But from the top of the steps, you couldn't beat the view. Across and beyond the rooftops of Agrigento, to the south, acres of ancient ruins lay as they had for hundreds, maybe thousands, of years.

To the west, new ruins were being made in Porto Empedocle and all along the coast road. Smoke filled the sky, showing all the variations of battle. Furious, dark, billowing clouds from the port, maybe an oil storage depot on fire. Gray smoke from buildings, caught on the wind and drifting toward us on the breeze off the sea. Here and there a pinpoint of flame and greasy smoke as a smashed vehicle consumed fuel and flesh. Along the coast road, dust and smoke from skirmishes produced a hazy glimmer in the harsh sun. Men were dying. We turned our backs and opened the door to the Duomo.

Standing in the doorway, I saw it was lighter inside than I had expected. Wooden crossbeams painted in bright colors with scrollwork, flowers, and dancing angels gave the interior a cheery look, compared to the dark and dank church in purgatory. This looked like a place you might actually find some happiness. I put my hand in my pocket and felt the crumpled silk handkerchief, cool to the touch, and wondered whom I would end up giving it to, or if it would be taken from me. I shivered.

"*Carne?*" a small voice asked. I nearly jumped, spooked by my own thoughts, and saw three children standing behind us, two little girls and a boy. He was the oldest, maybe eight or nine.

"*Carne?*" he said again, looking to Sciafani this time.

"Doesn't that mean meat?" I said, remembering a few Italian words I'd learned from Al DeAngelo that weren't swear words.

"Yes, but they use it to mean food. They honor us by asking for meat, since only rich men could give such a gift to a beggar." He shrugged, turning from them slightly, speaking with his body what he thought of them.

"*Carne?*" one of the little girls asked. I wondered if she thought we were debating how much meat to give them or what kind. Beefsteak or chicken? We had eaten Italian rations last night and I still had one crumpled packet in my shirt pocket. I pulled it out, the white wrapping dirty and ripped, but the words BISCOTTI DOLCI still stood out. Sweet biscuits.

"*Nessuna carne*," I said. "*Mi dispiace.*" I figured I should practice apologizing in Italian, and wondered how many languages I would learn to express sorrow in.

"*Grazie*," the boy said, putting his arms around the girls' shoulders and shepherding them away. The little girl who had taken the biscuits held them to her chest and looked at me over her shoulder, her dark eyes locked onto mine as her brother led her down the steps. An anti-aircraft gun on the hill behind us began firing, and she flinched at the noise, but held her gaze as she disappeared down the steep steps.

A pair of fighter planes zoomed overhead, British Spitfires, twisting and turning to avoid antiaircraft fire from the ridge behind the church. Straightening, they went into a shallow dive, racing across the city, their machine guns chattering at some target along the road. We couldn't see anything but the two fighters pulling up and away, arcing in the sky, gleaming in the sunlight over the Mediterranean. A puff of smoke appeared where they had strafed. This far away, it seemed inconsequential, like it must to those pilots, so high in the air. I wondered if they had ever killed a man up close, felt his blood on their hands. Or did they dream of blood at night, safe in comfortable beds?

I went into the church, glad to leave the ringside view. I didn't like the view up close, and I didn't like it from a distance either. There was too much dead and empty air, too much of everything between the living and the dead. Distance, memories, dreams, desires. Soldiers and civilians were losing their dreams of life down there in those little puffs of smoke, losing everything to the distant *rat-tat-tat* that almost sounded like a woodpecker at work on the old dead tree near the bird feeder in our backyard. They were dying amid screams and terror and noise so loud the ears of the living would ring for hours after.

There was so much space between us, so much of nothing, that there was room enough for the memory of my mother feeding birds, and how happy the sound of the woodpecker's beak against dead wood made her. She'd stand at the kitchen window, up on her tiptoes, straining to see that tree. *Tat-tat-tat.*

I couldn't look. Instead, I went to find happiness, following Sciafani into the church. He seemed more troubled by the children than the battle. Then again, the kids were right here.

"Look, a Caravaggio," he said, pointing to a painting. It was of a baby, but the canvas was so dark I couldn't tell anything more. The church door shut behind me, the distant sounds of battle muffled by the ancient wood.

"Is he famous, like Michelangelo?"

"Yes, my friend," Sciafani said, laughing. "He is famous. There would be *carne* for all the beggar children of Agrigento if the church sold that one! But don't worry, priests will feast their eyes on it over the centuries while the *bambini* starve. They always have."

"So it's been a while since you've been to services?" I said, trying to joke him out of his foul mood.

"Not since my parents . . ." He let the sentence drift off. "Not since my parents," he said more firmly.

We walked to the ornate altar, tiers of rose-colored marble rising to support a statue of Mary holding her baby.

"See, Billy? We Sicilians worship the Mother of Christ, the mother of us all. But we do not pay so much attention to her son. He should have respected her more and not drawn all that trouble down on the family. As soon as he was born, they had to flee to Egypt!" He shook his head dismissively.

Sciafani wandered off to look at the other paintings along the main wall. I was glad not to have to listen to him rant and rave about the church and paintings and mothers. Something was eating at him and it was ready to boil over, which would have been fine, except I couldn't afford to have him go off his rocker right here, right now, while I was searching for happiness. Where would Saint Felice be, and what would happen when I found him? I peered down the corridor that led off to each side of the altar. The transept, I thought, remembering my brief career as an altar boy back in Boston. It was an honor, my mom kept telling me, and I guess it was, but one I'd been eager to pass up. Getting up earlier than everyone else to prepare for Sunday services wasn't high on my list at that age. Every once in a while, though, as the organ played and I felt the eyes of the congregation following me as I carried the heavy candle to the altar, I had felt holy, deep inside. There was something about being up on the chancel, dressed in my small black cassock, that set me apart from everyday life, and I'd liked that. I would forget about my alarm clock and the lonely early morning walk to church, and I'd feel sorry for all those poor people in the pews who weren't part of what we were doing, who had to follow along as I alone carried the gifts of bread and wine for the priest to work his magic on. I guess the church knew what Mussolini knew, that blood alone moves the wheels, even if the blood was made miraculously from wine every Sunday.

I never would have admitted it to Dad, but that experience had a lot to do with my becoming a cop. It gave me a feeling of separateness, a holy isolation from the day-to-day drudgery of life. And it gave me a chance to set things right, the way they should be, which is what I always thought the best part of religion was about. *Do unto others as you would have them do unto you.* But I liked the blue coat better than the cassock, and the police revolver far better than the heavy candlestick.

I looked at the flickering votive candles along each wall. Some were about to go out, while others looked like they had recently been lit. For the first time it hit me that there was no one in the church. Where were the people who'd lit those candles? Where were the old women who came every day to pray? No priest listening to confession? No one taking refuge from the battle inching toward the city?

I saw a man at the far end of the transept. He hadn't been there a second ago, but now he stood square in the middle of the tiled floor, hands folded behind his black robe. He didn't move. He looked straight at me. I walked away from the altar in his direction.

He was gray haired but stood straight, the robe showing only a slight bulge around his middle. His nose was bent, broken once, maybe twice. His eyes stayed on me, tracking me as I came closer, sizing me up. He looked to me like a man whose business was firmly rooted in this world, not the next. Before I could get close enough to speak, he turned sharply on his heel and strode to a narrow wooden door. He opened it and stooped to enter, leaving it ajar. The entrance led to a small landing and a circular staircase made from the same soft stone as the building itself. I grasped the iron rail and walked down the steps, the faint glow of candlelight beckoning me below. I thought about calling to Sciafani, but didn't want to risk him saying something to offend Cristu himself in the bowels of a cathedral.

At the bottom of the stairs, low arched ceilings ran to the left and right. Stone beams supported the arches, and between them were dusty carved caskets, some of shiny marble, others of dull stone. Crosses and bishops' miters adorned the caskets, the dates on them hundreds of years old. Candles fixed to the arches were the only light in this grave-yard of priests and bishops. I followed the echo of clacking heels to a pool of golden light that bathed the cold stone. Inside a small chapel, rows of tall white candles lit the room, casting shadows in every direc-tion and drawing sparkling reflections from the polished gold that dec-orated an open casket. Inside I could see mummified remains, dressed in chain mail and a faded blue cloak. Next to the casket, as still as the ancient corpse, stood the black-robed man.

"*Buon giorno,* Padre," I said, using up a good portion of the Italian I could speak in a church.

"I'm not a priest, kid." He spoke in low growl, his accent as much Brooklyn as Italian.

"Who are you?" I said.

He answered with a little gesture, a tip of the head, eyebrows up and mouth turned down. A very Italian response. Who's to say, it all depends, who's asking, all rolled up into the twitch of a few facial muscles.

"Who are you looking for?"

"I've passed through purgatory twice, and I've come to find happi-ness," I said, looking at the figure laid out in the open casket.

"Ah, yes, San Felice. So, you have found him. Is this what you imagined happiness to be?" He raised one hand, palm out, inviting me to step closer. I did.

The chain mail and cloth rested on bones. The head was bare. Leathery patches of brown dried skin stretched over cheekbones and curled up where it had split and wasted away. The lips were gone entirely, leaving brown teeth grinning at the ceiling. White gloves enclosed the hands crossed on his chest. A sword in a scabbard lay at his side. Traces of leather wrapped around the scabbard were visible, turned almost to dust. Everything around the corpse was worn, frayed, dark, and limp, so heavy with age that it seemed to yearn for the con-cealment of the grave. Everything except the white gloves.

"Over a thousand years old, the priests tell me. The gloves are to keep the small bones of the hand from falling apart. We wash them every Easter."

"The gloves or the bones?" I asked.

"The gloves, of course. It is best to leave the bones of the dead alone as much as possible, don't you think?"

"I think somebody ought to have thought of that a thousand years ago," I answered, tearing my eyes away from the skull's hideous grin. Whatever sainted name this guy had been given, it was obvious he'd been a soldier, a soldier who had done something that marked him as a holy man or perhaps a holy warrior. Now he was a relic, a curiosity for the religious to pray to. I felt sorry for him, alone here among the living.

"Why have you returned?"

"You've seen me before?" Panic rose from my gut. I didn't remember anything about this church, this man, or this rotting saint.

"Yes, but you stood back, with the other one. The Englishman. What happened?"

"I'm sorry," I said, wishing we could get out of this underground chapel. "I don't remember everything that happened. I got separated from my friends, and I'm trying to find them."

"That is no concern of mine. I don't know you. I knew the man who came here, but all I know of you is that you were with him."

"I knew about purgatory," I said.

"It is a common enough expression," he said.

It was time to clinch the deal. I pulled the handkerchief out, held it by two corners and flapped it once as I unfurled it for him to see. Candle flames danced crazily in the brief breeze it created. He looked at it, reached his hand out to feel it, and rubbed it between his thumb and forefinger. His eyes went to mine, and he nodded. Had I done this before? I couldn't remember.

"Come," he said. "Put that away and follow me."

I followed him upstairs, glad to give the chambers of the righteous dead my back. In the transept, Sciafani leaned against the wall, waiting. He and the black-robed man stared at each other.

"This is Dottore Enrico Sciafani," I said. "He guided me here from Gela. And you are . . . ?"

"You vouch for him?"

"Yes, I do."

"Very well. I am Tommaso Corso, sacristan of this cathedral."

"I'm Billy Boyle, lieutenant, U.S. Army. Now, tell me—"

"Not here," he said, cutting me off with a wave of his hand. "Come."

We sat at a rough wood table in a small room off the sacristy, the place where the priest kept his robes and vestments, the chalice, all the special gear for the Mass. In a big church or a cathedral like this one, the sacristan was the guy in charge of all this stuff. Everything in the sacristy from candles to cassocks. Plus all the church property in the rest of the building, which really meant something when art treasures decorated the walls.

"You're American?" I asked as he poured each of us a glass of red wine.

"Only for a brief period," he said. Pulling off his robe and hanging it on a peg, he sat down with his glass, spilling a drop of ruby red on his hand. He wore a white collarless shirt and dark vest, like every other Sicilian man. But unlike many, he wore a shoulder holster with the butt of a big revolver sticking out from under his left arm. "I left Sicily as a young man, and went to America as many have done. Mr. Luciano gave me work in New York, with the unions at the docks. There was a disagreement with the authorities, and ultimately I was deported. I had become an American citizen in 1921, but they took that away from me in 1934 when they put me on a boat and sent me back."

"Are you still loyal to Lucky Luciano?" I asked.

"Loyalty is a precious thing, my young friend. An honorable thing, not a thing to be questioned."

"Please excuse Billy," Sciafani said. "He is not Sicilian, and does not understand these things so well. He is Irish."

"So," Corso said, as if that explained everything. "The answer is of course I am. I am also loyal to Don Calo, and he wants to see you very much. In order to be certain he survives the meeting, I want you to give me that little pistol you have stuck in your pants." With that, he drew his revolver and pointed it at me casually as he took another sip of wine.

"I always say it's better to give than to receive," I said as I pulled the Beretta out with my thumb and forefinger. I slid it across the table to him.

"Yes, especially with this monster," he said as he holstered his revolver. "It's an Italian sidearm from the last war, a Bodeo. Fires 10mm ammunition. Would make a hell of a racket in here. And a big hole in your chest."

"Are you really an official of this cathedral or did you kill him and take his place?" Sciafani asked. Even with his cynical view of religion, he seemed to be having a hard time believing this guy was for real.

"Yes, indeed, I am the sacristan here. I am also a member of the altar society. Does that surprise you?"

"Since the war, not much surprises me," Sciafani answered. "Only I have never seen a gun concealed by a church robe before."

"This is nothing, Dottor, compared to the Teutonic Knights and the Knights Hospitallers who established orders here in Sicily centuries ago. There is nothing strange about protecting holy property when rival armies are fighting across our land."

"Tommaso, I do want to see Don Calo, that's why we're here," I said, trying to focus on the present. "I have an important message for him, from the Allied Command, and from Lucky Luciano."

"Then why didn't you deliver it the first time?"

"Something went wrong in the Valley of the Temples."

"Maybe you are what went wrong there," Tommaso said, drumming his fingers on the table.

"Do you know what happened?"

"I know everything that happens in this city. It is the reason I am here. I know a platoon of Italian *soldati* encountered a small group of men shooting at each other on the same night I sent the three of you there for the rendezvous. Several were killed, and a few deserted in the confusion. One of them reported to me."

"Wait, you mean they ambushed us?"

"No. Gunfire broke out as they approached the Temple of Concordia, but it was not directed at them. Their lieutenant ordered them forward; he was killed in a grenade blast. Then most of them ran."

"Did they find any bodies?"

"Only of their own men," Tommaso said.

"So the two men I was with, they must've gotten away with Don Calo's men?"

"Yes, they had a car. The meeting place was at Il Tempio di Concordia. Is this what you can't remember?"

"Yes," I said. "I think that I killed my friend, by accident, during the fight. They must have taken his body away."

"I would advise you to revive your memory. Don Calo has questions for you."

"Does he want me dead?" I asked, remembering what Kaz had said about rumors of a contract.

"That will depend on your answers."

"Fair enough," I said, as if fairness had anything to do with it. "Who else knew about the rendezvous?"

"Don Calo himself told me about it, a week before you came. A British agent contacted him and asked him to see your party."

"Where's that agent now?"

"Dead. He was stopped by the Germans and tried to shoot his way out. Stupid."

"Do you know Vito Genovese? Joey Laspada?"

"I knew Vito back in the States. Then I was known as Tommy the C. Joey, him I met here a few times. Why?"

"Are they involved in this?" I asked, ignoring his question.

"Not that I know of."

"And you know everything that happens here," I reminded him.

"Everything that happens in Agrigento," Tommy the C said, stretching out his hands as if to include the entire province.

"Does the name Charlotte mean anything to you?"

"Other than a dame in Jersey, not a thing. And she didn't mean much. What are all these questions for?"

"We had a run-in with Vito and Joey a couple of days ago. They're working for the Allied Military Government as translators. They were looking for one of the guys I was with. And for the handkerchief."

"Vito usually gets what he wants," Tommy said.

"A company of German paratroopers got in his way this time. Tell me, is Vito well connected here?"

"Everybody in Sicily wants to go to America. Those who do and come back as men of honor, are respected. So, yeah, Vito has connections."

"With Don Calo?"

"Of course."

"And you are Don Calo's man, Tommy the C?" Sciafani said, breaking his silence, and pronouncing the strange American nickname with exaggerated correctness. He pointed his finger at Tommaso, and left it there, like a pistol pointed at the man's heart.

"Of course. I worked for Luciano in New York, and when I came back here, Don Calo honored me with the position of *caporegime,* in Agrigento. I am his lieutenant. Like you, Lieutenant Boyle. Aren't you somebody's man?"

Sciafani dropped his hand to the table but kept his eyes on Tommy, and spoke before I could answer.

"Do you find it easy, serving both God and Caesar?"

I knew my mind wasn't working at its peak. I also knew that its peak wasn't what it should be. I was still mixed up and tired out from days and nights on the run. Even so, I caught the charge in the air between the two of them. For some reason, Sciafani was challenging Tommaso—or Tommy—a man of God and of the gun, well-armed and inside his own cathedral. It was a sucker's bet and I couldn't understand what Sciafani was thinking, even if he didn't like priests keeping the riches of their churches locked away.

"Who do you serve, Dottor?" Tommy asked, as he began again to drum his fingers on the polished tabletop. "*L'americano?*"

"I have served the Fascists for three years, binding wounds and watching men die for them. Now, I serve myself."

"Serve who you wish. Men will still die," Tommy said, stopping the rhythmic drumming and pointing at Sciafani. "I will remember you."

"Good," answered Sciafani, as if this settled something.

"Listen, we don't want to make trouble," I said, trying to reduce the tension in the room. "Can you get me to Don Calo? The *dottore* is headed to Palermo now—"

"No, Billy, I promised I would guide you, and I will. Villalba is on the way. I will stay with you," Sciafani insisted.

"I don't care if you go with him or go to the devil, but you both must leave soon if you want to get out," Tommy the C said, slapping the palms of his hands on the table as he rose from it. "The Germans are coming down from the north, and it looks like the Americans will have secured Porto Empedocle in no time. Then we'll be caught in a vise between them. Wait here. I will arrange transportation for you."

He left us. Sciafani stood and paced, stopped, drank his glass of wine, then paced some more. The church bells rang and explosions boomed, more menacing as they crept toward us. Sciafani ran his hands through his hair as he looked out the narrow window.

"Will it ever stop?" He covered his ears but couldn't look away. More explosions ripped at the edges of the city below us, overpowering the small arms fire that rattled in the streets. Houses were burning. I thought of the old lady who'd pulled us in and hoped she was safe. *Whoever you serve, men will die.* Tommaso had gotten that right. I went to the window and stood by Sciafani. For a long time neither of us spoke.

"What is it, Enrico? What's eating at you?"

"Many bad things, my friend, many bad things."

We watched the explosions. They became less frequent and then stopped. But the fires they left burned and spread, red flame and black smoke engulfing the city.

CHAPTER • TWENTY

HALF AN HOUR LATER Tommy the C showed us out through the side door of a storage room beneath the sacristy. It led to a narrow courtyard between the cathedral and the city wall. He'd given Sciafani a small burlap sack stuffed with bread, cheese, and a bottle of wine, and the *dottore* wore it suspended from a strap over his shoulder, looking more and more like a hobo. A black sedan sat idling, its driver leaning against the hood, smoking a cigarette. Tommy had put on his black robe again, but the top was unbuttoned, his big pistol within easy reach. He nodded to the driver, who crushed out his cigarette. It was another Fiat—a Balilla—sort of a miniature touring car. It had running boards and a shiny grille, and would've looked pretty fancy if the driver hadn't been leaning against it with his arm draped over the roof. It looked like a half-size version of a 1930 Model A.

"Good luck with the Germans and Don Calo," he said.

He watched us get in the backseat, the driver alone in front, and opened the heavy wooden door to return to the cathedral.

"*Un momento,*" Sciafani said to the driver, holding up one finger. He scampered out, called "Signor Corso," and followed him inside. I wondered if he'd forgotten something or had decided to apologize or wanted to say a prayer. None of these options made sense. Less than a minute passed before the door reopened. Sciafani smiled an apology to the driver and slid into the backseat with me.

"What was that about?" I asked as the driver hit the accelerator.

"I had some unfinished business." He was breathing hard, looking back at the cathedral, as if we might be pursued.

"What—" My words were cut off as the driver took a hard left. I caught a glimpse of brown uniforms, hunched low, crossing the street ahead of us in the direction we'd been driving. It felt odd to be evading the American troops fighting to take the town. Sciafani turned to look and I noticed the cuff of his once white shirt was soaked red. Not the dark rusty color of yesterday's blood, but the fresh, unmistakable red of a fresh blood stain. I pulled his jacket aside. The Blackshirt's dagger was still tucked into his belt. He pulled his jacket tight once more and stared out the window, holding onto the empty passenger seat in front of him as our driver weaved in and out of narrow roads and alleys.

"Enrico," I said quietly. He shook his head before I could continue. The burlap sack was at his side, the strap still over his shoulder. It wasn't hard to see the butt of the big Italian Bodeo revolver crammed in next to the loaf of bread.

I didn't know if the driver spoke any English or whether he'd admit it if he did, so this wasn't the time to come out and ask Sciafani if he'd killed Tommy the C. Anyway it was obvious he had even if I didn't know why. A doctor would know exactly where to stick that dagger. Sharp on both sides, the thin blade was perfect for a surprise jab through the ribs and up into the heart. The victim would lose consciousness and die within seconds. Had Sciafani hesitated, I wondered? Long enough for Tommy the C to comprehend he was dying? As he pulled the dagger out had he looked into the dying man's eyes while a spray of blood soaked his shirt cuff? I watched him as he glanced away from me and out the window, not sure if he was looking for GIs or staring at his own reflection.

Whichever, it didn't amount to a hill of beans. I was stuck with Sciafani for now and had to hope we could get away before any of Don Calo's men heard about Tommy the C bleeding out in the cathedral basement. I wondered what would happen to us when they found out. I wondered if Tommy the C would end up in a special underground chapel for sacristans, his hands on his chest, wearing white gloves for eternity. I wondered about what would make a doctor turn killer, and who he might stick next with that dagger. It was a lot to wonder about.

The car swerved around a switchback as the road descended to the valley below, and the burlap bag slid on the seat. The pistol was halfway out and I started to make a move for it, but Sciafani was too fast. He clutched the bag to his chest and sighed as he turned his face away from me. I followed his gaze to the spare, rocky ground, dotted with cactus and spindly green trees. I recognized the place. I'd been here before. We were entering the Valley of the Temples.

The driver slowed, rolled down his window, picked up a long strip of white cloth, and held it out. It fluttered in the breeze like a banner, a flag of truce, as he shouted the same few phrases over and over again. I had no idea what he was saying, so I made up my own version, based on the cadence of his words. *Don't shoot, it's only a* mafiusu, *a demented doctor, and an amnesiac American. One of us is harmless, take your chances on the other two.*

We must have passed through the front lines. The GIs here were either standing around, marching in single file, or busy, stacking boxes and setting up an aid station by the side of the road. Ruins dotted the landscape for miles, some of them no more than heaps of rubble with two or three columns left standing. Others consisted of rows of columns holding up empty sky.

There was one that was different. What was it?

"*Viva gli americani,*" the driver shouted to a file of GIs trudging up the road, kicking up little clouds of hot dirt with their shuffling feet. They laughed and waved, but it all seemed distant, as if I were watching a newsreel. Troops on the move. Heat and grit from the road flowed into the car, and I had to rub my eyes to clear the sweat, dust, and fatigue away. My heart began to beat faster and faster as a cold shiver ran through my body and sweat trickled down my back. I felt dizzy, and the windows seemed to fog over, encasing the tiny vehicle in a hazy cocoon. I shut my eyes and clasped my hands over them, hoping when I opened them again everything would be normal. I breathed deep and heard the blood pounding in my ears as images flashed into life, brighter and clearer than they ever could have been, sharp and focused, so real I could feel them slashing and clawing at my eyelids.

A man in a black robe. The sacristan, one hand on my shoulder, the other pointing to the valley below the city.

"There," he said. "The only temple still intact. See it on the hill? The Temple of Concordia." *The setting sun lit it, casting fingers of soft yellow light along the narrow building.*

"Our contact will meet us there, you're sure?" *That was Nick.*

"It's all been arranged." *Tommy the C nodded and walked away.*

As in a dream, the scene changed swiftly. I saw myself standing at the bottom of the steps leading into the temple. Harry was there.

"Do you see anyone?" *Harry asked me, swiveling his head and squinting his eyes to pick up any movement in the fading light.*

"No. Nick?" *Nick had gone inside. He appeared, waving us on.*

We were all wearing the same thing. Nondescript khaki jackets. Khaki pants. Boots. We could have been anyone on a dark night. That was the point, I guess. I felt my boots clomp against the stone steps as I passed between two columns looming above us, blocking the light. Patches of stars showed through the ruined roof. Inside the columns was another building, supported by its own set of smaller columns. A temple. It was disorienting. I turned, looking for Harry. He was gone.

"Billy?" *Nick said in a whisper.*

"What?"

"Give me the handkerchief. Now." *I felt the hard, cold barrel of his automatic pistol press against my neck.*

"What's got into you?" *Panic fluttered in my chest.*

"Never mind. Give me the handkerchief and get lost. I don't want to shoot you but if I have to, I will."

"What did you do to Harry?" *I was trying to buy time.*

"I sent him to watch for the contact. Give it to me now," *he ordered. He made his point by pressing the tip of the automatic harder against my neck, so hard I could feel the front sight dig into my skin.*

"OK, OK," *I said.* "I don't want to get shot over a piece of silk."

I felt him relax. But the automatic was resting on my shoulder, still pointing at my neck.

"I'm sorry, Billy, I have to have it."

"OK, stay calm. It's in my jacket pocket." *I thrust my hand into my jacket. As I did, I swung away from the pistol and smashed him with my elbow* in the back of his neck. He went down with a grunt, but the automatic went off. The sound echoed off the temple walls, and I heard the zing of a ricochet.

"No, no!" Nick coughed up the words as he struggled to get up, one hand on his neck and the other clutching the automatic.

I drew my .45 and aimed it at his head. I heard footsteps running toward us and tried to comprehend Nick's actions. Had he gone mad? He seemed determined and anguished at the same time.

"Nick, drop your weapon."

He held onto the automatic, grasping it loosely in his hand as he rose to his knees. "I need the handkerchief," was all he said, his eyes cast down to the stone floor of the temple.

"What's this?" Harry said, stepping carefully around a column, pressing his back to it and keeping both of us covered with his Italian Beretta submachine gun.

"I need the handkerchief," Nick repeated, as if that explained everything.

Harry and I exchanged dumbfounded glances. Nick, with his Sicilian connections, was the key to this mission. We needed him, but it occurred to me that except for the handkerchief, he didn't need us.

Nick stood, placing his body between Harry and me. He didn't drop his weapon. He held my eyes and it seemed he was searching for something, an answer to an unfathomable question.

"Give it to me, Billy, and go hide out somewhere, both of you. I'll take it from here."

"I can't—"

He turned and squeezed off two shots, aiming high, over Harry's head, but close enough to drive him back under cover. He judged me right. I couldn't shoot him, not in the back anyway. He ran from me while angling away from the column Harry had hidden behind. I fired, high too, wanting to let him know I meant business but reluctant to hit him. He disappeared behind rows of columns and I followed, darting between the stone pillars, listening, trying to stay close but not too close.

I heard footsteps again, heavy this time, not like Harry's stealthy approach. I tried to see beyond the outer row of columns but it was too dark.

"Chi va?" The voice was demanding something, and more boots tramped the ground outside the temple. A single shot sounded in response, *and I figured that Nick was about to make his break, covered by a hail of gunfire. It was risky, but he probably figured every nervous Italian soldier standing in the open would keep his eyes on the temple as he blasted away.*

He was right. Shots rang out, bright flashes sparkling in a rough line that slowly moved closer. The soldiers were yelling, firing, advancing. I backed into the interior temple, hoping to find Harry and escape before they pulled the ring tighter. I made it to the rear corner of the temple and hid behind a wall that gave me a view along the perimeter of the colonnade.

More shouts from inside the temple, one voice, probably an officer, rising above the others. I couldn't understand but I was sure the words meant Come out with your hands up!

Boots scraped against the hard floor, moving in my direction. I needed to do something, to take the initiative away from them. I pulled a grenade from one of the big side pockets of my jacket. I holstered my .45 so I'd have both hands free and looked down the shorter row of columns that ran along the rear of the temple. It was clear. I stepped out and pulled the pin of the grenade, holding the safety lever down. I judged the distance and figured I could roll the grenade halfway down the length of the corridor formed by the two rows of columns. The explosion would distract the soldiers and force them to take cover, giving me a chance to beat feet out of there.

I stood exposed between two pillars, listening for the bootsteps to get closer. They were behind me. It was time. I let go of the lever and it sprang away, bouncing off the stone with a metallic twang. I threw underhanded, rolling the grenade perfectly, watching it bounce on the uneven paving and come to rest. I had about two seconds left.

I saw Harry. He came from behind a column, just a few feet forward of the grenade. I opened my mouth to warn him, but before I could make a sound, something hard hit me in the head and a blinding flash of pain sent me to my knees. I tried to shout, to warn Harry, but I couldn't fight through the sharp electric stabbing sensation in my skull. My hand went to my holster, there was a rapid babble of Italian, more pain, then an explosion, right where Harry had been.

I opened my eyes and saw the Temple of Concordia. GIs wandered around it craning their necks and gawking at the ancient columns. Did they wonder at the bloodstained floor inside? The stonework glowed softly golden in the bright sun. It was beautiful in the daylight,

not at all the place of dark shadows from my memory. I saw one officer focusing his camera on it, a tourist in dogshit brown, snapping photos to impress the folks back home while other soldiers fought house
to house less than a mile away. The temple receded from view as the
little Fiat sped down the road, churning up dust behind us, obscuring
the brightness and leaving me with my memories of betrayal and death
in the night.

My right hand shook as I recalled the feel of that grenade in my
hand, the grooved case iron cold against my palm. My heart was
thumping to beat the band and I glanced at Sciafani to see if he'd
noticed. It was hard to believe everything I remembered hadn't just
happened. Sciafani's head was slumped against the window as he stared
at something very, very far away, clutching the burlap bag to his chest.
I relaxed and shut my eyes again, wishing for oblivion, clasping my left
hand over my right to hide its trembling, hoping the visions wouldn't
return. Thanks for the memories.

So what did this tell me? Nick had betrayed us, demanding the
handkerchief for his own purposes. That was important, but there was
something else equally important. He had been desperate and anguished. Not cold and calculating. He wanted the handkerchief; no, he
needed the handkerchief. That meant he was under pressure to get it,
the kind of pressure that makes a man turn a gun on his friend and beg
him to give him what he wants and then leave. He'd gotten away, that
much Tommy the C had confirmed. Too bad Sciafani had killed
Tommy. I would have liked to ask him a few more questions, like who
we were supposed to meet and how they had eluded the Italian soldiers. He'd said their officer was killed in a grenade blast, and then
some of them deserted. That had to have been my grenade. With their
officer dead, the Italians must have lost interest and gone their separate ways, some back to their unit, one to report to the *caporegime* at the
cathedral, the rest headed for the hills. Except for Roberto.

Now it came to me. The cut on my arm had been from a bayonet.
One of the soldiers had stabbed at me when I tried to unholster my
.45. It had been Roberto. It was a halfhearted stab, more of a push to
dissuade me from shooting. His officer had stepped in front of us, his
pistol raised. If Roberto hadn't stopped me, he would have had plenty
of time to plug me. Roberto had saved my life.

Wait a minute. The Italian officer had stepped in front of us. The grenade was a few yards behind him, then there was a couple of yards more to where Harry stood. Would Harry have stayed rooted to the spot, out in the open, with an enemy officer yards away? Maybe yes. He might have advanced, to take him out before he could shoot. Maybe no. He might have ducked behind a column to take cover. Which was it?

"Enrico," I said, nudging Sciafani in the ribs.

"What?" He turned away from the window and answered, like a drunk at a bar who only wants to stare into his glass. His eyelids were lowered, half hiding the redness of his eyes.

"Ask the driver if he was the one who was to meet me and two others at the Temple of Concordia." He did, and the driver shook his head.

"It was not him," Sciafani said. "It was his brother."

"Jesus, man, ask him what happened. Ask him if one of the other two men died!"

Sciafani shrugged and obliged. They exchanged some rapid-fire Italian, and Sciafani shrugged again, that all-purpose gesture that I'd seen more of in Sicily than I had before in my whole life. "He says Don Calo will tell you what happened, if he wishes to, and to stop asking questions."

I was pretty sure Sciafani had added that last part himself.

CHAPTER ■ TWENTY-ONE

WE DROVE NORTH, on back roads through little villages. The Fiat strained up a dirt track climbing through orchards and olive groves until the road straightened out and we saw a small hilltop town in the distance. A signpost said Montaperto, and I could make out a collection of orange-tiled roofs clustered together on the highest point around. I looked back and was rewarded with a view of green rolling hills and a dusty, brown view of Agrigento farther out. The car slowed, and I saw an Italian soldier approach us carrying a shovel on his shoulder. He wore his *bustina* but no shirt and he was soaked in sweat. I tried to shrink into the backseat, to make my American uniform invisible.

It didn't matter. He and the driver chatted amiably as four packs of cigarettes were handed over to the soldier. They were Echt Orients, a German brand. I guessed the Mafia liked to spread its business around. The driver ground his gears as the Fiat struggled with the incline. The *soldato* called to his buddies and they left the entrenchment they were digging to claim their smokes. As we passed, the snout of a heavy machine gun was visible, protruding from the sandbags and covering the lovely valley behind us. A mortar was set up behind it, surrounded by sandbags and shells. Camouflage netting covered the emplacement, making it look like a natural fold in the terrain. By the time you got close enough to see it, you'd be dead.

"They are Sicilian," Sciafani said, as if that explained everything: the easy passage, the cigarettes, the deadly ambush.

We drove through the narrow street that cut through the village. The buildings were two or three stories tall, covered in faded stucco that had crumbled away in places, revealing rough brickwork underneath. Probably a few hundred people lived in these homes, crowded along the roadway at the top of the hill. I knew what would happen to them if our guys came up that hill and got hit by the mortar and machine gun. The *soldati* would take out a dozen or so GIs before they were pinned down. Some energetic lieutenant might try flanking them, but there was no cover on either side of the road. That would fail, and finally he'd radio Battalion HQ for artillery or an air strike. They might have to wait a while. Or maybe they'd have armor support coming up. Either way, the small emplacement would be smashed, along with a good portion of the village. People would hide in their cellars, and tons of brick would fall on them, fires would rage, and the ground would shake with each hit. A couple of hundred people would die, all because four Sicilian soldiers stayed at their post.

Had Nick betrayed our mission? Or could he have needed the handkerchief for something else? I couldn't think about him. Right now I had enough to worry about with Sciafani. He was armed and in his own strange world, and I had no idea how that was going to impact mine.

We cleared the village and the Fiat bounced over a potholed dirt track, descending into the valley due north. Sciafani pulled his dagger out and cleaned it, using the burlap bag to wipe it down. When he was finally satisfied, he smiled weakly, almost apologetically, and cut a piece of cheese and bread with it. He handed them to the driver, who took the food without comment or thanks. Then he cut up the rest and we shared it, washed down with wine from the bottle, which we passed around. A communion of secrets.

We picked up a good road and passed by more fields and orchards. Lemons hung heavy on branches, and the ground between rows was freshly turned. The air was cooler here, tinged with a hint of green richness emanating from the dark, fertile soil. There were no houses, no roadblocks or hidden entrenchments. It was peaceful, and part of me wished I could sit in the shade beneath an orange tree, drink wine, and sleep.

I did sleep, but when I opened my eyes I was still in the backseat with Sciafani, and the fertile fields were far behind us.

"What the hell is that smell?" I asked, realizing what had awoken me.

"The Vulcanelli di Macalube," Sciafani said, gesturing out to the grayish brown mud flats surrounding us. No more greenery, no smell of fresh-turned soil. Instead, the stink of sulphur and parched, cracked layers of mud, divided by streams of oozing gray liquid, assaulted my senses. I even wondered for a second if I was dreaming, but the smell convinced me I was wide awake.

"What is it, and do we have to go through it?"

"It is an area of natural gases, forcing the mud to the surface. See?" He pointed to a mound about a yard high, where bubbles of gray mud exploded out of the ground and ran down in rivulets, looking like pictures I'd seen of lava from flowing volcanoes. "It goes on for a few kilometers more. It is a safe passage; no one would put a roadblock here."

"You got that right," I said, trying not to breathe the rotten egg odor in too deeply.

"There is a legend that once a great city stood here," Sciafani said, staring out the window with that faraway look again. "The people of the city thought so highly of themselves that they forgot to thank the gods properly for their good fortune. This angered the gods, and they sunk the city beneath the earth, condemning the people to live forever underground. The only thing that comes to the surface is their tears."

We drove through the macabre landscape, past bubbling pools and streams of ooze, until finally we left the weeping city behind. I thought about the bomb damage I'd seen in London and the destruction across North Africa, the rumble-strewn streets of Agrigento. Nature—or the gods—had matched that devastation here.

We stopped in Aragona, where more cigarettes changed hands and *soldati* filled our gas tank from five-gallon jerry cans, taken from one of their own trucks. Our driver seemed to know everyone on this route, and I figured he was part of Don Calo's communication network. Nothing in writing or over the phone, nothing but reports and whispers between the *caporegimes* and their couriers.

We crossed the Salito River and saw Italian engineers, a *guastatori* unit, wiring demolition charges beneath the bridge. On the north side, two antitank guns covered the approach to the river, their barrels barely visible jutting out from the camouflaged bunkers. Again, cigarettes were handed all around, and our driver joked with the men, who were glad to take a break from their work. An officer stood apart from them, glaring at our car, but saying nothing.

"Many of the officers are not Sicilian," Sciafani said. "Mussolini does not trust us to lead our own men, so he puts Fascists in charge, men from the north." He uttered the phrase like a curse.

The sun was low in the western sky, beginning to touch the tips of the mountains we were traveling through. The road curved back and forth on switchbacks, slowly gaining altitude as we approached the crest and the mountaintop village of Mussomeli. The Fiat seemed to accelerate in thanks as the ground leveled out, and we passed a tall, rocky outcropping, a couple of hundred yards in height, with a small castle built into the top of the rock. Italian Army trucks were parked at its base, along with tents sprouting aerials, all covered by the usual netting. They definitely had artillery spotters up there, with a view for miles in every direction. As long as they had this observation post, anything that moved south of Mussomeli would get plastered by their artillery.

We headed down the north side of the mountain to the town. Mussomeli was at a crossroads, five roads intersecting near it. The town itself cascaded down the side of the mountain, a crowded assembly of gray stone buildings spread around a church with a tall steeple. A column of Italian soldiers was marching out of town, past a concrete bunker covering the main road. Our driver waved, and some of the men nodded back. Evidently he didn't have enough cigarettes for a whole company. He spoke to Sciafani, pointed back at the column of men with his thumb, and laughed.

"His sister-in-law's uncle is the *sergente* of that company, all Sicilians. He says there is a platoon of MVSN Fascists at the castle, and the commander of the town is a Fascist, and that the Sicilians will cut their throats as soon as the word is given."

"Whose word?" I asked.

"Don Calo's," Sciafani answered. "Who else?"

"It sounds like he's in a position to save a lot of lives."

"A man who can save lives can also take them, have you thought of that?" He spoke with a fierceness that surprised me. Ever since Agrigento he'd been subdued. Stunned by the realization of what he'd done. Now, as we drew closer to Villalba, I sensed a shift in him, an anger that overcame whatever guilt he felt, becoming stronger as the distance from his murderous act increased. Were we getting closer to another? I wanted to ask him directly, but I couldn't assume the driver didn't understand English. A man like Don Calogero Vizzini hadn't survived without playing every angle, and I figured he'd want to know anything that passed between us.

"Tell me about the village you were born in, Enrico." I had a suspicion that whatever secret he was keeping about his family was the reason for his actions. All of them, including killing Tommy the C and staying with me.

"It is not important," he said.

"What did your father do?"

"My father is a physician."

"Not your adoptive father. Your real father," I said. "What was his name?"

There was silence in the car. Sciafani put his hand to his mouth, as if to keep the name from slipping out. Leaning against the window, his eyes darted to the driver, who stared straight ahead. He switched on his lights, illuminating the winding road and the looming pine branches that crowded over it.

"Nunzio. Nunzio Infantino," Sciafani said, balling the hand pressed against his mouth into a fist so that the name was barely understandable. He closed his eyes and doubled up, as if in great pain, still holding his hand to his mouth. I waited. Finally he opened his hand and gasped for breath, exhausted from the ordeal of uttering his father's name.

The driver spoke, I think to ask Sciafani if he was going to be sick. He glanced back and Sciafani shook his head and gestured for him to keep driving. I nodded and was rewarded with another Sicilian shrug.

"Was your village like the villages we drove through today? All the buildings crowded together, maybe located at a crossroads?"

"No, there is no crossroads. But it does sit upon a hilltop, surrounding the Chiesa di San Filippo, where I was baptized. As Enrico Infantino."

I was watching the driver's eyes in the rearview mirror. I could only see half his face, but I saw him react to the name: a blink, a quick look in the mirror at Sciafani, then back to the road. Whether he understood English or not, he'd recognized that name. I tapped Sciafani on the arm, where the driver couldn't see, and signaled with my hand to keep it down. He nodded.

"Well, whatever General Eisenhower thinks about the Mafia, he'll be very glad if Don Calo cooperates. It will not only save American lives but Sicilian lives too, in all those small villages like yours. Many lives, Enrico."

He shook his head. Now that he'd spoken his father's name, I wondered if the whole history of his life that he'd kept buttoned up was aching to be released. But he'd gotten my warning about the driver, that maybe he'd said too much already. So he sighed and handed me the burlap bag with the big Bodeo revolver still in it.

"Yes," he said sadly. "Many lives, many innocent lives. You would think it would be a simple choice, wouldn't you?"

"There are no simple choices. People think there are because they don't think about their options. My father used to say that if people thought through what might happen before they acted there'd be a lot less killing on any Saturday night. He's a homicide detective, in Boston."

"He is wise, but some people need to act more and think less. A lifetime of thinking alone is no good. A desire that is never acted upon becomes pitiful. Do you know your Shakespeare, Billy? *Hamlet?*"

"Well, I had to read it in school. I had a hard time with it so my dad took me to see the play. They were putting it on at Harvard. It was a lot easier to listen to than read."

"One of my English teachers had us read Shakespeare and memorize passages as part of our lessons. In act three, Hamlet says:

Thus conscience does make cowards of us all;
And thus the native hue of resolution
Is sicklied o'er with the pale cast of thought,
And enterprises of great pith and moment
With this regard their currents turn awry,
And lose the name of action."

"I remember that part about conscience making cowards of us all," I said. I hadn't understood anything the actors were saying at first, and then all of a sudden I realized I understood everything, and that it was beautiful.

"It is very true. But I think if Hamlet had gone to war, that pale cast of thought would not have lasted. He had to revenge himself on the man who killed his father. Don Calo killed mine."

CHAPTER · TWENTY-TWO

WE CHUGGED UP A long, steep hill, surrounded by acres of wheat on all sides. Workers dotted the fields, cutting and stacking the crop, moving like a ragged line of infantry, stooping for cover and then moving forward again, mowing down the enemy that faced them in never-ending rows. We passed a donkey, laden with bundles of grain, led by a peasant woman. She wore a gray tattered dress, her stooped head covered by a black scarf. Adding to the donkey's burden, a man sat astride it, his feet scraping the road.

"He will wear out his wife and his donkey before he walks," Sciafani said. "Then he will have nothing and will look back with longing on the days when he used to ride an ass."

The driver laughed. I'd been right—he understood English. I looked at Sciafani, and he shrugged, an eloquent gesture that said, What can we do?

The car crested a rise and picked up speed as the village of Villalba came into view. The sun was setting behind us and lit the town, bathing the gray and brown stone walls in soft light, casting jagged shadows into the streets. Villalba sat on a gentle slope, surrounded by cultivated fields and a hilltop overlooking it to the north. It looked like any other town we'd passed through, but this was the end of the line, one way or the other. No troops were digging entrenchments; no machine guns covered the road into town. Villalba was not a crossroads, not a strategic center. Its only military value lay in what one man might or might not do, in how much weight a silk handkerchief carried, and how convincing I could be.

The car turned into a large *piazza*, anchored at one end by a two-story building with BANCO DI SICILIA in large letters at the top and at the other by a tall church tower. I wasn't surprised when the driver stopped right between them, in front of a house where a young man lounged against the wall next to an iron gate, his *lupara* slung over his shoulder. The windows were narrow and guarded with iron grilles. I wrapped the burlap bag around Tommy the C's revolver and shoved it under the seat in front of me. I glanced at Sciafani and he nodded wearily in agreement. There were bound to be more shotguns inside, and two guys bringing a dead *caporegime*'s pistol into a Mafia chief's house would mean a very short stay.

The driver got out and signaled us to follow the guard through the gate. As I did, I felt an odd satisfaction at having made it this far. A few days ago, I'd had no idea who I was or why I was here. I'd fought the Germans, escaped a Mob trap, been smuggled across the mountains, bombed, faced down bandits, and regained most of my memory in the process. Two men had been murdered, and others, including Harry, had died, all for this damn silk handkerchief stuffed deep in my pocket. I realized I didn't know exactly what to say to Don Calo, or if he'd understand me. Nick was the one who spoke the Sicilian dialect fluently, and who knew where the hell he had ended up.

The walls of the house were thick, and the entryway opened into a small courtyard with a covered walkway around it. The windows facing the inner courtyard were wide and open, with welcoming soft yellow light spilling out onto the stones. I heard the clatter of dishes and women's laughter. It was strange, delightful, and disorienting.

The guard put his palm out, signaling us to wait. He removed his cap, stamped his feet to shake off the dirt and dust, and opened a door, leaving us alone in the darkening courtyard. If it wasn't for the guard on the other side of an iron gate, I would've been tempted to run, grab the car, and head for the hills. Except we were already in the hills. Surrounded by Italians and Germans. I shivered, chilled by this thought and by the night air. Sciafani brushed at his suit and tucked in his shirt, doing his best to make himself presentable. With all the dirt, blood, and sweat he'd soaked up, it was hard to see any improvement. He looked nervous, and I wondered if this was the end of his mission too.

The door opened slowly, squeaking on its hinges. A silver-haired man with a slight paunch descended the two stone steps into the courtyard. His eyebrows were bushy and jet black, in sharp contrast to his slicked-back hair. He wore a short-sleeved white shirt, and his suspenders pulled his baggy pants above his waist. He had a broad face and a wide mouth and his eyes narrowed as if he was studying us, trying to understand exactly what we were. Behind him, a wide-shouldered man, his hands behind him, stood in the doorway and stared at us. He didn't have a paunch and his eyes were steady.

"*Benvenuto*," the older man said, approaching us and staring at Sciafani. He cocked his head, the way people do when they're trying to place a face.

"Don Calogero," I said, then surprised myself by nearly bowing.

"Welcome," he said, "but please wait."

He spoke slowly in a thick accent, holding his hand up and waving it back and forth, as if he couldn't be bothered with the first American soldier to make it to Villalba. He spoke rapidly to Sciafani, a stream of questions that reminded me of a small automatic snapping off a series of shots. Sciafani's face crumpled. A lifetime, perhaps, of knowing this man had killed his father, and decades of fear holding him back, until everything he'd seen and endured in this war had conspired to make him a killer. It all played out on his face as Don Calogero Vizzini, whom the Allies considered the single most important Sicilian, stood inches from him, asking who he was.

"*Lei è il figlio di Nunzio Infantino?*"

"*Sì.*" Sciafani drew himself up straight.

"They told me to kill the child too," Don Calo said to me, in that slow cadence of someone who is translating his speech, putting an emphasis on the last word to show how glad he was to be done with the sentence. He gestured all around him, meaning everyone had said to kill the child.

"So he wouldn't take his revenge as a man," I said.

"*La vendetta*," Don Calo said. "Yes, Nunzio and I fought, first with words, then with fists. Finally, with the *lupara*. Your father, he was stubborn. If I had known your dear mother was sick and would die soon, I might not have killed him." His dark eyebrows knitted in contemplation of what might have been as his shoulders threw off the burdens of the past.

"But you did," Sciafani said.

"*Sì.*"

"My mother?"

"Your mother, no, no. Nunzio and I fought in the hills, when he tried to take his wheat to the mills without paying the toll. I told him he had to pay, even just a little. If he did not, the others would soon make trouble. He would not give me a single lira, he was so stubborn. So we fought like men. He died at my hands, and I offered payment to your mother so you and she would not be put out on the street. It was then I found out she was dying. *Tubercolosi.*"

Don Calo took out a handkerchief and wiped his forehead. I thought about the one in my pocket, and how the sharp-eyed guy in the doorway might react if I pulled it out.

"My friends said it would be best to kill you after your mother died, that you would grow up to take your revenge, but I could not kill a *bambino*. So I did the next best thing. I gave you to a *dottore* and told him to raise you to be one yourself, if you were smart enough."

"The Sciafanis were your people?"

"They truly wanted a child, so what does it matter? Did they not treat you well?"

"Very well," Sciafani said, his eyes to the ground. "You wanted me to become a *dottore* so I would not easily take a life?"

"It was better than slitting your throat and burying you in the hills. Was I wrong?"

Don Calo jutted his chin forward, daring Sciafani to challenge his logic. He seemed affronted that this young man was not thanking him for sparing his life after Don Calo had killed his father.

"I cannot say, Don Calo."

"Have you deserted?" Don Calo asked.

"No, I have been released. I was captured but the Americans are releasing all Sicilian prisoners."

"The Americans are smarter than I believed then," Don Calo said, shifting his gaze to me, but still addressing Sciafani. "But how did you get blood on your clothes?"

"We were caught in the bombardment of Agrigento," I said. "Dottore Sciafani cared for the wounded Italian troops until the Americans set up an aid station." I hoped the killing of Tommy the C would not come out while we were here.

Don Calo nodded, tilting his head to the side as he did so, indicating that yes, perhaps, he might believe that. He sat on a stone bench set against the house, grunting as he exhaled. He mopped his face again, soaking tiny beads of sweat from his upper lip into his white handkerchief.

"This is a bad business," Don Calo finally said. "The Fascists from Rome hunted us, the Americans invade us, the Germans make our island a battleground, and now you walk into my home. Both of you have the smell of trouble."

I knew he was thinking it wasn't too late to correct his mistake in letting Sciafani live, and that I might as well be thrown into an unmarked grave in the hills with him. Don Calo scowled, looking back to the man in the doorway. He put his hands on his knees and pushed himself up, a grim look on his face.

"Don Calo," I said, stepping in front of Sciafani. To try to divert his attention, I was about to take out the handkerchief.

"No, we will talk later. It is Enrico I speak to now," he said. "It was wrong of you to wait so long to come here. If you were a hotheaded youth and I was younger also, we could have fought each other. But so many years have passed. You are now a *dottore*, and I have a position here, as the head of a society. When a man is on his way up, he uses everything he can to rise to the top. But when he gets there, he can no longer act like a bandit. Today I grant favors to people. If I can do a man a favor, no matter who he is, I will. So people do me favors in return: a vote or an errand, whatever they can. That is who I am now, not a young man with a *lupara* in his hands."

"The world is indeed turned upside down. You are *mafiusu* yet you tell me you don't wish to kill me. I have sworn an oath to protect life, and I would take yours," Sciafani said, sounding surprised at himself.

"Would you?" Don Calo asked. Sciafani opened his mouth to speak but no words came out. He cast his eyes to the ground.

"I will tell you a secret, Enrico. I sent you away in hopes that you would become a *dottore* not for myself, to avoid *la vendetta*, but for you also. I had no argument with your dear mother or you. You deserved a better life than the one your father and I left you. Don't be surprised that I include him now. If he hadn't been so stubborn we could have worked things out. But that was not his nature, nor mine."

"This is not what I expected," Sciafani said, raising his eyes to meet Don Calo's.

"You are a ghost I did not expect to meet today either. Now, if you can promise not to take your revenge tonight, I will offer you both the hospitality of my home. We will eat in one hour. Do you promise?"

"On my honor."

"Good. With a contented stomach, your heart is forgiving; with an empty stomach, the heart is hard."

CHAPTER TWENTY-THREE

SCIAFANI'S HONOR WAS GOOD enough for Don
Calo, and we were both escorted to rooms at the back of the house. I
was shown to a bathroom where a large tub, carved from a single piece
of limestone, was being filled with hot, steaming water. A straight
razor, brush, and comb had been laid out on a marble sink. Don Calo
evidently liked his dinner guests clean, and I obliged by soaking in the
water as an elderly man took my uniform away, making brushing
motions on it as he spoke a continuous stream of mournful Italian, as
if he were chiding me for getting my clothes so dirty. He was probably
actually saying he hoped all Americans didn't smell as bad as I did.

I fell asleep in the tub, awakening only when he returned, bringing
with him my shirt and pants neatly folded, boots polished, and a full
set of not-quite-GI socks and underwear. I would have been happy
never to see the ones he took away again. He smiled and chattered at
me, bowing as he left. I shaved, combed my hair, and dressed, mar-
veling at what a difference a hot bath and clean clothes made. I felt in
my pocket for the handkerchief. It was still there but folded precisely,
not stuffed into a ball. No wonder the old man was so much nicer when
he came back.

I found Sciafani in his room, putting on a new white collarless shirt. The only thing he'd gotten back was his shoes, polished to a shine.

"They took my dagger," he said, as he ran a comb through his thick dark hair.

"You might get the wrong end of it back when they discover what happened to Tommy the C," I said, keeping my voice low.

"It was my first step toward revenge, to strike at Don Calo, to take something from him. And if I could do it once, I would know I could do it again. I had to find out."

"Can you do it again?"

"I am not sure," Sciafani said. "He may not have been a good man, but I find I wish I could take my action back. I have seen so much death, I thought one at my own hands would not matter. But it does."

"There's an old Chinese saying according to my father," I said. "Before you embark on a journey of revenge, dig two graves."

"Did your father ever seek revenge?" Sciafani asked.

That was complicated. Among the Irish on the Boston PD there were often crosscurrents of loyalty and betrayal. There were IRA men like Uncle Dan, who organized money and guns for the cause in Ireland, and those who winked at their work. There was the day-to-day pilferage and graft, which greased the wheels for everyone but kept us all in the same boat. Then there was serious corruption, those who took payoffs from the Mob, guys who were after the big score, not satisfied with a little extra on the side. Guys like Basher, a cop who'd come up with my dad and gone really bad. Basher had shot Dad from ambush, to keep him from blowing the whistle on him. Only Basher wasn't as good at shooting as he was at being a crooked cop, so Dad had awakened in a hospital with Uncle Dan and a few IRA boys at his bedside. Basher was never heard from again, though they did find him floating facedown one fine day. I'd never thought about it before, but a year or so after that Dad started quoting Confucius to me.

"No," I lied, not wanting to have to explain or think more about this coincidence right now.

"He sounds like a wise man," Sciafani said.

Wiser than I ever knew maybe.

"Yeah. I guess he always hoped some of it would rub off."

I could see Dad clearly, standing on a wet sidewalk as the gray light of early morning found its way over the tenement roofs, his hands stuffed in his raincoat pockets, standing over a corpse in the gutter, prone, blood pooling against the curbstone. It was the first time he said it to me, and I had thought it was odd, since the argument that had led to this death had turned out to be a beef over a Studebaker, of all things. I'd listened, but not really. I'd listened with my ears, not my eyes or my heart, so it was only now, seeing someone else struggle with the demons of revenge and death, that I understood what my father had been telling me.

"Let's go find dinner," I said, patting Sciafani on the shoulder and moving him out of the room. He was subdued, harmless perhaps, but I had to keep my eye on him. He'd finally seen the man he'd agonized over killing and found him to be the person who'd shaped his life more than his own father had. It wasn't a good basis for *la vendetta*, but Sciafani had already started that ball rolling, and I wanted to get him out of there before he drew me into his scheme of revenge.

We tried to retrace our steps through the busy house, passing young smiling girls carrying laundry and a couple of dark, grim men who ignored us. We ended up in the small courtyard, then found our way into a large kitchen, where an old woman, her dull black dress flowing from her chins to her ankles, hollered at us, pointing the way out with an eggplant, which she brandished like a saber. Pots were bubbling on the cast-iron woodstove, and plates of cheese were set out, ready to be served. I felt a powerful surge of hunger, not because I hadn't eaten, but because I'd eaten poorly. The smells from the kitchen were so rich and tantalizing that they drew out the hunger that had been kept at bay by Italian rations and dry bread. I breathed deeply, anticipating nothing but food, putting all thoughts of *mafiusu* and revenge aside. We entered a large room, dominated by a long wooden table, a dozen high-backed chairs arranged around it. Don Calo stood at the far end of the room talking with a small group of men.

"Come, come in," he said, gesturing to us with both arms, welcoming us as if we were old friends. As he moved toward us, I saw the faces of the other men. And one ghost.

Harry. Lieutenant Harry Dickinson raising a glass of wine to his lips. I stopped, blinking, not sure that my mind wasn't still playing tricks on me. Harry was still there, his eyes fixed on mine.

"Billy!" He set down the wineglass hard, spilling the deep red liquid on the white lace tablecloth in his haste. "My God, I'd given you up for lost."

"I thought you were dead" was all I could say, in a faint voice. I should have been glad to see him, thrilled he was alive, but instead I was confused. Everything that had happened to me these last few days flowed from tossing that grenade and thinking I'd killed Harry, and here he was, drinking wine, hardly the worse for wear. Then I saw Nick, hanging back, watching me.

"And you—," I said, clenching my teeth as I felt anger flood me.

"Never mind that now," said Harry, holding up his hand. "No need for a scene, Billy."

"A scene? What, are you crazy? He—"

"You've got to tell me why you thought I was dead, Billy. But first I must introduce you to the other guests." Harry spoke as if we were at a cocktail party, not behind enemy lines at a Mafia chieftain's house. I didn't get it, but then again I could hardly take in that this was really Harry, alive and clapping me on the shoulder.

"I believe we have already met," a voice said from behind Nick. "In Algiers."

If seeing Harry had thrown me for a loop, this guy did it in spades. Harry and Nick were dressed in the same nondescript khaki uniforms they'd worn on the mission, nicely cleaned and pressed, but still the same. The other guest was dressed in khaki too, just as worn and sun bleached as theirs. The only difference was the cuff band that read AFRIKA with the palm-tree emblem of the Afrika Korps.

"Who. . . what?" I couldn't manage to say anything coherent. My mind felt rusty and slow, as if thinking back to Algiers was more than it could handle.

"Major Erich Remke," Harry said, "Lieutenant Billy Boyle, U.S. Army."

"Yes, it was in Algiers, in that unfortunate Vichy prison cell," Major Remke said. "I am glad you were freed." He extended his hand and I shook it, remembering the face and the circumstances. He was tall and lean with a weather-beaten face, his deep blue eyes set off by tiny white crow's-feet, a result of squinting in the sun.

"Yes, I was. Did your agent make it? The one with the student rebels?"

"No, no, Lieutenant Boyle," Remke said. "There are rules in this house. No weapons and no attempts at interrogation under Don Calo's roof. We are under his protection here, from each other."

I looked at Harry, hoping someone would take pity and explain what the hell was going on. He smiled at me, the kind of smile you give a young child who can't keep up with the grown-up conversation.

"Billy," Harry said, gripping my arm to get my attention. "We've all come here to see Don Calo. He's talked to us separately, and insisted we all remain here—as his guests—while he decides what to do."

"It is much simpler," Don Calo broke in, "to discuss things with both parties in the same house. It saves much driving about, and all it requires is that you do not kill each other under my roof. Now, come, eat."

Don Calo introduced Sciafani as a local doctor, as if he were an ordinary visitor. We sat, weaponless soldiers obediently making small talk with each other. Two thick-necked bruisers with arms crossed stood against the wall, watching the servers come in and out with plates of food. I wondered if this was Don Calo's real home or a house where he only did business. No wife or children were in evidence, only his men and servants, who moved like players in well-practiced parts.

"This wine is from our local grape, gentlemen, the Nero d'Avola," Don Calo announced, raising his glass. "*Salute.*"

We all raised our glasses and, following the others as if in a trance, I drank but tasted nothing. Candles were lit and bright pinpoints of light danced above the table. My enemy laughed at something my friend said, and they all seemed far, far away. Someone served me a small triangle of crispy eggplant. I bit into it and hot cheese oozed out. Sciafani, on my left, spoke to Don Calo in Sicilian, an easy flow of everyday banter, no trace of the avenging killer in his tone. Across from me, Nick stared down at his plate, the only one, besides me, who didn't seem caught up in the fantasy of Mafia hospitality.

Remke's eyes darted from Don Calo to Sciafani, and I knew he was following what they were saying. The last time I'd seen him, he was about to leave Algiers just before the Vichy gave up; Major Harding and I were in a police cell. Harding had figured out that Remke was an intelligence officer, and one of his agents had been picked up in the same roundup that had scooped up Diana. Remke had given us a few clues to help us find Diana, but only because he knew that was the best chance his agent had of getting out alive. I was here now because I'd been able to serve his purposes then. I wondered if I'd be as lucky this time.

"Lieutenant Boyle?"

"What?" I realized someone had been calling my name. It was Remke, eyeing me with a quizzical look.

"I asked you if your Major—Harding, was it not—was well?"

"Alive, you mean? Yes."

"Give him my regards. If you see him again," Remke said, then ripped a piece of crusty bread with his teeth.

"You can give him your own regards, from inside a POW cage," I said. It wasn't that I felt the need to insult Remke, but this whole setup didn't sit right with me. I didn't like Don Calo hosting blood enemies and making us play by his rules. I could be aiming my gun at that sun-bleached khaki tomorrow, and I didn't much like making dinner conversation with it today. I always tried to think about the uniform, not the man, when I was in combat. *It's just laundry*, my drill instructor had said once. *Shoot at the laundry, don't think about the guy wearing it. If he was in civvies they'd put you away for killing him. If he's wearing the right laundry, they'll give you a medal.*

"Billy," Harry said, narrowing his eyes and staring me down like a schoolmaster. "Not here, not now."

"Exactly," said Don Calo. "Everywhere else, you have dominion. On the sea, on the land, and in the air, you kill each other, as well as many innocents. But here, no. In this little village, in my poor house, no."

Remke nodded to Don Calo, acknowledging his wisdom while showing me up with his European patience. I felt like taking the damned handkerchief out and blowing my nose in it. Harry's eyes were on me, willing me to shut up. I avoided his gaze and stared at Nick, who looked as dazed as I felt.

"My apologies," I said. "Nowadays I try not to let my guard down, with enemies or friends."

"Very good," said Don Calo. "The virtue of an enemy is that you know he is your enemy, while your so-called friend may deceive you."

A plate of small rice balls came my way. I helped myself, the aroma nearly lifting me off my seat. It felt good to put everyone else on edge. It leveled the playing field, which I liked a damn sight better than being the odd man out.

"So we are all here, where you can keep an eye on us, and decide who is to be your new friend?"

"Yes, I do keep the eye on you all. As for becoming friends, we Sicilians do not need your friendship, we would prefer that you all go away. The Italians too. Leave us to our island, that is our wish."

"Then why do you have a German, two Americans, and an Englishman here, Don Calo?" Sciafani asked.

"*Un diavolo caccia l'altro*," Don Calo answered, and they both laughed. Remke raised an eyebrow, signaling his understanding. All I got was the bit about the devil.

"One devil hunts the other," Sciafani explained. "An old saying."

"Did you know that one, Nick?" I asked. "Sounds right up your alley, with your family coming from around here."

"No" was all he said, and meekly at that.

"Well, here's one for you then," I said, raising my glass. "*Faol saol agat, gob fliuch, agus bás in Éirinn.*"

"Gaelic?" Harry asked. "Aye," I said, the Irish lilt from Southie springing to my lips. "*Long life to you, a wet mouth, and death in Ireland. But any island will do.*"

Everyone but Nick laughed. I drank the wine down and the flavor danced on my tongue.

CHAPTER ▪ TWENTY-FOUR

REMKE WAS LEAVING. We watched as he shook hands with Don Calo and then opened the door of the Kübelwagen that had pulled up in front of the house behind two German motorcycles. We eyed the German riders as they spoke to each other and laughed as they glanced in our direction, their exchange barely audible above the rumbling machines. One of them revved his engine and took off, the thin slit of light from his taped headlamp casting a slash of brightness into the night.

"I hope to see you again, Lieutenant Boyle," Remke said as he pulled on his officer's cap.

"Each time a little closer to Berlin," I said, throwing him a lazy salute. He ignored that and drove off, the noise of the motors echoing harshly around the piazza.

This was the second time I'd encountered Remke, and like the first, there was a layer of repressed hostility between us. We were enemies, but he seemed to be having as much trouble with his allies as with us. First the Vichy French, now the Italians. I wondered how long it would be before the Germans stood alone, and if our next meeting would be somewhat less subdued.

In a minute, the sound of their vehicles was gone. It was quiet—

that dark, late-night, small-town quiet that can send a shiver down the back of a city boy. Don Calo walked a few steps into the square and looked up at the night sky. It was a silky black, the stars sparkling through the clean mountain air.

"We will talk in the morning," he said, sighing and waving his hand dismissively. "It is late."

"What did Major Remke have to say?" I asked.

"That the Germans and the Italians will drive you into the sea. That they almost did so and most certainly will. That you were foolish to come here, so far from your bases. That I would also be foolish to make cause with you." He looked at me, an eyebrow raised, daring me to say otherwise.

"I was there when they tried to push us into the sea."

"It is true that they almost did?"

"Almost, yes. But we killed many of them, and in the end, they ran."

"You are a solider then, not simply a messenger?"

I wondered about that. I'd done some fighting, but I wasn't at the front full-time, like the GIs who lived and died together. Clancy and Joe. It didn't seem right to lump myself in with them. And I didn't like the idea of admitting I really was a messenger boy, a general's nephew who had nearly screwed up his assignment.

"We'll talk in the morning," I said, and went inside. Don Calo followed, and I heard the iron gate clang shut and a key turn heavily in the lock.

"Wait—," Nick gasped as I grabbed him by the neck. Harry had signaled me to follow them into the room they shared. He wanted to talk but what I wanted to do was give Nick a thrashing and then find out what the hell he'd been up to at the Valley of the Temples.

"You son of a bitch," I hissed through clenched teeth. "Why did you draw a gun on me at the temple? Whose side are you on anyway?"

"Quiet," pleaded Harry. "Let him go, Billy, I'll explain." He pushed us apart, keeping the flat of his palm on my chest to make sure I didn't go for Nick again.

"It's not what you think," Nick said, rubbing his throat.

"Do you still have the handkerchief?" Harry asked me as he guided

Nick to a chair. I looked around the room and noticed their windows had iron bars like mine. The whole house was a prison. I nodded, thinking there might be someone listening outside.

I asked Nick in a whisper, "Are you working for Vito Genovese? He wants this handkerchief too. Pulled a gun on me like you did. Didn't get it like you won't."

"Then my family is dead," Nick replied in a whisper.

I backed away. There was sadness and resignation in Nick's voice.

"Sit down, Billy," Harry said. His was the only calm voice in the room. "I'll explain."

There were a couple of chairs around the small table where Nick sat. Harry pulled up one and I took another, wondering what could possibly come next. He pulled the cork from a bottle and poured three glasses.

"Grappa," Nick said, tossing his back and pouring himself another. "Made from the residue of grapes after they've been pressed. A bit like the war, isn't it? Just when you think the life has been drained out of you, someone else puts another squeeze on."

"Billy," Harry began, watching Nick warily, as if he'd been hitting the grappa too hard lately. "We can still salvage what's left of this mission, but Nick has a problem."

"Don't we all," I said, but decided to shut up until I knew more.

"They threatened Nick's family unless he cooperated with them," Harry said. "They said they'd kill all the men—his grandfather, uncles, cousins—unless he went along."

"They? Who are you talking about? And go along with what?"

"The heist," Nick said, looking into his empty glass.

"What heist, and who the hell are you talking about?"

"Someone in AMGOT, but we don't know who," Harry said. "And this Vito Genovese character you just mentioned, along with another gangster, Joseph Laspada."

"And their pal Muschetto, a local guy," I said.

"How do you know that?" Harry asked.

"They came looking for me. Or you, actually," I said, pointing to Nick. "You're their yegg."

He ignored my assertion and poured another drink for himself.

"What's a yegg?" Harry asked, moving the bottle out of Nick's reach.

"A safecracker. All you Naval Intelligence guys were taught the fine art of safecracking, weren't you, Nick?"

"Yeah," he said. "I'm pretty good at it too."

"Are you talking about a threat to your relatives here in Sicily?" I asked.

"My family name comes from the village of Cammarata. It's east of here, on the road to Palermo. They're holding my people there, every one. If I don't come through, they'll start killing the men."

"Come through with what?" I asked.

"I was supposed to eliminate both of you, take the handkerchief, and carry out your mission to Don Calo, with one little addition."

"What's that?"

" I have to steal two million dollars from the U.S. Army."

I drank down the grappa, felt it burn my throat and warm my stomach.

"Tell me everything from the very beginning," I said to Nick. I shoved my glass toward Harry and he poured. Nick talked, I drank.

"When I was a kid, I used to run errands for Luciano's gang in New York. Nothing illegal—getting coffee and sandwiches, delivering messages, stuff like that. I became a numbers runner for a while. Then I got serious about school and wanted to go to college, so I gave it up. I stayed in touch with my pals, and they knew I'd joined the navy right after Pearl Harbor. I was an ensign, and all of a sudden I get pulled from a cruiser and sent to the Office of Naval Intelligence. I took some tests, was promoted to lieutenant, and then they told me I'd been recommended by Lucky Luciano to work for them and infiltrate Sicily, since I spoke the language like a native."

"Most of that I knew," I said, getting impatient. "Who asked you to steal two million bucks? When? And whose money is it?"

"That's the funny part. I don't know. They had drummed security into us, so I never tried to find out. One day in Algiers, I got a memo on ONI stationery. No name or signature, just a notification that I'd be getting top-secret communications in the near future that I was not to discuss with anyone. And to burn each message, starting with that one. So I did."

Nick pushed his glass toward Harry, who shook his head.

"At first they were about the mission, the same stuff I was hearing every day. Then they mentioned the handkerchief, how I had to get it and present it to Don Calo. I thought it was just an ONI-versus-the-army thing, that maybe ONI thought it would be better to use a Sicilian-American to approach Don Calogero. Then, when we moved to the advance base in Tunisia, they hit me with the real reason. Someone was going to arrange for the Thirty-fourth Division payroll to come ashore with the first wave of the invasion. Six field safes, two million dollars in occupation lire. All I had to do was tell Don Calo that this had been arranged by Lucky Luciano as a gift to him. He'd get half. Don Calo would supply the men to take me there, and in the confusion I was supposed to hit the paymaster and open the safes."

"That's crazy," I said. "No one would ever send a division payroll in with the first wave. Paymasters arrive days later, when the area is secure."

"Whoever sent me the messages made it happen."

"You didn't . . . ?"

"No," Nick said, shaking his head. "First of all, Don Calo wouldn't bite, not without that damn handkerchief. Harry and I tried to convince him to use his influence to get the Sicilian troops to desert too. He wouldn't listen, not until he knew either or both plans had the blessing of Luciano."

"He puts a lot of store in a piece of cloth," Harry said.

"He's used them himself, it's a custom here. It means the owner trusts the person carrying it with his life, and that person will die rather than give it up, so that when the messenger delivers it, he can be vouched for."

"Lucky Luciano doesn't know me," I said.

"That's why it made sense to me at first. The army knew what they were doing when they gave you the handkerchief, they understood the tradition."

"How did you get these messages?"

"Each one was in a plain envelope. They'd show up under my door, stuck in my gear, on my pillow. Any number of people could have left them. Along with the note about the payroll, there was a threat. If I told anyone or didn't steal it, they'd kill my relations in Cammarata."

"Wait a minute," I said. "How could someone in Tunisia get to these thugs in Sicily to make all this happen? There had to be some-body already here to carry out the threat to your relatives." I stood then paced back and forth, trying to think things through.

"I guess someone high up enough could arrange phony orders to have the payroll go ashore early. The army issues enough screwy orders to make that plausible. But what happened when you didn't steal the money? You didn't, did you? That should've happened by now, right?"

"Fortunes of war, Billy," Harry said. "The surf was rough, and the landing craft carrying the safes capsized. They went in the drink, about a thousand yards offshore of Gela. We heard about it yesterday."

"So you're off the hook?"

"Oh no," Harry said. "Now we have to steal the money soaking wet, after it's salvaged."

"Are you still getting messages here?"

"Here I get instructions direct from Legs Laspada," Nick said.

"Does Don Calo know about the threat to your family?"

"No, he's supposed to think it's Luciano's plan, and that I'm in on it. He doesn't know I told Harry about the scheme. I had to, it was eat-ing me up."

"I have a feeling that if you managed to pull this off, Don Calo would never see his cut," I said. If Vito Genovese was in on this, what was Rocko's part? Evidently he'd no longer been important to Vito. It was probably Legs who'd murdered Rocko. What had Rocko offered that Genovese no longer needed? Supplies? Something was starting to make sense, but I couldn't quite put it into words yet. I kept pacing, tapping my finger on my lips.

"Billy?" Harry asked.

"I haven't had a chance to tell you yet, but I woke up in a field hos-pital with no memory at all. No idea who I was, or why I was here."

"From that knock on the head?" Harry asked, pointing to my bandage.

"Yeah," I said quickly, not wanting to talk about rolling that grenade and thinking I had killed him. Time enough for that later. "I woke up and this supply sergeant, Rocko Walters, was there. He was looking out for me, helping me, but he was after the handkerchief too. He tried not to tip his hand, since he was also trying to find out what had happened to their yegg."

"He was waiting for your memory to return," Nick said.

"Yes. But he waited too long. Someone killed him. That night at the Valley of the Temples, an Italian soldier led me back to the American lines. He only wanted to give up and get to America. I must've told him I'd help him. By the time I found him among the POWs, his throat had been slit."

"So there's someone back at HQ who both knew about the payroll and could manage to get orders changed so that the paymaster went ashore early. And a supply sergeant was in on it and a couple of mobsters who were already on the island," Harry said, summing up.

"Whoever is behind this had to be working with Vito and Legs from the outset. He'd have to, to get information to them," I added.

"How?" Nick asked. "I mean, how could he get all this dope to either of them? Who would have that kind of pull?"

"I don't know," I said. "Rocko was a classic wheeler-dealer, but he wasn't a headquarters guy. He ran the show at divisional supply. He's the one who could requisition the field safes. Maybe they recruited him then, or he smelled something fishy and cut himself in. He could get most anything, and knew how to work around officers. I heard him give a Signals lieutenant holy hell for not finding Roberto fast enough."

"Who's Roberto?" Nick asked.

"The Italian kid who saved my neck after the fight at the temple. He was bringing me back to our lines."

"Why would a Signals officer be looking for a POW?" Harry asked.

"I guess because he was in on the . . . wait a minute," I said, stopping in midsentence. My memory still felt as if rusty gears were grinding against each other. "Rocko had a corporal working for him. He was a technician fifth class, assigned to Rocko from the Signals Company. When he was killed at Biazza Ridge, Rocko was real shook up about it, which wasn't his style. He wasn't the sentimental kind."

"Billy, you may have gotten hit on the head harder than you realize. You're not making any sense," Harry said.

I tried to slow myself down, to lay it out step by step, but I was worried that if I didn't get it all out now it wouldn't make sense to me either. "Rocko didn't give a hoot about anyone but himself, but he took it hard when I told him Corporal Hutton was dead. That's because Hutton was a communications specialist. I overheard Rocko tell Vito that they had to get some sort of German piece of equipment working. A dialer of some sort, I can't remember its designation."

"So the plan called for a communications specialist. Hutton must have had the job of splicing into the local telephone wires. If he had had the right kind of equipment, he could have placed a call anywhere," Nick said. "Hell, he could have called Mussolini if he'd known the number."

"Hutton set up his equipment as soon as they landed and sent a message from Rocko to Vito, or maybe to Legs," Harry contributed.

"I'd bet on that," I said. "And when Hutton was killed, Vito and his pals had no further use for Rocko. He was just another loose end, like Roberto. Rocko hadn't gotten the handkerchief from me, so they came after me themselves."

"Well," Harry said with a tired sigh, "we still have a job to do. You've got to convince Don Calo to work with us, to tell the Sicilian soldiers to surrender, and you've got to do it tomorrow."

"One more thing," I said. "Is there a woman named Charlotte anywhere in this mess?"

They looked at each other blankly. "Why?" Harry asked.

"Something else I overheard. Vito told Rocko that Charlotte was worried."

"Did he ever refer to Charlotte as she?" Nick asked. "Like, 'I spoke to Charlotte and she's worried about you'?"

"No," I said. "it was, 'Charlotte is worried about you.'"

"I don't know if this means a thing," Nick said. "But ONI sent me to take a course at the Judge Advocate General school of military government, out in Charlottesville, Virginia. Most of the guys were from AMGOT, but there were a few other Sicilian- and Italian-Americans. Everyone called the place Charlotte. Don't know why, but they did."

"What the bloody hell is AMGOT?" Harry asked.

"American Military Government of Occupied Territories," I said. "The guys who take over after the fighting's done. They're the ones in charge of occupation currency."

"Right," said Nick. "They're planning on exchanging all the lire in Sicily for occupation lire, to keep inflation and black marketeering down. Someone high up in AMGOT would have access to the pay-master's orders."

"How much money are we talking about, in occupation scrip?" I asked.

"Nobody knows for sure. We're bringing enough in for divisional payrolls and for exchanging at the first couple of big banks we find. That will give AMGOT time to set up printing presses on the island, for turning out everything from newspapers to more lire."

"I hope they get your 45th *Division News* going first, if they are going to print newspapers. I do like the *Willie and Joe* cartoons," Harry said. "The blokes on my boat can't get enough of them."

"Patton hates them," Nick said. "I doubt that Mauldin kid will get much ink while he's in Patton's army."

I wasn't thinking about Bill Mauldin, who drew *Willie and Joe,* or the Sad Sack character, or Georgie Patton. I was thinking about Charlotte, a code name for someone in AMGOT, someone who'd attended a course at the JAG school in Charlottesville and probably knew Nick from there. Someone asleep in a warm cot right now, safe in Algiers or at the advance base for the invasion of Sicily, Amilcar, in Tunisia. He had two deaths on his hands already—Rocko and Roberto—and he'd nearly ruined this mission. No, make that three deaths.

"Harry, there's something else I need to tell you. Banville didn't make it. He and Kaz found me, and we were on our way here when the Germans showed up. Kaz and I escaped, but he didn't."

"Was he captured?" I saw the faintest hope in Harry's eyes and felt like a heel for not saying it straight out.

"No. He's dead."

"Bloody hell. There's going to be a score settled, the sooner the better. Get us out of here, Billy, first thing tomorrow."

I knew what he meant. I felt it myself, the urge for swift violence to right a wrong done to me. Sciafani had held on to his hate for too long, and when he'd finally done something about it, he'd found vengeance was darker and more haunting than he'd ever imagined. As I had in my own struggle with *la vendetta.* A knife in the ribs elimi-nated one problem, but another appeared in its place, one that all the violence I could ever summon up would never touch. I felt an over-whelming desire to sit on the front porch stoop with Dad and shoot the breeze for a while, the way we did when he had something impor-tant to say. He'd talk around it for a while, circling, easing into it. Maybe he could tell me something more about revenge than having to dig two graves. Or maybe he'd end up saying there simply wasn't any way around it. If that was true, it would be nice at least to hear it from him. But I wasn't anywhere near that front stoop in Southie, and I had to get the job done here and now. I had to convince Don Calo to sup-port the Allies, I had to figure out how to get Nick out of this mess, and I had to find the greedy bastard who'd taken three lives. Graves were going to be dug.

"I'll do my best, Harry. Nick, how far is Cammarata from here?"

CHAPTER ▪ TWENTY-FIVE

DON CALO WAS WAITING for me in the small court-
yard, drinking espresso in the early morning sun. I wondered if I was
supposed to bow, kiss his ring, or give the secret Mafia handshake. I
decided to use one of my few Italian phrases and then get to the point.

"*Buon giorno*, Don Calo. I have something for you."

"That is refreshing. People usually want something from me."

I drew out the handkerchief by an edge, and held it up so he could
see the L. "From Salvatore Lucania."

Don Calo took it, rubbing the silk between his fingers. "He was
born less than thirty kilometers from here, and he has never forgotten
his home. Salvatore Lucania is a good man. Sit, please, have some *caffè*
while we talk."

He snapped his fingers and a moment later a woman brought out a
small silver pot and poured hot, thick coffee into a tiny cup. As I took
my first sip, I watched Don Calo run the fabric through his hands. His
fingernails were manicured. Once his hands had probably been rough
and callused, when he was on his way up, hunting men in the hills. Now
he had others around him with rough, hard hands, and he sat in the sun,
pressing silk against his palms. I figured a guy like that would want to
stay on top, and that he'd go along with whoever could keep him there.

"We call him Lucky Luciano in the states, Don Calo, and I have a message from him for you but first I should tell you about the message I do not have."

"There are many messages you do not have, my American friend. Why should I care about those?"

"Because there are men who wish to use you, to put you in danger, with plans to steal from the American army. Lucky Luciano has no part in that."

"What do you mean?" He spoke with the calm, innocent assurance of a master liar.

"Money. Three million dollars in occupation scrip."

That made him flinch. He was ready to deny anything, but by adding the extra million to the haul I caught him off guard and made him wonder if Vito was holding out on him.

"Three million dollars? That is a lot of money. How could someone steal that much from your army?"

"Actually, I doubt if anyone could. But if someone happened to pull off such a thing, they would only come to ruin."

"How?" His tone was belligerent now, and I knew I had to convince him or this might be my last cup of joe.

"Don Calo," I said, leaning over the table, closer to him so I could speak in a whisper. "What do you think would happen to three million dollars' worth of stolen lire on an island, in the middle of a war? When thousands of armed men are moving through villages and towns? They would search for it. We're not just talking about the official search by the army, but every GI and probably every *tedesco* ripping this island to pieces to find three million in cash. There'd be no place to run. Every village would be torn apart. The simple people you protect would be the ones to suffer. They would lose far more than my army would. Anyone under even a hint of suspicion would be tracked down. And, it goes without saying, no one under suspicion could ever be trusted, after the fighting is over, in any position of authority."

I sat back, drained the last bit of strong brew from my cup, and watched Don Calo. He drummed his fingers on the table, as if they were calculating the odds. The drumming stopped, and his lower lip thrust out as he slowly nodded his head. He'd decided something, maybe which of his henchmen should take me out and shoot me or maybe that I wasn't as dumb as I looked.

"A true *mafiusu* would not weigh money against his people's welfare. And a man would be a fool to take such a chance, don't you think?"

"Well, it is three million," I said, giving my best shot at that all-purpose Sicilian shrug. "A man would have to think about it, even if he was only promised a half share. It is still a lot of money. But no, it wouldn't be worth it."

"You are sure about the amount?" Don Calo asked.

"I saw it loaded into the field safes myself, nine of them," I lied.

"You know all about this then. And you are certain the plan to take this money did not come from Salvatore?"

I had to tone things down a bit. I didn't want Don Calo thinking Luciano was trying to put one over on him, or else he might not believe anything else I told him.

"Don Calo, I was entrusted with this handkerchief as a symbol of Lucky Luciano's good wishes. There is only one message. Someone else is trying to use you for their own purposes, to manipulate you, to fool you into carrying out their plot. They threatened Nicholas Cammarata with the death of his relatives if he didn't bring that false message to you."

"Who did this?" I knew I had him. He was angry, and now his anger was directed at someone else, for a breach of honor.

"I will find out. Please don't blame Nick, he was in agony at the thought of his family being held hostage. They have threatened to kill all the men."

"You must know the names of these others. Who made this threat?"

"No names were given. I don't yet know who the guy at the top is. But here, I believe Vito Genovese, Joey Laspada, and a local man, a big fellow named Muschetto, are part of the scheme."

"Ah, Vito. That disappoints me. About Laspada, I am not surprised. This Muschetto, he is a *fuorilegge*, a bandit, not even a member of our society. He is nothing. The one in charge, the unnamed one, must answer to me. Are you sure you can find out who he is?"

"Don Calo, please don't hold this against me, but before the war, I was a police officer, a detective. I will find the person responsible and he will be brought to justice."

"Hold it against you? Lieutenant Boyle, I own some of the finest *carabinieri* in all of Sicily! I have nothing against the profession of policemen. As long as they take my money and then leave me alone."

"I do have a favor to ask," I said, ignoring the crack about owning cops.

"You have done me a favor by alerting me to this foolish venture. What can I do for you?"

"Give me a few men and transport. I want to pay a visit to Nick's relatives in Cammarata. Tonight."

He drummed his fingers again, more slowly this time. The odds weren't as great, so he finished sooner than before.

"Done. You will leave in the afternoon, to arrive well after dark. Now it is time we spoke of the message you do have."

I took a deep breath, trying to calm my jitters. I'm not the kind of guy who gets the big picture. When Major Harding and the ONI guys had explained it all to me back in Algiers, I hadn't taken the idea of palling around with the Mafia all that seriously. The mobsters I knew, like Legs and his gang, wouldn't give two hoots for anyone or anything that didn't benefit them. So I thought this was a joke, or maybe one of Uncle Ike's deception plans. Maybe there was something wrong with me, but I had to have a thing right in front of my nose before I got it. I had to see those narrow mountain roads covered by machine guns set up outside packed ramshackle villages. Nothing Harding could have said in a briefing would have gotten to me the way those antitank guns covering that bridge had. I could still smell the burning Shermans. So that's what I told Don Calo about—the odor of burning flesh and fuel spiraling out of blasted turrets. About Sicilian troops digging in at every crossroad, before every small village that straddled a pitifully narrow road, the soldiers working cheerfully in the sunlight, mopping their brows as if they were sowing crops for harvest. About our heavy artillery and fighter-bombers with their rockets and machine guns, and about bullets in the air so thick they trimmed blossoms from the wild-flowers in the meadows like a scythe.

I told him about Signora Patane dying in her bed, her kitchen left stocked and neat. I told him about the bombardment from the cruisers obliterating the militia emplacement outside Agrigento, leaving severed legs and puddles of gore spread over the hilltop. I told him about our forward observer teams—air corps and naval officers who went up front with the infantry and could instantly radio for air strikes or naval fire. I told him we would rain down fire and steel by the ton on any resistance, that we would not throw away our soldiers' lives to spare the enemy the suffering they would bring on themselves. I told him that once a town was taken, there would be food, medical care, and kindness, but that we would have no mercy beforehand. I told him the world had never seen a war with warriors so rich with the means of death and destruction, and never had so many factories labored so hard to produce so much to kill so many. I made us out to be vengeful prodigal sons, storming the Old World, ready to obliterate anyone who held up a hand to stop us. I felt righteous by the time I was done, and a little ashamed, but this was a *mafiusu* I was talking to, not some schmo from a street corner, so I had to lay it on heavy. Power. I wanted him to feel the power coming his way. The power to destroy and the power to elevate. They were one and the same.

I sat back in my chair and watched his face. He looked older by a decade. Maybe he was thinking about life before the war and how it would never be the same. Maybe he was thinking about his own mother, dying a peaceful death. I don't know. I did know that there was no need to go on, to hold out promises of position and wealth. He'd see to that himself. He looked at me with expressionless eyes, granting me nothing. I had brought a terrible message—the truth.

"A man does not live to rise to my position without being a good judge of other men," Don Calo said, after a minute of silence filled the space between us. "I am not surprised by the actions of Vito and his underlings. That is in character, all of it. It is an offense to me, but not a grave one."

He sighed as he looked around the peaceful courtyard. His violent anger was gone, replaced by disappointment and a wistfulness that seemed to weigh on him.

"And I think you have told me the truth about what will happen, to my island and to my children. We are a powerful society, my young policeman, you know that. We have strong hearts. But you, you bring a storm of steel, you and the *tedeschi*. I cannot let you sweep away the lives of my children and all that I have struggled for. The sooner you have your victory, the sooner you will leave us."

He nodded and stood. I did too, pushing back my chair, the metal scraping harshly against stone. Don Calo grimaced. I thought he might shake my hand, but instead he steadied himself against the table, as if against the terrible forces standing ready to overcome him. He pulled out a pocket watch on a long chain, the end looped around his suspenders.

"There is not much time," he said, and left me standing alone.

CHAPTER ▪ TWENTY-SIX

THE DAYS OF ROUGH travel had caught up with me. My legs felt like jelly, each step up the stairs winding me as I pulled myself along by the banister. I washed, cleaning the crusty lump on my head as best I could. I got rid of the bandage. I slept some more in my room behind barred windows. Later, I told Nick and Harry about what had happened, but I didn't feel like hashing it over. I wanted to get it done, and sleep some more. They asked me if Don Calo had decided to tell the Sicilian soldiers to desert, and I replied that I thought so. We ate, and I went into the courtyard and sat in the late afternoon sun, waiting. Nick and Harry followed, and Sciafani joined us.

Cars and a truck pulled up outside the gate, the sound of slamming doors and creaking rusty iron signaling the arrival of our convoy to Cammarata. Half a dozen men in white shirts with sleeves rolled up, black vests, and *lupare* slung over their shoulders, sauntered in. They were young and smooth skinned, thick dark hair curling from underneath their cloth caps. They watched us out of the corners of their eyes, two of them slowly walking around to where we sat, shotguns cradled in their arms. They stood behind Sciafani. Another guy, this one in a suit, about a decade older than the sawed-off gang, came through the gate. He didn't look at us as he hustled into the house, buttoning his jacket against his thick waist and pushing his slick hair back with his hands.

"*Che c'è?*" Nick asked, the Italian equivalent of asking what's up.

No reply. I threw Sciafani a look. It seemed like bad news had strolled in, and the worst news I could think of would come from Agrigento. He gave a nervous shrug, and grimaced. Not very Sicilian. More like Scollay Square after midnight, when a guy stops and asks you in a gruff voice for a light.

Footsteps pounded toward us from the house as we were each prodded to our feet by the hard end of a double-barrel. No one argued. Don Calo advanced on us, followed by the guy in the suit, whose lips were pinched tight into a thin line of anger. Don Calo clutched something in his hands, and the bottom fell out when I saw what it was. A burlap bag. The bag I'd left stuck under the seat of the car that brought us here.

Most people slow down as they get close to another person. Don Calo didn't. His rapid pace brought him right up to Sciafani as he drew the sacristan's big revolver from the bag and slammed it into the side of Sciafani's face, sending him crashing to the ground. Don Calo's momentum carried him right over Sciafani, so that he stood astride him as he lay on his side, holding both hands to his face. Blood leaked from between Sciafani's fingers.

"Why did you do it?" Don Calo demanded, his voice booming with violence. "Why?"

Sciafani, pulling one hand away, stared at his blood.

Don Calo kicked him, a vicious blow to the ribs. "Tell me!"

Sciafani opened his mouth, unable to take in enough air to breathe, much less speak. Don Calo brought his foot back again, but Sciafani rolled over, holding up one hand.

"I did it to hurt you, to take something away from you," he said between gasps. "I was going to kill you too, for my father. After all the death I have seen, I thought I could do it. But killing that man sickened me. I am a coward." Tears flowed from his eyes, mixing with his blood.

"My *caporegime* is dead, all because you wanted to try your hand at killing?"

Don Calo clenched his fists, fury knitting his brow. Sciafani's admission enraged him, and I could see him performing a cold, hard calculation, finding no solution that would make sense of his man's death. It was alien to him, and perhaps he saw Tommy the C's death as a waste, having come at the hands of a novice who found he didn't have the calling.

Don Calo raised the revolver and cocked the hammer. He aimed directly at Sciafani's head. Sciafani covered his eyes with blood-streaked hands, turning away from the sight of the barrel pointing at him. He offered no resistance. Don Calo's face was grim, and I saw the muscles tense in his forearm. He pulled the trigger.

The explosion in the enclosed courtyard rang from the walls. Birds rose up in flight from the roof. Don Calo stepped back, the revolver hanging limply from his hand. Sciafani looked up in shock and surprise. One of the *lupara* boys laughed and Don Calo silenced him with a look that could have cut glass. Sciafani got up, staring at the wisp of smoke curling up from a hole in the hard ground, next to where his head had been.

The guy in the suit snapped his fingers, and the others followed him out, casting backward glances at the man Don Calo hadn't killed.

"Come, sit, Enrico," Don Calo said, his voice calm and gentle.

Setting the pistol on the table, he guided Sciafani to a seat, taking out a handkerchief and pressing it to Sciafani's cheek, guiding his hand to hold it there. Don Calo sat down heavily, wiping his forehead with the back of his hand, a streak of Sciafani's blood leaving a thin trail over his eyes.

"They said I should have killed you years ago," Don Calo said. "But that was one death I could not cause either."

"*Perché?*" Sciafani said, one palm outstretched. Why? Why not then, why not now?

"I have done things that the law, and your American friend Billy, would call wrong. I call them natural to a man of our honored society. I have no regrets. But I do regret leaving you, a child, without parents. And some days, I regret the absence of men like your father, men who did not fear me. I am not a monster, and I could not solve the problem you presented by killing you, then or now. But, as of today, we are even. I regret the death of Tommaso, but it allows me to give you your life. I had to strike you, for the sake of appearances, you understand?"

"*Sì.*"

"Good," Don Calo said, standing and holding Sciafani by the shoulders. "Now go with these men tonight, and never return. If you do, I will kill you."

Sciafani stood, and I'll be damned if he didn't give the bastard who killed his father a double-cheek kiss, and if that Sicilian crime boss who promised to kill him if he ever saw him again didn't clasp him by the shoulders as he did.

Don Calo hollered into the house, and two old ladies came out to lead Sciafani away, dabbing at his cut cheek like cleaning up blood was a regular afternoon chore. I was speechless, and for me to admit that is saying something.

"There are weapons for you in the truck," Don Calo said, strictly business. "You are free to go."

"Are you with us then, Don Calo?" Harry asked, a little nervously, I thought.

"No, my English friend," he said, with a wink in my direction. "You are with me."

Don Calo led us to the gate. The little Fiat Balilla was there, with the older guy wearing the tight suit in the passenger's seat.

"This is Gaetano Fiore," Don Calo said, gesturing to him. He nodded to me as Don Calo spoke to him in Italian. All I heard was my name, but it sounded like it was said in a nice way. Bill-lee, just like Roberto had said it, stretching out those two syllables into something more Italian. Gaetano had a pencil-thin mustache surrounded by pudgy cheeks and a double chin. A British Sten gun rested on his lap, and it looked completely natural in his meaty hands.

"Gaetano," I said, sticking my hand out to shake his. I wanted to get some sense of the man before we roared off into the dark with him.

"Bill-lee," he said back, grinning as he shook my hand in a grip that could crush walnuts. "*Ci diverticemo*."

"He says this will be fun," Don Calo translated. "He never liked Laspada."

"A man of good taste. Thank you, Don Calo, for everything." I offered my hand but he ignored it, instead giving me a pair of kisses, just like the ones he'd traded with Sciafani. I was honored, since he hadn't even killed anyone in my immediate family.

The *lupara* boys cheered and Gaetano shouted my name. I mumbled my thanks again and tried to look as heroic as the situation called for. I climbed into the back of the truck with the others as the ancient engine rumbled into life, and after one of the *mafiusu* opened a crate of Sten guns and handed them around, off we went. Through the open canvas back I saw Don Calo waving, like a friendly relation after you've paid a visit and stayed a day too long.

It was after dark when we stopped. The drivers killed their engines at the same moment. A profound silence draped itself around us, broken too soon by the sound of men walking on gravel, the crunching of stones beneath booted feet ominously mixed with metallic echoes of bolts snapping back and driving home the first bullet into the chamber. Gaetano signaled us to stay quiet and stay put. One finger to the lips, then down to the ground, then two fingers to the eyes. No sounds, wait here, let your eyes grow accustomed to the dark.

I watched details emerge from the pitch-black night, hills and trees taking shape and showing detail beneath the cloud-darkened sky. A half moon glowed behind a break in the clouds, a sliver of silver light cascading over us. Breezes gusted and swayed the trees, leaves rustling and branches creaking, the perfect cover for approaching Cammarata; sounds and shadows we could get lost in as we descended on the village like ghosts with steel in our hands.

Gaetano nodded. We left the road and scrambled up a rocky hill, each man staying close to the one in front of him so we'd know who was who when the time came for it to matter. Sciafani stayed with the vehicles that had been pulled off the road in a grove of orange trees. I could tell he had no desire to kill again, to take part in this. The journey of revenge had broken him, uncovering his strength and his weakness, leaving him stranded in that second grave. For the rest of his life, the death of the sacristan would haunt him, a mortal sin he could never absolve himself of.

As I gripped the hard, cold metal of the Sten gun, the leather strap biting into my shoulder, I saw Villard, eyes wide open, mouth formed to ask a question I never heard. Why hadn't his death broken me? Was I too far gone for guilt and atonement? I envied Sciafani in a way. He'd gone as far as he dared, and now he knew he'd never go a step farther.

And here I was, creeping through the night with an intent to leave men bleeding or dead. Out there, ahead of Gaetano, someone didn't yet know he had seen the sun for the last time. He might be an evil man, cruel to his wife and children. Or maybe he loved them and kissed his children on the forehead before he went out with his shotgun. Either way, they would never see him again.

I wondered if Dad had ever thought about Basher like that. I'd bet dollars to doughnuts Uncle Dan hadn't, and that Dad had never told him about digging two graves. But he'd told me, and right now I wished he hadn't.

A hand went up in front of me, and I froze. We were near the top of a ridge, the outline of shrubs about chest-high. Gaetano moved back, signaling Nick and me to move up, low, with him. We crawled through the undergrowth until the glow of lights appeared below us. Cammarata wasn't much of a surprise. Church tower on a hill, big wall around it, houses tumbling down the slope. The ridge we were on faced the church, and the houses were below us on the opposite hill. The main road cut through the valley beyond the church. No vehicles or people were moving.

"*Guarda,*" Gaetano said in a whisper, pointing to a house at the end of a side road.

I tried to see what he was pointing at. Soft light, probably from candles, spilled from small, square windows in the gray stone house. Next to the door, the glow of a cigarette burned bright, showing a guard seated on a bench, shotgun across his legs. Opposite him in the street I could barely make out a dark mass that seemed to absorb the little light seeping out of the windows.

"What is that?" I asked Nick.

"*Le donne,*" Gaetano said with a grin.

"Women?" Nick said, squinting his eyes and crawling closer.

The clouds broke and a half moon lit the scene below, reflecting off the light gray stonework. I could make out a dozen women standing in a semicircle in front of the guard, who ground out his cigarette with his toe. Their long black dresses, black shawls, and black head scarves drew the night around them as they stood unmoving, silent, rooted to the road, watching the house where their men were imprisoned. The only contrast was a wisp of white hair poking out from under a scarf or two.

The guard lit another cigarette. He seemed nervous, one hand on the shotgun, the other tapping ashes. I didn't blame him.

Gaetano whispered for Carlo, the youngest of his *lupara* boys. Carlo crawled forward and after rapid-fire orders, gave Gaetano his shotgun and took off his vest and cap. Gaetano gave him a small Beretta and a bottle half full of grappa. Carlo scurried off as Nick and Gaetano spoke, the rest of the gang leaning in to listen. I looked at Harry and shrugged. It was a good Sicilian shrug. I was getting the hang of this.

"OK," Nick said. "Here's the deal: Carlo will come staggering down the street in five minutes, pretending to be drunk. If he can get close enough to use his knife, he'll take out the guard with it. If not, with the Beretta. Then I go in the front door with Carlo and Gaetano; the rest of you go around the back. Billy and Harry, you two stay outside to cover the front in case they have reinforcements. Gaetano doesn't want you inside since you won't understand him if he gives an order."

"Good plan," I said. "Can Carlo pull it off?"

"Carlo's good with his knife, don't let that baby face fool you. He already is a man of honor."

It wasn't the time to debate the definition of honor, so I nodded and followed Gaetano and Nick down a gully that gave us cover as we moved up to the rear of the house across the street from our target. We hunkered down behind it and waited. Two minutes passed like twenty. Finally I could make out Carlo, singing off-key and calling for Carmela. Taking advantage of the diversion, we ran to a wall that bordered the road and contained a small garden on the side of the house. Peering over the top, I could see the guard looking down the road toward Carlo. The women didn't move.

"Dov'è Carmela?" Carlo implored the women to help him find Carmela, going from one to the other, taking their hands and kissing one or two on the cheek. They ignored him and he turned to the guard, offering his bottle.

"Sai Carmela?" he asked the guard, who didn't accept the drink.

The guard rose and pointed his shotgun at Carlo, motioning him to move on. Carlo cringed, offering abject apologies, holding one hand palm out. The guard nodded and went back to his seat. He never made it. Carlo tossed the bottle to one of the women and had his knife out as soon as the guard turned his back. Before he took a full step Carlo had one hand under his chin as the other cut across his neck. Blood sprayed against stone, and Carlo let go of the guard's chin so he could catch the shotgun before it clattered to the ground.

As he kneeled over the body, looking like a feral child, Carlo's eyes darted up and down the street and back to the door of the house. Gaetano and Nick vaulted over the wall and ran to the door. Carlo blew a kiss to the woman holding the bottle and joined them at the door, shotgun at the ready. Gaetano put his hand on the latch, wrapping his fingers around it. As he looked to the other two men, the line of women silently parted, smartly leaving empty space between them in case gunfire erupted when the door opened.

I heard a faint creak, a hinge in need of oil, as Gaetano opened the door slowly. He froze as a voice from inside the house called out a name. He flung the door wide open and Carlo charged inside. Two explosive sounds followed as Carlo let go with both barrels. Light flashed bright in the hallway. Nick charged in with his Sten, then Gaetano with a pistol.

Harry and I ran to the house, taking up positions with our backs to each side of the wall, in case a surprise showed up from the back or the street. A murmur arose among the women, the first sound I'd heard from them. They looked at us as if we were from another planet. They'd taken a drunken kid slitting the guard's throat in stride, but my American uniform was a shock.

Another shotgun blast came from the rear of the house, followed by shouts, pistol shots, and a scream. Glass broke somewhere, then another shot, then silence. Harry and I looked at each other. Then a sound erupted at the side of the house. I swung my Sten around and waited, not sure if it was one of ours, theirs, or a neighborhood cat. A face showed itself, blood dripping down a cheek. He'd probably jumped out of a window, preferring jagged glass to shotgun slugs. He pulled back, then stepped forward again, a revolver aiming straight at my chest, but I was ready with the Sten. I fired a long burst, shell casings spitting out and pinging against the stone wall as bullets hit him. He collapsed onto his knees, the pistol firing once into the dirt as a spasm gripped his hand. I kicked the pistol away, but he wasn't going to be firing it again anyway.

A yell, sounding like a warning, echoed in the hallway, and caught me by surprise. I heard one shotgun blast and then saw a broad back retreating through the front door, a *lupara* aimed into the house. It was Muschetto, bleeding from one shoulder. He fired again, emptying the second barrel, then stumbled as he turned to run. Harry and I both had our Stens on him, but trying to escape down the street he careened into the clutch of women. He swung the short *lupara* like a club, trying to clear a path through them, but they closed in around him and he fell, roaring his anger as the silent women kicked at him, striking his face and wounded shoulder. He howled in pain and then in fear as kitchen knives appeared from within the folds of their skirts. They slashed at him as he curled up, hands protecting his neck. The women kept at him, knife blades turning red. A last gurgling howl rose up from the ground as one of them found his throat. The frenzy ended and they stepped back from the widening pool of blood, watching Muschetto twitch one last time.

"Jesus," Harry said quietly. Nick appeared in the doorway, lowering his Sten as he took in the scene in the street.

"He was hiding in a closet," Nick said. "Got the jump on us."

"But not on them," I said, watching the women clean their knives. They did not seem to have a problem with revenge.

CHAPTER TWENTY-SEVEN

IT WAS QUITE A party. Muschetto stiffened out on the street as Nick's relatives kissed us on both cheeks. They hadn't known why their menfolk had been held hostage and seemed to care less about that than being visited by an American relative and his pals. Bottles of wine were opened as glass was swept and blood mopped up from the kitchen floor. Carlo was a favorite of the women, who pinched his cheek after they kissed him. He blushed: a shy killer. One of Gaetano's men had brought Sciafani in, and he sat across from me, polite to the family but subdued. Family reunions were probably not high on his list right now.

"Ask if they've seen Legs or Vito," I said to Nick, as one of the gray-haired women put bread and olives in front of us.

From his seat of honor at the head of the table, Nick said, "That's my great-aunt Lucia! And this is my great-uncle Andrea!" He slapped the shoulder of the man sitting to his right.

"That's great, Nick. I'm glad to meet him. Now ask about Legs and Vito."

He leaned over to Andrea and started talking, gesturing with his hands, pointing to us, his relatives, Carlo and Gaetano, and everyone else. Between the gestures and the names sprinkled throughout the conversation, I could almost understand him. We had been sent by

Don Calo to rescue them. Muschetto was a bandit, recruited by Vito Genovese to do something Don Calo had no part of. There was arguing back and forth between the men, disagreement about some detail or other. Great-Aunt Lucia cut in on that exchange and everyone nodded.

"This is Lucia and Andrea's home. Vito came here once," Nick said. "Vito told them Don Calo had a favor to ask of the family, and he needed to speak with all the men. When they gathered here, Legs and Muschetto showed up and took them prisoner: Andrea, his two brothers, and four nephews. They kicked Lucia out. She went and got the other women and they stood in the street for three days, watching the house."

"They underestimated the women," Harry said. "I have made the same mistake."

Nick translated and the men laughed while the women nodded knowingly.

"So Vito hasn't been here since? What about Legs?" I asked.

"Right," Nick said. "Legs came by every day except today. Yesterday, actually."

"That could mean they're making their move on the payroll."

"But remember Vito needs me, to crack the safes," Nick said. "That can't be it, unless he was planning to pick us up at Don Calo's today."

"You may not be needed yet," I said. "If they're pulling the safes up from the bottom of the bay, the occupation scrip will be soaking wet. The paymaster might have to open up the safes and dry the paper first."

"Right," Harry said. "There will be guards everywhere with the money loose like that. Vito would want to wait until it was locked up again so the paymaster would relax his guard."

"Do you think they would have let my family go?" Nick asked.

Sciafani said. "The threat to your family would keep you from informing on them after the robbery as well."

Nick looked into his wineglass, lost in his thoughts again.

"We've got to get back to Gela," I said. "And stop them."

"That's not all I want to do to them," Nick said.

He spoke some more with his uncle and the other relatives gathered in the kitchen. He slammed his fist into his palm twice as he named Vito and Legs. He outlined a plan, and everyone seemed to approve.

It was after two in the morning. We were to wait until first light, not wanting to take a chance on dark roads with fully armed Germans, Italians, and Americans between us and our destination. Lucia gave us blankets and we tried to sleep in the other room as Nick's relatives kept up the celebration in the kitchen. But the sound of laughter and the clink of glasses and plates carried through the house. I liked it. It filled my mind with thoughts of home, Dad and Uncle Dan and a few buddies in the kitchen, Mom fussing over everyone, while my kid brother Danny and I tried to behave ourselves so no one would kick us out when the men started telling their stories. Funny stories about comic crooks and crooked politicians, sad stories about men they knew who had died—cops, soldiers, IRA men. It was all the same, I thought at first. When I was too young to understand, I thought we Irish were always at war with someone. The English landlords, the Protestants up north, the Kaiser and his soldiers, the criminals in Boston—in my child's mind they were all ranked against us, but I wasn't scared because between Dad and Uncle Dan, they'd fought them all and came home every day to sit at the kitchen table, Mom laughing with them or frowning at their curses.

And here I was, at war with Fascists and bandits. What kind of stories would I have to tell?

I tried to settle in and get some shut-eye. I should have felt satisfied with myself. Hell, I had regained my memory, completed my mission, found Harry and Nick, and now we were about to head back to the American lines. Something felt wrong, though. When I finally slept, I dreamed I was in Algiers, searching for Diana in the Hotel St. George. But I couldn't find her anywhere. The girl of my dreams was gone.

The floor was hard, the morning cold, but the espresso was hot and the warm kitchen cozy as Great-Aunt Lucia wrapped fresh bread in a cloth for us. She looked about eighty, but no worse for wear after knifing a bandit and staying up all night drinking wine and baking bread. I willingly kissed her goodbye and submitted to Andrea's whiskered double-cheek pecks. Nick, Harry, and I loaded what gear we had into the Fiat. Gaetano had told Nick we could have the car. He'd take his men back to Villalba in the truck.

Someone had removed Muschetto during the night, but his blood-
stains were dark beneath my feet as I opened the door to the Fiat.
Sciafani stood between the two vehicles, unsure where to go. I hadn't
thought about it, but he was close to home now, and it was time for us
to part.

"Enrico," I said. "What are you going to do?"

"I am not sure," he said. "I cannot go with them to Villalba."

He looked at the ground, then up and down the narrow street. He
was silent for a while, and I waited for him to speak.

"I do not think I can stay in Sicily anymore. There is too much
pain here. I don't want to live the life Don Calo has charted out for me.
It is not the way to honor my father."

"Do you think he meant it, about killing you if he ever saw you
again?" I asked.

"Yes. It was only the romantic notion of my father as a worthy
adversary that kept him from killing me. If he held back again, it would
be seen as a sign of weakness, and that is one thing he cannot afford."

"Come with us then."

"Where?"

"Away from here."

Sciafani looked at the rust-colored stain on the street and nodded,
his fingers rubbing his chin as he came to his decision. Without a word,
he got into the Fiat. Evidently, we were going in the right direction.

"*Un minuto,*" Gaetano said, beckoning Nick and me with his finger. He huddled with Nick, speaking low and fast, gesturing with open
hands, glancing at me several times.

"He says that we must leave Vito Genovese alone," Nick said.
"Don Calo instructed Gaetano to bring Vito to him if he found him
here. Vito is an honored member of the society, and he must not be
turned over to the authorities. If we find him, we are to let him go.
Gaetano is instructed to make Don Calo's apology, but that is the way
it must be."

"Or else?"

Nick consulted with Gaetano.

"Don Calo considers this part of his agreement with you. If you
break it, it will be on your head."

"We're only talking about Vito?"

"Yes. Joey Laspada is not an honored member of the society here."

"Do we have any choice?" I asked Nick.

"Don Calo is used to getting his way. If he doesn't, he'll back out of the deal."

Let Vito go? I knew I would find him sniffing around the two million in occupation scrip, and I hated the idea of watching him go free. But maybe he wouldn't be so free if Don Calo was angry with him. Especially since I had told Don Calo there was three million involved, not two. Maybe. Maybe not. We didn't have a choice, so what did it matter?

"OK," I said, nodding to Gaetano. I got into the car.

"What's going on?" Harry asked from the backseat.

"Sciafani's coming with us," I said, knowing that's wasn't what he meant.

"I can see that, he's bloody well sitting next to me. I mean all that with Gaetano. You two don't look happy."

I started the car, wondering how to tell Harry that the guy responsible for Banville's death, among others, was going to walk. Yet I had no real evidence against Vito to bring to the army. I realized that I hadn't been thinking about evidence, I'd been thinking about vengeance. Finding Vito, shooting him. Another Villard, my own retribution for a killer the law couldn't, or wouldn't, touch.

I backed the car into the street and put it into gear. I felt the tension in my gut ease as I understood that, for whatever reason, the responsibility for bringing Vito Genovese to justice, for his punishment, now lay with others. The army or Don Calo. Not me. I still had Legs to worry about, but Vito was off the books.

"I am happy," I said. "I don't have to dig two graves."

Nick explained what Gaetano had said and gave directions to the road south. Harry fumed, swearing a blue streak. Sciafani looked out the window, a smile turning up his lips, watching the landscape of his home disappear. I drove and whistled a happy tune. About ten minutes later, I laughed out loud.

"What's so funny?" Nick asked.

"Never mind. Too hard to explain."

It was. I'd been thinking about my father's advice about Al.

Remember who you are.

I'd thought about that a dozen times in the last few days without realizing that was exactly, literally, what I needed to do. Whatever I had done about Villard, it didn't mean I had to keep going down that path. Right or wrong, that had had to be done. It was personal. But it didn't define who I was. I did that. It was the very thing I had been worried about when I'd awakened with my memory gone. Was I a killer? An assassin?

The answer was no. All I had to do was remember. Remember who I was, even if I didn't recall everything that had happened to me.

But now I did remember everything, including who I was. I knew which of the three kinds of people in the world I was. I knew the world could throw a mean curve ball at me and at the ones I loved, but that wouldn't change me unless I let it.

Thanks, Dad, I whispered to myself, as I put the rising sun to my left and headed back to our lines.

CHAPTER ▪ TWENTY-EIGHT

"HOW'S THE LEG?" I asked Harry, glancing into the rear-view mirror.

"It hurts. Maybe your doctor friend should look at it," Harry said in a low angry voice. He hadn't spoken a word since we'd left Cammarata, unhappy with the Mafia edict that left Vito Genovese safe beyond our reach.

"I would be glad to," said Sciafani.

"Bugger off," Harry said. "I've had enough of you Mafia bastards. Your pals kill my first mate, and now we can't touch Genovese because he's such an honored man on this bloody island. Get me back to civilization."

"I am not *mafiusu*, and they are not my friends," Sciafani said, holding a hand over his heart as if he were swearing a holy oath.

"Who the bloody hell are you then?" Harry demanded, echoing my own thoughts. "Don Calo killed your father, you killed his man, he protects the killer of my friend, and you embrace like blood brothers. Who are you people anyway?"

"It is complicated to be Sicilian," Sciafani said, his hand dropping to his lap. "Let me know if you wish me to look at your wound, but I cannot answer your questions." He turned to stare out the window again, his eyes focusing on distant hills.

Silence filled the car as dust, hot air, and recriminations swirled between us. Time passed, and we descended through dry fields of harvested wheat, the yellowing stalks arrayed like soldiers cut down in ranks. Switchbacks snaked up and down the mountain roads that slowly took us south toward the American lines. Toward Vito and Legs, Charlotte, and all their plots and schemes. I had to protect the promise I'd gotten from Don Calo to intervene with the Sicilian troops, and at the same time do what I could to obtain justice for Roberto, Banville, and even Rocko. Glancing again at Harry, still grim faced, I made a note to keep him away from Vito Genovese. I couldn't let him take his own private revenge.

Damn, I sounded like Harding: complete the mission, and the hell with your personal feelings. I was sure Harding had them, but they weren't on display for all to see. I considered myself his complete opposite, but now I was thinking like him. I couldn't help it. I'd lost myself in Sicily, and as I discovered my own identity the grit and heat and passion of the island had worked their way under my skin. God help me, but I understood Sciafani and Don Calo, their brutal and honorable ways. Sometimes you had to stand and fight, bloody your knuckles, take a life. And sometimes you had to make peace with the past, even when harm had been done. I understood Don Calo, turning the brutal events of his earlier life into a romantic tale of bandits in the hills, Robin Hood reluctantly taking the life of his great rival, sending away his child and then waiting a generation for his return, to remind him of the man he had once been.

And Sciafani? What did he take from the embrace? If his father was defined in death by his enemy, then Sciafani would be forever defined by the man who had let him live. His father gave him life, but so did Don Calo. The old man with blood on his hands had washed a bit of it away. It must have made the old man feel good, but what about Sciafani?

Vito, he was easy to understand. The Mob was all about money and power, and Vito generated enough of both. Don Calo wanted to protect his cut, so Vito was safe. I didn't like it, but at least it made sense. No different than an insurance company or a car dealer rewarding their top salesmen. In the same way, giving up Legs was no different than laying off your most unproductive man. Good business.

I didn't necessarily like understanding this, but there you were. A cop gets pretty close to the criminal, close enough that the lines can get blurred. Like with me and Al. Trick was to remember who you were while understanding who the other guy was. I figured that would have been the next lesson from Dad if the war hadn't interrupted things. I wished I hadn't had to learn that one the hard way.

"Look," Nick said, pointing ahead.

"What?" asked Harry, craning his head forward.

"Town up ahead," I said. "Looks like a bunker covering the road."

"They wouldn't shoot at a car, would they?" Harry asked.

"Only if they're trigger-happy or Germans or Fascist militia," I said, considering the possibilities.

I decided the best thing to do was keep going. The town was gathered under a church steeple on the highest point of a small hilltop. Brown stone buildings, faded orange roof tiles, cisterns on nearly every roof. It looked like every other Sicilian village we'd driven through, even down to the concrete bunker at the edge of town. I downshifted, keeping my eye on the bunker's long narrow slit, imagining a gunner tracking us with his machine gun, sweaty finger on trigger, waiting for the perfect shot, a burst to the engine and one through the windshield. That's how I'd do it.

I drove faster. I couldn't help myself.

Nobody shot at us. I stopped even with the bunker. No gunner, no machine gun, no Fascists, no Sicilian soldiers.

"Could it be?" Nick asked.

"Maybe they were ordered elsewhere," Harry said.

"Or perhaps Don Calo has already kept his word," said Sciafani.

"We'll see," Harry said, sarcasm weighing down his voice.

We did see. Over the next few hours, we drove through towns with deserted entrenchments, empty bunkers and machine-gun nests with weapons idly pointed toward the sky, as if in surrender. Or indifference. Rifles and shovels lay strewn across the ground. Antitank guns sat alone, crates of ammunition stacked around them, abandoned like kids' toys at the beach.

"Well, I'll be damned," Harry said as we crossed a narrow bridge, the snouts of two antitank guns pointed harmlessly at our backs.

"Who won't be?" I asked. Nobody answered.

The road erupted in front of us, a blast of fire, smoke, and dirt that I drove through before I could hit the brakes. The smoke blinded me and I struggled to keep the car on the road, but it hit the crater, swerved to the left and rolled over. I coughed and gasped for air. I heard shouts and grunts, crunching metal, and smelled the sharp odor of gasoline, all in the split second before I passed out, with barely enough time to hope I wouldn't burn alive.

I heard someone calling my name. The smell of burned rubber coated my nostrils and throat as the sound of my name mingled with the crackling of flames. I panicked, not wanting to be toasted to a crisp inside a tiny Fiat. I fought to raise my eyelids, to get my body to move, but part of me wanted to lie there a few moments more, fire be damned.

"Billy!"

I recognized the voice and opened my eyes. I was on the ground at the side of the road.

"Billy, are you all right?" It was Kaz. His face was scorched black, his sandy-colored hair singed and smoking. His eyes were wide and desperate, and I knew how I had gotten out of the car.

"Think so. Good to see you, buddy." My voice came out a choked, harsh whisper.

I coughed some more as Kaz pulled me up by the shoulders. I hacked and spit black soot.

"What happened? The others?" I looked around and saw the car in flames, churning thick black smoke into the sky.

"They are all fine. Fine," said Kaz. "We got everyone out before the car's gas tank went up."

"You look like it was a close shave," I said.

"This little fella saved your butt," a sergeant in tanker's overalls said, chewing on an unlit cigar as he stood in back of Kaz. "You were on the bottom, with the car on its side. My crew got the other three out, then the gas tank went up. He climbed in and pulled you out, just in goddamn time too."

I got up on my knees and waited to see if I could stay there. That worked out well, so I tested my memory. Name, hometown, rank, it was all there. Time to stand. I took Kaz's hand, and he winced.

"Just a little burn, Billy. It is nothing," Kaz said, gracing me with a bashful smile.

I let go of his hand, startled by the sight of the angry red skin beneath his blackened shirt cuff. I took in the scene around me, awareness edging the fogginess out of my brain. Nick, Harry, and Sciafani leaned against a jeep, talking with some GIs and drinking from canteens. A couple of Sherman tanks were pulled off the road behind them, guarding our flanks, while a half-track sat in the road, a GI manning the .30 caliber machine gun, scanning the sky for German planes.

"You were looking for us," I concluded, as Kaz's presence with the patrol dawned on me.

"Major Harding sent out patrols toward Villalba, but the defenses were too strong," Kaz said, the words spinning out as he rapidly explained. "Then yesterday a patrol reported no resistance on the main road to Mussomeli and Villalba, so I asked him for permission to look for you on the back roads. I thought you would come in that way, rather than the main road."

"Smart thinking, Kaz. But what was the explosion?"

"That was me, Lieutenant," the tanker sergeant said, without much in the way of apology. "We heard a vehicle coming, and it looked like an Italian staff car, so I told my gunner to fire. Lucky for you he has a hard time with moving targets."

"Yeah, well, if I was really lucky you wouldn't have fired on us in the first place."

He spat, and turned away, yelling to his crew to mount up. That was my dad's response anytime he was told he'd been lucky not to get hurt any worse than he was. Now I understood why he said it. It was damn irritating to hear about my luck from a guy who had fired on me from inside a Sherman tank.

"Nice guy," I said.

"Well, he didn't like being ordered to drive straight up these roads, past other Shermans that were not so lucky. We all saw the bunkers and antitank guns. But now they're deserted, except for a few stray Germans. General Patton is halfway to Palermo already. You did it, Billy, you did it. Didn't you?"

"Yes. I spoke to Don Calo and he saw reason, once he laid eyes on

Luciano's handkerchief. It was strange, but I'll tell you about that later. It looks like he actually managed to get the Sicilians to vanish."

I don't know if I was surprised. But it was a shock to see how complete the desertions had been. Driving north, Italian troops had been digging in everywhere. Now, at the snap of Don Calo's fingers, they had disappeared.

"All right, let's get back to Major Harding," Kaz said. He gave a hand signal to the tanker sergeant and pointed down the road.

"Are you in command here?" I asked.

"Yes, Billy, I am," Kaz said, raising his singed eyebrow. "It is quite exciting."

A few months ago, Kaz had been translating documents at a desk in London. The quiet Polish academic with a bad heart was the last guy you would expect to see leading an armored combat patrol in the hills of Sicily. But here he was, ordering Sherman tanks around and rescuing me from the flames. It just showed that you never knew who was going to step up and put himself in harm's way for you, and who was going to turn and run.

Harry handed me a canteen, and I washed the soot out of my mouth, spitting onto the dusty road. Harry and I piled into the jeep with Kaz and his driver, while Sciafani and Nick climbed aboard the half-track. The vehicles roared to life, the tracks grinding up the roadside as they reversed and turned. The little Fiat burned away, the ferocity of the fire fading as the flames consumed the gasoline. Kaz had not been able to save Daphne from another burning car not too long ago. I was glad for his sake, as well as my own, that he had been able to pull me out, and did not have to witness another awful immolation.

Kaz had given no indication that he was thinking about the past, and perhaps the time had come when he could experience something like this without his first thought being of her death. Right now he seemed to be focused on the mission. Memory is such a strange thing. I had spent the past few days struggling to remember, glad of every little recollection and image that popped into my mind. Kaz probably prayed every night to forget most of the things he remembered.

"It's good to see you, Kaz," I said, speaking loudly over the sound of the jeep racing down the road. I put my hand on his shoulder and squeezed.

"You are remembering?" he asked me, looking over his shoulder. His voice was low, with a slight quaver to it. Then I knew I'd been wrong. He was in control, but he hadn't forgotten a thing. His eyes were moist, maybe from the dust, maybe from the pain of recollection. That charred frame of the little Riley Imp was burned into his brain, never to be forgotten. He needed to know that I remembered it all too.

"Yes, Kaz. I remember everything," I said. As I did, I thought of my father leaning close to me to say something important, his words a whisper brushing against my cheek. The dust got in my eyes too.

CHAPTER · TWENTY-NINE

"LIEUTENANT ANDREWS IS DEAD," Major Harding said, starting off my day with bad news.

"Throat slit?" I asked, not surprised that another sap involved in this mess had stopped breathing.

"Hard to tell," Harding said. "He got caught in the open by a couple of Messerschmitts. Truck he was in exploded."

"Was he alone?"

"No. We found him in the back of the truck. Two GIs in the cab, also dead."

Harding's answers were crisp, like his uniform. Even in the field, his brown wool shirt looked as if it had been ironed. Actually, Harding looked as if he had been starched and ironed at birth, like the uniform stood to attention when he put it on. He sat straight, his torso at a perfect angle, his boots polished, the few gray hairs at his temples evenly distributed, though there might have been more of those gray hairs than when I'd first met him in England a year ago.

"Who killed them?" I asked.

"Probably someone named Fritz or Hans. I do not think the Germans are in on this conspiracy," Kaz said. Everyone's a comedian.

"Did anyone see the attack?" I asked.

"No," Harding answered in that patient tone reserved for explaining the obvious to thick-headed lieutenants. "The bullet-ridden burning truck was a clue, though."

Another dead body in another flaming wreck. I saw Kaz's eyes flicker to the floor and close for a second. Then he was back. He had only been half kidding about the Germans.

I leaned back in my chair and looked out over the Valley of the Temples. Rows of olive trees curved over the hills around us, silvery leaves bright in the morning light. The view would have been pretty if it hadn't been for the 20mm antiaircraft gun set up several yards in front of us and the fuel cans shaded by camouflage netting strung from the farmhouse. The night before, Kaz had taken us to Harding's headquarters outside of Agrigento, a small farmhouse between the city and the ancient ruins. I'd reported to Harding, telling him everything from waking up in the field hospital to all the things I'd gradually remembered. When I told him about Don Calo and the deserted defenses in the mountain towns, he pointed to a map showing the advance of Patton's infantry and armor into the interior of the western portion of the island.

"You saved lives with this one, Boyle," he'd said. He'd patted me on the back and ordered me to get some sleep, which was his version of awarding me the Silver Star. That was six hours ago, and now I was trying to get enough coffee in me to stay awake and talk through our next priority—finding Legs and Vito before they could heist millions in occupation lire.

Harry, Kaz, and I sat outside with Harding, all of us on rough wooden straight-back chairs, arranged in a semicircle to take advantage of the view. It felt strange to be back here, my memory returned and the journey to Don Calo over, looking out at the Temple of Concordia where things had first gone so wrong. I was glad to see Harding and have him in charge of what happened to me. I sipped the hot coffee, ready for him to decide what our next move was, tired of days of making decisions on my own.

"OK, Boyle, if you're satisfied with the circumstances of Lieutenant Andrews's death, what's our next move?" Harding said, as if he'd read my thoughts. So much for the subordinate relaxing.

"First thing is to track down where the payroll is. I assume they've brought it up from the bottom of the bay by now. We head to where it is, then watch for our Mafia pals."

"Makes sense," Harding said. "First, we secure the payroll. Then find out who Charlotte is. I understand that we need to let Genovese walk, but that doesn't mean we can't squeeze some information out of him first."

"What will happen to Nick?" Harry asked.

Nick was being held in a locked storeroom in an outbuilding behind the farmhouse. It wasn't the stockade, but he wasn't sipping coffee in the sun with us either.

"I'm not sure," said Harding. "He endangered the mission, even if I understand why he did it."

"He did deliver our request for cooperation to Don Calo," Harry said. "But without that yellow handkerchief, the old man wouldn't listen to him no matter what he said."

"He could have shot me at the temple and taken it," I said. Would that argument help or hurt Nick?

"I have to think about it," Harding said. "He could be court-martialed or simply sent back to the States. We can't trust him with anything vital if he can be so easily manipulated."

Back to the States. For screwing up. Maybe that would make Nick happy or maybe he wanted a chance to prove himself. Me, I had to stay here since I had done such a great job. Indispensable me.

Indispensable. That made me think about Andrews again. Hutton and Andrews had both been in the Signals Company. The two of them must have been the communications link between Charlotte and the other conspirators. But how had they worked their part of the scheme?

"Where was Andrews when the truck was hit? Where was he headed?" I looked to Kaz and Harding. They had no answers.

"I have a report in the office," Harding said. "Is it important?"

"I have no idea," I said. "But it might indicate what they were up to. Was his outfit moving out? Were they under orders? Or was he on a joyride?"

Harding got the report and I read it.

"Says here they took a truck from the motor pool and were headed to Vittoria. No mention of orders. I know his Signals Company is still in its original location. All our phone wires are strung to their position at Gela."

"What does it mean?" asked Kaz. Vittoria was a couple of hours east of Gela, past Biazza Ridge.

"Maybe nothing. If it had been official business, I'd have less doubt about Andrews being alive when they were hit. But the way people have been turning up dead, I wouldn't be surprised to find out he was already a corpse in the back of that truck. Maybe they didn't need him anymore."

"Why wouldn't they?" Harding asked.

"They wouldn't if Charlotte was already in Sicily. Maybe Charlotte can run his own communications now. Maybe Andrews got cold feet, or maybe that was someone else's body in the truck. I don't know, but it makes me wonder."

"What's in Vittoria?" Kaz asked. He was getting pretty good at this detective stuff.

"Let's put that number one on the list," I said. "Could be important."

"One more thing," Harding said. "What about your Dr. Sciafani? Where does he fit in?"

"He helped me when I needed it," I said.

"He could have gotten you killed too, by knifing Don Calo's *caporegime*," Harding noted. Harry grunted in agreement.

"He wasn't acting rationally," I said. "He fell apart and found out the hard way it wasn't in his nature to be a killer. He was a big help to me, no matter what else he did. I don't think I could have gotten to Don Calo without him. But he can't stay in Sicily, that's for sure."

"What do you want me to do?" Harding asked.

"Can you get him to the States?"

"Only way to do that is via a POW camp. We're not accepting enemy prisoners as immigrants."

"But he's not a prisoner. He was paroled, he has the paperwork to prove it. Why couldn't he go back on a hospital ship? He's a doctor, he could help with the wounded."

Harding stroked his chin, struggling with the notion of bending army regulations. "I don't know about the States, but I could easily get him to North Africa. We have lots of Italian prisoners there. They need medical care. He could work for us, in one of the POW hospitals."

"He wouldn't be a prisoner?" I asked.

"No. He'd work for AMGOT. They hire many civilians. And he

would be out of Don Calo's reach, and once he's on staff he'd have a better chance of making it to the States."

"As long as his boss isn't named Charlotte," I said.

"Then find Charlotte. I'll work on getting Sciafani to Tunisia. You let him know he's to stay put for now."

"OK," I said, standing. "How about I check out what Andrews was up to back at the Signals Company? Kaz and Harry can track down the location of the payroll." I had a hunch we might end up in the same place.

"Fine," Harding said. "Take a jeep there now. They can contact the 45th Division headquarters by radio to find out where the payroll is. All of you report back here tonight or radio in if you can't. If you find these mobsters, bring them back too. As our guests, of course. Mr. Genovese can stay for dinner."

"Will you wait until we return to decide about Nick?" Harry asked. He and Nick had grown close during their stay with Don Calo, and he was clearly on Nick's side. It also helped that Nick hadn't pointed a gun at Harry. I wasn't so sure, although I thought the best punishment for Nick would be to keep him here, not to send him packing—home.

"He's not going anywhere for a while," Harding said. "I might be able to use him as a translator, with an MP posted at the door."

"Fair enough," Harry said.

Fair had nothing to do with it, but Harry had his illusions. If life were fair, Vito Genovese wouldn't have a free pass and Roberto would still be alive, working on a plan to get to America. Hutton wouldn't have taken a bullet in the head, and Rocko would be alive, serving a sentence in the stockade for selling army inventory on the black market. Fair was a fairy tale.

I left after talking to Nick and Sciafani, trying to sound upbeat about their respective futures. Freshly shaved, in a clean uniform, with the familiar feel of a Colt .45 automatic at my side, I pulled onto the main road to Gela and let the breeze blow away the heat and dust of the day. I had given the Beretta to Kaz as a souvenir; he liked having a backup gat. Or maybe he liked saying *gat*, rolling the hard gangster slang around his Oxford-educated tongue. Me, I liked the feel of my new clothes, the open road, and the sure knowledge of where I was going—all things that had been in short supply recently. A medic had removed the stitches from my arm and cleaned out the cut on my head. It was a relief not to sport white gauze anymore.

The open road soon lost its allure as I choked in the smoke and grit of a convoy of deuce-and-a-half trucks. Traffic crawled along, and I was glad of the goggles that had been left on the passenger seat. I tied a handkerchief, plain army-issue khaki, over my nose and mouth, and ate dust for a dozen slow miles.

I tried to think things through, wondering how I could get a line on Charlotte. Was he already in Sicily, or still back in North Africa? Some AMGOT staff were already here, I knew, setting up basic services in liberated towns. They started with burying the dead, working their way up from there, helping to establish a normal life for civilians while at the same time insuring the army had everything it needed. That meant food, transportation, road and rail access, all the things civilians wanted. It wasn't an easy job, and it required lots of patience both with our own bureaucracy and with civilian complaints. Sort of like Boston politics, but in the middle of a war zone.

So, how to find Charlotte, a bad apple in a big barrel? I had hoped to interrogate Lieutenant Andrews, but the Luftwaffe, or somebody, had eliminated that option. It was too convenient. But that didn't stop me from craning my neck in every direction, scanning the skies for enemy planes. Our convoy would be a juicy target, and I didn't want to get caught at the tail end of a strafing run.

It would be great if Harry and Kaz found Vito and Legs, and brought them in without a fight. I'd like to question Vito myself. I'd bet he would give up Charlotte in return for his freedom or his life.

I wondered about Nick. Would Vito still be after him either as revenge for killing his henchmen in order to free his family, or for his services as a yegg? Not the latter, I concluded. All those lira notes had to be dried out. If they were left in the safes, they would turn to moldy paste in no time. Someone had to have opened those safes by now. So somewhere in Sicily, two million dollars' worth of occupation scrip was drying in the sun. In Vittoria, where Andrews had been headed? Why would a communications guy go there? I needed to know what was in Vittoria. And if Andrews had started the trip dead or alive.

CHAPTER • THIRTY

WITH GELA AND Porto Empedocle in our hands, not much was still coming in via the beachhead. The mountains of supplies were mostly gone, moved inland with the troops. I drove past the field hospital where I'd awakened, the single tent now multiplied by four, all connected and marked with large red crosses on a white background. It was quieter now, no rush of wounded on stretchers, no kids left on the ground to die alone. Maybe making a deal with the devil was worth it if it kept a few GIs out of that place and above ground.

Was Signora Patane still coughing up blood in her bed? Or had she died in the night, unaware of the quiet Don Calo had ensured for her last moments? I couldn't understand why anyone, even a crime lord like Don Calo, had to be convinced to avoid bloodshed. Why had I endured all this to convince Don Calo to save the lives and homes of his own people? It seemed the more power people had, the less they were likely to use it to make something good happen, as if they needed to bank it for a rainy day. I hadn't seen it rain in Sicily yet.

The Signals Company was easy to find. More wire had been strung, and tall poles had been erected along the shore road to carry it. All lines led to the communications center, which sprouted aerials and antennas from tents, trailers, and trucks. I parked the jeep and looked for an officer.

The sides of the tents were rolled up to allow the sea breeze to provide ventilation. GIs scurried around tables piled high with communications gear, others sat at switchboards and radios, listening and transmitting with an intensity that was electric. Static crackled in the air.

"Can I help you, sir?"

I nearly jumped, but instead managed to turn and see who had surprised me. It was an MP, his white belt and painted helmet gleaming. I remembered all the things Dad and Uncle Dan had told me about the military police in the last war, but decided not to hold it against this guy.

"I'm looking for the officer in charge."

"And who might you be?"

I studied him for a moment while trying to perfect the kind of look Harding gave me when he wanted me to shake in my boots. He was a buck sergeant, a bit on the short side, which probably accounted for his chosen branch of service. As an MP, he could be a big guy, even at five foot two.

"I would be a lieutenant, looking for another officer, *Sergeant*," I said, leaning on his rank to make my point as obvious as possible.

"No problem, sir. I can take you to the CO, but my orders are to check out everyone entering the area. We've had some trouble lately."

"What sort of trouble, Sergeant?" I looked over his shoulder and saw several other MPs patrolling the area. I picked up another one inside the main tent. This was more than a normal guard detail.

"If you don't mind, Lieutenant, tell me what you're doing here first."

"I'm Lieutenant Billy Boyle, attached to Seventh Army HQ." I turned to show him my worn shoulder patch. "I'm here to ask a few questions about Lieutenant Andrews."

"He bought it a few days ago, so he won't be able to help you, Lieutenant Boyle."

He started to walk away, dismissing me as if I were the enlisted man and he the officer. Not caring much for officers above the rank of second lieutenant—which meant all others—I would have admired his style if I hadn't clearly said I had questions about Andrews, not for him. I decided to try a little Harding out on him.

"Sergeant!" I barked, loud enough to draw stares and send privates scurrying out of my line of sight. "Stand at attention!"

"Yessir." He did, but without turning to face me. Well, my fault for not giving the order. I walked around him, taking my time and studying his uniform. It was clean, his boots were polished, and his haircut recent. He was braced, chin up, chest out, the perfect example of a tin soldier.

"Have you put in for transfer to a line company, Sergeant . . . what's your name?"

"Cerrito, sir. No, I haven't. I don't understand."

"You don't understand, what?" I linked my hands behind my back and marched back and forth in front of him, playing the martinet and enjoying it a bit too much.

"I don't understand, sir."

"Well, I'll explain, Sergeant Cerrito. I bet you've been itching to get up to the front lines. I bet Bouncing Betty mines and German 88s don't scare you one bit. But your CO can't do without you, right? So you figure to piss me off enough to get you transferred. You probably figured it out as soon as you saw my HQ patch."

"Bouncing Betty? Sir?"

"A mine, Sergeant. You set it off and it launches up about waist-high and explodes. Good news is that it hardly ever kills you."

"OK, sir. I don't need to hear the bad news, I get it." Cerrito was still at attention, but a line of sweat was working its way down his temples. He spoke through gritted teeth, and I knew he was as afraid of the other men's hearing him give in as he was of making Betty's acquaintance.

"Stand at ease, Sergeant Cerrito, and let's start over." I clapped him on the shoulder so everyone could see we were pals.

"You look like you could use a cup of joe, Lieutenant. How about we sit and talk?"

I must have had dog tired written all over my face. Coffee and a seat that wasn't in a vehicle driving on a bad road sounded fine.

"Lead the way, Sarge."

My new best friend crooked his finger at me and led me over tent pegs and lines drawn taut. Eyes from inside the tents glanced out from beneath canvas flaps and quickly looked away. Cerrito began to whistle a tune, showing how casual this all was. "Mister Five by Five," a song about a singer in Count Basie's band who was as wide as he was tall. I remembered that Mister Five by Five had quite a line of jive, and wondered what made Cerrito pick that tune.

He was a pretty good whistler, and I was humming the tune myself by the time we came to a long tent with all the flaps rolled up. I could tell it was a mess tent by the smell, which wasn't a compliment to the chef. Burnt toast, soapy water, and soggy eggs combined their odors into a single nauseating smell. A GI dumped a garbage can full of greasy water in front of us and we sidestepped the scummy remnants of a few hundred washed-out mess kits. Breakfast was over, and the cooks were cleaning up and preparing lunch. Dishing out army chow to GIs who had to wait in long lines for it was probably the most disheartening job on the island. No one had much good to say about dehydrated potatoes, eggs, and milk.

Cerrito nodded to a cook in a white T-shirt and apron who had the look of another noncom. The cook nodded back, ash from the cigarette hanging from his lips flavoring whatever was in the aluminum pot he was stirring.

"Hungry?" said Cerrito. "Sir?"

"Coffee will do," I said.

We poured steaming, thick coffee out of a pot scorched black from the embers of a dying fire. It smelled like wood smoke and eggshells. We sat on crates of U.S. Army Field Ration C under camouflage netting, the dappled shade a relief from the increasing heat.

"So who ordered you to give the cold shoulder to anyone asking questions?" I asked, blowing on the hot coffee.

"Just doing my job, Lieutenant," Cerrito said.

"Does your job include protecting a murderer?"

"Who said anything about murder? We're here to protect the equipment and personnel, that's all. That means limiting information about what goes on here."

"Who are you protecting them from?"

"Thieves, black marketeers, you name it. The Mafia is supposed to be active around here too," Cerrito said.

"Yeah, so I heard. Who told you all this? Who sent you here?"

"Listen, Lieutenant, you got me in a tough spot," Cerrito said, moving closer and leaning in as he glanced around to see if anyone was listening. "You're only a second louie, but you're from HQ, so maybe you could send me wherever you want. But it was a major who gave me my orders, and they were to keep everyone away from Signals

Company, and not to answer any questions. I asked what the problem was, and he told me about thieves stealing communications gear, and how we had to keep a lid on things. That's all. If I spill more to you, then I'm in dutch with the major."

I drank the coffee. Cerrito was nervous, but not big-league nervous. That comment about the Mafia would not have come out so easily if he were involved in any of this. There was no tell, no flickering of the eyes, no rubbing the nose, no involuntary gesture to show he was concerned about how that statement would sound to me. I had to gamble that he was being straight with me and guilty of nothing more than being a pompous MP afraid of being sent to the front. That meant I had to scare him more than the major did.

"I don't think you need to worry about him, Sarge," I said, giving him a knowing smile. "Didn't you think it was odd that a major from AMGOT was giving orders to guard a Signals Company?"

"How did you know that?" Cerrito's eyes widened, as if I had guessed the card he'd picked out of a deck.

"You don't think I happened to stop by today, do you? You look too smart for that."

"I did think about it, but the army doesn't always make sense, does it?"

"No," I agreed. "But in this case, you were on the right track. Who else knew about the orders?"

"Besides Major Elliott?"

Bingo.

"Yeah. Besides him," I said.

"Captain Stanton, CO of the Signals Company. No one else."

"OK, Sarge, that's a help. Now I want you to keep this conversation between us. Can you do that?"

"Sure I can, sir."

Damn straight he would. He was willing to let the officers fight it out among themselves.

"Good. I don't see any reason to include your name in my report. So far, anyway."

By the time I finished my coffee he was ready to give up his grandmother if it would get me out of his hair quicker. Cerrito even took my mess tin and washed it out for me. Major John Elliott, Civil Affairs

Officer, had originally been with AMGOT HQ in Syracuse, but was now in Gela, as CAO in charge of the Agrigento and Caltanissetta provinces. It put him right in the thick of things. I listened to Cerrito whistle again as he walked away. This time it was "Shoo-Shoo Baby" by the Andrews Sisters, about a sailor saying goodbye to his girl. I couldn't read much into that one, but damned if he wasn't a good whistler.

CHAPTER ▪ THIRTY-ONE

"I'M SORRY, LIEUTENANT, but you're not authorized to enter," the MP said. He held his carbine at port arms, blocking me from the tent. He was polite, none of Cerrito's initial insolence about him. I took him more seriously. Besides, he was bigger than me. A lot bigger.

"That's Captain Stanton in there, isn't it? I can see him from here," I said. A private had pointed him out to me moments before. Stanton had bright orange-red hair, a hard guy to miss with his helmet off.

"This is the Code Section, sir. Only authorized Signals personnel may enter. No exceptions, not even for lieutenants from headquarters."

I was sure that last part was sarcasm, but I let it go. He was a corporal, and I couldn't blame him for giving an officer a hard time when he could. And, like I said, he was big, a head taller than me and about twice as wide in the shoulders. The carbine looked like a peashooter in his massive hands.

"I'll come back later," I said. He wasn't interested in my plans for the day.

The next tent was larger than the code tent, and unguarded, so I decided to try my luck there. A crude sign painted on a plank of wood read MESSAGE SECTION. No one stopped me or even paid attention to me as I walked in. Despite the rolled-up canvas flaps, it was still hot inside. The tent was thirty feet long, with all sorts of tables lined up on either side—folding tables, a fancy dining-room table, a door on a couple of sawhorses—all holding communications equipment that crackled and buzzed with static. Wires and cables wound their way from one table to another, connecting to other cables that snaked out of the tent to the tall camouflaged antennas outside. A teletype machine clacked away while GIs sat at radios and switchboards, connected to someplace far more dangerous.

"Love Mike, this is Sugar Charlie. Over. Love Mike, this is Sugar Charlie. Over." The operator leaned over, pressing the headphones against his ear, straining to pick up a response. He slammed a pencil down on a blank pad, leaving a sharp mark like a ricochet.

"Words twice, Dog Victor, words twice," the guy next to him shouted, grimacing at the noises that made him ask for the transmission to be repeated. Mortars maybe?

Tension throbbed in the hot air trapped under the canvas roof, the smell of sweat, cigarette smoke, and stale coffee making me wish I hadn't come in.

"Anything from Love Mike?" A lieutenant, his sleeves rolled up above his elbows, leaned over the operator who had been listening for Love Mike's call sign.

"Nothing. Maybe their radio's out. Maybe."

"Dog Victor?" the officer asked the other GI.

"I couldn't make him out," he said, a weary sigh escaping his lips. "Explosions. Then gunfire. They're off the air."

"Where is all this going on?" I asked. The operators went back to their headphones as the lieutenant took notice of me for the first time.

"Gangi, north of Enna. Those call signs are the First and Second Battalions of the Sixteenth Regiment, and they're in trouble. Who the hell are you?"

"Billy Boyle, from Seventh Army HQ. I have a few questions about Lieutenant Andrews. You have a minute?"

"Sure," he said, extending his hand. "Frank Howard."

"You in charge here?"

"I have the Operations Platoon. We do most of the work here, except for coding. Captain Stanton takes care of that. Let's talk over here."

Howard was a second lieutenant, just like me, the lowest of the high. Close-cropped sandy hair, a sharp nose, and blue eyes with dark bags drooping below them. He had a distinct New York accent, the word "work" coming out "woik," the way the Three Stooges said it. I'd taken enough guff about my Boston accent that I didn't comment on it. I figured if he dropped a few r's, we added them in Boston, so it all worked out. Maybe we could argue baseball, though. That might be fun except that, last I heard, the Yankees were leading the division.

"You're from New York?"

"Neither of us can hide where we're from, can we?"

"You got that right. What did you do before the war?"

"Crane operator, mostly on the docks. My old man was in the union, so I got my card and managed to work fairly regular. How about you?"

"I was a cop. My dad too."

"Doesn't hurt to have connections, especially when times are tough."

True enough. Plenty of guys without them got no work at all during the Depression. Depending on family connections might not be fair, but it sure beat standing in a soup line.

Howard stopped to talk to a noncom and went over a sheet of orders with him. He had a few years on me and seemed firmly in control of this operation. He finished with the noncom and I followed him to the end of the tent, where he had his office set up. An empty spool of communications wire on its side supported a field desk, one of those portable boxes that opened to show a variety of drawers and cubbyholes, big enough to hold all the forms, stamps, and red tape needed to run a company. A field telephone and tools rested on another upturned spool, and a wool blanket hung heavily from a line strung from the end pole, half hiding a cot stuck in the corner of the tent.

"All the comforts of home," I said, as he sat in a swivel chair that looked like it came from a lawyer's office. He pointed to a crate of rations, 10-in-1, for me to perch on.

"Nothing like you boys at HQ enjoy, I'm sure," Howard said, lighting up a Lucky without offering me one, and blowing blue smoke above my head. He eyed me with a studied wariness that told me he hadn't found lieutenants from headquarters of much use in this war.

"I've been too busy lately to check out the accommodations," I said, ignoring the jibe. "I've been looking into something that may involve Lieutenant Andrews. Did you know him well?"

"We went through training together at Camp Gordon. He had the Supply Platoon, and did a fine job. We weren't close, but friendly enough. Poker games, baseball, stuff like that."

"You don't seem surprised I'm asking about him," I said.

"I knew somebody would, sooner or later."

"Why?"

"Because of what he did to my corporal. He got him killed."

I tried not to jump out of my seat. This was more than a lead, it was a real clue. "Do you mean Hutton? Aloysius Hutton?"

"Yeah, Hutton. He didn't like his first name much."

"I thought it was a good solid name," I said, thinking about what it had been like to be without a name, when I gave Hutton's to Clancy and Joe, and how speaking it had felt like ashes in my mouth.

"You know what happened to him?" Howard asked.

"I was there when he died," I said. "But first, tell me what Andrews had to do with getting him killed."

"So they even shanghaied a headquarters louie up on Biazza Ridge?" He gave out a sad laugh as he shook his head in disbelief at the thought of a staff officer on the front line. "Andrews was in charge of our supplies, obviously. Rocko Walters was a sergeant who ran the division's Supply Company, and I mean ran it. His CO was a goof-off who left him in charge of the whole show."

"I met Rocko too. When a paratroop officer came looking for men and supplies for Biazza Ridge, he vanished."

"Sounds like him. He was a rat, and someone finally caught up with him."

"I know," I said, letting it go at that.

"Anyway, Andrews had to go through Rocko for our requisitions. Back in Tunisia, I noticed radios starting to go missing. They were marked down as lost or broken, but I knew we'd never gotten them."

"Rocko was selling them on the black market," I suggested.

"That would have been my bet, but I couldn't prove it. I think Rocko gave Andrews a big payoff and did all the work, to get him hooked." He ground out his cigarette and spit out a piece of stray tobacco.

"And then put the squeeze on him," I said.

"You got it, junior."

"But how did Hutton fit in?"

"Hutton was a genius with radios and telephones. He could repair any damn thing, using spare parts from German equipment if he had to."

"But what would that mean to Rocko?"

"My guess is, it meant Rocko could communicate with anyone he wanted, anywhere."

"You mean anywhere you had wire strung, right?"

"Come with me. It's easier to show you," he said.

I followed him out to a smaller tent, about eight by ten feet, not far from Howard's office at the end of the Message Section tent. He pulled open the front flaps and tied them back. Except for a cot stuck in a corner, it looked like a warehouse for radio and telephone parts. A workbench at the far end was littered with tools, wire, tubes, and the guts of gadgets I couldn't identify. A switchboard sat next to an SCR-300 radio, and other electrical hardware encased in canvas or wood with U.S. Army markings stood stacked shoulder-high. I looked more closely at a device connected to the switchboard. It was a long wooden case with black dials set into it and connectors for a dozen or so wires along the top. The faceplate was marked in German.

"What the hell is all this?" I asked.

"Hutton was a loner, and he liked to tinker, so I gave him his own workshop. He came up with some ingenious stuff. This is a BD-72, our standard field switchboard. We can bring in twelve lines and route calls between them. But, like you said, it's only for calls on our wire. We can connect two of these and increase the capacity, but it's still a closed loop."

"But Hutton tinkered with it, right?"

"He sure did," Howard said, with a hint of pride as he tapped the unit next to the switchboard. "This has some god-awful long German name, which translates to something like Special Exchange Telephone Interface. See the line coming out of it?"

I nodded, following the black wire up and out the rear of the tent, where it was tied together with a bundle of other insulated wire.

"That line is spliced into the civilian telephone network. With this dialer, also German, you can call any number in Sicily."

"Who did Hutton talk to on this thing?" I was having a hard time imagining Aloysius Hutton as the kingpin of a Mafia conspiracy, huddled in here calling mobsters all over Sicily.

"I don't think he talked to anyone. He didn't speak Italian, and he wasn't much of a talker anyway."

"But he could make a call and route it to anyone connected through this switchboard?"

"Sure," Howard said. "Or anyone connected through any of our switchboards."

"Like the divisional Supply Company?"

"Definitely, along with division HQ, Corps HQ . . ."

"What about AMGOT?"

"Yep, we have them too, the Syracuse HQ and the Gela Civil Affairs Office," Howard said. "Connect this with our high-frequency radio, and I could give Ike himself a call in Algiers."

"Get much radio traffic between AMGOT and the 45th?"

"Fair amount. The Civil Affairs officers call in from towns all along our front."

"What about a Major Elliott?"

"Yeah, I've seen his name on a lot of messages. Some coded, some in the clear."

Now I knew why Rocko was so broken up to hear Hutton had been killed. Hutton was his way to contact Vito, Elliott, and whoever else was in on this.

"So Lieutenant Andrews arranged for Hutton to be assigned to Rocko at the supply depot, so he could keep an eye on him and have him make a call whenever he needed to," I said, spelling it out. "But Hutton was in *your* platoon—right?—not Andrews's. How come he was sent to work for Rocko?"

Howard answered, "I didn't have any choice about assigning Hutton. Orders came from division."

"From who, exactly?"

"Don't know. That's what Captain Stanton said. He wasn't too happy about it either. You figure something funny is going on here?"

"Rocko was killed. Murdered," I added, stressing the distinction.

"You think Hutton was mixed up in something illegal?"

"Hard to figure him for a crook."

"I agree. He was a good kid. You got any idea who's behind all this?"

"I'm working on it."

"What a waste," Howard said as he looked at the contents of the tent, the tools lined up neatly on the workbench, dust starting to settle on the hardware.

"Just so you know, Hutton did OK up on Biazza Ridge. He stood his ground."

"Good for him. I hope he didn't suffer when he got it," Howard said.

"No," I said, remembering the hole in his forehead and how he had quietly slumped over his rifle. "I don't think he knew what hit him."

"Thanks. You seem OK for a headquarters louie."

"All depends on who you ask. Mind if I look around here a bit?"

"Knock yourself out, pal. Just don't make any long-distance calls."

Howard left and I began to search the tent. For what exactly, I had no idea. With so much funny business going on, there was sure to be some sign of something shady, if only I could recognize it when I saw it. There were technical manuals stacked everywhere, so I flipped through the pages, looking for notes or maybe Mussolini's phone number. A couple of well-read *Popular Mechanics* issues from 1940 had loose pages falling out. I lifted up every piece of equipment and looked underneath. Nothing but dust. Checked the few items of clothing that were left scattered around and felt under the cot frame. Nothing but a wad of chewing gum.

There weren't any of Hutton's personal effects; those must have been picked up to be shipped home. If there was anything out of place, Howard would probably have noticed. Which meant if Hutton had left anything, he'd had a hidey-hole. I tried to put myself in his place. A loner, he liked to tinker with things. I remembered his hands were smooth, with long tapering fingers. Perfect hands for working with tubes and connections in cramped spaces. He didn't talk much, didn't bunk with anyone, so he probably didn't have a lot of pals. Where would he place his trust? What would seem to be a safe place to him?

I picked up a thin screwdriver from the workbench and eyed the piles of equipment. There were a lot of screws holding these things together, and I tried to guess which one he'd pick. It had to be one he knew no one else would use. The BD-72? No, I'd seen half a dozen others in operation in the Message Section tent. Someone might need a replacement and take his. But no one would need German equipment, right? I got to work on the dialer and the exchange device, unscrewing a wooden side panel from each and looking inside. Nothing. I screwed the sides back on and decided Hutton would not have risked taking these things apart—too many things might go wrong.

I sat back in his chair and stared at the thing. A thin metal plaque was fixed to the side with a diagram of the circuits and a bunch of German writing. Howard had been right about the name— Umtauschtelefonschnittstelle—it was a mouthful. I found a flashlight on the workbench and shined it on the metal. Four small screws held it in place; two of them had very small scratches at the end of the slot. Of course. No need to take it apart at all.

I found a smaller screwdriver and took out three screws. The plaque swiveled down, hanging by the single bottom right screw, as a small piece of paper fell to the table. I picked it up and read five rows of numbers, printed in a neat, precise hand.

92221166
09137422
32290664
71910900
230933

If I hadn't been sitting down, you could have knocked me over with that slip of paper. I had no idea what the first four numbers were, but I knew the last one by heart. It was the main phone number of the Hotel St. George in Algiers. General Eisenhower's headquarters.

CHAPTER ▪ THIRTY-TWO

I REPLACED THE PLAQUE and put Hutton's tools back where I'd found them. I felt sorry for the kid. I was sure he had been dragged into this by Andrews to get Rocko off his back, and had only been doing what he was told. This, clearly, had been his world: wires and gizmos, radios and transceivers, the stuff of colorful *Popular Mechanics* covers. A page that had fallen out of one of the magazines lay at my feet. It was headlined RADIO GOES TO WAR! Problem was, it didn't always come home.

"You!"

I swiveled in my seat to see a finger pointed at me. At the other end was Captain Stanton, his red hair no match for the color rising up from his neck.

"Stand up, goddamn it," he said. "Now!"

I wasn't as worried about the finger pointed at me as I was about the carbine held by the same MP who had kept me out of the Code Section. It wasn't at port arms anymore.

"Sure thing," I said, standing up, keeping the piece of paper folded in the palm of my hand. "What's the problem, sir?"

I placed my hand on my hip, as if my back were sore, slipping the paper into my belt. The MP got nervous, stepping forward and motioning "hands up" with the carbine.

"Hold on, fellas," I said, reaching for the sky. "We're all friends here, right?"

Neither of them wanted to be my pal. The MP held the carbine up to my neck as he took my .45 from the holster then shoved me out of the tent.

"What's going on?" I asked, looking around for a friendly face.

"You're not asking the questions here, Boyle, so shut up," Stanton growled.

"Actually, I am, Captain. I'm here from HQ with some questions—"

"Take the wind out of his sails," Stanton ordered.

The MP moved his carbine and whacked me in the stomach with the butt, high, in just the right spot to send me to my knees sucking air and watching little starry lights dance before my eyes. I took heaving, gasping breaths that didn't seem to carry any oxygen into my lungs. I had to admire his technique. He'd used the corner of the wooden butt, knocking the wind out of me without breaking a rib. A billy club was better for this move, but he was doing the best he could with what he had.

My breathing calmed down and I was able to lift my head in time to catch a view of Stanton's backside as he trudged off to the Code Section.

"You . . . a . . . cop?" I asked, needing a few gasps to get the words out.

"Yeah. Patrolman, Detroit. Don't tell me—"

"Detective. Boston."

"Sorry, Lieutenant," he said, helping me up. "If you had your shield you could've tinned me back there."

"You bring yours with you?"

"Yep. Here, take a look." He pulled out a bright silver badge, Detroit police all right. "Got me out of trouble in Norfolk before we shipped out, and I even got a ride from a French *flic* in Oran one night. I was drunk as a skunk."

"Good to hear that cops stick together the world over," I said.

"Yeah, well, sorry I had to put you on your knees. You OK now?"

"I think so. What are you supposed to do with me?"

"Watch you until a Major Elliott gets here. Come on, let's get out of the sun and take a load off." He led me by the arm—that insistent yet inconspicuous cop grip that left no doubt who was in charge—into the shade of the Message Section. We sat on folding wooden chairs inside, our backs to the rest of the tent. His chair creaked under his weight, but held. He tossed his helmet onto the ground and brushed back his brown hair. He had blue eyes, broad cheekbones, and a nose that looked like it had been broken at least once.

"Smoke?" He offered a Lucky from his pack. I shook my head.

"So what's your name, Patrolman?" I asked.

"Miecznikowski. You can call me Mike."

"Billy Boyle, and you can forget the lieutenant stuff. When there's no one around, who cares." I stuck out my hand and he shook it.

"You look young for a detective," he said, squinting at me through rising smoke as he lit up.

"I made the grade right before Pearl Harbor. Boston PD is a family business."

"Your old man?"

"Yeah, and uncle too, plus a few cousins."

"Not bad, Billy. You like it, being in the family business?"

"It's all I ever wanted to be. I grew up watching the men in my family carry badges like yours. It's all I know really." It occurred to me that there was a big difference between wanting to be something and becoming something because it was all you knew. Maybe I did want it, like Mike wanted it, all on his own.

"It's good work, especially for us Poles and you Irish. Jobs don't come so easy when you got too many c's and z's in your name," he said.

"Or an O in front of it," I said.

"Can you imagine a half Polack half Mick? O'Chmielewski? He'd starve to death before he ever got work!"

We laughed and swapped stories of walking the beat, desk sergeants, and run-ins with politicians and sons of the high and mighty who ran our towns. Things weren't that different in the Motor City, except that Mike didn't have a bunch of relatives to pull him up the ladder. He was a couple of years older than me and still hoofing it in his bluecoat. Or was.

"I work with a Polish guy," I said. "Talks like an Englishman but he's a Polish baron or something."

"A *Szlachta*, one of the Polish nobility. My old man used to tell us stories of the old knights and their battles. Nothing like this war, that's for damn sure."

"Kaz lost his whole family in Poland."

"That's tough. Fuckin' Germans. Yet we get along fine with them in Detroit, used to go to their church before we got our own built. Something about the old country must make them nuts. What's your pal's full name?"

"Piotr Augustus Kazimierz," I said, giving it the full treatment.

"Don't know the family," Mike said, after giving it some thought. "Say *pozdrowienia* to him for me. Tell him to settle in Detroit when the war's over. We got a nice neighborhood—Poletown, they call it."

"I'll tell him," I said, smiling at the thought of Kaz settling down in Poletown.

"Gotta hand it to you Irish," Mike said. "You made your own place in Boston when you were turned out everywhere else. It's good to have your own people running things instead of being run, ain't it?" He fieldstripped what was left of his Lucky and let the shreds of tobacco drop through his fingers.

"Yeah. That why you brought your shield with you? To stay connected with your own people?"

"Never thought about it really. Just seemed like the logical thing to do. Something to hang on to, you know? To remember what life used to be like, back when I took everything for granted."

I understood what Mike meant. More than he could realize. Having lost all memory of my life, rediscovering it was like seeing it all for the first time, a new and gleaming, shiny thing full of promise, but distant now, unattainable. He was hanging on to his own former life, his shield a talisman of things past, a promise of a future.

"I know" was all I said. It was too much to explain, too much to put into words. But our eyes locked for a second, and I said it again, so he'd realize I understood. "I know."

We sat in our chairs, letting the silence linger, the background noises of typewriters, static, chatter, and engines rising into it. The line of shade crept toward us as the harsh sun climbed in the sky.

"I gotta go to the latrine," Mike said.

"Hope you're not going to handcuff me," I said.

"We're brother cops; I draw the line at that," he said. Then he leaned back in his chair, turning his head slightly as a PFC rushed by, a stack of papers in his hand and a pencil stuck behind his ear. "Hey, Reynolds. Watch this guy, willya? Don't let him escape."

He said it in a low voice, winking at me as he did. When he got up, he took out his shield and held it up for me to see.

"Badge number 473. In case you ever make it out to Detroit. Ask for Big Mike."

And then he was gone.

A moment later, so was I.

CHAPTER ▪ THIRTY-THREE

I WAS ON THE run again. I could count on MPs and Major Elliott from AMGOT, Legs, and maybe some local muscle to be on my trail. Not that different from last time around, except now I knew the score. Elliott had to be the man I was after. Why else would he hotfoot it over to the Signals Company and have me held there? Maybe Stanton was in on it too, or maybe he thought he'd apprehended a dangerous criminal. The small fry didn't matter. I wanted Vito for questioning. I wanted Legs for the deaths of Roberto, Rocko, and even Aloysius Hutton, who would have been alive and tinkering in his tent if it hadn't been for this scheme to grab an army payroll. And Elliott for engineering it all, betraying his own side, and throwing me to the wolves.

I eased the jeep onto the main road, keeping my helmet tilted low and my head down. What I needed right now was a radio, so I could contact Harding and find out where Kaz and Harry were. Too bad I was persona non grata at the Signals Company. I had to find another unit with a radio fast, before the MPs issued an all-points on me.

I scanned the roadside for rear-area units as I drove east to Vittoria. With nothing else to go on, I figured it made sense to check out what Andrews had gone looking for. I passed a supply depot, but didn't see a telltale antenna. A hundred yards on, a hand-painted sign reading TWENTY-SIXTH RGT. MOTOR VEHICLE MAINTENANCE pointed to the left. I took it, following a wide, rough road of crushed stone and hard-packed dust, to an assembly of tents grouped under ancient gnarled, thick-trunked olive trees. Their shade was sparse but, supplemented by camouflage netting, provided defense against the sun, not to mention the Luftwaffe.

Trucks of all sizes, in various stages of dismemberment or repair littered the landscape. Thick logs had been set up in tripods, lashed together with heavy chains, to yank motors out of vehicles by greased pulleys. But what interested me was sticking up through the netting: a single antenna. I parked the jeep in the shade and ducked under the low-hanging net. The radio rested on a couple of empty crates in a tent half tied above to the trees to give full protection from the sun and the rain, if it ever came. A GI in an oil-stained shirt, his sergeant's stripes barely visible through the grime, sat in front of it, headphones on, writing intently with the stub of a pencil.

"OK, got it. Baker Seven out." I waited while he continued to scribble, stopping once to lick the tip of the pencil. He finished with a sigh and took the headphones off.

"Sarge, could I use your radio for a minute?"

"Jeez," he said, standing up as the chair fell over backward. "Don't sneak up on a guy like that. Lieutenant."

"Hey, sorry. I just need to radio my CO. Only take a minute."

He ripped off the top sheet of the pad he'd been writing on, and lifted the chair. "Knock yourself out, sir."

I sat at the SCR-510, a vehicle radio that had obviously been removed from a disabled jeep or tank. I set it for Harding's frequency and began to transmit.

"White Bishop, this is White Rook. Over."

Static blasted my eardrums. I tried again and heard a faint voice acknowledge.

"White Rook, this is—" Static again. I repeated my call sign and as I waited, picked up the pencil and began doodling on the pad. I drew Kilroy, then began filling in his face. I repeated the call sign again.

"White Rook, this is White Bishop One. Come in." I recognized Harding's voice. As I held the pencil poised to write down a message, I could see the faint outline of a word beneath my drawing. I rubbed the pencil lightly over the pad.

"White Bishop One, this is White Rook. Do you have location of White Knight?" That was Kaz and Harry. Then I saw a name appear. "Boyle" showed clearly where the motor pool sergeant had written his message on the top sheet, along with the words "report" and "hold."

"Scoglitti, on the coast, southeast of Gela. Do you read? Over."

"Understood, White Bishop. Keep destination top secret. From all. Do you read? Over."

"Not surprised, White Rook. Out."

I changed the frequency and took the top sheet with me. I looked for the sergeant but didn't see him anywhere. Maybe he didn't waste much time on radio orders from MPs or AMGOT. I didn't go straight to the jeep. Instead, I walked around inside the netting, staying behind vehicles and supplies so I could get a good view of the road. I wanted to be sure there were no surprises waiting out there. I edged behind a deuce-and-a-half truck with the hood open and heard voices, the slap of cards, and laughter. Nowhere left to go, I walked around the truck and gave them a friendly grin.

"Hey, fellas, at ease," I said, as the first of the four mechanics spotted me. "I'm looking for your sergeant." They sat on crates around a broken table, its two missing legs supported by a stack of K rations.

"He went to the mess tent to fix himself a sandwich. That way," one of them said.

"All the Spam you want—help yourself, Lieutenant," another said, as the others laughed at his wit.

"Raise you ten," the first guy said, heeding my "at ease" and doing everything he could to comply. Then I noticed the pot. It was a stack of ten-dollar bills higher than a fist.

"How much is in that pot?" I asked, trying not to sound like an officer. "I usually play for nickels."

"Nothing, Lieutenant. Here, have one."

I took the ten-spot. It looked real, until I turned it over. On the back was a German eagle grasping a swastika and a message in Italian.

"Are they all the same?" I asked.

"Yeah, same serial number on all of them. We found a bunch blowing around in the field over there, then a whole box of the damn things."

"Anybody know what it says?" I asked, my curiosity keeping me there when I should have been driving off.

"Tony, tell the lieutenant what you figured out. Tony speaks the lingo pretty well," one of the players said proudly.

"Well, there's a whole bunch of stuff about how we killed plenty of women and children bombing Sicily. And bombed a hospital ship. Then about how all Italians should hate the Americans and the English for that, and that the blood of innocent victims cries out for revenge. Stuff like that."

"We do any of that stuff, Lieutenant?" the youngest of the card-players asked me.

"Can I keep this?" I asked.

"Sure," Tony said. "We play for nickels too. That's what each one's worth to us, in the game anyway. Otherwise they're only good for the latrine. Easier to play with paper, even if it's funny money."

The kid still wanted an answer.

"That's propaganda. Don't take it seriously."

"Sure. That's what I thought, sir. Thanks."

"Call."

I left as Tony won the pot with three jacks. I didn't know about any hospital ships, but I figured a fair share of the bombs we dropped on Sicily killed civilians, without regard to age or sex. Maybe Mussolini was right, that blood alone moves the wheels of history, but I didn't see any reason for a kid who didn't shave regularly to worry about that before he went to sleep each night. A little lie to soothe the conscience seemed right.

I folded the phony bill and walked the long way back around the tent to my jeep, in the opposite direction from the mess tent. I figured there was only so much Spam a guy could eat before he realized he should have asked me my name. I stepped around guy-wires support-ing the radio antenna as a wrecked truck caught my attention. It had been dumped in back, in an open area where olive trees had been cut down. It was a charred hulk, bullet holes visible in the cab and frame, showing it had been shot up and then burned. Could this have been the truck Andrews had been caught in? Lots of vehicles had been shot up and burned, but this was the road to Vittoria, so it would make sense. I looked at my jeep, then back at the wreck. Another few min-utes couldn't hurt.

I trotted over and looked inside the cab. The windows were gone, shot out or broken in the crash. Inside, it smelled like death and burned rubber. Bullet holes in the door left jagged edges that tore at my pants. My hands came away black with soot, and I headed for the back of the truck. The metal supports for the canvas covering were bent and broken. I hoisted myself up on what was left of the truck bed and tried to comprehend what I was looking at. A pile of charred cans could have been anything. Spam, peaches, who knows what. A faint dark outline showed on the charred floor. About the size of a body. Bodily fluids and burning fat always left their mark. It made it more likely that this had been Andrews's truck. I scuffed through the debris, wondering what a clue would look like after all this.

A flicker of white caught my eye. I pushed aside a blackened pile of something and saw more white. I kneeled and picked it up. Paper. Charred paper. Small pieces fluttered from my hand, none larger than my thumb. It had been a roll of paper, far larger than what I saw here now. The innermost layer of a roll of blank paper, protected from the fire, crumbled at my touch.

Paper. I took the folded fake ten-dollar bill and placed two of the larger pieces inside it, then carefully put it in my shirt pocket and buttoned it. This had been Andrews's truck, I was sure of it. Big rolls of paper could mean only one thing. For Andrews, though, all it had meant was that his luck had run out. Legs or the Luftwaffe? It didn't matter. Dead was dead, and I had to move.

I decided to walk straight to the jeep. There was no unusual activity in the motor pool, and I needed to put some miles between me and this place. Sooner or later someone would figure out it had been Boyle who'd stopped by. And maybe sooner, if anyone had been monitoring Harding's frequency. If they had been, then they knew Vittoria was my destination and might be waiting for me there. But I had to have a next move. That was easy to figure. Get things out in the open, in a place where the odds were in my favor. I thought about Kaz, great in spirit and small in stature, and Harry with his leg still hurting from the bullet he took in Algiers and I had to amend that. Not in my favor exactly, just not stacked against me.

I hopped in and started the jeep. I tried not to make any unusual moves, but I couldn't stop myself from looking at the radio. I could see the sergeant, standing at the set, holding an earphone to his head, looking straight at me and nodding. I gunned it, but not before I heard a "Hey, stop!" and other shouts, which I left behind in a cloud of churning dust.

Damn! Now they knew where I was and could guess where I was going. Elliott could pull anyone he had between here and the coast into the search: MPs, mobsters, renegade GIs, you name it. All I had was a .45 and a nagging thought at the back of my head that I'd been led on a wild goose chase ever since I'd awakened in that field hospital.

CHAPTER ■ THIRTY-FOUR

WHEN MY LITTLE BROTHER Danny was in junior high school, he got a Mysto Magic Kit for his birthday. Practicing and reading up on magic and magicians, he quickly became a junior Houdini. He did magic shows for neighborhood kids, charging two cents apiece, and he'd usually end up with enough copper in his pocket to stock up on penny candy—when I could talk him into it. Otherwise, he preferred to save to buy more magic tricks. Or illusions, as he called them.

He got pretty good. He could pull off card tricks using the dove-tail shuffle, pull a coin out of your ear, all that stuff. Once he got serious about magic, he refused to tell me what the secret was to each trick. The simple ones I could figure out, after insisting, in a big brotherly sort of way, on a hint or two. But otherwise, all he'd say was that it was based on distraction. What you saw was not the illusion; how he distracted you was the real trick.

I hit the brakes as I came to the main road and looked behind me. No sign of pursuit, but I was pretty sure a confirmed sighting of an AWOL lieutenant was being radioed back to Elliott, who would have concocted some sort of cover story—maybe the black market or simply desertion. Or could he have alleged something far more serious, a crime that would allow the MPs to shoot on sight? Yeah, that sounded right. Rocko's murder, maybe.

I had to hide in plain sight while getting to the coast road. I couldn't risk being spotted, but traffic was light. Solitary jeeps, ambulances, heavy trucks, and motorcycles passed by, and I slammed my fist against the steering wheel in frustration. Then the rumble of engines and a low, rolling cloud of dust came to my rescue. A convoy of trucks, big GMCs, some towing artillery pieces. Slow moving, tightly packed. I let the first four go by, then pulled out and accelerated, nosing the jeep between the snout of a 150mm gun and the cab of the next truck. The driver yelled something about my mother and I waved back, like a happy idiot who wanted to eat dust and grit in the noonday heat. I buttoned my collar and pulled on a pair of goggles. This wasn't going to be fun.

But it was safe. Thirty minutes later, a jeep with three MPs, traveling at top speed, passed the column. They didn't give me as much as a glance as they sped by, holding onto their helmets and shielding their eyes, eager to get ahead of the dust cloud.

I was keeping my lips tightly shut so the grit wouldn't work its way between my teeth, otherwise I would have cheered. Not at temporarily outwitting a few MPs, but at finally seeing what was so obvious. Nick had said it back in Villalba, but we were so focused on the payroll heist that it hadn't registered.

Say Elliott and his crew pulled off the theft. It was like I'd said to Don Calo—every GI and Sicilian who heard about it would be on the lookout for it. What could they do with it? As soon as anyone flashed a wad of occupation scrip, they'd be immediate suspects.

No, tempting as it was, the 45th Division payroll was not the real target. It was the distraction. While we were worrying about Nick's relatives and protecting the payroll, someone was pulling off the real theft. The German phony ten-dollar bills had got me thinking about it. When I found the remnants of paper in the burned-out truck things had finally clicked.

It was like Nick had said. AMGOT would need lots of occupation scrip to replace all the lire in Sicily. So much that they'd be printing most of it here, once they were established ashore and could get the printing presses rolling. Andrews had been heading to Vittoria with a supply of printing paper. I'd bet my Boston PD pension it was the same paper they used for the scrip back in North Africa. Supplied by Rocko, of course, before he flapped his lips too much for his own good.

If you had the right paper, running off extra scrip from AMGOT plates would be the opportunity of a lifetime. Especially doing it as soon as possible after the invasion, before things got too organized. He'd have the plates and all he'd need would be enough paper to run off sufficient high-denomination notes. He'd need to find printing presses and supplies, of course, but that would be normal procedure. AMGOT would take over the first print shop they came across. No one would ever be the wiser. A guy like Vito could launder the cash through enough banks and businesses that no one would ever guess the scrip was crooked. And it wouldn't be, that was the beauty of the whole deal. It would be official currency, not actually counterfeit.

There had to be a connection between Elliott and Vito. That I could sort out later. It was obvious Rocko had been a key player, coordinating supplies and equipment. And Hutton, with his skills at radio and telephone communications, had been the link between them, communicating with AMGOT, Vito, and Lord knows who else. Using shortwave radio, civilian phone lines, whatever it took, he had been the linchpin. But now all the players were ashore, and the army was moving deep inland. And Elliott had arrived as planned from Algiers, the rear echelon following the first wave by a week or more.

I had to slam on my brake as I heard the squeal of protesting brakes ahead of me, followed by the sound of tires crunching gravel. As the column came to a halt, the dust from the road settled around me, coating the jeep with an even thicker layer of grit. I tried to spit, but my mouth was too dry. I drank warm water from my canteen and felt the grime wash away.

"Hey, Mac, now's your chance," the driver behind me motioned. He was right. No one in his right mind would pass up a chance to move ahead of a halted convoy. So I waved "so long, pal" and pulled out. I floored it, letting the hot wind blow away the road dust and fumes. Not ten minutes later, there was a fork in the road. Crudely painted signposts pointed to Vittoria, 4 miles; Scoglitti, 12 miles; and back the way I had come, New York City, 4,380 miles. No GI putting up road signs could resist the temptation to add the mileage to his hometown.

I took the right to Scoglitti and put another few miles between me and the Statue of Liberty. The lane narrowed, stands of cactus and tall grass crowding the roadway. I could smell the sea, the salt heavy in the heated air. I rummaged in the pack on the seat next to me, looking for a D Bar of chocolate from the K ration I'd brought along. As I looked down for the chocolate, I took the jeep around a curve. I was only distracted for a second or two, but when I looked up there were jeeps blocking the road ahead of me. Military police jeeps, both of them. One had a long whip antenna tied down in front. Damn, they'd probably been radioed to look for me. An MP faced me with his hands out, signaling for me to halt. I looked to both sides of the road. Tall stands of cactus stood like walls on either side. I couldn't turn or back up fast enough. So I stopped, smiled, and tried to think of a way out of this one.

"ID, Lieutenant?" the MP in the road asked. Two other guys sat in one of the jeeps, one of them holding a clipboard, the other a Thompson.

"Lost my dog tags. Took a hit to the head and woke up in a field hospital without 'em."

"You got orders?"

"Yeah, I got orders. I got a major waiting for me in Scoglitti who's pissed off because his jeep broke down. You want to let me through before he blows a fuse?"

"What's your name?" He didn't seem to care about an angry major.

"Dick Newsome." I had been thinking about the Red Sox for some reason, and Dick Newsome popped into my mind. At least I wasn't thinking about Pinky Woods. Worse name, worse pitcher.

"Hey, just like that pitcher for the Sox."

"Yeah, I get that all the time."

"What's the major's name?"

"Huh?"

"The name of the major what wants the jeep, Lieutenant."

"Oh, yeah." Don't think about baseball, I told myself. "Major Elliott. He gets pretty sore when he has to wait." I figured he might have run into Elliott and it made the story more plausible.

"Hey, that's funny too. We got a Major Elliott right here."

I'd run into some really smart MPs in this war and some dumb ones. This guy either had a real subtle sense of humor or he was on the deep end of dumb. The guy with the clipboard got out as his partner started the jeep.

"Major John Elliott, Lieutenant Boyle. We've been looking all over for you."

He smiled, his mustache rising at the corners. He was a short, barrel-chested guy, dark haired and on the far side of thirty. He looked entirely too happy to have me in his paws.

"Miller," he said to the MP who was still trying to figure out if there really were two Major Elliotts. "You take this jeep. Boyle, you come with me."

"No," I said. I slammed the gear into reverse. I had to count on Miller being slow on the uptake and a lousy shot with the carbine that was slung over his shoulder. The other MP's hands were on the steering wheel, and Elliott hadn't made a move for the .45 still snapped shut in his holster. It wasn't much, but it was all I had. I tried to figure my chances, but a distant sound hummed in my ears, growing louder and breaking my concentration.

"Don't do it!" Elliott yelled. Miller looked up, and so did Elliott. Two dark forms took shape in the air. Twin-engined Me110s, German fighter-bombers. They came from the direction of Gela, probably heading home from a raid on the harbor and looking for a few more Americans to strafe. They were so close to the ground I could see bright sunlight reflecting off the cockpit canopies.

Then came the sparkling of machine gun and cannon fire from the nose of each plane. The ground around us exploded as shells hit rocks, cactus, and the hard-packed earth. Elliott and the two MPs hit the dirt, making themselves as small as possible in the ditch running along the side of the road. I didn't even think about it. I jumped from my jeep, vaulted into the MP's jeep in front of me, and threw it into first, punched the accelerator, and kept my head down. Metallic tearing sounds and bright white lines surrounded me as phosphorescent tracer shells snapped at the vehicles. Twin explosions boomed behind me, not the sharp cracks of bombs, but the *whump* and *whoosh* of gas tanks igniting.

I chanced a look backward and saw the tail fins of the Me110s as the aircraft gained altitude and sped away. Three figures rose from the ditch, stumbling around the wrecked and burning jeeps, and I saw one shake his fist at me. God bless the Luftwaffe.

I kept my foot pressed to the floor. The wind whipped at my face as I outraced the swirling clouds of churning dust my tires kicked up. I smelled smoke and saw the charred hole in the passenger-seat cushion where a tracer had ignited the stuffing. There were two more holes in the floorboard. I'd gotten off pretty easy. I downshifted to take a sharp curve and felt an odd sensation in my right arm. I took my hand off the gearshift and watched rivulets of bright red blood trickle into my palm. It didn't hurt, but it surprised me. I looked at my arm, wincing as I drew it across my body. The cushion wasn't the only thing burning. I slapped at the smoldering black and glistening red above my elbow, trying to hold onto the wheel with my right hand, now sticky and slippery with blood. Oh damn. It started to hurt.

Good, I thought. If it hurts, it means I'm not going into shock. I think. I looked again at the big holes in the floor and realized that half an inch in the other direction and the slug would have taken my arm off. Of course, half an inch the other way, and I wouldn't have been breaking out in a cold clammy sweat. I took a deep breath and tried to calm myself. It was only a bad scratch. I got away from Elliott and was almost to Scoglitti. It wasn't so bad.

Then I laughed and pressed hard on the accelerator, picking up speed. I was bleeding, on the run from mobsters and MPs, and driving like a maniac to rendezvous with my friends in a stolen, shot-up jeep. I loved it. I had been wondering who I was only days ago. This was who: I was on the hunt, enjoying the chase, living by my wits. Living or dying. That sobered me up. Then I thought it was funny again and laughed, a mad cackle that ended as I coughed and hawked up road dust.

The next turn took me close to the beach, flat grassy land on either side, the wind bending the stalks across my path. A small peninsula jutted out from the town ahead, a church tower dominating it, shimmering against the deep blue sea beyond. The sun was at my back, illuminating the stark, bleached, almost blinding whiteness of the church. I didn't know what was going to happen next or who would be waiting for me and at that moment I didn't care. Not many people experienced a single moment of knowing exactly who they were and what they were made for. But now I knew. This was me. All the doubts about identity, guilt, and death were swept away in the gleaming sunlight.

I was the guy who did what had to be done. I might suffer for it, I might wonder what it had done to my soul, but while the Rockos of this world ran and hid from the fight, God help me, I couldn't. I saw the wounded paratrooper drop his sling in the road while his buddy limped along with him to the sound of gunfire on Biazza Ridge. I saw Villard, a look of surprise in his dying eyes, and knew I'd paid the price, and that I'd pay it again. I heard Dad telling me to remember who I was, and understood that as long as that voice echoed in my head, I would never forget, no matter what sins priests demanded I confess.

CHAPTER THIRTY-FIVE

I PASSED BEACHED fishing boats, tangled nets hanging over their gunwales. A wooden dock stood in pieces, gaps from age or war or both creating little wood islands in the sea. Squat stone houses lined the edge of the water, and the air smelled of salt, seaweed, and dead fish. A wrecked LST lay on its side on the beach, waves crashing around it. This was CENT Beach, the easternmost invasion area for the 45th Division. I turned away, hoping all the GIs had gotten out after the landing craft had been hit.

The street widened, a few two- and three-story buildings telling me this was the town center. Down a side street, I saw a gaggle of army vehicles, and figured that's where I'd find Kaz and Harry. I coaxed the jeep forward, hoping my driving—or the hits it had taken from the German shells—wouldn't bring it to a grinding halt. I pulled into a spot next to a flatbed truck and killed the engine. Sitting on the bed, beneath a mounted crane, were six U.S. Army field safes, doors wide open.

"Billy, where did you get that jeep?" Harry asked as he stepped out of the building in front of me. It was the biggest one on the street, great gray granite blocks painted over with a picture of Mussolini. Two GIs stood guard on either side of the door.

"Where's the money?" I asked him, not wanting to explain right then about the manhunt for me.

"Drying out, up above us. This used to be the local Fascist head-quarters, and it has a nice flat roof. Just the place to dry out two million dollars' worth of scrip, don't you think? What are you doing in a shot-up MP jeep?"

"And how far away are the people who are chasing you?" That was Kaz, right behind Harry. He knew me well.

"Not far, but now they're walking. How did you get the safes here?"

"We didn't. The navy raised them," Kaz said. "The landing craft had swamped in only ten feet of water, so once the divers found them it wasn't difficult to get them ashore. We have a platoon guarding the building."

"Who?" Harry asked.

"Who what?" I returned as I got out of the jeep and scanned the street. They had guards at every corner.

"Who is walking?"

"Some MPs and an AMGOT officer named Elliott. Long story . . ."

"You're wounded," Kaz said, looking at my right arm. "Come with me."

He didn't seem fazed. Not by my bloody arm or the military police jeep with bullet holes and a smoldering seat cushion. I let him lead me inside, past Mussolini's jutting chin in a framed photo. We ended up on the roof, under an awning, watching sailors in their blue dunga-rees spread out drenched occupation scrip.

I had to hand it to those Fascists, they didn't scrimp when it came to setting up shop. The building had a long meeting hall, offices with ornately carved wooden desks, and an ocean view from this terrace, where we sat in the shade, watching money dry.

"You may need this stitched up," Harry said as he cut away my shirt and cleaned the wound with sulfa powder from a first aid pack. He unwound a roll of gauze for a bandage.

"No time now, just wrap it up tight."

Harry finished cleaning the wound and squeezed some sulfadi-azine ointment over the burn, which was worse than the cut.

"What happened?" Kaz said, peering through his thick glasses at the wound.

"I was stopped at a roadblock when a couple of Me110s strafed us. The MPs hit the ditch, and I took off in one of their jeeps. A tracer round nicked me in the arm."

"You're lucky to have an arm at all," Harry said, pulling tightly on the bandage as if to emphasize his point.

"Ow! Listen, we've got to get to Vittoria fast."

"We can't leave the payroll," Kaz said.

"Yes, you can. It's under guard, and that's not what they're really after."

"What?" Harry and Kaz said at the same time.

"There's a lot to explain, but that can wait until we're on the road. I—"

The *crack* of a rifle shot was followed by a buzzing sound past my ear and a shower of granite fragments from the wall behind me.

"Get down!" Harry yelled, pulling Kaz and me to the floor as a second shot shattered a large pot resting on the railing next to where I'd been sitting. Then more shots rang out amid a lot of screaming and hollering until someone yelled louder and more calmly than anyone else, "Cease fire, cease fire!"

We scrambled down the stairs to the sidewalk. The guards were aiming their rifles up, swiveling left and right, searching for a target.

"Did anyone see anything?" Harry asked the sergeant who trotted over to him.

"Not a damn thing, sir," the sergeant said. "The two shots came from that building. Then the boys started firing at shadows. No one saw anything." He was pointing at a two-story cinder-block store, with a picture of a fish on a wooden sign. The single window had been shot out.

"From the roof?" I asked.

"Think so. That window was intact before my guys shot back. I don't think it was open."

In the distance, we could hear the sound of an engine start up and fade away.

"Probably the shooter," I said. "No way to catch him now."

"Who do you think it was? Was he shooting at you?" Kaz asked.

"I'd say so. I felt the bullet pass by my head."

"Mafia?" Harry asked.

"Maybe Vito didn't get the word that he was getting a pass on all this. Or maybe it was Legs. He never liked me much back in Boston."

"But why—"

"Never mind," I said. "We gotta go—now!" I had caught sight of an ancient farm tractor chugging down the road, weighed down by two MPs and one pissed-off AMGOT major. With the MPs to back him up, he could take over command of the guard platoon and hog-tie the three of us. I ran and hoped Kaz and Harry followed.

I jumped into the nearest vehicle, a Dodge Command Car. It was bigger than a regular jeep and outfitted with a radio in the back. Kaz got in next to me and Harry leaped into the rear.

"Hey, that's ours!"

"Sorry, Sarge, we're commandeering it."

"The hell you are, buddy. I don't know who you are and I'm not letting this vehicle go on your say-so. Or on orders from a couple of Brits. No disrespect intended, sirs."

He nodded politely at Kaz and Harry while keeping his M1 leveled at me. I had no shirt other than my OD undershirt and so no HQ shoulder patch or lieutenant's bars to impress him with.

"You can believe him, Sergeant," Harry said. "Colonel Routh, division paymaster, will be here soon to collect the money. Turn it over to him and provide a guard detail."

"Yes, sir," he acknowledged politely, still keeping me covered. "Now you get out of the vehicle."

It was a damned odd situation.

"I'll return it in one piece," I said, with all the sincerity I could muster as I jammed the gear in reverse and backed out. The tractor was halfway down the street.

"My captain will have my head if I lose that vehicle." The M1 was aimed square at my head.

"It won't be lost. We're taking it to Vittoria. If you shoot, try not to hit either of these two, it's not their fault." I hit the accelerator and worked the gears to get us up to top speed before anybody started firing. I glanced back to see the sergeant lower his rifle and curse. Elliott was waving his fists again.

"Why did you tell them where we are going?" Kaz asked.

"Because Elliott already knows. Everyone knows. Everyone except us."

CHAPTER ▪ THIRTY-SIX

WE DROVE NORTH, out of the deserted town and through mudflats bearing tufts of brown dry grasses that lay limp in the dead air. Away from the sea breeze, the land was scorched and arid. The only good thing was that there was no cover, no hiding place for a sniper to ambush us. I drove fast.

"What have you discovered, Billy?" Kaz asked, holding onto his cap in the hot wind.

"More like figured out, finally. I found the truck that Andrews was killed in. It was burned, but there were remnants in it of big rolls of paper. And I remembered something that Nick had said, about AMGOT setting up printing operations on the island."

"Yes, to produce newspapers and more occupation currency," Kaz said.

"*Willie and Joe!*" Harry said from the backseat.

"Right. It makes sense to print stuff here instead of shipping it all from North Africa. But someone had the bright idea of adding to the printing runs on the sly, and getting rich without seeming to steal anything."

"I still don't understand about the payroll. Why aren't you worried about that?" Harry asked.

"It came to me when I thought about what I'd told Don Calo. About how every German, Italian, American, and British soldier would turn this island upside down if it got out that someone had three million bucks' worth stashed away. I was saying it to persuade him that stealing the payroll was a lousy idea. Well, the more I thought about it, the more I understood that it really was a lousy idea. Let's say someone did pull off the heist. What would he do with it? Deposit it? No. Spend it? No. If you're a GI, you shouldn't have more than your pay and what you might win in a card game. Hide it? But for how long? Sooner or later scrip will be replaced by Italian currency and any GI with a huge bundle of it to exchange would be a suspect. There's no point in stealing that much money unless you can launder it. It wouldn't make sense."

"Tell us something that does make sense," Kaz said.

We all arched our necks at the sound of aircraft engines, but they were ours. Thunderbolts. I pulled onto a main road and had to slow down to keep pace with the big trucks lumbering along.

"Here's how I figure it. Someone who knows Vito Genovese also learned about the plans to print currency here."

"Someone in AMGOT?" Harry asked.

"Right. My guess is Elliott. He arranges for his guy in the Signals Company to be their go-between. Once they land, Hutton can link up with the civilian phone network and call Vito or somebody who can get in touch with him."

"Which would explain a criminal like Genovese offering the army his services right after the invasion," Kaz said.

"Bingo. Now Hutton can communicate both ways. With Vito, through his linkup with the civilian phone network, and with AMGOT back in Algiers. He could get in touch with HQ by shortwave radio. Hell, maybe he could patch the calls together, I don't know."

"I still don't get it about the payroll," Harry said. He sounded like I used to in algebra class.

"OK. Our guy is planning this out. He's going to organize the printing of extra occupation scrip. Maybe by extra runs on an AMGOT press, maybe a secret print run with his own printing press and stolen plates, I don't know exactly. He still has to involve people. Hutton and Rocko, not to mention Andrews. At some point, he gets nervous. Maybe he thinks someone's gotten wind of his plans."

"So he creates a diversion!" Harry said. "He distracts us by focusing our attention on the payroll. Bloody hell."

"Yeah. And he blackmails Nick into going along, agreeing to crack the safes. But think about it. Between an ONI agent and the Mafia, it wasn't going to stay quiet for long."

"So if there is an investigation, the first thing they'll find out about is the plot to steal the payroll," Kaz said, rubbing his fingers on his chin. "But then the payroll never made it to shore and you ended up poking your nose where it does not belong, as usual."

"Exactly," I said, as I pulled out and passed two deuce-and-a-half trucks. "Which worked out well for them, since it kept their cover story alive."

"And all the while, Genovese and Elliott were planning to quietly print up all the occupation scrip they wanted which no one would suspect. Vito is the perfect choice to launder money on this island. It's genius," Kaz said.

"Why were Rocko and the Italian chap, Roberto, killed?" Harry asked. In the rearview mirror I could see his face scrunched up with the effort of working it out, and imagined what I'd looked like to my poor sainted algebra teacher.

"Maybe greed, maybe caution. Rocko had served his purpose, procured all the supplies they wanted, so they didn't need him anymore. They may have worried he'd panic and talk. Or both. Maybe Rocko found out the payroll heist was a blind, and asked for a bigger payoff. As for Roberto, he had seen Rocko take me away, and could identify him. That would be a connection Vito wouldn't want to come up later. Rocko nearly killed Roberto on the spot, but a patrol came along before he could finish the job."

"Who shot at you then?" Harry asked. This time he wasn't confused. "It wasn't Elliott—he was on that damned tractor. Vito or Legs? Why try to kill you? As far as they know, you were there to celebrate your victory in saving the payroll. Andrews is dead, Rocko is dead, and Nick, even if he is more involved than we know, is in Major Harding's custody. Who's left?"

Kaz looked at me, one eyebrow raised in question. Now Kaz is a really smart guy, the kind of guy who reads philosophy and poetry in a bunch of different languages. If he didn't have an answer, I sure as hell didn't.

"Somebody we don't know about," I said.

I hated not having an answer. I drove with my lips clenched, tired of talking and swallowing road dust. I had thought I'd hit a home run with this one. Or had all the bases covered. Why was I thinking so much about baseball anyway?

"Is there anything to eat in this jalopy?" I asked. I hadn't had any food since early that morning. Nothing but coffee and the thought of a chocolate bar. I could hear Harry rummaging around in the backseat.

"Dear me, British rations," he said. "Sorry to do this to you, Billy. They must have been trading. For what, I have no idea. Ah! Here's some chocolate. Rollos, not too bad."

He passed me the chocolate and some packages of crackers. They were labeled WELFARE BISCUITS, which didn't do much for my appetite.

"Tins of Bully Beef, made from select meat parts," Harry said, reading from another label. "Approved by the ministry of food for front-line troops. Nothing too good for the chaps doing the fighting, although I'd love to see this stuff approved for General Staff consumption."

I ate dry crackers washed down with warm water. What had I missed? One thing you could count on with criminals was a willingness to do whatever it took to get what they wanted. Beatings, killings, threats, bribes—they were as natural to crooks as punching a clock or taking the trolley to work every day. Knocking me off had to make sense to them in a way that a working stiff could never figure out. That's why a little streak of backroom larceny could make for a really sharp cop. It made you think like a gangster every now and then, which was helpful if it didn't become your regular line of thought.

Maybe Vito had gotten it into his head that I had to be killed, and even when it didn't make sense anymore, he and Legs couldn't let go of that idea. They were men of honor, after all.

"Harry, get Harding on that thing and let him know where we're headed, willya?"

"Aye aye," said Harry, and began fiddling with the dials.

"Billy, there's something else that bothers me," Kaz said.

"What?"

"We met Colonel Routh, the paymaster for the 45th Division. He showed us the orders that came through from II Corps Headquarters, ordering him to take the payroll ashore with the first wave of the invasion. He said such an order was completely unexpected."

"And?"

"No one at II Corps HQ had any idea about that order. He checked afterward. There was no name attached. It did say 'By order of Lieutenant General Omar N. Bradley,' but all Corps orders say that."

"Maybe AMGOT wanted to get the occupation scrip into circulation as soon as possible?"

"Yes, but no other unit had their payroll go ashore that early. It does not all add up, does it?"

"I don't know, Kaz. I hope we find some answers in Vittoria."

I took a right at another road sign pointing to Vittoria. Brooklyn was to the left. Same joker probably painted all the signs on this road. Forty-four hundred miles from home. Maybe it would be an even five thousand before the war was over.

"Harding left for Vittoria an hour ago." Harry spoke up from the rear. "He sent us a message to find you and bring you there."

"Anything else?"

"No, there's too much static."

"Message delivered," I said. "Harding's a day late and a dollar short. By the time he gets here we should have this all wrapped up."

"Piece of pie," Kaz said.

"Piece of cake, not pie."

"Thank you, Billy. American colloquialisms are so difficult to remember. They make little sense to begin with."

"Yes, why cake and not pie?" Harry asked.

"I would say cakes are harder to bake than pies," Kaz said.

"Right. One mistake with a cake and you've got a lopsided mess," Harry concurred. "With a pie you can simply cover it up with crust."

"How many cakes have you baked?" I asked them both.

"I've tasted quite a few," said Harry.

"I prefer pies. Tortes, actually," said Kaz.

I was still hungry, and this talk of food made me think of my favorites, all currently off the menu. I should have thought of my mom's cooking, which was great, but the picture I saw in my mind was a good old American hot dog, slathered in mustard, served up at Fenway Park with a cold beer. I hadn't thought about baseball since the last *Stars and Stripes* I'd read in Tunisia, and today it kept popping up. I hoped the Red Sox had climbed up in the standings and were ahead of the Yankees by now. It had been a long time since 1918.

We drove into the city proper. It was mostly intact with some shops open for business. The local Banco di Sicilia was open too, and I wondered if any phony money was already deposited in secret accounts there. Not actually phony, though, so there was no way to tell which was legit and which wasn't. GIs strolled down the street and a group of officers sat at an outdoor café, sipping glasses of red wine. I passed them by, a bit nervous about ranking officers right now. One of them could be an AMGOT pal of Elliott's.

The road got narrower, and after a few twists and turns it dumped us out into the central *piazza*. The usual church was at one end with a fountain in the center. A statue of a woman and a bunch of fish stood ready to spout water, but the basin was bone-dry. A group of GIs sat on the church steps, reading newspapers, their field packs and rifles scattered around them. As I got closer, I could see it was the *45th Division News*. A clue, or at least a lead to a clue.

"Hey, fellas," I said as I stopped the car next to the fountain. "Do they print that paper around here?"

"Yeah, but they're gettin' ready to pull out," a corporal said, a cigarette dangling from his lips. "We're waitin' for transport ourselves."

"Where to?"

"Dunno," he said. "North, I guess. Followin' the division. The front's so far up this ain't even the rear of the rear no more. AMGOT took over the town yesterday."

"Where can we find them?" I asked.

"AMGOT?"

"No, the newspaper staff, the print shop."

"If they ain't moved out yet, head down the street to the left of that church. 'Bout a quarter mile or so there's some tin-roofed buildings. One of them has printing presses and that's where they been workin' outta."

"Do you chaps have an extra copy?" Harry asked.

"Sure," the corporal answered, signaling one of his squad to hand over a newspaper. He eyed me, with my undershirt and bandage for a uniform, then Kaz in his British field blouse with "Poland" stitched on the shoulder, and finally Harry, his bleached-out naval cap at a rakish angle, his blond hair flowing out from underneath. "What kinda out-fit you boys with, anyway?"

"Would you believe General Eisenhower's staff?" I asked.

"You better git movin' before somebody comes along what ain't got a sense of humor," he said, flicking the ash off his butt and field-stripping it.

It was good advice. Taking the turn past the church, I drove slowly down a residential street, flowers and drying laundry decorating the small balconies three and four stories above us. People were going about their business—leaning out windows, laughing, arguing—much like you'd find in any neighborhood back home on any normal day.

But normal didn't mean good. Normal meant you let your guard down. I looked at the rooftops and balconies ahead. I took the first side road I could.

"Where are you going, Billy?" Kaz asked.

"I'm going to find the back way in, and then we walk."

"Why?"

"Because our sniper could be waiting, and I don't want to give him a second chance. We might even crawl."

"There's no *Willie and Joe* in this!" Harry said from the backseat, more upset at the absence of Mauldin's cartoon than the idea of a sniper.

"There's a war on," I said helpfully as I parked the car behind a roofless building.

This street had a dilapidated look, as if times had left it behind. A rusted motorcycle with two flat tires and no engine lay in the alley, probably right where it had fallen over a couple of years ago. A few small shops with iron bars on the windows were doorless, broken fur-niture and other debris marking the trail of looters. From the looks of things, they hadn't had heavy burdens. Down the road was an empty stretch, then the tin-roofed buildings the corporal had mentioned. It was as if people had simply used up all their luck here and moved on down the road to try again.

"What do we do now?" Kaz asked.

"Well, since we can't sit and read the funny papers, let's take a walk."

I got out and checked my .45, worked the slide, and flicked the safety off. Harry had found a carbine in the back of the car, and Kaz had his Webley revolver. Not exactly heavy weapons, but they'd do the trick. All we had to do was get close.

We walked single file, keeping close to the empty buildings. The sound of our footsteps in the rubble was loud, rock and debris slipping and scraping beneath our boots. The same sound, softer, echoed from around the corner. I stopped at the last building, leaning against the crumbling brick, and listened to the footsteps headed our way. Pressing my back against the wall I motioned Kaz and Harry to halt. Two sets of heavy feet, no voices. I held up the .45, the grip resting in the palm of my left hand. A curse sounded as one of them slipped, the tone and words familiar to me from North End neighborhoods.

"Porca l'oca!"

Two Italian soldiers, rifles slung from their shoulders, came into view. One was hopping on one leg, rubbing his ankle. The other was square in my sights, his mouth twisted open in shock, as if he wanted to scream but was lockjawed. The .45 was cocked and locked, my finger against the trigger, only the slightest muscle tension needed for two quick head shots. My vision flickered across them, registering something odd about their uniforms, but I kept my eyeballs on those slung rifles. One move and they'd both be dead.

The guy with the hurt ankle looked up. He knew it. Slowly, while his pal stood rooted to the pavement, he raised his hands, palms out. He had bent over to tend to his ankle so he looked like he was rising from prayer, the fear of God written across his face.

"Non sparare, non sparare," he said quietly, soothingly. *"Carabinieri. Siamo carabinieri."*

He turned, showing the large white armband that had caught my eye. In bold English letters, it read:

CIVIL POLICE
PERMIT PASSAGE
AMGOT

"He says not to shoot, Billy," Kaz said, walking up to them, his

Webley still in his hand.

"That much Italian I've learned," I said, lowering the .45. "Ask them where they got those armbands." Kaz spoke to them, gesturing with the business end of his revolver at the white armbands.

"He says they are from a *carabiniere* unit, the national military police. They have been put to work by AMGOT, patrolling the town and preventing looting."

"Ask him what there is to loot out here."

While the man closest to me finally managed to shut his mouth and stop attracting flies, the other pointed to the buildings, where we were headed. He was taller, and his uniform wasn't as dirty as his buddy's. He spoke emphatically, gesturing to the buildings, to everything around us.

"He says there is machinery in those buildings. A tool-and-die firm, and a printing company. The Americans are employing many locals there. They publish a newspaper and print important proclamations. He and his companion are to guard against looting, so they patrol this entire area. AMGOT is located in the city hall, back in the town center."

"Tell them to beat it, and to keep their mouths shut."

Kaz rattled off some Italian and pointed back the way we'd come with his revolver. The tall fellow drew himself up and replied without moving, pointing to Kaz, Harry, and me. The other guy's mouth opened again.

"He asks what we are doing here, interfering with their duties, and why we have weapons drawn in this rear area," Kaz said. "And he threatens us with arrest."

Great. An honest Sicilian cop and a brave one, to boot. Kaz was smiling. It was just like him to enjoy this predicament.

"OK," I said, holstering my automatic. "Tell him I'm a cop too. Tell him we are on the trail of an American who's involved with the Mafia. Ask him if he wants to help us apprehend him."

That will separate the men from the boys, I thought, as Kaz translated. When he was through, the tall man put his hand on the other man's shoulder, and spoke to him quietly, nodding in the direction of the town center. Looking relieved, the little one shut his mouth and darted off, away from us and the Mafia.

"Sergente Renzo Giannini, *al suo servizio*," the tall one said, snapping a crisp salute my way.

"Ask him why he's willing to help us," I said to Kaz as I returned the salute and studied Renzo. His face was long and his nose was watched over by thick eyebrows that met in the middle. He had an intense look about him as his eyes searched each of us. He looked at me as he answered Kaz.

"Because if you are lying and we are thieves, he will arrest us. The people of Vittoria need this work, they have suffered enough. And if you tell the truth, then he wants his revenge. The Mafia killed his father, who was also a *carabiniere.*"

I looked at Kaz and Harry. A shrug and a nod, and Renzo was in. Now all we needed was a bar to walk into.

CHAPTER ■ THIRTY-SEVEN

THE FIRST BUILDING WAS long and narrow. Stalks of dried dead grass stuck out from sagging drainpipes. Open windows revealed machinery sitting idle in the darkness. Lathes, maybe, I don't know. I never liked getting close to factory work. Long hours doing the same thing while worrying about losing fingers never held any attraction for me.

Peering around the corner, I saw a single deuce-and-half truck parked near the open door at the front of the building. GIs wearing the 45th Division shoulder patch were loading up boxes and gear, pulling out, like the corporal had said. Watching the windows as I walked toward them, I tried to sense any movement inside, any furtive shuffling or shadowy figures. There was nothing, only the beat of my heart and the thuds of heavy cartons being dropped on the truck bed.

I smiled, my best friend-of-the-enlisted man smile. "Hey, fellas, anyone else around here?"

"Who you looking for? Hey, Renzo, *come sta?*"

The private, who looked like he was ready for his sixteenth birthday, exchanged some halting Italian and sign language with Renzo, grinning. He gave him a pack of Luckies and they shook hands warmly.

"Renzo's a great guy," he said. "What are you all looking for? Kind of an odd bunch, aren't you?"

He didn't even try to salute Kaz or Harry. Me, I could've been their driver in my OD undershirt and bandaged right arm. I liked his attitude right away.

"We're looking for an AMGOT print shop. We're supposed to meet a guy there," I said.

"You came to the right place. They're taking over our joint now that we're moving out."

"You're the chap who draws *Willie and Joe*," Harry said. "I saw your picture in the newspaper back in Tunisia. How come no drawings in the paper here?"

"That's me, Bill Mauldin's the name. We're heading up to Caltanissetta now, and if we can find a photoengraver and zinc plates, *Willie and Joe* will be back in business. Wasn't enough here to work with. Gotta go," he said, as the engine started and the other GI newspapermen climbed aboard.

"Wait," I said. "Where's the AMGOT print shop? Is anybody there?"

"Next building over, down at the far end. They're using a small press they found there, but they're going to move into this place as soon as they get reliable electricity. Turning presses by hand is a bear of a job!"

The truck pulled away, Mauldin waving and calling out to Renzo, "*Arrivederci!*"

Everyone was cheery, but my arm was throbbing and I didn't like standing out in the open.

"Let's get inside," I said, glancing up at the roofline of the building across from us.

We went through the double doors. Tables held tin cans full of cigarette butts, empty wine bottles, and scattered pages of the *45th Division News*. It was dark and cooler inside, the concrete walls damp and musty. Behind the tables was a printing press, the huge rollers idle but still glistening with ink from the last run. The room smelled of ink, oil, and tobacco, with the yeasty smell of old wine and sweat thrown in. Any newspaperman I'd known in Boston would have felt right at home.

"Lieutenant Boyle."

I jumped at the sound of my name, startled that someone had come up behind us without our hearing him. The voice came from a figure in the doorway, but my eyes weren't adjusted to the darkness yet and with bright sunlight behind him, I couldn't make him out right away. I could only see his outline and the position of his hands. None of it was threatening. Then his face became clear.

"Howard?" It was the Signals Company lieutenant. Kaz looked at me, one eyebrow raised and the Webley pointed in the general direction of the doorway.

"Yes. Lieutenant Frank Howard, 45th Division Signals," he said, extending his hand to Kaz and Harry, who introduced themselves. I was trying to think why he might be here or how he'd known we were. Perhaps Harding had told him, but before I could ask, he and Renzo were shaking hands.

"*Sono contento di conoscerla, Sergente,*" Howard said, returning Renzo's salute.

"What the hell are you doing here?" I asked.

"I have a message for you."

"How did you know I was here?"

"I wasn't certain you would be. Can we talk privately?"

"If it's about the matter we discussed earlier, Kaz and Harry work with me. They know everything I do." Or don't. But I didn't bother saying that.

"OK," Howard said, leaning against a table and pulling out a crumpled pack of Luckies. He lit one with a shiny Zippo, took a deep drag on it, and spoke as the smoke wafted from his mouth. "There was an uproar after Corporal Miecznikowski let you get away. Or I should say Private, since Stanton busted him and threatened to have him court-martialed for leaving his post. What happened to you anyway?" He seemed finally to notice that I wasn't in the same shape as when he'd last seen me.

"Little run-in with the Luftwaffe. That's too bad about Big Mike."

"Yeah, well, no good deed goes unpunished. Mike's a stand-up guy, and if he thought you were on the level, then you're OK in my book. So when a message came through for Major Elliott from AMGOT in Gela, I took a look."

"What did it say?"

"That you were headed here, to the AMGOT printing facility in Vittoria, and that Elliott should follow to make certain you arrived. There are two Mafia gunmen waiting and a thousand-dollar contract out on you. In real greenbacks, not occupation currency."

"They said that in an open radio message?" Harry asked.

"No, it was in code, to be delivered to Elliott. He's on the road but he's got a communications jeep. I had to let it through, but I thought I should warn you."

"How were you able to decode it?" Harry asked.

"We have all the low-level codebooks. It only took a few minutes, then I passed the message down the line to be transmitted to Elliott."

"Thanks, Howard," I said. "I appreciate it."

"I've got my own beef with these guys. Hutton was one of my best men, and he'd still be alive today if it wasn't for them. I'll stay with you here until things get straightened out." He patted his .45.

"Someone has already taken a shot at Billy," Kaz said. "It may have been the Mafia."

"If there is a contract out on me, I can't believe it comes from Don Calo," I said. "More likely Legs or Vito, working their own deal."

"You don't mean Vito Genovese? And Don Calo, the Mafia boss? You guys travel in strange circles," Howard said.

I walked back and forth in front of the printing press, thinking. Elliott was probably on his way here, with official or unofficial muscle. The shooter who had ambushed us in Scoglitti could be waiting in the next building for another try, or near enough to get off a clean shot as we headed into the AMGOT print shop. They were closing in from two sides; it was time to push back.

They were too damn close to pulling it off, using this big press to run off sheets of scrip with whatever high-denomination plate they had managed to steal or copy. I knew they couldn't have done it yet, not with Bill Mauldin and his crew hanging around. But now that they'd left all that stood in their way was a Sicilian cop and four junior officers with sidearms and one carbine. Well, if they wanted a fight, this was the time to oblige. With Howard's tip-off, we finally had an edge. A small one, but an edge.

"OK, here's what we do," I said, turning to face the others. "Kaz and Harry, get up on the roof and keep a lookout, one on each end. Watch for Elliott on the road, and the local shooter and his pals in one of the other three buildings."

"What are you going to do?" Frank asked me.

I wasn't sure. There were three long, narrow concrete buildings on our side of the road. We were in the front of the first one. The AMGOT print shop was at the other end of the middle building, which was the largest of the three. It stood two stories tall, wider than the buildings on either side, and was a grimy unpainted gray.

"I'm going to go in quietly, through the other end of the big building. They'll be expecting me to walk in through the print-shop entrance."

"What do you want us to do if Elliott shows up?" Harry asked.

"Shoot over his head or disable the jeep if you can hit it with that thing," I said, pointing to his carbine. "But keep your head down. Depending on who he has with him, you might be outgunned."

"And he is a superior officer," Harry said. "His Majesty frowns on his subjects shooting their allies."

"This could all turn out badly," I said. "No reason not to bow out now, if anyone wants to. Probably would be the smart move."

Kaz and Howard both spoke with Renzo, quick bursts of Italian and hand gestures.

·"*Sono con lei*," Renzo said. He unshouldered his Italian carbine and worked the bolt. I didn't need a translation.

"We'll go with you," Howard said, pointing to Renzo. "You'll need somebody to watch your back once you're inside."

A stairwell at the end of the building led up to the roof. We shook hands all around, and then Kaz and Harry clambered up the steps, out through a small shed and onto the open tin roof. Four air vents stuck up at intervals, the blades of their fans idly turning in the rising heat. The roofline had a slight slant, and I hoped it was enough to keep both of them hidden while they stood watch.

I couldn't worry about Kaz and Harry for long. I had other things to think about, like whether Renzo and Howard were going to be more help or hindrance. And whether someone was waiting around the next corner to put a bullet in my head.

We went out through the double doors we'd entered by. I put my finger to my lips to signal for silence, and they nodded. Good so far. Then I pointed across the road, to a small cinder-block building. Then motioned forward for them to follow. I took off running low, listening to the sounds of their boots scuffing across the hard-packed dirt. We circled to the back of the cinder-block building, skirting piles of rotting garbage. Coming around to the front, we faced the big gray building with the AMGOT print shop at the other end. I motioned them to get down, and they obeyed, out of breath and looking puzzled.

I never liked frontal assaults. Not as a soldier in the army or as a cop. What sense was there in crossing open ground or banging down a front door? That was always where the firepower was focused. Me, I liked the oblique approach. That's what Dad called it. By the time they shut the door, we'll be coming through the window, he used to say. And then Uncle Dan would chime in, When they shut the window, we'll be coming through the door. It's some old kids' song, and ended with them coming through the floor. They always thought it was hilarious. I wasn't so sure about that, but I got the point. "Hit 'em where they ain't." Even though that one came from New York Yankee Wee Willie Keeler, I still liked it. I liked Willie too, a little guy who played smart. He made it sound simple.

So that's what I was doing. Going through the window while they were watching the door. I motioned forward and we ran, crouching, hoping the bad guys didn't have anybody up on the other roof.

They didn't. We leaned against the wall next to the door, waiting for our breathing to slow down. It was hot in the late afternoon sun, and sweat dripped into my eyes. I wiped it away, grimacing as I raised my arm. I ignored the pain and put my hand on the iron door handle, which was already starting to rust. I pushed it down, feeling its grittiness against my sweaty palm. The door opened with a creak, and I stepped aside, ready for a hail of bullets. None came. I pushed the door with my shoulder, opening it wider. Signaling for Howard and Renzo to follow me, low and to the right, I moved in, keeping my back to the wall and sidestepping right. I kneeled and they followed suit.

It was dark inside. There were only two small windows. One was broken, taped over with newsprint. The other was filthy, barely letting in any light. I pointed to my eyes: Wait here and get adjusted to the darkness. It was cool; the concrete at my back felt damp and refreshing after the hot sun. Things came into focus: a workbench, wooden boxes of tools stacked on the floor, machine parts on the tables. Some sort of workshop. The room took up the width of the building. Another door faced us at the far end. When I thought we could see clearly enough not to stumble over a pile of wrenches and pliers or knock over a table, I got up and walked to that door.

Another creak and it opened. The second room was huge, and I guessed that the third one would contain the printing presses; there wasn't that much more building left. Large double doors on tracks faced each other from opposite walls. This was a garage of sorts. A broken-down truck, tires gone and engine removed, stood next to us, doors hanging open. Chains and pulleys hung from the ceiling, and there was a pit in the middle, so the mechanics could work underneath the vehicles. It wasn't the neatest shop I'd ever seen. Oil drums leaked dark fluids, and bolts and other discarded parts littered the floor. It was dark in here too, but the coolness was marred by the rancid odor of spoiled food. A table held plates of unrecognizable shapes, buzzing with flies and decorated with mouse droppings. I wondered why people weren't back at work by now, or at least cleaning up. Then I realized the present tenants probably didn't encourage visitors.

We eased our way around the hanging chains, stepping over anything that might make a sound. I thought I heard a noise, a shout from outside. I signaled Howard and Renzo to stop. Then three shots rang out in quick succession, the *pop pop pop* sounding like Harry's carbine, and before I could even think, two explosions sounded in the darkened room—*boom boom*—amid flashes that burst white against my eyeballs. Renzo fell backward, his white armband spattered with blood, before Howard turned from him in a single swift motion, bringing the butt of his automatic up to the side of my head.

My brain came to before my body. Not that it had been all that much help to me that day. But I had to give it credit—it had been sending me messages. Baseball messages. The New York Yankees. New York. Lieutenant Frank Howard, from New York City. Who worked on the docks, where Lucky Luciano and Vito Genovese controlled the unions. At the center of the II Corps communications network, in charge of the Message Section. Not the Code Section, where Captain Stanton held sway. So there had been no coded message. That was only an excuse, a pretext for Howard to tag along and take me by surprise.

Why was I still breathing? Why had Howard killed Renzo? Or had he? Was he was waiting for Elliott to show up?

Sounds worked their way into my awareness, along with the feel of rope tight around my wrists, the cold cement floor, and that increasingly familiar feeling of blood in my hair and a throbbing headache. I opened my eyes and saw the ugly face of Vito Genovese staring down at me. He wore nicely pressed U.S. Army khakis, and an officer's garrison cap with no rank insignia. I couldn't help noticing that the braid was gray and gold, the colors of the Paymaster Department. I had to laugh, even though it hurt.

"It's good to keep your sense of humor," Vito said. "What's so funny?"

"Do you know the braid on your cap is in paymaster colors?"

"No, I didn't. That is pretty funny, I gotta admit." He kneeled down to look me in the eyes. "But what's gonna happen to you if you don't talk, now that ain't funny. How much do you know, and who else knows it?"

"I know that you're going to kill me either way. And everybody else knows you're a lying crook too."

"You're a real comedian, Boyle. Ain't he a riot, Box Hook?"

"I'm not laughing yet," Howard said. Box Hook? I didn't have to think hard about how he got that nickname on the docks. A longshoreman's hook was an ugly weapon.

"OK, OK," Vito said, waggling his hand back and forth. "Listen, Boyle, I know I'm safe here. You got a deal with Don Calo and I'm it. I can hide Box Hook out so the army'll never find him. So we don't gotta kill you. But we do need to know who else knows what you know. Tell us, and we leave you here, tied up but alive. Someone'll come along."

Vito hadn't risen in ranks of the Mob by leaving witnesses alive, so I knew he was spinning one for me. It seemed like a good idea to buy time and wait. For what, I wasn't sure.

"Hey, Box Hook, any idea where Vito will hide you? Now that he doesn't need you? I'd say six feet under but the ground is pretty hard around here. I'd bet two feet, maximum."

"Nice try, Boyle, but Vito and me go way back. I got no worries on that account."

"Stand up," Vito said, and I noticed for the first time that he was holding my .45. Howard had Renzo's carbine, and then I saw how it was going to happen. A renegade Sicilian shoots me, then Howard plugs him. But what about those first shots? Nobody was mentioning Elliott. I didn't get it.

Vito rapped on the door to the print shop. It opened, and Legs appeared, dressed in army khakis like Vito's, holding an automatic. I could see a small vertical printing press, not one with rollers like the big one Mauldin and his crew had been using. It had a big plate. A lever press, I think they called it. Next to it was an ornate iron paper cutter, its sharp blade a yard long. Stacks of neatly tied occupation lire filled the space along the wall.

"You've been busy," I said.

"Shut up," Howard replied and shoved me into the room.

Kaz stood in the corner, his hands on his head and his holster empty. Legs had the Webley stuck in his belt.

"I'm sorry, Billy," Kaz said. "We tried to warn you with the gun-shots—"

"You shut up," Legs said, pulling his gun hand back as if to smack him. Kaz flinched, and Legs laughed. "Fucking four-eyed Polack."

"All right, let's get this over with," Vito said, waving with his pistol for Legs to bring Kaz closer. Legs stuck his gun in Kaz's back and prodded him forward. "I know you want to play by the rules and not tell us anything. But perhaps the rules won't mean as much when we cut your pal's hand off. For starters."

"No!" Kaz shrieked as Howard grabbed his left hand and shoved it under the blade. He held it there while Legs walked around the cutter and grabbed his wrist from the other side. Kaz yelled and writhed in Howard's grasp.

"OK, I'll talk," I said, blurting out the words in the hope of stemming Kaz's panic.

"What would be the fun in that?" Legs asked. The paper cutter had a large wheel on top, about five feet up. He had one hand on that, the other clasped around Kaz's wrist. Below the wheel was a curved arch above the long blade. He looked through it at Kaz, still squirming in fear.

"Take it easy, Four-Eyes, it'll be worse if you don't stay still," Legs taunted. It was obvious he relished Kaz's fear.

"Don't! Please, don't," I said to Vito.

"It's too late. You need to learn who is in charge here."

"Hold onto him, Box Hook," Legs said. "I'm gonna enjoy this."

Kaz kicked out and Howard's grip loosened. I saw a small pistol appear in Kaz's right hand and fly up. A flash and a loud blast and Legs's left eye disappeared in a blur of red. Kaz twisted as Howard tried to keep his grasp on him. Kaz jammed the pistol to Howard's chest, fired twice, then a third time.

I lifted my bound hands and slammed them into Vito, sending him sprawling against the stacked piles of lire. His .45—mine, actually—slid across the floor.

Howard dropped, finally releasing Kaz from his embrace. Legs, whose bloody head had been resting against the cutter's iron plate, rolled off and thumped to the floor.

Kaz pushed his glasses up on the bridge of his nose. "I do not appreciate ethnic slurs," he said, turning the pistol on Vito. "Do you, Mr. Genovese?"

"You can't touch me, Don Calo's orders!"

"Billy, would you say Don Calo meant we could not arrest or kill this man?"

"Exactly, Kaz," I said, trying to get my rapid heartbeat back to normal. I picked up my .45 and held it with bound hands, trained on Genovese. "That leaves us with a lot of latitude."

"You can have it all, don't shoot me. Please!"

"Is it too late?" I asked Kaz. "Does Vito need to learn who's in charge here?"

"No," the mobster said, as if he couldn't believe what was happening. My finger closed around the trigger. It felt good. My Irish was up, and I would have no regrets about shooting this bum, who moments ago had given the go-ahead to a sadist to take Kaz's hand off. But I had made a promise, and it was a promise worth keeping. Not the one to Don Calo. The one to myself. I wasn't going to kill an unarmed man.

"Get out," I said to Vito. Kaz nodded.

Vito got up stiffly, his eyes darting between the dead thugs and the two guns leveled at him. He made a show of brushing himself off, deciding, with the shrewdness that had kept him alive this long, that neither of our bullets had his name on it. He walked to the door, picking up two bundles of thousand-lira scrip as he did so. He looked at the corpses again and shrugged, whatever emotion he felt contained in that small gesture. He left us, a tiny fraction of the fortune he had planned on reaping tucked under his arm.

I really didn't care.

CHAPTER THIRTY-EIGHT

"YOU HAD THE BERETTA," I said, when I had recovered enough to notice the automatic in Kaz's hand.

"Yes, my backup gat, Billy. I had it inside my shirt, under my belt. It was uncomfortable, but it proved its value when I finally got my arm free."

"Are you OK, Kaz?"

"Yes. Now I am."

I clapped him on the shoulder and smiled. I seemed to be more concerned about what had almost happened to him than he did. But nonchalance was an art form with Kaz, and he was becoming tougher to read. A hard shell had formed over his soul, and I wondered if I'd ever see it revealed again.

"What were those first shots I heard?"

"Harry was trying to signal you. When I looked down at the jeep in which Lieutenant Howard had arrived—you must explain his nickname to me later—I saw a rifle partially hidden under a blanket. I thought we would have a better chance at shooting out Elliott's tires with a rifle, so I went down to look. It was a sniper rifle, with a telescopic sight. I knew he must have been the shooter. But Legs was waiting, and captured me as I ran between the buildings."

"I'm glad he was the type to underestimate guys who wear glasses. Let's get out of here." The flies were already gathering on the corpses. Kaz retrieved his Webley and as we left, I glanced at the stacks of bound notes. How much dough was this anyway? They were farther along than I had expected, not as far as I had feared. If we had been much later, Vito and his crew would have been busy laundering this small fortune, probably starting a major black market operation.

We walked across the space between the two buildings, and heard the distant sound of a jeep driving off. So long, Vito.

"We ought to find you an ankle holster for that Beretta," I said.

"That would be quite excellent—"

Two shots interrupted us. Harry's carbine from the roof again.

"Elliott," I said, and we broke into a run. Return fire echoed against the buildings, the sound of braking jeeps and squealing tires mixing with shouts and orders. It sounded like Harry had taken on an entire company.

"Up here!"

I looked up to see Harry in a second-story window. He tossed down his carbine, and I caught it, looking around for a target. Harry dangled from the windowsill and dropped, hitting the ground hard. The impact must have jarred the healing wound in his leg.

"There's half a dozen jeeps out there," he said, limping along with us. "Some MPs. I figured it had to be Elliott and fired above their heads to slow them down. We have to get out."

"Come on," I said, helping Harry along as he half ran and half hopped.

"What happened in there? Where's Howard?"

"I'll tell you when we get clear," I said.

"Box Hook. His name was Box Hook," Kaz said, still excited over a new bit of gangster jargon.

We ran along the edge of the building, away from the road. At the corner, we squatted low and scanned the terrain. Flat ground all around. A line of trees about fifty yards out, then an olive grove. If we could make it that far, we could vanish. I checked the clip in the carbine. Three shells left. I handed it to Harry.

"Any more ammo?"

He shook his head.

"OK. Don't shoot unless it's absolutely necessary. Three of these will only make them angry."

"Whatever you say, Billy. Shall we run for it?"

Kaz tapped me on the shoulder. The sound of racing engines rattled against the walls, and I heard gravel spitting and gears grinding as jeeps came around both sides of the building. Clouds of dust filled the air and within seconds four jeeps had blocked our escape, while two others drove around the other buildings, checking for more of our accomplices. I wondered what Elliott would say when he found Howard and Legs stiffening up in the print shop.

"Lieutenant William Boyle?" I instantly recognized the voice. It was Elliott. I shielded my eyes against the dust settling around us where the jeeps had slammed on their brakes. I could make out several Thompsons and one jeep-mounted .30 caliber machine gun pointed at us. Harry let the carbine drop to the ground.

"That's me," I said, standing with my arms raised high. I didn't want to give him a chance to shoot first and ask no questions later. "These two aren't with me, I just met them here."

Elliott vaulted from his jeep and walked straight up to me, holstering his automatic as he did so.

"Lieutenant Boyle, you are one dumb son-of-a-bitch flatfoot, I'll tell you that right now." His mustache twitched in what was almost a smile. I didn't like being caught much, and I liked being caught and insulted even less.

"Listen, Elliott, I'm sick of you and your Mafia pals. Do what you have to do and be glad you didn't end up like your flunkies in there."

"Who are you talking about?"

"Legs and Box Hook.

Elliott stood there, looking at me, Harry, and Kaz for a long time, shaking his head sadly.

"Major," he yelled, not taking his eyes off me. "Major Harding! Come over here and take charge of these three."

All the guns moved off us. An MP came running from the print shop and reported to Elliott, who listened and did that mustache twitch again. I saw a figure in the far jeep remove his helmet.

"Gentleman," Harding said, "I'm glad to see you are all right, but not happy at being shot at by you."

"We thought . . . who . . . ?" That was about all I could get out.

"This is Major John Elliott, Criminal Investigation Division. He's been working undercover as an AMGOT officer to track down a series of supply thefts and rumors of a counterfeit ring."

"You're not one of them?" Kaz said, pointing to the print shop.

"Hell no, and I'm glad of it, from what I just learned. I've been on their trail since North Africa."

"Rocko and Andrews," I said, remembering what Howard had said about Rocko suckering Andrews in. I figured that part was true enough.

"Right. First radios, then more equipment went missing. We had some good leads, but when Rocko turned up dead and I lost Hutton, the trail ran out."

"Lost Hutton? What do you mean?"

"Hutton was CID too. He worked in our communications center. We needed someone in the Signals outfit, and he volunteered."

"That's why he had the number of the headquarters in Algiers written down. He was reporting to you."

"Yep. He had several numbers in Algiers and at Forward Headquarters in Tunisia."

"But how did you glom onto me?"

"I tracked down a couple of boys from the Eighty-second, Joe and Clancy. They told me about Hutton buying it up there, and once I convinced them I wasn't on a chickenshit detail, they told me that you'd given them his name as yours."

"And that's when you started looking for me."

"Right. Turned out Major Harding and I were both looking for you. CID had no idea about the operation you were involved with. The major filled me in."

"Well, at the time, Major, neither did I. When I tried to put the pieces together, your name kept coming up. Then when I heard you had the MPs at the Signals Company looking for me—"

"You figured I was gunning for you. I was trying to help you, but you are one slippery customer."

"I can vouch for that," Harding said. "Do you need us for anything now, Major?"

"Not unless you want to watch a fortune in scrip go up in smoke."

"I'll be happy never to see another lira again," I said.

"Come on, boys," Harding said, leading us over to his jeep. In the passenger seat sat Sciafani, dressed in GI fatigues with a medic's bag in his lap.

"Enrico! What are you doing here?"

"I told Major Harding you would probably have been hit in the head again. Was I right?"

"And the arm," Kaz added helpfully.

"I think I reinjured my leg," Harry said, like a kid who didn't want to be left out.

"Patch 'em up," Harding said. Sciafani grinned and dug into his medical kit. "How about you, Lieutenant Kazimierz, any wounds?"

"I almost had my hand cut off, but I am quite fine, thank you."

I hadn't often seen Harding at a loss for words, but he looked at Kaz with a stunned expression, then regrouped.

"Glad to hear it. Boyle, any loose ends here?"

"We let Vito Genovese go," Kaz said flatly, as if he already regretted it.

"It's for the best, in the long run," Harding said, in a hesitant whisper. He didn't like it much himself.

"As long as these MPs don't stick too many thousand-lira notes up their sleeves, that should do it. Frank Howard, otherwise known as Box Hook back in the New York dockyards, must have been the primary contact with Vito. He could run everything out of the Signals Company."

"Who killed Rocko?" Harding asked.

"Don't know for sure. Probably not Vito, although he came to see Rocko that night. For that sort of dirty work, I'd bet it was Legs. Anyway, the whole song and dance about stealing the division payroll was a red herring. This was the real thing all along. Running off thousand-lira notes that no one knew about and laundering them through Mafia operations."

"Smart. Made us focus on the payroll and all the time they were planning on printing their own money," Harding said.

"Who is Charlotte?" Harry said, rubbing his chin.

"Had Howard been at the military government school at Charlottesville?" I asked.

"He had," Elliott said. "He took a course on civilian communications—maybe that was where he got the idea to link into the civilian phone lines. Since he didn't actually work for AMGOT, using Charlotte as a code name worked. Besides hinting at a female, if anyone overheard they might draw the conclusion it was someone from AMGOT, like me."

"It had us wondering, all right. Ow!"

I winced as Sciafani checked the lump on my head and cleaned the dried blood from my hair. Harding passed a canteen around and we all took thirsty gulps. I felt the water wash away the grit in my throat and ran my tongue over my teeth. Everything was so hot and dry here that the air was always filled with the fine dust kicked up from the ground. The simple act of walking stirred up the ground and sent tiny bits of Sicily into your body, coating your lungs, staying with you, no matter how hard you tried to wash it away.

A sharp pain pulled at my arm, and Sciafani smiled apologetically as he drew another stitch across the wound. The pain reminded me how lucky I was to be alive.

"There are a couple of loose ends, Major," I said. "There's a third body in that building, a Sicilian *carabiniere*. Renzo Giannini. He was with us, and Howard shot him. I don't want anybody thinking he was part of the Mob. He volunteered to help us out."

"I'll tell the local authorities," Harding said.

"And I probably got an MP in a lot of hot water. He was detailed to hold me back at the Signals Company. Corporal Mike Miecznikowski. Turned out he was a cop too, and we got to talking, and pretty soon he looked the other way. We didn't know about Elliott being with CID. Anything you can do?"

"Jesus Christ on a crutch, Boyle! Did you enlist your own police force today? MPs, Sicilian cops. What's next?"

"Sorry, Major. But I do owe the guy."

"Well, I already let Nick go back to ONI without telling them about the blackmail attempt. Springing one more pal of yours who doesn't follow orders shouldn't set back the war effort too much."

The heat must have gotten to Sam Harding. Bending the rules twice in one day?

"There, you should be fine," Sciafani said. "Stitches out in a week, keep it clean. You are lucky you did not get hit on the head in the same spot as before."

"If I was really lucky, I wouldn't have gotten hit at all. My kind of luck seems to be limited to getting hit on the head in two different locations."

"Do you remember everything now?"

"Yes. I am no longer the most fortunate of men. I won't be discovering myself all over again."

"Good," Sciafani said as he unlaced Harry's boot. "As long as you are satisfied with what you found the first time."

I thought about that. Was I? Sciafani taped up Harry's ankle while Kaz watched. He held his left arm cradled in his right, the arm that had been under the blade. I saw that it trembled. His face was a mask of indifference, the scar down his cheek hiding the sadness in his eyes. I stood by him, casually draping my arm around his shoulder.

"Yes. I am."

CHAPTER ▪ THIRTY-NINE

THE NEXT MORNING, I watched a Sicilian dust cloud churned up by the twin engines of a C-47 transport as it took off from the Comiso airfield. The ground fell away and beneath me I saw the great buildup of Allied forces, the vision of the New World's might I had conjured for Don Calo made real. Acres of supplies. Aircraft lined up on the runway, bombers and fighters waiting for their next mission. Convoys snaking along the narrow roadways. Ships docked and disgorging men and machines. Destroyers cruising close to shore, cruisers off in the distance.

I wondered if the gold silk handkerchief was in Don Calo's pocket right now, and how many lives it might have saved, and for how long. As the plane banked to head for North Africa, I could see a thin line of land on the horizon, across the Strait of Messina. Mainland Italy. We still had a long, long way to go.

"Never been in a plane before," Big Mike said. He sat stiffly in the seat, as if moving his big body around might jar the aircraft off course.

"Neither have I," said Sciafani, watching his homeland slip away as the C-47 rose and flew through white, fluffy cumulus clouds.

Harding had sprung Big Mike and gotten him his corporal's stripes back. Officially, Harding had him assigned to his command to transport an Italian ex-POW to Tunisia. The best Harding could do for Sciafani was to get him a job with AMGOT as a doctor in an Italian POW camp there. It was the only way to get him out of Sicily and away from Don Calo, who could be counted on to keep his promise if their paths crossed. Sciafani wasn't happy about the POW camp, where he'd be only a step above a prisoner. But it beat a knife across his gullet, so he packed a medical kit and made the best of it.

"Perhaps I will visit you in Boston, Billy, after the war," he said. "Or you in Detroit, Mike."

"Sure," Big Mike said, kneading his thighs with his hands. "How much longer before we land?"

"Relax," I said. "It'll be a few hours."

A few hours. A few hours until I'd be on the same continent as Diana again. I was heading back to North Africa to give Uncle Ike a report on our contact with Don Calo, and everything that had followed from that. Harding had also ordered a full medical check for me, to make sure I was recovered from the whacks I'd taken and my amnesia. I didn't mind a few pokes and prods if it gave me an extra day or so with Diana. Harding had allowed Big Mike a couple of days before he had to deliver Sciafani to the POW camp, in case I could work anything out for Enrico. The States, or maybe England, but that was doubtful for any Italian outside of a POW cage. Still, for me it would mean a few days of doing relatively little. Sleeping in, eating regular chow, clean clothes, nobody shooting at me. It's the little things that make life bearable.

Then it would be back to Harding in Sicily, unless Uncle Ike needed me for something else. Maybe a colonel stealing a general's scotch, or a visiting congressman getting mugged in the Casbah. Either way, I'd be back in trouble soon enough.

Harry had been given two weeks' leave for his troubles, time for his leg to fully heal, and had talked his way onto an RAF flight to England. Kaz was staying with Harding, waiting for something else to keep him amused while he decided if he wanted to live another day or so. He'd seen me off at the airfield, and I watched his hand for any telltale shakes. There was nothing, no hint of any break in the shell. But I knew. I knew his heart would never heal. I knew too what a good and true friend he was to me, to watch me leave, knowing I would soon be reunited with Daphne's sister. I'd be in her arms tonight, and Kaz would be sitting outside Harding's HQ, his scarred face turned to the stars, dreaming of Daphne. Alone.

Not for the first time, I wondered at my good fortune, and Diana's. We were alive. After Dunkirk, after Norway, North Africa, and now Sicily, we still had each other. I'd been a fool to let my worries come between us, my rage at Villard and my juvenile, insane, perverse fear of what being raped had done to her. Or to me. It had hurt both of us, and now it was time for me to put it behind us. If I could.

Didn't it say something in the Bible about the truth? Know the truth, and it will set you free? Sometimes I think being a cop made me too literal, always looking for physical evidence, a confession, the stolen silverware. Real things, not concepts like freedom and the truth. I'm not a slave, so why do I need the truth to free me?

Big Mike had gotten over his terror and was zonked out, sawing logs. Sciafani watched the clouds, and I felt the ache in my gut as I thought about Diana. Half fear, half joy. Not the best mix.

The drone of the engines dulled my thoughts until I fell into a half sleep, startled by every patch of rough air. Finally we began descending, the North African coast visible below us, clear blue water churning up white foamy waves on sandy beaches. Peaceful, sandy beaches. We touched down at an airfield outside of Amilcar, north of Tunis. General Eisenhower didn't have a full staff here. Forward HQ occupied a villa overlooking the ocean. I don't know how nice it was for the WACs and GIs living in tents behind the villa, but the senior staff sure liked it.

And a staff car was waiting for us. It brought me straight to headquarters, dropped me off, and took Big Mike and Sciafani to the tent they had assigned us. I walked up the front steps, returning the salutes of the two guards by the door. As I entered, I had to pass Uncle Ike's toughest guard post. That was the desk of Sergeant Sue Sarafian, secretary and receptionist to the general. With the general and other senior officers, Sue and the others were always formal, calling them by their rank. It had taken me a while, but I finally convinced her to call me Billy.

"Welcome back, Billy," Sue said, gracing me with a smile. "The boss is expecting you."

"Thanks, Sue. Who else is here from Algiers?"

"Tex is with the boss, and I'm sure you know Ensign Seaton is here. She's at a briefing with General Clark but will be back this evening. There's going to be a dinner party. When the boss heard you were coming, he decided to go all out. Now get in there and don't keep him waiting!"

This last part was delivered in a conspiratorial whisper. The girls in Uncle Ike's office worked around the clock. They were there when he showed up early in the morning and only left after he did, late in the evening. The mess tent was usually shut down by then, so food was a source of endless discussion. Especially any food different from the usual army fare. I knew Sue was glad to see me, but what she was excited about was the possibility of a real meal.

I knocked on Uncle Ike's door and it was opened by Captain Tex Lee, the general's aide.

"Go on in, Billy, we're all done," Tex said as he held the door for me.

I stepped into the room and came to attention. "General," I said, standing as straight as I could. I never assumed he wanted to be informal. There were times when he was "the boss," as Sue called him, when he had to be the commanding officer and not a relative. I was careful to let him be the one to set the tone.

"William," he said, standing up from his desk and crushing out a cigarette. "How are you, son? Sit, sit."

He gestured to two chairs facing a window overlooking the courtyard. The white stucco gleamed in the bright sun against a deep blue sky. I sat, trying to stop myself from relaxing. The last week or so was catching up to me.

"How are you feeling? I heard you'd lost your memory for a while. Are you all right now?"

"Yes, sir, it all came back after a few days. I'm fine now."

"When we met on the road in Sicily, how long was that after it happened?"

"Not long, sir. I'm afraid I was a bit mixed up then. I knew who you were, but I still didn't have everything straightened out."

"My God, William," Uncle Ike said, sitting back and lighting another one of the Lucky Strikes that he smoked by the gross. "Wandering around Sicily trying to figure out who you were, and you still completed your mission. Amazing. Patton went through the mountains to Palermo like a hot knife through butter after your visit with that Mafia fellow. I'm not saying it was all due to your efforts—Georgie and his boys are doing a fine job—but not having to stop and clear out every mountain crossroads has saved us time and lives."

"That's what I told Don Calo." As I said it, I wondered about Signora Patane and whether the *tubercolosi* had taken her yet. Was Signor Patane pressing the dried herbs in the kitchen to his nose right now, remembering the smell of them on her hands as she tied them?

"Did it make a difference to him? Saving Allied lives?"

I knew Uncle Ike didn't mean to leave out Sicilian lives. American and British were the ones he was responsible for, the lives he thought about every day. To add to them the burden of civilian lives in an enemy country was more than I could bear to think about.

"Yes. Yes, it did."

"William, are you sure you feel all right?"

"Yes, sir. I'm OK. A good night's sleep and I'll be ready to go."

"I'm sure the past week has put a lot of stress on you. Major Harding has you set for a medical exam tomorrow. Let the doctors check you out and tell me what they say. If you need a rest, you can stay here a while. Take Miss Seaton to the beach, go for a swim. How does that sound?"

"Great, Uncle Ike. Thanks."

He rose and placed a hand on my shoulder and stared out the window. It was something he did often, whether it was at Grosvenor Square in London, the St. George Hotel in Algiers, or here in Amilcar. It was as if he were watching for a sign or a judgment. I couldn't tell which, or if he hoped for or feared it.

"We've come a long way, William, since London."

"Yes, sir." I didn't think he meant the two of us.

"We've occupied enemy soil and toppled Mussolini. The King of Italy has appointed Badoglio prime minister. Italians are surrendering everywhere. There's a good chance they'll come into the war on our side. All because of our success in Sicily. And you played a vital role in that, William."

"Yes, sir."

"You've already done more than most of my generals. I wish I could promise you more than a few days' rest. You've proved your worth to me, William. But it's still a long way to Berlin, and I'm going to need you to help us get there."

"Every day, a little closer to Berlin, General," I said, remembering what I had told Remke, and trying not to think about what the future held for me. It came out choked, like a line you rehearsed a hundred times but blew when you tried to say it.

"That's the spirit, William. The harder we work at this, the sooner more of us will be home again."

"Yes, sir." I noticed he didn't say all of us. I thought about the Me110 bullet grazing my arm. How much longer would my Irish luck hold out?

"Now, you be sure to write your mother," he said, looking me in the eye with an uncle's admonition. "I sent a note telling her you were fine and how proud I was of you. The invasion news may alarm her, so be sure to write soon. That's an order, William."

"Yes, sir, I will," I said as I rose from the chair and looked Uncle Ike in the eye. He nodded, and walked me to the door.

"Come for dinner tonight with Miss Seaton. We're putting on the feed bag for General Alexander and some of his group. Have some good food, enjoy yourself." He put his arm around my shoulder and smiled.

I thanked him and walked down the hall, remembering how Kaz had looked when I put my arm around his shoulder to buck him up. I was glad there wasn't a mirror handy.

I saw Diana on the balcony, turned away from everyone, touching up her lipstick, her eyes focused on the mirror in a gold compact. She clicked it shut, slid it into her uniform pocket. She glanced around the group gathered on the veranda, but didn't notice me coming up the stairs. She looked incredible. Her light brown tropical-weight FANY uniform fitted her perfectly, which meant she'd regained some weight since I'd last seen her. Her face was tanned, giving her a healthy, robust look. The honey-colored hair tucked under her FANY cap had been tinted blond by the North African sun, which lit the people on the veranda now with a glowing, horizontal light, making them look like characters in a painting. She waved to someone and smiled, and at that point I couldn't wait a second longer. I went to her and she turned, her face lighting up with a smile.

"Billy," her lips said, without making a sound. We embraced, forgetting for a moment that the highest-ranking Allied generals in the Mediterranean were watching us. We forced ourselves apart, and she sheepishly looked at her shoes. We clung to each other's arms like dancers.

"You look great," I said, feeling like a shy schoolchild.

"You look like bloody hell," she said. "What's this?" She felt the bandage on my arm under the shirtsleeve.

"A few stitches, that's all." I touched my forehead, where a bruise had spread from my hairline. "And a bump, nothing much."

Diana ran her hands over my chest and arms. She bit her lip, tears leaking from her eyes.

"You're a terrible liar. Come with me," she said, linking her arm in mine. We walked down steps inlaid with colorful tiles to the beach. White sand and palm trees stretched along the curving shore, a cool evening breeze blowing at our backs. It felt clean and fresh after Sicily.

"I want to hear about it," she said.

"I don't know where to start."

"General Eisenhower told me what you managed to do. He's quite proud of you. But what I want to know is, what happened to you? You were injured and lost your memory, that's all I know."

Her grip tightened on my arm as she spoke. We stopped.

"I knew who you were. I remembered you. Not your name at first, but you came to me in my dreams. When I couldn't remember anything, you were there. I thought of you as the woman of my dreams. Then one night, I dreamed I couldn't find you."

We leaned into each other, foreheads touching, hands clenched together. I felt tears on my cheeks, and I was embarrassed.

"I had the same dream," she said. "I waited for you somewhere, and you didn't come back, from somewhere. You know how it is in dreams. I tried to find you, but I kept getting lost."

I put my arm around her waist, and we walked through the soft sand.

"When I was trying to figure out who I was, I ran into a Sicilian doctor. He told me about amnesia and said I was the most fortunate of men because I was about to discover who I was. He told me some philosopher once said the unexamined life is not worth living, and that I was being given the opportunity to examine mine."

"How did he know you'd get your memory back?"

"He had studied amnesia. He called mine psycho something and was sure I'd remember everything in time. The last thing to return, he said, would be the event that had caused it. He's a smart guy. I brought him back here with me."

"Why?"

"Listen," I said, "It's a long story. Right now I want to tell you something else."

"What, Billy?" She stopped and put one hand on my arm, the other to her breast, as if holding me back and protecting her heart.

"He was right. I did learn who I was. Some of it was a shock, mostly about how I treated you."

"What do you mean?"

"After Villard," I said.

Then I started over. "After Villard raped you, all I wanted was revenge. But it was for what he'd done to me, not to you. I thought going after him would help, but it didn't."

"I wanted him dead too," Diana said, her lips clenched.

"I know. And he deserved it. But I should have let you know that what he did, whether he was dead or alive, it made no difference. It wasn't about us."

We walked again, and she was silent for a while.

"Does it?"

"What?"

"Make no difference, about us?"

"No. What's done is done. It's real, it happened, and we can't forget about it, and I can't pretend killing Villard made it go away. But it's not who we are. I didn't tell you the truth about this," I said, touching the bandage on my arm. "It isn't serious, but it could have been. It was a shell from a German plane. One more inch and I would have lost my arm. Six more inches and it would have taken my head off."

"What's done is done. No use pretending it didn't happen."

"Right," I said. We walked some more, the sound of the surf enveloping us.

"But no sense dwelling on it. Either of us could be killed tomorrow."

"Right."

"All right, Billy, all right." She leaned her head into my shoulder and held onto my arm with both of her hands, uncovering her heart. "All right."

CHAPTER ▪ FORTY

WE MADE IT BACK to the party an hour later, after the sun had set and we'd shaken the sand out of our clothes. Everyone was still outside drinking cocktails. Candles lit the veranda, their flames reflected in all the polished brass.

I spotted Sciafani. Big Mike had organized a suit for him to wear. I'd alerted Sue that a local doctor would be attending, and she got him past the guards after they'd given him the once-over. It wasn't exactly a lie, since he was local, now that he was here. I figured we had at least a chance, among all the American and British muckety-mucks getting gassed on Uncle Ike's booze, of getting someone to intervene for him.

"Ah, so this is the Sicilian doctor who knows his Socrates," Diana said when I introduced them.

"An honor, Miss Seaton," he said, bowing and kissing her hand. If I'd known he was going to show off like that, I would have left him to play cribbage in the tent with Big Mike. I got us drinks and scanned the crowd for a likely candidate. I didn't want to bother Uncle Ike for a personal favor if I could work it out myself. He had enough of that all day long. It looked like Enrico and Diana were hitting it off, so I buttonholed a British major with medical insignia on his uniform. Turned out he was a dentist and was being transferred to Cairo, so I gave up on him after apologizing for not listening to yet another story about tooth extractions gone bad. Then on to an American colonel who was on the G-1 staff at HQ, which meant personnel. No dice with him either.

I found Diana and Sciafani as the group filed in for dinner, talking with none other than Uncle Ike. I had to hand it to Diana, she took matters right to the top.

"I was just telling Dr. Sciafani that civilian immigration is outside of my jurisdiction," Uncle Ike said. "I wish I could repay you for the help you've given William, but there's nothing I can do. Except, of course, to make certain you are well supplied for your duties in the POW facility."

"Thank you, General. That is most generous. I am honored," Sciafani said, shaking Uncle Ike's hand.

"Let Sergeant Sarafian know whatever you need. Now, excuse me, I have to play the gracious host." He gave us all his famous grin, that friendly gaze right into your eyes. It got me every time.

"He is a great man, and gracious," Sciafani said.

"Yes, runs in the family, they say," I said.

"Tell me, Enrico, is it true that losing one's memory causes a swelled head?" Diana asked.

By the time we explained the double meaning in English, we were seated, drinking fine red wine, and laughing like old friends. The room glittered, and Diana's voice was like champagne, sweet and heady, making me aware I was blessed every time her eyes turned to look at me. Once I saw Uncle Ike talking with General Alexander, and as he listened, he glanced toward us and smiled. We were blessed. Alive, together.

Late that night, in Diana's quarters, we lay in tangled sheets under mosquito netting, our uniforms scattered on the floor where we had discarded them on our way to her bed. It was a small room in a local hotel that had been taken over for women officers. I was glad she wasn't in a tent with a rickety cot.

"Billy?"

"Yes, I'm here." I ran my hand down her back. Tiny beads of sweat decorated her backbone.

"I'm going back to the SOE. They said I was fully recovered."

"Did they order you back?" I could feel my heart sink, and I was ready to protest the injustice of it all.

"No."

"You volunteered?"

"Yes."

"I don't want to lose you, Diana." It came to me then. On the beach, she'd said *either* of us could be killed any day.

She faced me. "Those dreams we had, about losing each other? Those weren't about the assignments we were on, or the danger either of us was in. It was about how we'd let Villard come between us. It was about how separated we had become, even when we were together. Don't you see? As long as we love each other, nothing can get in the way."

"Are you certain? About volunteering, I mean?"

"I have to, Billy. All I do here is shuffle papers from one damn meeting to another. Some captain asked me to make tea for him last week!"

"One of the first things your sister told me about herself was how she brewed horrible tea and coffee, just so they'd stop asking her."

"She truly made horrible tea. I can't imagine her attempting coffee."

We laughed, and I watched the happy memory turn sad, and then saw the return of her smile, as the joy of recollection overcame the pain of loss. It's not that time heals all wounds, it's more that it lets you stay happier for a bit longer every day when you remember someone you lost.

"I miss her," she said.

"Kaz does too. I doubt a minute goes by he doesn't think of her."

"Poor Kaz. We've got to find him a woman, Billy. Someone he can have a bit of fun with."

"Wait a minute!" I wasn't going to allow myself to be distracted. "Weren't we talking about you and the Special Operations Executive? Secret missions and all that?"

"All right. I have to make a contribution. Knowing I can and not doing it is driving me crazy."

For me, the opposite would be true. I would much rather Diana stayed at headquarters.

"When?" I asked.

"I have no idea. Nothing is on right now. I'm all yours, for these few days at least."

"Well, what's done is done."

"Right," she said. She drew closer, nestling into my arms. I realized that although I was afraid of losing her, I wasn't surprised at all that she'd volunteered to go back. It was who she was.

"Remember who you are," I said softly. I felt her breath on my arm as she fell asleep. I couldn't tell if she had heard me. It didn't matter. She knew well enough.

CHAPTER ▪ FORTY-ONE

"TRAUMA TO THE HEAD, psychogenic amnesia. Return to the Zone of the Interior authorized. Honorable discharge due to medical reasons."

I read the paper in the file the nurse had handed me. It was signed by the doctor who had talked to me after a bunch of other doctors had examined and prodded me all morning. The file held a bunch of other papers. Travel priority AA. Orders to report to Fort Dix, New Jersey, for separation.

Zone of the Interior. That was the States. Honorable Discharge. Separation. Home.

Words that I'd waited more than a year to hear. Beautiful-sounding words.

Separation.

I was fine physically. The last doctor was a psychiatrist. He thought I was OK, sort of, but didn't like that amnesia episode one bit. It was grounds for a discharge, and that's what he gave me. I was sure he expected thanks, but I couldn't take it in. I left his office to wait for the paperwork. Then I stood outside the hospital tent, reading my orders over again. Home. Boston by way of Fort Dix. Travel priority AA. Not the highest, but not bad. I could get on an airplane bound for the

States as soon as there was an empty seat or I could bump some poor schmo with a single A priority.

Nothing seemed real. I walked the mile to General Eisenhower's villa, watching the trucks and jeeps roll past, everyone going somewhere in a hurry. Going to war. I was going in the opposite direction. Home. Zone of the Interior.

All of a sudden I was returning the guard's salute and standing in front of Sue.

"Is the general in?"

"No, he flew to Algiers this morning. Anything I can do for you, Billy?"

"Sure. Can you call the airfield? See if there's a seat for me?" I gave her the folder. "Do you have a paper and pen I can use?"

"Sure, Billy. There's stationery on Marge's desk. Is this for real?" She flipped through the folder and looked at me. Couldn't blame her really; I did have some experience with forged orders.

"They're real. Top secret, OK?"

"Mum's the word." She picked up her telephone. I sat at the other desk and found a fountain pen. I thought about what to say and the best way to say it. I wrote a long letter, long for me anyway, and then sealed it in an envelope. I scrawled a name on the outside and stuffed it in my back pocket. Sue hung up the phone.

"With these orders, you can get on a plane at 1400 hours. Are you leaving now? Without—"

"See ya, Sue. Thanks for everything."

I hotfooted it over to our tent. Sciafani was sitting in the sun, reading an old *Life* magazine.

"Big Mike around?" I asked.

"He is at lunch and is coming after that to drive me to the POW camp. Nothing worked out last night?"

"Nothing, Enrico. Sorry. Listen, I need a favor. Will you drive me to the airfield?"

"Should I be driving a military vehicle? Here?"

"Hey, you've been in the army. Come on, you'll be back in time for Big Mike to take you to the POW camp."

"Well, it was in a different army, but what can they do to me?"

"Right, come on. There's a two o'clock flight." I enjoyed using civilian time, a lot more than was normal. Maybe it was like a connection, like Big Mike carrying around his shield.

Big Mike had drawn a jeep from the motor pool to take Sciafani south to the POW camp. We got in and drove down the busy road to the airfield.

"Thank you for everything you've done," Sciafani said, speaking loudly above the road noise.

"I didn't get anything done."

"I mean back in Sicily. It was remarkable, really."

"Stubborn is more like it."

We pulled up at the gate and I showed my orders. The sentry waved me on. I followed the markers to a waiting transport. A line of officers and civilians stood near it as GIs loaded gear into the rear. An MP held up his hand for us to halt.

"You on this flight, sir?"

"Got the orders right here."

"Both of you?"

"No, just one."

"OK, get your gear out, have your orders ready, and then get this vehicle out of here." He blew his whistle at another vehicle and stalked off to tell the driver to get a move on.

"This is it, Enrico." I stuck out my hand and we shook.

"Where are you going, Billy?"

"All depends. But you, my friend, are going to Boston. Massachusetts General." I took my dog tags off and put them around Sciafani's neck.

"What?"

"Don't ask any questions. Stand in line, get on the plane, don't talk to anyone." I handed him the file and a wad of greenbacks that I guessed would buy a train ticket from New Jersey to Boston.

"But this is a discharge for you."

"Bad timing. Busy right now. Get going before I change my mind." The MP blew his whistle again.

"Get a move on. One of you on board, one of you out of here! Sir!"

I liked polite cops.

"Are you certain?" Sciafani asked.

"God help me, I am. Here, one more thing. When you get to Boston, go to this address." I handed him the envelope. "He's an old friend of mine. Alphonse DeAngelo. He'll help you. I'd send you to my family, but I don't want them to know that I could have come home."

"If this is truly what you want, Billy, I will go."

"Go."

He grabbed his bag with the few belongings he had packed for the POW camp.

"Don't get hit in the head again, Billy. Promise me that."

"Odds are against it."

Sciafani waved, a grin lighting up his face. He ran to the line, showing his orders to a bored PFC who hooked his thumb toward the open door of the transport without looking up from his clipboard. I smiled, wheeled the jeep around and floored it, certain I had done the right thing for Sciafani, and for myself.

But that didn't mean I wanted to watch him fly away to the States. I didn't want to think about what I had given up. As I heard the engines cough and turn, I kept my eyes on the road stretching ahead of me.

I drove fast, the wind whipping my face, bringing tears to my stinging eyes. This is who I am.

AUTHOR'S ■ NOTE

Readers may wonder how much of this story is based in fact. The extent to which the narrative is based on documented history is sufficient to prove the old saw that truth is stranger than fiction.

It is true that Lucky Luciano cooperated with the Office of Naval Intelligence from his jail cell at the Great Meadows penitentiary in New York. Through the Mob's connections with organized labor, a careful watch was kept on the docks in New York City and other ports in the Northeast. They reported on suspicious activities and threats of sabotage to ONI and also cracked down on union activities that might impede the war effort. Even commercial fishermen supplying the Fulton Fish Market were enlisted to watch for German submarines.

As planning proceeded for the Allied invasion of Sicily, ONI again worked with organized crime to recruit Sicilian-American agents who could be landed on the island prior to the invasion. These agents, trained in commando tactics and in safecracking, went ashore armed with introductions to Sicilian Mafia contacts provided by Luciano and his gang. One of them did pull off a significant coup by breaking into the safe at Italian naval headquarters, securing valuable intelligence about Axis naval forces.

Numerous accounts of Luciano's involvement with the invasion of

Sicily mention the yellow silk handkerchief with the large *L* embla-
zoned on it. Some say it was dropped to Don Calogero Vizzini by
Allied aircraft via parachute. Other stories relate that it was delivered
by a secret agent, and that Don Calo rode on an American tank, waving it like a flag, convincing hundreds of Italian soldiers to desert.
While these stories sound fanciful, it is a fact that secret agents were
sent ashore to make contact with members of the Sicilian Mafia, and
that a handkerchief was used to serve as a message from Luciano to
Don Calo. Whatever the exact truth, Don Calo was ultimately made
mayor of Villalba by the American Military Government of Occupied
Territories (AMGOT). Lucky Luciano had his sentence commuted in
1946 and was deported to Sicily, the land of his birth.

Vito Genovese did flee to Italy in 1937 to avoid murder charges in
New York. When the Americans landed, he offered his services as a
translator, and soon became a valued assistant to AMGOT officers. As
the war progressed, AMGOT enlisted Genovese to help clean up
black market activities in Naples and southern Italy. Black market
activity disappeared, and AMGOT was pleased with his success until
they learned that Genovese had simply eliminated the competition and
taken over all black market operations himself, sending convoys of supplies to Don Calo in Sicily. He was sent back to the United States to
face the murder charges from 1937, but by then all the witnesses had
conveniently disappeared, and he was again a free man.

The disastrous night paratroop drop described is unfortunately
true. Through either miscommunication or sheer nervousness, naval
and ground antiaircraft fire hit the reinforcing wave of 82nd Airborne troopers, causing 319 casualties (88 dead, 69 missing, and 162
wounded).

While I have tried to weave history into this fictional narrative, it
is ultimately a work that springs from my imagination. I am inspired
by real events, to which I hope I have remained true in spirit, if not
always in precise fact.

The battle for Biazza Ridge, described in Chapter Three, is a little-
known but crucial action that held the Germans back from the beachhead on the day after the invasion. Colonel (later General) Jim Gavin
did lead a mixed force of paratroopers, infantry, and some rear-area
personnel to hold the high ground and keep the German force from

breaking through and wreaking havoc on the buildup along the southern coast. The battle, as seen through Billy's eyes, is recreated based on eyewitness accounts, which include mention of the tears Gavin shed at the burial of the men who died there.

I had the opportunity to visit this site while my wife and I were on vacation in Sicily. The battlefield is on the property of a Sicilian farmer, who raises artichokes and oranges beneath the ridge where the fight took place. He has kept the bunkers untouched, and respectfully cares for the land where so much blood was shed. He and his family invited us in to share their Easter Monday celebration and showed us around the farm and took us into the bunkers below the ridge. On the outer wall of his farmhouse, facing the road to Gela, is a monument attesting to the lives sacrificed there. It reads in part:

> *Extreme were the losses. Supreme was the heroism, and from the sacrifice of these men is created the new history of Europe.*

Who could say more?

reading group guide

1. The novel opens with the main character suffering from amnesia. How does that help—or hinder—the narrative?

2. The title comes from a quotation by Italian dictator Benito Mussolini, who said, "Blood alone moves the wheels of history." Discuss how true that statement really is. How does it relate to this novel?

3. Ethnicity plays a large role in the world of Billy Boyle. Discuss how Billy's worldview is colored by ethnicity in terms of his own Irish origins and how he sees others with whom he comes into contact: Poles, Italians, Sicilians, and English.

4. Billy's English lover, Diana Seaton, has had a role in each title in the series. Where would you like to see that relationship go? Does it enhance the story, or get in the way?

5. Another recurring character is Dwight David Eisenhower. How does the presence of this historical person help the character of Billy Boyle reconcile himself to his role in the war?

6. The historical character of Bill Mauldin, the cartoonist famous for the creation of Willie and Joe, makes a cameo appearance in *Blood Alone*, as does Colonel Jim Gavin and gangster Vito Genovese. Are there any other real people you'd like Billy to encounter in future novels?

7. Discuss the role of Enrico Sciafani in the story. In what ways does his presence move the narrative along and help establish the setting?

8. What does it mean to be *mafiusu*? Is Billy Boyle *mafiusu* at heart?

9. Did you view *Blood Alone* as primarily a war story, or a mystery? Or something else?

10. What did you learn about World War II that most surprised you, from this or any other of the Billy Boyle novels?